Neo-Victorian Young Adult Narratives

Sarah E. Maier

Neo-Victorian Young Adult Narratives

Sarah E. Maier
University of New Brunswick
Saint John, NB, Canada

ISBN 978-3-031-47294-7   ISBN 978-3-031-47295-4 (eBook)
https://doi.org/10.1007/978-3-031-47295-4

© The Editor(s) (if applicable) and The Author(s), under exclusive licence to Springer Nature Switzerland AG 2024

This work is subject to copyright. All rights are solely and exclusively licensed by the Publisher, whether the whole or part of the material is concerned, specifically the rights of translation, reprinting, reuse of illustrations, recitation, broadcasting, reproduction on microfilms or in any other physical way, and transmission or information storage and retrieval, electronic adaptation, computer software, or by similar or dissimilar methodology now known or hereafter developed.

The use of general descriptive names, registered names, trademarks, service marks, etc. in this publication does not imply, even in the absence of a specific statement, that such names are exempt from the relevant protective laws and regulations and therefore free for general use.

The publisher, the authors, and the editors are safe to assume that the advice and information in this book are believed to be true and accurate at the date of publication. Neither the publisher nor the authors or the editors give a warranty, expressed or implied, with respect to the material contained herein or for any errors or omissions that may have been made. The publisher remains neutral with regard to jurisdictional claims in published maps and institutional affiliations.

This Palgrave Macmillan imprint is published by the registered company Springer Nature Switzerland AG.
The registered company address is: Gewerbestrasse 11, 6330 Cham, Switzerland

Paper in this product is recyclable.

*For my daughter, Violet …
always, always.*

Acknowledgements

My first thanks are to Allie Troyanos at Palgrave for her steadfast encouragement for this project and others and to the reviewers for their enthusiastic suggestions. To the wonderful artists who have made this work beautiful, my gratitude to Angela Morgan for her neo-Victorian painting, "the reality of retrograde," which graces the cover; to Lita Judge for her generosity to let me include her remarkable work on Mary Shelley; and to Glynnis Fawkes for her enthusiastic permission to let her images do some of the explanation on the Brontës.

Glennis Byron, Patricia Demers, Ann Heilmann, Gary Kelly, Marie-Luise Kohlke, Mark Llewellyn, Juliet McMaster, Deborah Morse, Naomi Schor, Joanne Shattock, and Elaine Showalter who have been my professors, mentors, and friends. I am in your debt for your amazing work and support over the years. To try to follow your paths are journeys worth taking. Brenda Ayres, your willingness to share indefatigable wisdom is a gift.

It is imperative that I thank the library staff at the Hans Klohn Commons at the University of New Brunswick; when I thought research material was out of reach, they would inevitably find it for me. Jenna Granger deserves extra credit for her gentle reminders to me to fetch or return them.

To the very special people who make me laugh and fill my life with love and friendship, you have my gratitude—Lars Stuijts, for your shared fondness of reading and book-title swapping on spies, YA, and everything in between over these many years; Christine Coleman, for teaching me the value of words carefully chosen and the steadfastness of quiet understanding in a friend; and Rachel M. Friars, for wisely reminding me that waffles are essential for the best scholarly work.

My life is blessed. Even though I miss the silence I shared with my Mum as we sat reading our huge tomes with a cup of tea in hand, my Dad—and the world's best Gido—continues to surround us with strength and love every moment of every day. This work is, as always, for my extraordinary daughter who is the pure joy and wonder in my world.

Contents

1 Neo-Victorian Young Adult Narratives   1

2 Re/articulated Monstrosity: Mary and Her Creature   21

3 Mash(ed) Up: Maidens, Monsters, and Mad Scientists   55

4 Illustrative Genii: The Brontës' Genius   83

5 The Odd(est) Brontë: Portrait(s) of Emily as a Young Author   109

6 Irregulars: Sherlockian Youth as Outsiders   137

7 The Mis(s) Education of Young Women   163

8 ~~Deviant~~ Young Womanhood: Liminal Queerness, Mad Femininity, and Spectral Subjectivity   185

9 Things as Yet Undone: Encountering the Past Through the Present   209

Index   213

List of Figures

Fig. 2.1	Mary's Monster (2018, 2) courtesy of Lita Judge	34
Fig. 2.2	Mary's Monster (42) courtesy of Lita Judge	36
Fig. 2.3	Mary's Monster (258–59) courtesy of Lita Judge	40
Fig. 4.1	Charlotte Brontë working on *Jane Eyre* in *Charlotte Brontë before Jane Eyre* (2019, 86). (Courtesy of Glynnis Fawkes)	92
Fig. 4.2	Emily and Anne's celebration in *Jane Eyre* in *Charlotte Brontë before Jane Eyre* (2019, 87). (Courtesy of Glynnis Fawkes)	93

CHAPTER 1

Neo-Victorian Young Adult Narratives

At some point after Harry Potter, but before Edward Cullen and Katniss Everdeen, arrived in novels to spark the literary imaginations of young people, the non-adult section of the bookstore started to become very interesting. To me, children's literature had always been wonderful; working in the children's section of an independent bookstore was a delight of picture books, classic stories, and new genres, and then a different kind of book began to arrive that needed an area of its own—the not quite children's books but not quite adult books section. These books crept onto shelves just outside the children's zone, oddly placed between picture books and nonfiction computer manuals, an odd juxtaposition if there ever was one. Divisions multiplied between narratives for children, tweens, teens, young adults, and now, new adults and with those expansions—or narrowings, depending on your opinion—subjects changed, characters diversified, and genres shifted. The search for the "next big thing"—a series that could keep young people reading—continues with multiple genres and possibilities continually joining these new classics on the shelves.

    Heather Scutter, in *Displaced Fictions*, believes there is a need for increased scholarship on young adult novels and readership because "books for teenagers and young adults belong neither here nor there, neither in the free market of adult books nor in the closed shop of children's books" (1999, 2). The ambiguity of "Young Adult Literature" does not help focus the discussion. When asked recently in *The New York Times* how to distinguish between young adult and adult books, Judy Blume replied,

© The Author(s), under exclusive license to Springer Nature Switzerland AG 2024
S. E. Maier, *Neo-Victorian Young Adult Narratives*,
https://doi.org/10.1007/978-3-031-47295-4_1

That's a tough question. It's a marketing thing. It's how they're published and how they're sold. If I look at the shelves in our Y.A. section right now there will be more fantasy than reality, heavy on dystopian and futuristic stories, L.G.B.T.Q.+ characters. Often the books will be longer in length than adult fiction. Think Harry Potter. Good against evil. It might be part of a series. Y.A. is read by kids as young as 11 and goes on to appeal to adults in their 20s. Realistic fiction isn't as *in* today as when I was writing in the 1970s and '80s. There was no official Y.A. category then. But it's all cyclical so who can say what the next Big Thing will be? (quoted in Clarke 2023, n.p.; emphasis in original)

Clear as mud, but young adult literature is definitely "a contemporary term used to define a market, an audience and a developmental category" and "is a construct rather than a stable term that neatly defines an age bracket" (Beckton 2015, 1). A "young adult" is variously defined as young people anywhere from ten to eighteen, or more often thirteen to nineteen; of course with the *Harry Potter*, *Twilight*, and *Hunger Games* series, age suggestions did not stop crossover interest, much to the chagrin of some critics but to the delight of open-minded adult readers.[1]

The increased interest in these works saw some readers advocate for "the literary character of young adult literature and the importance of finding some way of acknowledging, encouraging, and underscoring that fact" given "its art, its innovation, its creative energy, and its vitality" (Cart 2016, n.p.). There is an argument that young adult literature, especially if read by adults, is purely escapist; however, Virginia Zimmerman rightly points out that is a misconception

> probably because so much of young-adult literature overlaps with genre fiction—plot-driven books that fall into one specific genre, like fantasy, romance, or sci-fi…. The YA books that have been popular with adults are dark and serious and hard…. People might to go to YA literature to sink into a reality different than their own, but I think they sink into that reality to encounter feelings, challenges, and relationships they recognize from their own lives. (quoted in Kitchener 2017, n.p.)

More likely, the bias is age discriminatory and subjectively based rather than on any serious intellectual argument.

Groups who advocate for censorship have created arguments over appropriateness, and too-easily availability, due to some of the realistic topics and themes in the new books. S. E. Hinton's *The Outsiders* (1967) and J. D. Salinger's *The Catcher in the Rye* (1951), early exemplars of fiction betwixt and between children's literature and adult literature, introduced uncomfortable subjects that were of interest to readers even as the debates continued, with Hinton's novel still frequently challenged because of gang violence and underage sexuality, and Salinger's for what is perceived as blasphemous language, overt sexuality, and undermining of family values (Mydans 1989, 22). Newer entries like *Perks of Being a Wallflower* (1999) by Stephen Chbosky are still banned in some places for themes of non-heteronormative LGBTQ+ sexuality and supposed anti-family values. PEN American experts Jonathan Friedman and Nadine Farid Johnson are righteously concerned that with fifty or more groups pushing for book bans, "More students [are] losing access to literature" because of the documented number of books banned in the 2021–22, a deeply undemocratic move. They list 2532 instances of individual books being banned including 1648 book titles written by 1261 authors, illustrated by 290 artists which affected the "literary, scholarly, and creative work of 1,553 people altogether" (2023, n.p.). Marsha Lederman in the *Globe and* Mail recently warned that vigilance is needed to make certain that U.S.-style book bans do not happen in Canada (2023, n.p.) and/or that anti-intellectualism does not take hold. Nearly half of the titles banned were young adult novels with the vast majority of the books including LGBTQ+ and/or BIPOC characters with central themes of sexuality and racism being deemed inappropriate. The result is that an increasing lack of diverse reading is having "multifaceted, harmful impacts: on students who have a right to access a diverse range of stories and perspectives, and especially on those from historically marginalized backgrounds who are watching their library shelves emptied of books that reflect and speak to them" (n.p.).

Richard Jackson suggests that when "people worry about bleak stories, they are worrying on behalf of the audience about the readiness of young readers to face life's darkest corners" but those same people forget that there are "kids *living* in those dark corners" and even "children in the sun will enter the darkness. They *all* need our tenderness. And we need our tenderness as art inspires us to feel it" (quoted in Cart, n.p.; emphasis in original). Instead, some groups make it their mission to ban or remove these "bad books" to the adult section of bookstores[2] but are taken to task for such arbitrary decisions by equally resistant campaigns by others.[3] No matter the debates, literature for young adults has become progressively sophisticated to match the increased worldliness of its readers. Of course, shifting books from one corner to the other corner of a bookstore or a library is not going to make them less appealing; if anything, young people's curiosity is piqued by rumblings of topics supposedly beyond their understanding.

Shifting Centuries

Some concerns of young adults are, to a certain extent, without temporal borders which makes reaching into history for insight relevant. Adolescence is a difficult period of transition—an "awkward age"[4]—for most individuals, past or present, and offers particular challenges for the writer. In fact, Stephen Peacock, the author of *The Boy Sherlock* series, claims

> The funny thing about writing for Young Adults is that, if you want your novel to have literary aspirations and depth, then you are in for a greater challenge than writing for adults. In an adult novel a character can stare at the horizon for 50 pages, but try having him/her do that for more than a sentence in a YA novel and you are in serious trouble. So if you are an ambitious YA novelist, you must stay on the plot at all times while employing literary techniques and giving your story depth. That is often very difficult to pull off. (quoted in Ue 2010, 40)

Long interested in the Victorian age, Peacock was "adamant that [he] would challenge them, create something dark and literary, with a deeper subtext" (2008, 17); with a protagonist set in the era, he fully believed that young readers could and would handle the historical context. Such historically located texts are "those well-known and popular novels which are both intensely self-reflexive and yet paradoxically also lay claim to historical events and personages," and which include "a theoretical self-awareness of history and fiction as human constructs (historiographic *metafiction*)" which make possible the "rethinking and reworking of the forms and contents of the past" (Hutcheon 1988, 5; emphasis in original)

The genre of historical fiction—and, by extension, neo-Victorian narratives—can be enticing to young adults even without extensive knowledge as a productive means to access the past to see how it relates to the readers' present. Kim Wilson argues that what is "distinctive to the genre of historical fiction … is that readers of fiction are situated to absorb a sense of the past from the privileged position of personal re-experience" (2011, 3). James Goodman sees the task of "fictional history" to be daunting because it has the "task of re-creating characters who are as engaging and believable and true as great fictional characters—all of whom have the distinct advantage of never having lived real lives" (2005, 246) unless they are "real characters in real historical settings" (244).

Neo—What?!

The next step to a neo-Victorian narrative, for any age of reader, becomes—as defined by Ann Heilmann and Mark Llewellyn—"*more than* historical fiction set in the nineteenth century" and must instead be "*self-consciously engaged with the act of (re)interpretation, (re)discovery and (re)vision concerning the Victorians*" (2010, 4; emphasis in original). This reminder of the textual project as active will, then, hopefully encourage the reader to be engaged in the exploration of the past to elucidate his/her/their present or future. Young adult interest in the persons, characters, and issues of the long nineteenth century create the opportunity for reflection on the past and what it can tell us about the present. Kate Mitchell points out that such fiction contains "complexities as a unique historical moment that is now produced in a particular relationship to the present" (Mitchell, 2010, 3).

It is not enough for a narrative to be set in the historical past; rather, it must engage with previous eras or isms in a self-aware manner. One difficulty that might unwittingly lead the reader away from cognisance of bias is presentism, defined by Marie-Luise Kohlke as

> the creative process whereby artists insinuate current attitudes and sociocultural contexts into the historical worlds they recreate for present-day consumption. Hence, presentism may produce unintentional misreadings of the past in so far as individuals remain unaware of (or in self-denial about) the extent to which their modern mindsets infiltrate, inform, and possibly distort their assessments of another age and its cultural products, discourses, and ideologies (2018, n.p.)

but that most "neo-Victorian fictions, however, foreground their presentism overtly" (n.p.) and challenge the conflation with a "self-analytical drive" (Heilmann and Llewellyn 2010, 5). Kohlke allows that "genuinely neo-Victorian works, then, seem obliged to acknowledge both their recycled 19th-century and contemporary contexts and to duly reflect on the present *in tandem with*—rather than *at the expense of*—the past, lest they be accused of disingenuousness or even historical distortion" (2018, n.p.;

emphasis in original). Llewellyn argues rightly that the neo-Victorian includes "those works which are consciously set in the Victorian period (or the nineteenth century—there is a difference ...), or which desire to rewrite historical narratives of that period by representing marginalized voices, new histories of sexuality, post-colonial viewpoints and other generally 'different' versions of the Victorian" (2008, 165).

Sonya Sawyer Fritz and Sara K. Day introduce their collection, *The Victorian Era in Twenty-First Century Children's and Adolescent Literature and Culture*, with an appreciation of the dual potential of the "Victorian as both iconic and malleable" (2018, 2) and an explanation of how the period is attractive to writers and readers as a moment where the "figure of the child, then, becomes a key point of both connection and differentiation between the nineteenth and twenty-first centuries" (3). Even if there is no one long nineteenth century but only a range of (re)interpretations of it (Heilmann and Llewellyn 2010, 3), there is in those (re)interpretations a series of open spaces wherein to address similarities and differences between the past and the present as they are (re)presented to young readers. A neo-Victorian narrative invites the young reader to muse upon history and/or the historical, then asks scholars to contemplate "what texts mean as acts of reading, as spaces of intellectual exchange" when they are "fundamentally concerned ... with the ontological and epistemological roots of the *now* through an historical awareness of *then*" (4, emphasis in original). Neo-Victorian young adult narratives may not be able to rely on the prior knowledge of the Victorian by the reader, but it may be that these (re)writings act as a primary experience, a first encounter with the long nineteenth century "through a more complicated literary experience, priming readers for a more complex interaction ... with the original Victorian work later in life" (Fritz and Day 5). Scholars might come to a neo-Victorian text with a great deal of knowledge with which to contextualise it or challenge its representation of the age, but a young adult will more likely come to read the narrative to experience vicariously the Victorian, then later seek out knowledge to fill in the unknowns.

The neo-Victorian project, according to Nadine Boehm-Schnitker and Susanne Gruss, "looks into the desires and contexts that tinge and shape the perspectives of our contemporary construction ... moreover, it explores the changing purposes with which we fashion the past—and with it, ourselves" (2014, 1). Consequently, Rosario Arias and Patricia Pulham believe that neo-Victorian fiction, for adults or young people, is haunted by its representation of the Victorian; often, the recent text represents a "double" of the Victorian text mimicking its language, style, and plot and even its massive size. The text plays with the conscious repetition of tropes, characters, and historical events; it reanimates Victorian genres, for example, the realist text, sensation fiction, the Victorian ghost story and, in doing so, seemingly calls the contemporary novel's "life" into question; it "defamiliarizes our preconceptions of Victorian society; and it functions as a form of revenant, a ghostly visitor from the past that infiltrates our present" (2010, xv). These rewritings "do not claim to be all-encompassing reconfigurations" (Llewellyn 2008, 165) but they may be reparative, exploratory, or redemptive. In this new area of creative expansion and critical engagement, it is important to embrace what Llewellyn calls the "f(r)iction" (2008, 170) between the past and the present with a desire to understand the past to articulate its relationship to the postmodern present in these works. If "neo-Victorian novels have so readily found a home in the sphere of young adult fiction which has always welcomed literature with a social purpose" (Stetz 2013, 142), then they may "contribute to the social and aesthetic transformation of culture by, for instance, encouraging readers to approach ideas, issues, and objects from new perspectives and so prepare the way for change" (Reynolds 2007, 1). This attention to the details of the past in neo-Victorian young adult texts includes issues, themes, and motifs that lead to "sympathetically portraying the alienated pains and pleasures of adolescence, through enacting adolescence with all its turmoil, writers bring young readers face to face with different forms of cultural alienation itself: the legacy of colonialism, political injustice, environmental desecration, sexual stereotyping, consumerism, madness, and death" (Hilton and Nikolajeva 2016, 1). These insights create a "new consciousness about the possibilities of re-visioning nineteenth-century cultural *Ur*-texts" to begin "articulating perspectives that were textually marginalized and yet imaginatively central to the original text" (Heilmann and Lewellyn 2014, 498–99).

A consideration of neo-Victorian young adult narratives reaches into the neo-Gothic when new texts about Mary Shelley and her Creature delivered powerful examples of just how revelatory their representation of adolescent writers and their creations could be. Mary Shelley is, by all accounts, a Romantic, but her concerns speak to the challenges that will rise in the Victorian age over science, gender, subjectivity, and authorship, particularly for young people grappling with a changing ideological landscape, issues which travel forward to the lives and writings of the young Brontës that are also explored in "neo-" narratives.

The trick is to parse out the differences between them. Two terms are of significance here; the first, the neo-Victorian has been well-defined, but the more amorphous second is the neo-Gothic and what, exactly, is its difference from the Gothic. To discuss the Gothic is to enter well traversed literary territory; in the traditional Gothic, particular tropes manifest in discussions of good versus evil just as characters who align with good or evil take their places in various scripts with physical restraint, sexual exploitation, uncontrolled madness, and other excesses that locate the Gothic as unerringly difficult to pin down. Fred Botting points out that the Gothic engages with "Movements across time and place", which are "double (desired and feared; frightening and comforting) because they are bound up with figures and conventions—mirrors, portraits, ghosts, hallucinations, doubles, misread manuscripts—that link a sense of reality (or unreality) to structures of fiction: tensions between perceptions and misperception, understanding and misreading, fancy and realism" to "provide the condition and problem of gothic texts" (2014, 5), encouraging us to see the Gothic as applicable to more than one era and opening the potential for a revisiting a self-conscious intention in our reading. There is the threat to using Gothic too widely or easily because it then lessens its usefulness and makes any referentiality to different versions of Gothicism difficult, just as to use Victorian as a single term is far too vague for all of its concerns and characters. The combination of the two terms into one, neo-Victorian Gothic, has been the means by which critics have sought to get around this barrier.

Marie-Luise Kohlke and Christian Gutleben claim "neo-Victorian fiction enacts Gothic principles and, as such, takes part in the constant reactivation of the Gothic" (2010, 3); then, they assert it follows that "*neo-Victorianism is by nature quintessentially Gothic*: resurrecting the ghost(s) of the past, searching out its dark secrets and shameful mysteries, insisting obsessively on the lurid details of Victorian life, reliving the period's nightmares and traumas" (2010, 4; emphasis in original). Surely this consummation of one term with the other is too overwhelming. Similar features sometimes occur in each—spectral visions, overlapping time, secrecy, and shameful acts—but not necessarily in the same way or purpose. The use of a third term, neo-Gothic, allows for a reseparation of the terms where the neo-Gothic stands apart. The ubiquitous use of Heilmann and Llewellyn's definition of the neo-Victorian makes it essential to consider a parallel discussion for some modern texts that evoke the Gothic. In similar manner to the neo-Victorian project, neo-Gothic narratives consciously, and with intent, revise, rewrite, or reconsider the original meanings or presentations of Gothic *Ur*-texts and/or their inheritors. A major difference is in the ability of the neo-Victorian to allow for lightness of subject while the neo-Gothic often struggles in the darkness of liminal subjects.

The neo-Gothic young adult narratives discussed here take what is accepted as the Gothic in order to deal with "a post-postmodern, sometimes posthuman, world to expose the ambivalence and banality that now greets questions of evil, to address questions of memory, violence and traumatic experience, to investigate non-linear identities as well as spectral selves and to give voice to multifaceted cultural, scientific and artistic complexities in a time of complexity" (Maier and Ayres 2020, 4). Potential features of the neo-Gothic narrative include an understanding of the fragmentation of subjectivities which includes the recognition of and reconstruction of those subjectivities, an understanding of transgression as movement across socially delineated boundaries, a breakthrough of silenced voices from inner perspectives that, in particular, give credence to unknowable or unspoken selves to rehabilitate those cast by society as monstrous selves/others. Gender, sexuality, context, and non-heteronormative lives are investigated as unthreatening but potentially disruptive to the historical contexts that may have cast individuals as monstrous aberrations from the norm. The disavowal and unmasking of society as a means of entrapment is outed as such and tragic outcomes for non-conformists are exposed, delayed, or overturned in the new texts. Finally, the neo-Gothic is not as emancipatory as the neo-Victorian; if a cost must be paid to society, the protagonist often suffers a strong sense of loss and anger. If the neo-Victorian Gothic gives precedence to the neo-Victorian as grounded in a particular era, the neo-Gothic expands across eras to revisit the original Gothic in a particular period by postmodern intervention into the life of the once-labelled monster or self-blaming monstrous subject.

Indeed, the tensions between fact and fiction, past and present, are a defining feature of neo-Gothic, neo-Victorian, and young adult literature—the grey matter of the "in between"—which leads naturally to the combination of the two kinds of literature. The purpose of a strong neo-Victorian storyline seems that it must appeal to the "audience's desire for knowledge" but at the same time, provide "the detailing of historically accurate situations, the fetishistic displays of wealth or poverty, the struggle between personal and parental or social desires" (Montz 2019, 91).

The inclusion of "equal (or horizontal) power relations between the major characters within the text" is important so that the young adult reader has "the power to see the opposing ideologies at play" (Cadden 2000, 146), which then allows for a dialogue not only between characters within a Victorian context but also with the present reader of the neo-Victorian narrative.

The voices of not often heard Victorian adolescents are restored in neo-Victorian young adult narratives and may be investigated through self-conscious and self-aware intersectional readings of trauma studies, gender studies, psychiatric history, or any other means righteously invoked in the study of adult fiction. *Neo-Victorian Young Adult Narratives* provides some literary, critical responses to young adult fiction, and to the need to "theorize young adult fiction as a type of literature that has its own constellation of concerns that mark it as distinctive from literature for either children or adult" (Pattee 2017, 218). Scholars of children's literature are duly cautioned that there is a question of un/knowability that underpins such literature and are warned to be aware of the vertical power relationship "when an adult writer speaks through a young adult's consciousness to a young adult audience" (Pattee 225). The same facts apply to adolescent works. Even sympathetic portrayals are, for the most part, constructed by adults for young adult readers; very few novels written for youth are written by a young person. Ideologies seep into the texts and, in those portraits of the individual in a particular context, there is often a link between society's "most pressing and disturbing issues" and the "adolescent's quest for identity" (Hilton and Nikolajeva 2012, 9), often at a moment of crisis for the protagonist.

One could just as easily add that these positionings between political awareness and personal agency—the "capacity to act independently of social restraint" (McCallum 1999, 7)—allow the young adult to investigate "themes of constructedness, intersectionality, and feminist revision" (Clasen and Hassel 2016, 4) as an evolving reader. In addition, any young adult neo-Victorian narrative necessarily "exists at the intersection of several cultural forces and discourses: twenty-first-century young adult (YA) literature and film, the growing body of works that reimagine Victorian fiction or culture, and the afterlives of that canon's most prominent literary icons" (Temple 2021, 24). Clearly, the acculturation and civilising of young persons via literature is an important moment for their awareness of the need to understand the "individual potential suited to a future in which societies could be different in some significant ways" (Reynolds

2007, 2) when the dialogue is opened between the past and the present. This very entanglement in some texts—of the *Bildüngsroman* (2023) and *Künstlerroman* (2023)[5]—becomes apparent in the cross-era dialogue contained in the stories that elucidate the complexity of neo-Victorian character(s) who may exhibit radical potentialities, silent strengths, creative ideas, and subversive politics when they can be re-visioned outside of their historically contextualised moments.

Scholars of children's and adolescent texts see them as multidimensional and complex, as well as narratives of artistic sophistication with a richness of language that mobilise literary devices, intertextuality, metanarrative as well as multiple genres to engage with young adults. Intertextuality alone is a complex pattern that arises in neo-Victorian young adult narratives. Maria Nikolajeva points to the past problematic and "common misunderstanding that, compared to adult literature, children's books are characterized by a simpler narrative structure, poorer language, and inferior artistic resources"; she argues tenaciously that it is "the right of children's literature to be literary, to be part of a *discourse* instead of a mere children's book" (1996, 7; emphasis in original). The intertexts may appear as quotations, allusions, irony, and/or pastiche, or as "intertextuality with a single oeuvre which may provide clues to an interpretation of a difficult multidimensional text" (10).

Neo-Victorian Young Adult Narratives focuses on the conflation between young adult and neo-Victorian narratives, how they elucidate the past for the present, and how the similarly aged characters are embodied in those narratives. For example, historical fiction for this age group, "while concerned with the past at the level of content, is additionally concerned—because of the future to which it is moving—with the present views of that historical past" but even more striking is how the humanistic metanarrative of positive progression attempts to disclose the cultural, social and/or political ideologies of the time in which it was produced (Wilson 2011, 5). Young adult literature foregrounds "adolescent protagonists who strive to understand their own power by struggling with the various institutions in their lives" (Trites 2004, 8). The parallel between readers and characters invites an "inquiry into imbalance, inequality, a symmetry between different social groups; an umbrella concept for several critical positions dealing with power and discrimination generated by the difference in gender, class, nationhood, or race" (de Certeau quoted in Nikolajeva 2010, 8). Novels engaged with history have "outlived groundshaking changes, responding, adapting, and freely crossbreeding with other genres. Its inherent interest and vitality have not staled" (Rahn 1991, 1) and deserve more scholarly attention as to how and why the historical past can elucidate the present for young readers.

Writers combine this self-awareness of history with an individual's personal growth to contemplate adolescence as a metaphor for social change. In her discussion of adolescents in the novels of Charles Dickens, Elizabeth Welburn makes a point salient here: that "age *is* fundamental to social and political change" (2006, 223; emphasis in original). She expresses the importance of how adolescents create their "formation of identity against the norm of the previous generation, the conscious struggle to speak, and the adolescent perception that a concrete identity and the right to speak are fundamental to personal agency, all suggest that adolescents are uniquely poised to enact social change" rather than be "merely victim to or victors of the social system, passive recipients of their parents' lifestyles" (223). The focus here is on how adolescents engage with the Victorian in neo-Victorian literature for young adults with no qualification to discuss actual psychological development. It is, however, immensely helpful to consider this description of generational learning and movement as a way to understand the looking back to the long nineteenth century for the consideration by, and illumination of, the twentieth- and twenty-first-century reader. Through "sympathetically portraying the alienated pains and pleasures of adolescence, through *enacting* adolescence with all its turmoil, writers bring young readers face to face with different forms of cultural alienation itself: the legacy of colonialism, political injustice, environmental desecration, sexual stereotyping, consumerism, madness, and death" (Hilton and Nikolajeva 1; emphasis in original). These works encourage the young person, in reading neo-Victorian narratives that speak back to the long nineteenth century, to interact with the complexity of the historical past.

The very prevalence of the Victorian in the young adult genres of bio-fiction, juvenile writings, graphic novels, Gothic revisions, and mystery and crime fiction, in twentieth- and twenty-first-century narratives for young adults opens to a plethora of readings of long-nineteenth-century creators and/as character afterlives, young Victorians and/as character(s), as well as various imaginings and/as neo-Victorian critiques. *Neo-Victorian Young Adult Narratives* interrogates the complicated relationship between the Victorian past and the use of Victorian modes of thought on literature, history, and morality to explore coming-of-age in the present day in relation to subjective development, personal agency, gender presentation, and sexual expression. There is potential for (re)visiting young people in history and as historical characters; further, the neo-Victorian's relation to the Victorian age and our current age should not be seen as a gimmick or trend but as a socio-political, literate commentary on century/ies end(s) that is mobilised in the young adult context via issues of character(s), gender, convention, class, race, and exclusion. For example, there must be more to stories that feature, are written by, are created for, or are read by young people than to think neo-Victorian fiction might have over "emphasised (or capitalised upon)" the "presentation of children as molested, abused, or murdered, casting neo-Victorian fiction as their 'rescuer' and righter of historical wrongs" against children (Kohlke and Gutleben 2011, 24). While definitely a brilliant and necessary question to ask, it is surely neither the limits of reading as scholars or young adults, nor is it the purported intention of authors to set themselves as historical exploiters or saviours.

Creators and/as Character Afterlives

Amid bicentennial celebrations and new scholarship dedicated to nineteenth-century authors, there has been an increasing interest in the lives of those authors and their character(s). One of the most famous and well-examined authors in biofiction for young adults is Mary Godwin Shelley; such a focus on her life and works in the genre comes as no surprise when her most famous novel, *Frankenstein; or, The Modern Prometheus* (1818) was written when Shelley was only eighteen or nineteen. The mythos surrounding Shelley's life and her seminal text are, like her creature, revived in considerations in fiction and graphic novel form. Chapter 2, "Re/articulated: Mary and Her Creature," reads Antoinette May's *The Determined Heart* (2015) and Lita Judge's *Mary's Monster* (2018) as neo-Gothic texts that enact a kind of double vision, wherein they return to the historical past through Shelley and her creature to illuminate the connection between monstrosity and adolescence by framing Mary Godwin Shelley and/as her creature. Such a conflation is particularly significant in framing and subverting gendered codes—a common trope in young adult biofiction about famous female authors. Shelley's alignment with her creature underscores both her genius and her defiance of convention, interrogating the established social codes that resonate with young adult readers.

Following an examination of Mary Godwin Shelley's biofictions, chapter 3 constitutes a similar (re)engagement with how the Gothic "is constantly being reinvented in ways that address the current historical moment, as is the cultural construction of monstrosity, which is historically conditioned" (Smith and Moruzi, 2018, 9), including for a younger readership. "Mash(ed) Up: Maidens, Monsters, and Mad Scientists" advocates that authors of neo-Gothic young adult fiction return to the figure of the "mad scientist" to reinterrogate the assumption of male dominion over science, women as objects of experimentation, and ethical concerns over transgressive scientific practices. In Megan Shepherd's trilogy—*The Madman's Daughter* (2013), *Her Dark Curiosity* (2014), and *A Cold Legacy* (2016)— and Theodora Goss' Extraordinary Adventures of the Athena Club—*The Strange Case of the Alchemist's Daughter* (2017), *European Travel for the Monstrous Gentlewoman* (2018), and *The Sinister Mystery of the Mesmerising Girl* (2019)—the texts focus on the narratives of young women who are either the biological or scientifically created children of their scientist fathers, men whose motives are by turns questionable and corrupt. These stories of females who are othered in various ways—through their liminality, their dual status as powerless girls and unwilling Creatures—seek to reframe science and systems of knowledge-seeking as no longer the property of their male fathers. Indeed, the protagonists in these novels quickly surpass their male progenitors as they consider some ethical questions that are so often only pointed to or elided in the Victorian *Ur*-texts.

Young Victorians and/as Character(s)

Moving away from revisions of early nineteenth-century Gothicism into a genre that is no less concerned with issues around authorship, creation, genius, and girlhood, the "Illustrative Genii: The Brontës' Genius" will consider recent neo-Victorian young adult biofictions. *The Glass Town Game* (2017) by Catherynne Valente and *Worlds of Ink and Shadow* (2016) by Lena Coakley, explore the fascinating Brontë family in fiction that collapses the space between their actual lives in Howarth and their imaginative lives in their juvenilia worlds. Two recent graphic novels, *Charlotte Brontë Before Jane Eyre* (2009) by Glynnis Fawkes and *Glass Town: The Imaginary World of the Brontës* by Isabel Greenberg (2020), further explore the conflation of juvenilian narratives with biographical suppositions. These fictions make the case for how the sibling writers' lesser-known juvenilia become a biofictional realm that highlights the importance of the Victorian juvenile imagination to young adult authorship. For readers, encountering the creative genius of the Brontës engenders a kind of sympathy with the plight of the children; not only can the reader understand the siblings' attachment and devotion to their imagined worlds into which they would escape, but they may also empathise with the children's psychological and literary transition from childhood to adulthood. Like the earlier narratives focused on Mary Godwin Shelley, these biofictions enact a double perspective wherein the representation of the Brontës and their worlds inspires the young adult reader to consider their contemporary environment and the drive to create worlds that provide escape.

The Brontë family continues to fascinate young adult readers—some individual members more than others. In several cases, the paradoxical contrast between the quiet life of Emily Brontë and her passionate fiction offers no complete picture of the young woman in spite of the myriad biographies, legends, and myths about her life or the crushing number of critical responses to her fictions. Into this gap, neo-Victorian (re)visionings of and a (re)voicing of personal history allow for a reconsideration of Emily Brontë's interests. To that end, chapter 5, "The Odd(est) Brontë: Portrait(s) of Emily as a Young Author," considers *Always Emily* (2014) by Michaela MacColl and *The World Within: A Novel of Emily Brontë* (2015) by Jane Eagland. Both biofictional narratives reconstruct an image of Brontë despite the scant archival evidence available primarily because, like adult readers, adolescents are interested in the who and why of writers' lives; in addition, readers seek a greater insight into the famous characters that such an author may have invented in their texts. Eagland's and MacColl's portraits of Brontë bring together issues of girlhood, authorship, and biography as they illustrate the life of one young woman and her quest for autonomy through her irrepressible genius.

Imaginings and/as Neo-Victorian Critique

Chapter 6, "Irregulars: Sherlockian Youth as Outsiders," explores the ways several series now take as their point of departure the early life—or developing character(s)—of Sherlock Holmes: how did he become "the" detective? Stephen Peacock's The Boy Sherlock Holmes (2007–12) series and Andrew Lane's equally excellent series, Young Sherlock Holmes (2010–15), trace the developing, particularised and nonconformist education of the young man that convincingly foreshadow the later man in the fictions of Sir Arthur Conan Doyle. It has also arisen in neo-Victorian mysteries for young adults that young female detectives are literally and/ or figuratively the offspring of Sherlock Holmes. The second section of this chapter focuses on Enola Holmes to demonstrate that neo-Victorian narratives of crime use the differing experiences of a young woman who is nonconformist in her actions and agency uses her strengths of observation and detailed consideration to take up the Sherlockian legacy.

Following from these narratives of autodidacticism and self-fashioning, "The Mis(s) Education of Young Women" considers how neo-Victorian young adult narratives of girlhoods and girl cultures in boarding-school books examine and critique the socialisation of young people alongside ideas of "proper" femininity. The school stories of Libba Bray speak to historical issues of concern to young people like queerness and difference. There is, in narratives for young adults, a consistent interest in the past; in particular, the dialogue between the past and the present has a dual purpose of engagement. Such novelists surely "want to bring the culture of some former age to life for a generation with little or knowledge of it" (Rahn 1991, 3). Bray's Gemma Doyle trilogy—*A Great and Terrible Beauty* (2003), *Rebel Angels* (2005), and *The Sweet, Far Thing* (2007)—features young female characters who are on a quest for agency and independence in a system that seeks to regulate their bodies and minds. It is only when they become aware of the social strictures that confine them that they begin to live more authentic lives. "Mis(s)education" suggests that these novels return to the nineteenth century to examine the role that extremely binarised gender roles play in both Victorian and contemporary conceptions of girlhood, and how young women must work to think beyond these ideologies. The four unconventional women of Bray's trilogy embody uncomfortable social issues and/or political interests of unheard voices of the Victorian past, highlighting strategies of resistance to heteropatriarchy, including alternative sexualities, social defiance, and found families.

Last, "~~Deviant~~ Young Womanhood: Liminal Queerness, Mad Femininity, and Spectral Subjectivity" addresses Victorian conventions and restrictions on historical youth, particularly unconventional young women's bodies, and minds. Libba Bray's Gemma Doyle trilogy (2003, 3005, 2007), Jane Eagland's *Wildthorn* (2009), Cat Winters' *The Cure for Dreaming* (2014), and Mindy McGuiness' *A Madness So Discreet* (2014) all feature the trials and tribulations of young adult women who live their lives outside of normative conceptions of gender, sexuality, or politics. This chapter suggests that, while young adult fiction's inclusion of these women highlights many of the obstacles faced by queer people and othered subjects of the past, these texts also figure their female characters as liminal subjects who are in a period of transition—between spaces and places, as well as between rules and rebellion—as they pursue autonomy and selfhood independent of their social circumstances. Such a liminality is one with which contemporary young adult readers can sympathise since the transition from girl-child to adult woman is marked by its own liminality in adolescence, where bodies and minds change, develop, and alter. In neo-Victorian fiction, the characters' transgressions allow for a reconsideration of Victorian social conventions that remain central to the lives of young women.

Neo-Victorian Young Adult Narratives explores our current culture's self-conscious fascination with Victorian authors, characters, and narratives as well as the implications and concerns of potentially appropriative rewritings of persons, texts, tropes, and characters—factual, fictional and f(r)ictional—of the long nineteenth century in new iterations and how the popular imagination has turned back the clock to engage, embody, and document young adults as people and/or characters. The discussions that follow are based on the premise that proof of the oft-demonstrated misjudgement of the savviness of readers in the tween to young adult age groups is found in the range of narratives focused on authors and their books from the long nineteenth century. Historical narratives can captivate young readers, extending knowledge of personages and their writings, or social issues still pertinent today.

Notes

1. See, for example, Ruth Graham's "Against YA" that informs adult readers they should be embarrassed to read writing for children (2014, n.p.).
2. On their American website, one can find their criteria for decision making, such as "good taste" or whether a particular book is "necessary" (n.p.).
3. While book banning is not unique to the United States, it is particularly virulent over the past few years. For examples of those fighting back, see Odette Yousef (2022) or Amna Nawaz (2022) on conversations taking place.
4. Sarah Bilston uses this excellent phrase (see 2004).
5. The nuances between these terms are particularly of interest in the study of young adult narratives which, for the most part, focus on young persons in development. The *OED* defines them as follows: the *Bildungsroman* is a "novel that has as its main theme the formative years or spiritual education of one person" while the *Künstlerroman* is a composite, the former narrative but also "about an artist."

Bibliography

Arias, R. and Pulham, P. Eds. *Haunting and Spectrality in Neo-Victorian Fiction.* Basingstoke: Palgrave, 2010.

"Bildüngsroman, N." *Oxford English Dictionary* Oxford: Oxford University Press, July 2023. https://doi.org/10.1093/OED/5794340722.

Bilston, Sarah. *The Awkward Age in Women's Popular Fiction 1850–1900.* Oxford: Clarendon Press, 2004.

Boehm-Schnitker, Nadine, and Susanne Gruss. Eds. *Neo-Victorian Literature and Culture: Immersions and Revisitations.* London: Routledge, 2014.

Botting, Fred. *The Gothic.* London: Routledge, 2014.

Beckton, Denise. "Bestselling Young Adult Fiction: Trends, Genres and Readership." *TEXT* Special Issue 32 (2015): 1–18.

Cadden, Mike. "The Irony of Narration in the Young Adult Novel." *Children's Literature Association Quarterly.* 25, no. 3 (Fall 2000): 146–54.

Cart, Michael. "Young Adult Literature: The State of a Restless Art." *SLIS Connecting.* 5, no. 1 (2016): n.p. https://aquila.usm.edu/cgi/viewcontent.cgi?article=1099&context=slisconnecting.

Clarke, Rebecca. "By the Book: The Best Book Judy Blume Ever Got as a Gift? 'Lady Chatterley's Lover.'" *The New York Times.* April 23, 2023: n.p. https://www.nytimes.com/2023/04/19/books/review/judy-blume-by-the-book-interview.html?action=click&module=Well&pgtype=Homepage&section=Book%20Review.

Clasen, Tricia, and Hassel, Holly. Eds. *Gender(ed) Identities: Critical Rereadings of Gender in Children's and Young Adult Literature.* New York: Routledge, 2016.

Friedman, Jonathan and Nadine Farid Johnson. "Banned in the USA: The Growing Movement to Censor Books in Schools." *PEN America 100.* September 19, 2023. https://pen.org/report/banned-usa-growing-movement-to-censor-books-in-schools/.

Fritz, Sonya Sawyer, and Sara K. Day. Eds. *The Victorian Era in Twenty-First Century Children's and Adolescent Literature and Culture.* London: Routledge, 2018.

Goodman, James. "Fictional History." *Rethinking History: The Journal of Theory and Practice.* 9, no. 2–3 (2005): 237–53.

Graham, Ruth. "Against YA." *SLATE.* June 5, 2014: n.p. https://slate.com/culture/2014/06/against-ya-adults-should-be-embarrassed-to-read-childrens-books.html.

Heilmann, Ann, and Llewellyn, Mark. *Neo-Victorianism: The Victorians in the Twenty-First Century, 1999–2009.* Basingstoke: Palgrave, 2010.

Heilmann, Ann. and Mark Lewellyn. "On the Neo-Victorian, Now and Then." In *A New Companion to Victorian Literature and Culture,* edited by Herbert F. Tucker, 493–506. Somerset: Wiley-Blackwell, 2014.

Hilton, Mary and Nikolajeva, Maria. *Contemporary Adolescent Literature and Culture*. New York: Routledge, 2012.
Hilton, Mary, and Nikolajeva, Maria. "Time of Turmoil." In *Contemporary Adolescent Literature and Culture*, edited by Nikolajeva and Hilton, 1–16. New York: Routledge, 2016.
Hinton, S. E. *The Outsiders*. New York: Viking Press, 1967.
Hutcheon, Linda. *A Poetics of Postmodernism*. New York: Routledge, 1988.
Kitchener, Caroline. "Why So Many Adults Love Young-Adult Literature." *The Atlantic*. December 1, 2017: n.p. https://www.theatlantic.com/entertainment/archive/2017/12/why-so-many-adults-are-love-young-adult-literature/547334/.
Kohlke, Marie-Luise. "The Lures of Neo-Victorianism Presentism (with a feminist case study of *Penny Dreadful*)." *Literature Compass*. 15, no. 7 (2018): n.p. https://compass.onlinelibrary.wiley.com/doi/abs/10.1111/lic3.12463.
Kohlke, Marie-Luise and Christian Gutleben. Eds. *Neo-Victorian Tropes of Trauma: The Politics of Bearing After-Witness to Nineteenth-Century Suffering*. Amsterdam: Rodopi/Brill, 2010.
Kohlke, Marie-Luise and Christian Gutleben. Eds. *Neo-Victorian Families: Gender, Sexual, and Cultural Politics*. Amsterdam: Rodopi/Brill, 2011.
"Künstlerroman, N." *Oxford English Dictionary* Oxford: Oxford University Press, July 2023. https://doi.org/10.1093/OED/1199810879.
Layne, Bethany. "On the Limits of Biofiction: Bethany Layne Talks to David Lodge." *Literary Hub*. November 20, 2018: n.p. https://lithub.com/on-the-limits-of-biofiction-bethany-layne-talks-to-david-lodge/.
Lederman, Marsha. "U. S.-style Book Bans Could Happen in Canada Too, If We Are Not Careful." *The Globe and Mail*. May 26, 2023: n.p. https://www.theglobeandmail.com/opinion/article-us-style-book-bans-and-censorship-could-happen-in-canada-too-if-were/.
Llewellyn, Mark. "What Is Neo-Victorian Studies?" *Neo-Victorian Studies*. 1, no. 1 (2008): 164–85.
Maier, Sarah E. and Brenda Ayres. *Neo-Gothic Narratives: Illusory Allusions from the Past*. London: Anthem, 2020.
McCallum, Robyn. *Ideologies of Identity in Adolescent Fiction: The Dialogic Construction of Subjectivity*. London: Routledge, 1999.
Mitchell, Kate. *History and Cultural Memory in Neo-Victorian Fiction: Victorian Afterimages*. Basingstoke: Palgrave Macmillan, 2010.
Montz, Amy. "Unbinding the Victorian Girl: Corsetry and Neo-Victorian Young Adult Literature." *Children's Literature Association Quarterly*. 44, no. 1 (Spring 2019): 88–101.
Mydans, Seth. "In a Small Town, a Battle Over a Book." *The New York Times*. September 3, 1989: 22. https://timesmachine.nytimes.com/timesmachine/1989/09/03/568690.html?pageNumber=22.

Nawaz, Amna. "National Debate Over Parental Rights and Censorship Enters School Board Race." *PBS News Hour*. PBS. August 23, 2022. https://www.pbs.org/newshour/show/national-debate-over-parental-rights-and-censorship-enters-local-school-board-races.

Nikolajeva, Maria. *Children's Literature Comes of Age: Toward a New Aesthetic*. London: Garland Publishing Inc., 1996.

Nikolajeva, Maria. *Power, Voice and Subjectivity in Literature for Young Readers*. New York: Routledge, 2010.

"Parents Against Bad Books in Schools." www.pabbis.com. Accessed March 2023.

Rahn, Suzanne. "An Evolving Past: The Story of Historical Fiction and Nonfiction for Children." *The Lion and The Unicorn*. 15 (1991): 1–26.

Reynolds, Kimberley. *Radical Children's Literature: Future Visions and Aesthetic Transformations in Juvenile Fiction*. Basingstoke: Palgrave, 2007.

Pattee, Amy. "Between Youth and Adulthood: Young Adult and New Adult Literature." *Children's Literature Association Quarterly*. 42, no. 2 (Summer 2017): 218–30.

Peacock, Shane. "The Creation of *The Boy Sherlock Holmes*." *The Baker Street Journal*. 58, no. 4 (2008): 17–21.

Salinger, J. D. *The Catcher in the Rye*. New York: Little, Brown and Company, 1951.

Scutter, Heather. *Displaced Fictions: Contemporary Australian Fiction for Teenagers and Young Adults*, Melbourne: Melbourne University Press, 1999.

Smith, Michele J., and Kristine Moruzi. "Vampires and Witches Go to School: Contemporary Young Adult Fiction, Gender, and the Gothic." *Children's Literature in Education*. 49 (2018): 6–18.

Stetz, Margaret. "The 'My Story' Series: A Neo-Victorian Education in Feminism." *Neo-Victorian Studies*. 6, no. 2 (2013): 137–51.

Temple, Erin. "In Conversation with *Enola Holmes:* Neo-Victorian Girlhood, Adaptation, and Direct Address." *Victorians Institute Journal*. 48 (2021): 24–42.

Trites, Roberta. *Disturbing the Universe: Power and Repression in Adolescent Literature*. Iowa City: University of Iowa Press, 2004.

Ue, Tom. "The Boy Wonder: Interview with Shane Peacock." *The Baker Street Journal: An Irregular Quarterly of Sherlockiana*. 60, no. 3 (2010): 33–40.

Welburn, Elizabeth. "In Such a State of Ink: Adolescents in the Novels of Charles Dickens." *Literature Compass* 3, no. 2 (2006): 218–29.

Wilson, Kim. *Re-visioning Historical Fiction for Young Readers*. New York: Routledge, 2011.

Yousef, Odette. "Book Bans and the Threat of Censorship Rev Up Political Activism in the Suburbs." *All Things Considered*. NPR. March 21, 2022. https://www.npr.org/2022/03/21/1087000890/book-bans-and-the-threat-of-censorship-rev-up-political-activism-in-the-suburbs.

CHAPTER 2

Re/articulated Monstrosity: Mary and Her Creature

In "My Hero: Mary Shelley," Neil Gaiman tries to imagine how, in that "the cold, wet summer of 1816, a night of ghost stories and a challenge moved a young woman to delineate the darkness, and give us a way of looking at the world" when she gave us *Frankenstein; or, The Modern Prometheus* in 1818. Gaiman explains:

> It was the place where people learned we could bring life back from death, but a dark and dangerous and untamable form of life, one that would, in the end, turn on us and harm us. That idea, the crossbreeding of the gothic and the scientific romance, was released from into the world, and would become a key metaphor for our times. The glittering promise of science, offering life and miracles, and the nameless creature in the shadows, monster and miracle all in one, back from the dead, needing knowledge and love but able, in the end, only to destroy ... it was Mary Shelley's gift to us, and we would be infinitely poorer without it. (2014, n.p.)

Two hundred years later, the monstrous—predominantly Victor Frankenstein's Creature—increasingly appears in young adult narratives that combine in a mindful combination of Gothic and Victorian rewritings, a kind of neo-Gothic Victorian text.

Young adults, as readers or transmedia viewers, are very receptive to Gothicism as a whole; whether Gothic romance (*Twilight* Saga by Stephanie Meyer) or Gothic fantasy (*Clockwork* Trilogy by Cassandra

© The Author(s), under exclusive license to Springer Nature
Switzerland AG 2024
S. E. Maier, *Neo-Victorian Young Adult Narratives*,
https://doi.org/10.1007/978-3-031-47295-4_2

Clare) as examples, a proven receptiveness to Gothic themes of liminality, monstrosity, transgression, romance, and sexuality (James 2009, 116) exists in such readers. Robyn McCallum suggests there are three narrative strategies integral to young adult literature and the quest for identity:

> First, the double, or *doppelgänger*, is used to represent intersubjective relationships between self and other as an internalized dialogue and the internal fragmentation of the subject-the split subject. Second, characters are seen to experience temporal, cultural or psychological displacement and marginalization and the third is intertextuality. (2012, 68–9)

These three requirements appear in retellings of Mary Shelley or her Creature when narratives about them are stitched together from letters, biographies, letters, and suppositions.

Although written when Mary Godwin Shelley was a young adult—between eighteen and nineteen years of age—the enigmatic nature of her text, with its startling engagement with the promise but dangers of scientific discovery as well as with pervasive and potentially damaging dark Romanticism, are evoked in many novels that fall in the lineage of *Frankenstein*. The young adult shelves include *Dr. Frankenstein's Daughters* (2013) by Suzanne Weyn, *Man Made Boy* (2013) by Jon Skovron, *Mister Creecher* (2013) by Chris Priestley, *This Monstrous Thing* (2015) by Mackenzi Lee, *The Monsters We Deserve* (2018) by Marcus Sedgwick, and *The Dark Descent of Elizabeth Frankenstein* (2018) by Kiersten White. The re/articulation of the long nineteenth century in such neo-Gothic Victorian texts offers "a new take on the evolution of canonical monsters" (Connors and Szwydky 2012, 88). This new perspective results in a direct questioning of the self-alienation and self-questioning that is prevalent in young adult narratives which trace the development of an articulate, intellectual individual in the conventional world that often conflicts with adolescent self-discovery. The two narratives of interest here are Antoinette May's *The Determined Heart* (2015) and Lita Judge's *Mary's Monster* (2018), both of which rearticulate the relation between Mary Godwin Shelley and her Creature.

Mary Godwin Before Shelley

Mary Godwin's life story before the writing of *Frankenstein* is integral for understanding its germination. On August 30, 1797, one of the most radical foremothers of feminism, Mary Wollstonecraft, gave birth to her second daughter, Mary Wollstonecraft Godwin (later Shelley), with the philosopher William Godwin;[1] eleven days later, little Mary Godwin's mother died of septicaemia.[2] In her mother's physical absence, her father encouraged her from girlhood to remain connected to Wollstonecraft through her extensive writings—*Thoughts on the Education of Daughters* (1787), *Vindication of the Rights of Men* (1790), *Vindication of the Rights of Woman* (1792) as well as *Mary: A Fiction* (1788) and *Maria: or, The Wrongs of Woman* (1798)—and to become the educated, intellectual, progressive woman for whom her mother wrote. From a young age, Mary Godwin received an education from a governess and a brief six-month stint in 1811 at a Ramsgate boarding school, and a tutor.

William Godwin remarried to have help raising his daughters, Frances "Fanny" Imlay (Wollstonecraft's eldest daughter by Gilbert Imlay), and Mary. In December 1801, the widow Mary Jane Clairmont joined the household after their marriage and brought with her two children, Charles and Claire (née Clara Mary Jane).[3] Mary Godwin, according to her father, was precocious and intellectually astute, often acting "singularly bold, somewhat imperious, and active of mind. Her desire of knowledge is great, and her perseverance in everything she undertakes almost invincible" (Spark 1987, 15). These traits led to clashes between his wife and daughter; Mary even admitted in a letter on October 28, 1814, to Percy Shelley that she "detested" her stepmother (quoted in Seymour 2000, 61). Godwin's solution in 1812 was to send Mary to live in Scotland with the Baxters, a family of Dissenters with four daughters who were known for their radicalism (Seymour 74–5). While there she entered into an intense friendship with Isabella, one that would end when Isabella married her husband, David Booth.

Returning to London puts Mary Godwin on the path to meet Percy Bysshe Shelley[4] a youthful poet who, at the age of twenty, was already separated from his wife, Harriet, and his first child, Ianthe. Godwin and his wife had started the publishing firm M. J. Godwin, with an accompanying store, but it was increasingly insolvent, and it was through the generosity of fellow literati and public intellectuals that he remained out of debtor's prison. As an aristocrat, Percy Shelley carried the promise of wealth; in reality, he had been cut off by his father, Sir Timothy Shelley for exceeding his *noblesse oblige* and for his abandonment of his family. Entranced by the twenty-year-old young Shelley, the fifteen-year-old child Mary met him in secret at her mother's grave and, when they told her father of their relationship, Godwin was unwilling to trade his daughter's reputation for his theoretical political beliefs. July 28, 1814 was the day they left her father's home for France, taking Claire Clairmont along with them (Spark 24); since Shelley was already married, Mary Godwin was a fallen woman ruined in the eyes of society. Pregnant and penniless, Mary was shocked when her father refused to acknowledge her. Adding to Mary's reputational loss, Shelley's wife gave birth to their second child and his heir, Charles, on November 30, 1814.[5] Mary's own daughter was born prematurely on February 22, 1815, and shortly thereafter, died. She writes on March 6 to their friend James Hogg:

> My dearest Hogg my baby is dead—will you come to see me as soon as you can. I wish to see you—It was perfectly well when I went to bed—I awoke in the night to give it suck it appeared to be *sleeping* so quietly that I would not awake it. It was dead then, but we did not find *that* out till morning—from its appearance it evidently died of convulsions—Will you come—you are so calm a creature & Shelley is afraid of a fever from the milk—for I am no longer a mother now. (quoted in Spark 45)

Shortly thereafter, she gives birth to a son, William, on January 24, 1816, and by May 14, 1816, Shelley, Claire, and Mary travel to stay for the summer with George Gordon, Lord Byron, and Dr. John Polidori at Villa Diotati near Lake Geneva. It is here that Mary Godwin would begin to sketch out the narrative that would become *Frankenstein*.[6]

The Gothic/the Neo-Gothic Victorian

The undead in the present are doubly reflexive; the return to the past means it is never dead and, indeed, if postmodernists do, in fact, "reject the notion that there is a universal acceptance of a single denotation of good versus evil, and that morality is relative, then of course, contemporary Gothic works are going to reflect that *zeitgeist*, and its expression through the Gothic is new" (Maier and Ayres 2020, 2), then this particular *zeitgeist* defines neo-Gothicism. In like fashion, Marie-Luise Kohlke writes that any cultural and critical practice that re-visions the nineteenth century and is latter-day aesthetic and ideological legacies in the light of historical hindsight and critique, but also fantasy—what we *want* to imagine the period to have been like for diverse reasons, including affirmations of national identity, the struggle for symbolic restorative justice, and indulgence in escapist exoticism. (2014, 22; emphasis in original)

For young people, even without the biographical information, the knowledge that *Frankenstein* is a mainstay of popular culture invites a reading of new narratives which reawaken the text from a postmodern perspective.

According to Fred Botting and Catherine Spooner who investigate the contemporary Gothic in their collection *Monstrous Media/Spectral Subjects*, "relationships multiply and numerous configurations emerge" that are "Underpinned (and undermined) by disturbing and obscure movements of monstrosity and spectrality, of monstering and spooking, a key polarisation [that] is sustained in interrelations of political, normative systems and subjective orientations" (2015, 1–2) in the name of progress. Danel Olson has considered, but not defined, the usefulness of such a term, admitting "we need an understanding of how and why the alien will within the neo-Gothic has cast such a spell on us" (2011, xxiii) and how it conjures such "macabre emotional territory" (xxvii).[7] Kohlke and Christian Gutleben argue that "*neo-Victorianism is by nature quintessentially Gothic*: resurrecting the ghost(s) of the past, searching out its dark secrets and shameful mysteries, insisting obsessively on the lurid details of Victorian life, reliving the period's nightmares and traumas" while it "tries to understand the nineteenth-century as the contemporary self's uncanny Doppelgänger," and still "celebrat[es] the persistence of the bygone even while lauding the demise of some of the period's most oppressive aspects.... Clearly there exists a generic and ontological kinship between Gothic and the neo-Victorian phenomenon" which then questions but reinforces the "neo-Gothic cultural craze" (2012, 4; emphasis in original).

A strong argument can be made for the seductiveness of the neo-Gothic novel set in the long nineteenth or Victorian era—neo-Gothic as the larger umbrella term and neo-Gothic Victorian narrative as a focused term specifically dealing with the rewriting of Victorian age Gothic texts—and its transgressive ideas as having a strong pull for young adult readers. Darkness and subtexts encourage "reverberations of past literatures, the hauntings that scientific reasoning has never been able to exorcise" because neo-Gothicism "is that which cannot be controlled, the infectious Other that cannot be scientifically or objectively contained" (Maier and Ayres 4). There is a postmodernist propensity to be "fundamentally concerned … with the ontological and epistemological roots of the *now* through a historical awareness of *then*" (Kaplan 2007, 4), including in literary adaptation and revisioning of past texts and their authors. In particular, the neo-Gothic—like the neo-Victorian—calls out "cultural systems that continue dehumanisation, domination, and objectification practices to those who are Other to the norm" wherein such fictions seek to expose an individual's situational displacement in often non-linear, "fragmented narratives that revisit themes of contamination, collision, transgression, and excess while revisiting Gothic precursors including Dark Romanticism, Victorian Gothic(s), and representations of truth therein" (Maier and Ayres 5).

The young adult section of bookstores is filled with a high percentage of Gothic and neo-Gothic works because many readers, and authors, are seemingly "fascinated by monstrosity and its dark correlation with adolescence" (McInnes 2018, 220). Some of these are neo-Gothic texts—like novels, graphic novels—in that they question tropes, settings, characters, and scenarios that present themselves to invoke the Gothic in a revisitation of earlier texts to reinvent the narrative for a new era. A young reader is encouraged to see doubles, intersubjective relationships, temporal or cultural displacement, and intertextuality (McCallum 2012, 68–9) to see how and where these retellings locate the author and/as her Creature. In particular, the confusion of both Shelley and Creature, as well as author as Creature, parallels the "liminality of the YA period" which is "expressed in troublesome, transitional moments, testing times, identity crises amidst social and environmental crises" (Wisker 2019, 390). In this respect, the Gothic as predecessor to the neo-Gothic "reflected and contributed to the evolution of the radically unstable, unpredictable and trustworthy modern subject, which at best *performs* rather than constitutes a unified, rational, and defensibly self-secure ego" (Kohlke and Gutleben 2012, 8) and the neo-Gothic young adult narrative contains protagonists who seek to reconstruct that sense of self into a coherent subject with the agency to act.

In this way, Mary Shelley's *Frankenstein* "still speaks to very modern fears" and "contemporary anxieties" (Ahuja 2018, n.p.). There are many young adult adaptations of various aspects of *Frankenstein* where strategies both advocate for giving voice to the doubleness of the texts, the complexities of the characters' self-perception, and the appropriateness of neo-Victorian and neo-Gothic projects for adolescent subjectivity. Rather than a sympathetic character, the appeal of a character's dark persona is often challenged by the protagonist as she/he/they move towards personal agency. In the case of re/articulated neo-Gothic fiction, the "monstrous Other is nearly always a sympathetic character in Young Adult horror fiction" (Pulliam 2014, 12). One such monstrous coupling occurs when Mary Shelley and her Creature become *doppelgängers*, reflections of and on each other, in their miseducation, their desire, their loss, their trauma, and their suffering.

Mary Shelley and/as Her Creature

In *Monstrous Bodies: Feminine Power in Young Adult Horror Fiction*, June Pulliam remarks that horror fiction for young people "deserves feminist scholarly inquiry because it uniquely explores the process by which teen girls become gendered subjects" because such fiction "does not simply reproduce through the form of the monstrous Other sexist ideas about women; rather, it uses the tropes horror to deconstruct sexist ideas about women's supposed essential nature, which have been used to justify their subordination" (2014, 11).

The movement from Victorian Gothic *Ur*-texts into neo-Gothic reconstructions continues the suturing of authors to their texts or characters, brought together for the re/articulation of the female authors as biofictional subjects. Male authors, like Charles Dickens and Edgar Allan Poe, do not seem to have the same draw as does the ongoing intense interest in women writers like Charlotte, Anne, and Emily Brontë, Louisa May Alcott, and Emily Dickinson,[8] or those young writers who grew up in unusual circumstances, expressed non-heteronormative behaviour, or defied convention. Young adult fiction presents readers with a certain degree of biographical and historical information about an author of similar age in whom they might see their own double.[9]

In Victorian texts, a young female's maturity is controlled and set by others; the assumption that the protagonist(s) will grow into a sense of selfhood that leads to increased autonomy is further complicated for a young woman who must negotiate far more barriers than, say, a twenty-first-century reader, including having to "fight against cultural and institutional expectations which would deprive them of agency" (Pulliam 12) in the developmental journey. The trajectory of a *Bildüngsroman* or novel of development in the Victorian age is highly complicated by gender and, as a result, so is a neo-Victorian novel. Any such path of a female subject towards education, growth, and agency—that same path taken intentionally by male subjects—would, in fact, be "extraordinarily progressive, and be an invitation to personal development beyond social accomplishments and wifehood, both of which—to some extent—framed the life of the real Victorian young woman" (Maier 2007, 319). Neo-Gothic, Victorian, and neo-Victorian are, to an extent,

> fictions of development [that] reflect the tension between the assumptions of a genre that embodies male norms and values of its female protagonists. The heroine's developmental course is more conflicted, less direct: separation tugs against the longing for fusion and the heroine encounters the conviction that identity resides in intimate relationships. (Abel and Abel 1983, 11)

Female self-definition via a single identity is impossible when considered within the complex historical situation which, once experienced and witnessed by the female authors, then produces their complex heroines of fiction wherein "woman's 'place' is, by definition, multiple—daughter, sister, teacher, lover, wife, surrogate mother figure—in both fact and fiction" (Maier 2007, 320). The multiple perspectives on an appropriate young woman's role, as embodied in these works on Mary Godwin Shelley and her creature, lead the reader to see how, in Shelley's own life, and "in the world of *Frankenstein*, one woman must die so that another can self-actualise" (Mitchell 2014, 114). In neo-Victorian fiction, these defined roles are interrogated for the limitations they place on the development of a young woman within Victorian conventions, but the neo-Gothic exposes the monstrous costs of patriarchal manipulation.

Monstrous Young M/Other

Reconsiderations of Mary Shelley's *Frankenstein*, and of the parallels between her Creature and herself, recreate the despair and confusion of the young author in challenging circumstances. Gina Wisker reminds that the "radical, creative, troublesome spirit of much Gothic" is often "aligned with the disturbance and questioning of that equally troublesome teenage period in our lives" (2019, 378). One appeal of the Gothic for some young adults may be that difference is drawn between the abject and the subject "through the figure of the monster, a type of Other and a double. Teen girls have firsthand experience with the Other: in a patriarchal culture, they *are* the Other, even when they successfully contort themselves into a restrictive normative femininity" (Pulliam 15; emphasis in original). To become the Other in neo-Gothic texts is to become monstrous.

Antoinette May's *The Determined Heart* speaks less of a heart undeterred from surviving Percy Bysshe Shelley's free love than as a daughter determined to write her heart to take a place in her mother's literary legacy. Many texts or films that depict Shelley as a character include her as, according to Megen de Bruin-Molé, "a reproductive writer (effectively a sidekick whose true skill is in observation rather than imagination, or in bearing and nurturing the male 'seed' of productive genius), as an unreliable hysteric, or as the lone, 'unnatural' female genius in a male-dominated world" (2018, 238). More recently, the film *Mary Shelley* (2018) makes the case for a young woman who is intellectual and thoughtful; while young, she spends a great deal of time at her mother's tombstone, communing with Mary Wollstonecraft's memory through reading.

In May's novel, a similar scene gives the reader an intellectual woman, frustrated by her position as judged by society. The young girl traces Wollstonecraft's name on her tombstone and "a sense of familiarity enfolded Mary like welcoming arms. How many times had she sat before this simple monument, pouring out her heart in the hope that love could transcend death?" for truly, "Mary needed her mother badly. There was so much she longed to share: frustrations, dreams, and sadness. What was Mary to do?" (May 2015, 85). Shelley's exhortations to run away together have won the young woman's desire to follow in the choices of her radical mother. The pair are shocked to learn that although they rely on *Political Justice* (1793) to pave the way for their unconventional choice to be together, Godwin's intellectual hypocrisy denies them approval. He asserts his refusal with "Don't tell me what I wrote!" because "Mary is my *daughter*. Do you think for one moment that I would permit her to ruin herself by running off with a married man?" (May 91; emphasis in original). Dismissed from the outset from the discussion about her own future, Mary understands she is to be disowned and cast out of the family.

Separated from paternal understanding, the most important relationship explored in this biofiction is Mary's own with her absent mother; in a sense, the Creature is a representation of her need to express how misunderstood her mother was and, indeed, how the young woman feels monstrous in her need to be understood by the one who created her. Once in France, "She thought often of her mother and tried to picture the Paris of her day … aware that her mother had experienced her greatest joy in Paris"; while she "visited the newly reopened Louvre, Mary imagined her mother walking there with her lover, Gilbert Imlay, among the first public visitors after the Revolution" (121). In the Tuileries Garden, Mary imagines her mother walking with her, feeling strongly "*Mother was here, she saw it all*" and hopes her "her life had taken on a wild and wonderful new direction of its own" (121; emphasis in original). There is the implicit belief that Wollstonecraft would have understood her refusal to bow to tradition. Mary's increasingly introverted, inward existence begins to collapse the boundary between her life and her fiction.

In May's narrative, Mary Godwin's deep connection to her parents' literary legacies and political values gain her admittance to Byron; he practically swoons from his material contact with their heir. "'*Political Justice* seared my mind,' he said, picking up a well-worn copy from a marble-topped side table. 'And *A Vindication of the Rights of Woman* was a daring manifesto. I cannot say that I agree with its premise, but I recognize the genius from which it sprang'" (189), a man's confession that a strong, independent woman is a disagreeable though even if expressed by such a woman. He contemplates how a seduction of Mary might allow him to commune with the spectral literary legacy of the dead authors. Byron continues to pull at Mary's long-standing connections with the literati of the day. He watches the group "like a puppet master" (220), mentions her connection to Samuel Taylor Coleridge, then reads aloud the recently published Gothic poem *Christabel* (1816), while Henry Fuseli's painting, "The Nightmare" (1781), overhangs them all.

This description of the scene has Mary contemplate, "*Do I appreciate being frightened? ... Sometimes, surely, and would it not be splendid to possess the power to frighten others with* my *written words?*" (May 221; emphasis in original). May's biofiction portrays the young woman as an intentional author who invokes and refutes received notions of the female/daughter/author refusing to act as a conduit of male ideas. In response to Byron's demands and Mary's own strength, Percy Bysshe Shelley becomes hysterical, possessed by a laudanum-induced hallucination of her "naked, your eyes blazing out at me from where your nipples should be" (222). Perhaps it is emblematic of how her intentions are no longer to mother the poet Shelley but to return the male gaze, and to mother her own ideas since "the others stared as if she were a monster" (222) or as the "Mother of Monsters" because her confidence, resourcefulness and independence are seen as masculine and unnatural in portraits of her as a character (Ralston and Sondergard 1999, 200–01).

To break the social tension, Byron throws down his challenge, and Mary asks, "'what if electricity—this lightning crackling across the sky—could create a life force?'" (May 224) for which the men have no answer. Even later, after she writes, the social and literary milieu in which Mary comes to write is radically male-centric; May sketches out what a woman might be allowed to write. When her father asks after her "little book" and whether it is "a romantic tale?" to which Mary responds "Hardly … It is neither little nor romantic. I am writing of a man and the monster he creates. You might call it a tale of abandonment" (246). Not unsurprisingly, the father who quickly ignored her needs and grief, "hardly knew what to make of that" (246). In the next few days, the narrator tells the reader she drew from "experience—the loss of her mother and insensitivity of her father, the separation and social ostracism following her elopement—Mary wrote of the anguished monster" (250). She wonders, "Might a monster be her salvation?" (262). Publishing anonymously like many women authors, *Frankenstein* is—factually and fictionally—reviewed as beyond blasphemous and the hunt is on for the author, not authoress, because "All agreed that such challenges—some called them scathing attacks—to both science and religion could not possibly have been written by a woman" (270). *The Determined Heart* allows May to posit an answer to a question many readers of Mary Godwin would have: how might she have felt about the dismissal of woman as author? Perhaps, in this case, "mistreatment, interestingly enough, is redemption" (Coats and Sands 2016, 242). The patriarchal refusal to see a young woman as the author builds her resolve to be recognised by the literati of her time.

In fact, this argument over the parenthood of the novel has continued into the twenty-first century with the subtextual belief that a girl of eighteen could not have written the novel alone. Mary Shelley's clear response to critics was "I certainly did not owe the suggestion of one incident, nor scarcely of one train of feeling, to my husband, and yet but for his incitement, it would never have taken the form in which it was presented to the world" (Shelley [1831], preface). Clearly, her lover's enthusiasm was encouraging, but his pen was not needed beyond as an editorial function, one author to another one. Writing on the 200th anniversary of *Frankenstein*, critic and biographer Fiona Sampson asked in *The Guardian*, "Why hasn't Mary Shelley gotten the respect she deserves?" (2018, n.p.). She noted that in "recent years Percy's corrections, visible in the *Frankenstein* notebooks held at the Bodleian Library in Oxford, have been seized on as evidence that he must have at least co-authored the novel. In fact, when I examined the notebooks myself, I realized that Percy did rather less than any line editor working in publishing today" (n.p.).

The speculation over, and ghosting of, the abilities of a young woman's authorship make Mary's story compelling for a young adult reader who might share a sense of ownership over their own imaginative, intellectual property. Incensed, Mary answers, "I suppose I should be annoyed. I *am* annoyed. I wish I'd insisted on putting my name on it in the first place. Really, to think that a woman could not attempt a scientific theme! But … I'm also pleased that so many are taking my book seriously" (May 270; emphasis in original). Mary comprehends her poet partner is jealous when she overhears him claim "*Frankenstein* is a charming little book" to which her internal reaction is "Her frightful monster *charming*? Really?" (280; emphasis in original). The life she expected and hoped for is not the disillusioned reality of her life. Her reality includes intense grief over the tragedies that befall her children, losses that lead to the fear that the "child she carried, a tiny soul gestated in such strain and suffering … might it be a … monster? Mary shuddered involuntarily, then quickly promised herself to be a better parent than her Dr. Frankenstein" (313). In *A Determined Heart*, Mary's inward existence begins to collapse the boundary between her life and her fiction.

Illustrating Mary

A continuation of this approach to Mary Godwin/Shelley is collapsed with her fiction in the graphic novel, *Mary's Monster*, by Lita Judge. Although "comics" were once seen as a genre for young children and then teen-aged boys (Clemens 2010, 71), the expansion into serious subject matter and less-gendered readership has followed.[10] Since the publication of Art Spiegelman's autographic biofiction *MAUS* (1980) about his family's experiences during the Holocaust, the once dismissed sense of "comic books" has given way to a view of how the genre—and visual stories in general—have increasingly been used, by adults and young adults, to confront "fundamental questions about the interpretation of visual images and about their power to relay affect and invoke a moral and ethical responsiveness in the viewer regarding the suffering of others" (Whitlock 2006, 965) who are in the present or in the historical past. Specifically, "iconic drawings of the human face are particularly powerful in promoting identification between reader/viewer and image" (976). The use of a graphic form as a catalyst for discussion has proven effective for the story of the Brontës, both to discuss their lives and their juvenilia, and *Judge* proves the graphic novel is useful in the neo-Gothic Victorian mode. There is a particular joining of the visual and the narrative which invokes binocularity for such a conjunction asks the reader to move back and forth between the materiality of words as well as the discursive nature of the narrative images (Hirsch quoted in Whitlock 966), thus a way to think about "life narrative that focuses on the changing discourses of truth and identity that feature in … representations of selfhood" (Whitlock 966),[11] a dialogue that might be particularly evocative for a young reader.

It is unsurprising that Mary Godwin, as a young—in fact, teen-aged—unmarried, grieving young woman, mother, and author is of fascination. The audience for Gothic fiction was, historically, "presumed to be young and female" (Spooner 2017, 134); in addition, Gothic/neo-Gothic fiction, expresses the "underlying tensions between challenge and dis-ease, guidance and conformity … and a sense of transition, of liminality" (Wisker 378) in young adults. Such commonalities in anxieties between the readers and the protagonists prove why young adult fiction "littered with reanimated corpses and other things that should be dead but are not" (Coats and Sands 2016, 242) of interest. When combined with "experiencing oneself as an outsider" as a teen who feels "monstrous, clumsy, trapped in a body he or she does not understand, and rejected by peers. Social rules and conventions make this experience even more traumatic" (242).

Jill Lepore's celebratory bicentennial consideration in 2018 of *Frankenstein* included a poignant description of Mary Shelley:

> Like the creature pieced together from cadavers collected by Victor Frankenstein, her name was an assemblage of parts: the name of her mother, the feminist Mary Wollstonecraft, stitched to that of her father, the philosopher William Godwin, grafted onto that of her husband, the poet Percy Bysshe Shelly, as if Mary Wollstonecraft Godwin Shelley were the sum of her relations, bone of their bone and flesh of their flesh, if not the milk of her mother's milk.... *Awoke and found no mother.* (2018, n.p.; emphasis in original)

The Creature and its true creator, Mary, are much alike.

Mary's Monster reverses course and has the Creature act as the narrator of Mary Godwin/Shelley's story (see Fig. 2.1), instantly raising the improbability of his own creation because "Most people didn't believe

Fig. 2.1 Mary's Monster (2018, 2) courtesy of Lita Judge

Mary Shelley, / a teenage girl, unleashed me, / a creature powerful and murderous / enough to haunt their dreams" (2018, 1). Her Creature admires how unconventional she is at the same moment Lita's black/grey/white image has Shelley look directly at the reader. He recalls the pain her difference caused her when "They expected girls to be nice / And obey the rules. / They expected girls to be silent / And swallow punishment and pain" (3).

The next two pages contain one illustration with images of three crows hovering while the monster is behind Mary Godwin, twice her size and powerful; rather than preying upon her vulnerability, the Creature seems to hover in protection over his teen-aged mother. He physically embraces her, thankful that,

> She conceived me.
> I took shape like an infant,
> not in her body, but in her heart,
> growing from her imagination
> till I was bold enough to climb out of the page
> and into your mind. (7)

Gratitude fills the Creature and, as an act of kindness, he seeks in his immortality to tell the reader Shelley's own story. Quoting Mary Wollstonecraft's *A Vindication of the Rights of Woman*, the Creature prefaces the narrative with "A great proportion of the misery that wanders, in hideous forms, around the world, is allowed to rise from the negligence of parents," a commentary on his own fictional parent, Victor Frankenstein, and his true creator Mary Godwin's own father who sent her away in exile (10). The narrator switches to the young woman as she finds herself a fourteen-year-old who feels "left to feel / completely alone" (13), without money, and full of despair at her father's betrayal.

The Gothic, as a historical genre, includes "anxiety … characterized briefly as a fear of historical reversion; that is, of the nagging possibility that the despotisms buried by the modern age may prove yet to be undead" (Baldick 1992, xxi), a truth still seen in the twenty-first century. The very progressive nature of Godwin's politics gave his daughters the right to assume he at least, if not society, would embrace their own progressive attitudes; however, his own radicalism does not extend to his daughters' lives, proving patriarchal conservatism still dictates convention from fathers to daughters. Judge's interpretation shows how Godwin had given the girls, Mary and Fanny Imlay, their mother's books; he had encouraged them to read, to know that "independence is admirable / and imagination indispensable" (Judge 19) but then had succumbed to his second wife's swift judgement that Shelley was "an awful child" (23) because she reacts against authority. Exiled, the young woman is much more comfortable with the radical Baxter family and while there, she learns much more of her mother.

Young adults, like all age groups, deal with loss and grief at the death of a parent. At a desk with a book, a despairing Mary is—in Judge's full-page illustration (see Fig. 2.2)—watched over by Wollstonecraft (42–3) in a light pencil drawing that evokes the ghostly and the ephemeral, a haunting legacy of resilient strength in spite of her own life's difficulties.

Fig. 2.2 Mary's Monster (42) courtesy of Lita Judge

Mary knows her mother was "mother to a rebellion / before she was mother to me" who braved rebellion and witnessed revolution, standing against abuse where "unfair laws toward women" allowed men to beat their wives; she knows the power of mind and words with which her "mother challenged a world of angry men / with the soft feather of her pen" (43). Reading *Maria* in the Baxter's library, and alongside Isabella and with her emotional support, the young girl feels reborn, taking to heart the advice she finds there:

> Death may snatch me from you, before you can weigh my advice, …
> I would then, with fond anxiety, lead you very early in life
> To form your grand principle of action…

Gain experience—ah! Gain it—
While experience is worth having, and acquire sufficient fortitude
To pursue your own happiness; it includes your utility, by a direct path. (44–5)

With comfort in the words and, in the illustration, the embrace of Wollstonecraft, Mary knows in that moment "Her dreams become my own" (44). Mary seeks the life her mother would have wanted her to have, reading science, poetry, fiction, and filling her mind as her body grows into young womanhood until she confronts the reader with her direct gaze. At sixteen, the spectral images of her mother are now gone, and she is ready to grasp hold of her life with "I am no longer a girl / weary with disappointment. / I have become rock / and wind and fiery sea" (48).

The lack of restrictions in Scotland allows Mary to develop in a kind of idyllic youth; the return to the confined, prescribed urbanity of London wreaks havoc on her sense of self as it does for many young people who have to move unwillingly at such a crucial point of maturation. Unhappily recalled, Mary reflects in a window looking out, admitting to herself, "I miss the brightness of Isabella's smile, and most of all / I miss my mother, / because she felt alive to me there" (70). Looking back at how much she has changed, the reader literally sees she is vulnerable. Crucially, at the same time, Godwin boasts of a new follower who calls himself a Godwinian and, for Mary, "The day Percy Bysshe Shelley / walks into my life / is as if a bolt of lightning / shoots through my soul" and the girl believes "the entire landscape / of my existence changes" (74). Lita Judge's panel captures the poet in a Byronic moment; collars high, hair mussed, eyes full, and hand extended, the attuned neo-Gothic reader sees an image that is evocative of a vampire being invited in.[12] Shelley encourages her mind's development as "galvanism, / alchemy, / gravity, astronomy / become a secret language" (83) between them. It is in a graveyard where Mary finds her desire; the next three sections—"WANT," "BESIDE HER GRAVE," and "OUR LOVE IS REAL"—are the moments where proximity to her mother, in body and mind, coalesce into the determination of the young woman. Her stepmother tells her, "*He's in love with the idea of your mother ... more than with you!*" (94; emphasis in original); a modern reader might, in fact, see the wisdom and awareness of the mature woman regarding the young poet's motives.

Viewing herself in a broken mirror, Mary sees how her "Father promised / freedom, love, equality / for women" (96) but does not grant the same to her. Lisa Diedrich, generally thinking about mirrors and mirroring in *Frankenstein*, points to how reflective surfaces, like Mary's window in Judge's graphic novel, "are a prominent prop for staging the identity question" (2018, 388) for young people. Now choosing to define herself as the lover of the poet, Mary is forced to leave. In Europe; her own status as displaced leads her to empathise with women and children she sees huddled together until "Images of the poor / pile up like waves in my imagination / and threaten to drown me" (Judge 127). Judge's illustration of the haunting presence of such women overwhelms Mary into a corner. The return to London makes clear the women are social outcasts and, unlike Shelley, who may still move amongst the aristocrats and the literati, "There is a special curse / reserved for girls / who dare to run away / without a wedding ring" (140).

Giving Birth to Pain

Mary's circumstances continue to devolve as they suffer continual humiliation. Her disillusion is dark and compelling when her father passes her on the street without acknowledgement, but Shelley's moods move to a kind of madness when "he leaps out the window / to escape the terror that stalks him" (148), a terror Judge's drawing personifies as a giant shadow following his escape. While Shelley's behaviour is erratic, Mary must act with reason and intention. She gives birth to her daughter, Clara. With her birth, Mary thinks,

> Suddenly, I understand.
> I didn't steal my mother's life
> when I was born.
> She gave it, just as I have now given
> my daughter life. (156)

Ten days later, Clara is dead; Mary turns seventeen. In her desolation she has a moment of epiphanic thought not uncommon for a neo-Gothic heroine; Mary is now alone—"I am daughter to a ghost / and mother to bones" (160)—but the drawing of huge, sad, spectral eyes watching over her suggest her own mother's care and compassion continues.

More travel, more pain, more death follows Mary until, at Byron's Villa Diodati, the great contest to write begins. Byron watches them in "LIKE A VAMPIRE" (207) and the images Judge uses become darker and more chaotic with lightning strikes in the windows and wind screaming to interrupt sleep with nightmares. The men speak of science and galvanism, but after the deaths of her children[13] Mary Godwin divulges, "I am sickened they talk so easily of men, / not women, / creating life" because "WHAT DO MEN KNOW OF CREATING LIFE"; she is afraid of "What will happen if they assume the power / to create life?" (Judge 216), a question raised by the neo-Gothic text as one that is as pertinent now as it was then. Surrounded by the men's arrogant talk of dead dogs and reanimated life, Mary is

> seized by a wakeful dream.
> I see a pale student of unhallowed arts
> kneeling beside the thing
> he has put together.
> A hideous phantasm of a man
> with watery eyes and blackened lips
> stirs with motion. (224)

Mary is about to give birth to her fictional Creature when "the dark presence of another begins to whisper / from the corners of my mind, / and his shadow grows and touches my own" (228) as Judge frames an image of paper and a feather pen on a desk, and indicator of Mary's imagination made manifest. Mary's emotional devastation continues with Fanny's suicide and with Percy Shelley's wife's suicide by drowning. As death fills her dreams, she keeps writing "until my pen scratches pain/ as loud as screams" (255). With "no longer my own voice I hear. / It is the Creature's" words she hears as a being appears by her side in the drawings. When she writes, Judge's alternate font suggests there is a whisper of "now, Mary, / you begin to see" as if her mother is a voice encouraging her enterprise (255).

The conflation of writer and Creation is exemplified by Judge's clever palimpsestic image (see Fig. 2.3) superimposing Mary's eyes onto the Creature next to the central poem, "I AM":

> I am an exiled girl who feels so rejected by her father,
> she must create a family from ghosts.
> I am a poet who feels persecuted
> because society loathes him for his beliefs.
> I am a sister shackled by illegitimacy and despair,
> lying down to die along.
> I am an abandoned wife standing beside a river,

Fig. 2.3 Mary's Monster (258–59) courtesy of Lita Judge

> no longer able to endure living.
> I AM the rage and shame
> that burn like embers through you.
> I AM THE WORDS torn from your mind
> until they pulse like a BEATING HEART.
> I am your Creature. (256–7)

Now a composite image of the young Mary and her Creature, Mary is becoming her own creation.

Mary steps into her role as woman author, acknowledging her own complexity; on the next two pages, the images separate to stand side by side, creature and creator. In the replication in the panels and windows, as well as the images of Mary and the dead women, or Mary and the Creature, Judge's text separates what Mary may say and what the Creature is free to narrate of her fragmented life in a literal reflection of what Diedrich calls "a collision between interior and exterior, subject and object, self and non-self, and between sympathy or fellow feeling" (390). Mary's Creature will speak these truths in her novel.

Shelley will nourish her writing as her creation all the while learning about herself because "Creating is bone crushing" and "like learning how to breathe again" (260) as the two grow into maturity and until

> my fingers take up the ache
> my heart can no longer hold
> ...
> till the words save my soul
> by creating your own. (263)

In return, he embraces her as she lets fly the crows, now "FEARLESS" (265) to continue. "NINE MONTHS AFTER / I BEGAN WRITING" she declares she has a "new offspring, / …my Creature" (270) with whom she identifies as "Anonymous, / just like my unnamed Creature" (276) until, years later, it is proven she is his Creator.[14] In the Epilogue, the Creature takes back the narrative to remind the reader, that although she has died, "her spirit whispers / eternally through me, / her creature" (298) as he keeps vigil by her grave.

Frankenstein's Offspring

The turn from creator to character leads to a reimagining of Victor Frankenstein as a youth. In this prequel there is a intertextual investigation of the hubris of men that worried Judge's Mary Godwin Shelley, man usurps the place of both God and women in his search to create life from death in the form of an inanimate being re/articulated from the dead. Oppel's texts look back to Frankenstein's adolescent development, his early influences, and his intellectual interest, all of which are hinted at in *Frankenstein*. This story combines literary characters, authors, and philosophers to create the history of Frankenstein when he is the approximate age of the reader. In Kenneth Oppel's *This Dark Endeavour* (2012) and *Such Wicked Intent* (2013), "Monstrosity, duality, [and] performativity" are "the vertices of Victor's adolescent personality" (McInnes 2018, 25).

This Dark Endeavour begins with a chapter titled "Monster" wherein a play, written by Henry Clerval, and two identical twin brothers—Konrad and Victor—appear to do battle against a beast in an effort to save the cursed girl trapped within and to establish masculine primacy between them. Victor, the younger, asks, "Why was it only me you attacked?" to which the girl, Elizabeth Lavenza, answers, "It is you … who is the real monster" (Oppel 2012, 2) in a foreshadowing of what is to come. The reader learns that Konrad and Victor, as well as their cousin Elizabeth, are raised in a progressive, liberal household where the father recognises that all men were created equal, but must be reminded by his wife that women are equal to men and that more would be worthy of such an evaluation "if the education of girls were not designed to turn them into meek, weak-minded creatures who waste their true potential" (26). Mrs. Frankenstein will have none of such submissive girls, "Not in this house" (26). All four young people receive lessons in Greek, Latin, literature, science, and politics from the two parents as well as tutors brought in on other subjects. On Sundays the family make and serve the servants' dinner to emphasise their non-conventional beliefs in equality that echo those of Mary Shelley's own radical theorist and political reformer mother.

Much of historical Gothic fiction takes issue with religion;[15] here, God and faith are debated in this neo-Gothic text an "outmoded system of belief that has controlled and abused people, and that will wizen away under the glare of science" an idea from which Elizabeth recoils since having considered it carefully, she finds "no other possible explanation for … all of this!" (31) than God. Their contention on this point sets up an important moment of contrasting understanding; Victor decries her argument based on lack of proof, to which she counters, "There is *knowing*, and there is *believing*" where "Knowing requires *facts*. Believing requires *faith*. If there were *proof* of God's existence, it wouldn't be a *faith*, would it" (32; emphasis in original). Elizabeth aspires to be an author, telling Victor,

> "I will write a novel," Elizabeth said with decision.
> "What will it be about?" I [Victor] asked, surprised.
> "I don't know the subject yet," she said with a laugh. "only that it will be something wonderful. Like a bolt of lightning!"
> "You'll need a pen name," Konrad said, for the idea of a woman writing a novel was scandalous. (33)

Like Mary Godwin Shelley, Elizabeth believes her own name will suffice, a clear indicator of her desire to retain her own identity. When Konrad brings up the idea of marriage, she rebuts with "It would take a remarkable man to make me marry" (34). Victor's goal is clearly a brazen one full of ego because he declares he will "*create* something, some great work that will be useful and marvellous to all humanity…. In any event, I will be remembered forever" (34; emphasis in original) and thus hopes to win her from his brother who hopes to marry her.

Unlike Mary Godwin Shelley's obvious oppositional pairing of Dr. Frankenstein and his creature, Oppel's creation of identical twins embeds the *doppelgänger* into the narrative. Konrad falls ill; as his twin, Victor experiences empathic illness which upsets Elizabeth because, as she rebukes him, it was "merely in your head" (42). She makes a crucial suggestion of Victorian understandings of hysteria, brain fever, madness, or mental illness, an early indicator for Victor's later degeneracy. Elizabeth's concern for Victor's interest in alchemy, as a means to heal Konrad, sets them at odds. Victor disdains her prayers, while she is concerned with his obsessive search in his books for cures. "Someone has to" he claims, "I cannot pray, but I must do something, or go mad" (47).

Such a turn from faith to science, as in the *Ur*-text *Frankenstein* but also in a post-Darwinian world, leaves the young adults feeling unmoored as to where they might find answers if not in books. With Clerval, the friends discover the secret, ancestral Dark Library of the disgraced alchemist Wilhelm Frankenstein in the house. Desperate to help his brother, but also to gain potential power, Victor dreams of a tree, covered with bones amongst which there "was also fruit—red and luscious. And from the highest branch—for the tree was already taller than me—" from which "blossomed a book" (51). Signifying Eve leaning for an apple of knowledge, Victor fiercely demands they return to the Dark Library for answers where they find mention of a *Vita Elixir* by Paracelsus—in a cryptic language called the Alphabet of the Magi—with references to Cornelius Agrippa. After a search for Julius Polidori in "Wollstonekraft Alley" (68), Geneva, he agrees to translate the recipe because he understands that "When a loved one falls desperately ill, and all else fails, any risk is worth the taking" (73). The question Mary Godwin Shelley's Frankenstein does not ask when he makes his Creature is crucially rearticulated by Henry for the young adult reader: "Even if Polidori can translate the recipe, is the elixir something that should be made?" (84). Oppel's Victor gives a verbal response that is in line with the actions of the original: "damn the consequences!" (85).

The young adult text explores how desperate Victor, as a young man with no control over what is happening, turns to a kind of Faustian bargain to save his brother. Victor's belief in alchemy is countered by the science of healing. As they work on the recipe, experts are called; the skeletal and learned Dr. Murnau arrives from Ingolstadt, and for those in the know, a joke is made about his ghoulish appearance: "He's like a vampyre" (91).[16] Murnau, in spite of his folkloric appearance, discovers that Konrad has a "self-generated abnormality of the blood" (97) causing his wasting fever that, the doctor believes, can be counteracted with a clear fluid injected directly into his bloodstream. With Oppel's eye on the implications for scientific development, a connection to his modern reader, the author has Murnau believe that blood includes "Tiny enclosed compartments—invisible to the naked eye—inside of which all sorts of important work is being done" (98), does not know why Konrad's cells are trying to self-destruct. Victor's alchemical experiments begin in the dungeon below the Chateau's boathouse where, in comparison to Murnau's modern knowledge; the question then arises if the use of alchemy for healing might be sinful, precisely the kind of question which evades Victor's thinking in Shelley's *Frankenstein*. Elizabeth decides, "No … God is the Creator, and anything on this earth is here by His permission. I cannot think He minds if we use His creations—only how" (105).

The juxtaposition of alchemy and faith is countered by reason as well as the belief that knowledge must be earned through experience. Their father uses his own past as an arrogant young man looking for answers as an example with which to warn his son.

"But, Father," I objected, "you yourself have said that the pursuit of knowledge is a grand thing."

> "This is not knowledge," he said. "It is a *corruption* of knowledge. And these books are not to be read…. I keep them, dear, arrogant Victor, because they are artifacts of an ignorant, wicked past—and it is a good thing not to forget our past mistakes. To keep us humble. To keep us vigilant." (Oppel 2012, 23; emphasis in original)

The novel makes clear the presumed bifurcation of thought between the fantastical/alchemical and the "methodical and scientific" (125) with the former based in ego and madness while the latter is based on reason and knowledge.

Gothic texts, as do Oppel's neo-Gothic ones, often explore rapacious sexuality—like Matthew Lewis' *The Monk* (1796)—where the sense of entitlement of a man leads to the victimisation of a young woman. In addition, a romantic triangle is a standard trope of many young adult novels, like Jacob-Edward-Bella in *Twilight*. The reader learns Victor's dark thoughts are not limited to Konrad's illness; Victor's belief in the various potential uses of alchemy leads to the creation of a drug, not unlike a modern date-rape drug, for Elizabeth. With predatory instinct, he goes to the book by Ludividicus Eisenstein where he looks for a "Preparation of the Flameless Fire" (140) so he might find a means to force Elizabeth from Konrad. Victor premeditates a lie that will bring her to him. Believing she is talking to Konrad of their future wedding night, she admits she was troubled by a dream where, at the altar, she "heard a voice.... It was a most malignant voice, one I have never heard, and it said, *I shall be with you on your wedding night*" (143; emphasis in original) invoking Shelley's novel and its horrific consequences for the original Elizabeth. The neo-narrative conflates Victor and/as the Creature both of whom—past and present versions—see Elizabeth as a means to an end. Oppel's parallel for Shelley's Creature has now been revealed when the reader realises Victor is monstrous. By morning, Elizabeth has found him out. Victor's alchemical work "purges" (156) Elizabeth from his thoughts, but he sees her as property with his avowal, "*I will have Elizabeth as my own*" (162; emphasis in original) even if it includes violence because he has a "powerful urge to crush her against me and drink in her heat and scent" (120), a reminder of the violence perpetrated on Elizabeth on her wedding night that leads to her death.

Upending the tradition of a passive woman, and leaning towards the female Gothic's more active female protagonist, according to Sean P. Connors and Lissette Lopez Szwydky, Oppel's novels offer yet another new model of "the historical bad girl" who is

> intelligent, strong-willed, fearless and outspoken. She is also popular, attractive, athletic and competitive, and regardless of the historical time period in which she lives, she is unaffected by her society's conservative gender norms. Instead, she embodies aspects of post-feminist ideology, thus inviting a critique of the role that this figure plays in perpetuating the assumption that gender discrimination is an individual rather than structural problem. (2012, 88)

Long-nineteenth-century patriarchal discrimination against women was systemic, and in reaction, Oppel's Elizabeth exhibits the desire for freedom of gendered assumptions and dress. Elizabeth embraces the feeling of boyishness when she wears Victor's clothes. Although she does not enjoy the tightness of the breeches on her thighs, she admits "it is quite wonderful to feel so light, after so many layers.... No wonder you men manage the affairs of the world. It is far less tiring in lighter clothes!" (106) framing a causality between the restrictions of being a woman as represented in her clothing and the freedom of movement from being male. Oppel invokes the historical Wollstonecraft who had made the same comparison. For women, "IGNORANCE and the mistaken cunning that nature sharpens in weak heads as a principle of self-preservation, render women very fond of dress, and produce all the vanity which such a fondness may naturally be expected to generate, to the exclusion of emulation and magnanimity" (Wollstonecraft [1792] 2004, ch XIII). Elizabeth, like Mary, believes that given the opportunity for rational dress and educational interests, women would be less focused on their bodies and fashion leaving room for intellectual and character development.

Mary Godwin Shelley's mental and emotional turmoil, as written by May and Judge in these young adult narratives, is paralleled in Oppel's novels. Described as a spectral figure, an oft somnambulist who, according to the father, had a mind "temporarily disordered by the great changes in her life, and even in sleep it would not let her rest, and would make her walk in the house in the early hours of morning, trying to puzzle things out" (2013, 86). Her understanding of somnambulism is a clear indicator of distress.[17] When the sleeping young woman comes to his bed, Victor notes Elizabeth "seemed to emanate an eerie power. She was herself, and not herself" (86).

One power women hold that men do not is to give birth to a child. Elizabeth connects the impact of childbirth and loss with Mary Godwin Shelley with "Boys never remember these stories properly.... Girls do because we know it awaits us. You [Victor] ... nearly killed your mother" (2013, 176). Shelley was haunted by the image of a Creature brought alive before her:

> I saw the pale student of unhallowed arts kneeling beside the thing he had put together. I saw the hideous phantasm of a man stretched out, and then, on the working of some powerful engine, show signs of life, and stir with an uneasy, half vital motion. Frightful must it be; for supremely frightful would be the effect of any human endeavour to mock the stupendous mechanism of the Creator of the world. (Shelley [1818] 2013, 350–51)

Her dream is reimagined for her own novel where, "by the glimmer of the half-extinguished light," Dr. Frankenstein

> saw the dull yellow eye of the creature open; it breathed hard, and a convulsive motion agitated its limbs ... his eyes, if eyes they may be called, were fixed on me. His jaws opened, and he muttered some inarticulate sounds, while a grin wrinkled his cheeks. He might have spoken, but I did not hear; one hand was stretched out, seemingly to detain me. ([1818] 2013, 83)

In one scene described by Victor is reminiscent of both Mary Godwin Shelley's own dream and her Creature in *Frankenstein*, Victor tells the reader how in one of her somnambulist visits,

> When she turned to me, her face was stricken with anxiety. In her arms she cradled and old doll. I shivered, for her gaze seemed to look right through me, to someone just behind me.
> "The baby's not dead," she said fiercely.
> "No," I said.
> "She's just cold."
> "Yes," I said.
> "She needs warming...." (2012, 87)

This Dark Endeavour then rewrites these ideas in a dream Victor has of Konrad, dead and in his coffin. Victor stands by in silent rage; he envisions himself speaking "words of power" while applying unguents and attaching "strange machines to his limbs, his chest, his skull" (Oppel 2012, 204). Victor continues, "And then I gave a great cry, and energy erupted from within me and arced like lightning from my body to his. His hand twitched. His head stirred. His eyes opened and looked at me" (205). Konrad's illness requires a similar awakening; the alchemical process is used to create the elixir which is then given to the sick young man. He revives and even though there is no scientific proof there is possible causation—the elixir contained bone marrow from Victor, the suggestion being that there might be scientific reasoning just not yet discovered. Problematically, Victor now sees Konrad not his patient, but his "*Creation!* ... Come now, you must feel *something*! You have the Elixir of Life in you!" (288; emphasis in original). Their joy collapses when Konrad dies in his sleep. Victor rages at Elizabeth,

"You said—*you* said—He would listen and heal Konrad. Why didn't He?"
"He heard us. But sometimes He says no."
"He is not there at all," I [Victor] said savagely.
She shook her head. "He is there."
"Make me believe you. Convince me, *here*." I beat at my head with my hands. (294; emphasis in original)

Again, the faith of one leaves the intellect of the other bereft of explanation, only disgust at his own failure.

Such Wicked Intent opens with the destruction of the contents of the Dark Library. Books are burned, and as Victor "prowled the margins of the fire … hungry for destruction" there is only the smell of "burning paper and ink and reeking leather" (Oppel 2013, 1) to satiate his grief. Desperate for answers, he finds one book that will not burn and studies it, declaring "My faith in all things is shaken. Modern science failed me. Alchemy failed. I trust nothing but am ready to try anything" (16) including the occult. One in a line of "adolescent protagonists who strive to understand their own power by struggling with the various institutions in their lives" (Trites 8), Victor represents a critical moment in the rational limits of a construction of selfhood. Elizabeth, invoking Faust, chastises him: "Admit it…. You'd make your own deal with the devil if you could play God" (22). This slight is particularly apt since Elizabeth plans to join a convent, leaving the men to fend for themselves as Victor vows he will not subscribe "to any rational system again. Nothing will bind me…. If it makes me mad, so be it. But leave me to my method" (24). Victor's solution for the loss of Konrad is to create a Golem, the "mud creature" for which Victor wonders "if this made me his father" (133). It is a body created for Konrad to inhabit if he can return from his otherworldly existence in a kind of limbo.

There is another reference to the collapse of Edenic society when the trio of Elizabeth, Victor, and Henry deconstruct an oil painting of the Frankenstein who built the chateau: "But there's symbolism to it as well…. The apple's always a sign of the forbidden fruit of the tree of knowledge and … that one there has a bite out of it" (27), and indicator this narrative's new endeavour will end as badly as the first did in *This Dark Endeavour*. The experiment fails, but Victor's desire for power over life and death does not wane; the last scene is of friends parting while a storm rages as Victor muses about the "*astonishing power*" (310; emphasis in original) of the lightning. The neo-Gothicism of these young adult narratives illuminates, like the flash of the lightning, the moment of movement into the neo-/Victorian reproduction of newly articulated generations of texts which continue the Gothic's lineage in a rigorous critique of what has come before to leave some neo-Victorian young women disillusioned and disenfranchised by their Gothic elders.

Notes

1. Mary Wollstonecraft and William Godwin lived, respectively, April 27, 1759–September 10, 1797, and March 3, 1756–April 7, 1836.
2. According to Christine Hallett, puerperal fever "affected women within the first three days after childbirth and progressed rapidly, causing acute symptoms of severe abdominal pain, fever and debility" (2005, 1); in Wollstonecraft's situation, infection most likely occurred when bacteria was introduced into the female reproductive tract after childbirth by the physician in attendance.
3. From 1814 onwards, Mary's half-sister decided to use the name "Claire" and is how she will be referenced throughout this chapter.
4. Shelley was born on August 4, 1792, and died in unclear circumstances, by drowning, on August 4, 1792.
5. This elopement with a girl-child was not Shelley's first; he had already seduced Harriet Westbrook when she was only sixteen and married her in Edinburgh on August 28, 1811. On June 23, 1813, Harriet gave birth to Eliza Ianthe Shelley. He remarried her in London to secure the rights to their child in March of 1814.
6. The lore of how the challenge to "each write a ghost story" occurred has been well rehearsed by scholars, but for the most accurate version according to Mary Shelley's "Introduction" to the 1831 edition.
7. Other authors refer to neo-Gothicism, but they do not define the term; see Mary-Ellen Snodgrass (2011), Barbara Frey Waxman (1992), Lucian-Vasile Szabo and Marius-Mircea Crisan (2018) who evoke, but do not define, the term neo-Gothic.
8. The last few years have seen enquiries regarding these women such as renewed interest in Alcott's sexuality in "Did the Mother of Young Adult Literature Identify as a Man?" (Thomas 2022), the film about the Brontë family *To Walk Invisible* (2015) and another about the middle sister, *Emily* (2022), and the TV series *Dickinson* (2019–2021). Most pertinent here is the biofictional film *Mary Shelley* (2017).
9. There are several tween and young adult adaptations of Poe's life and tales including *Eddie: The Lost Youth of Edgar Allan Poe* (2012) by Scott Gustafson, *Masque of the Red Death* (2012) and *The Fall* (2014) by

Bethany Griffin, *The Raven's Tale* (2019) by Cat Winters, and *His Hideous Heart* (2019) edited by Dahlia Adler.

10. *Frankenstein* has been rewritten and adapted, loosely and otherwise, many times into comics and graphic novels (see Murray 2016) as well as other transmedia creations (see Friedman and Kavey 2016).
11. Edward Said has argued effectively, and pertinent to the argument here, that comics can defy "the ordinary processes of thought, which are policed, shaped and re-shaped by all sorts of pedagogical as well as ideological pressures.... I felt that comics freed me to think and imagine and see differently" (qtd in Whitlock 967).
12. According to vampire lore, a vampire must be invited in for the first time (Gelder 2002, 35).
13. Clara died of dysentery at the age of one, and William of malaria at three and a half (Seymour 2000, 214 and 231).
14. Ledore sees the historical questioning of Mary Shelley's authorship as insulting and as a supposition that the text is "more assembled than written, an unnatural birth, as though all that the author had done were to piece together the writings of others, especially those of her father and her husband" as if "this enduring condescension, the idea of the author as a vessel for the ideas of other people—a fiction in which the author participated, so as to avoid the scandal of her own brain" (n.p.).
15. For an excellent critical discussion on the Gothic strain of anti-Catholicism in popular fiction, see Diane Long Hoeveler (2014); however, for seminal examples of such novels, see Matthew Lewis' *The Monk* (1796/2016) and Ann Radcliffe's *The Italian* (1797/2017).
16. F. W. Murnau's silent German Expressionist film, *Nosferatu* (1922), was an unauthorised adaptation of Bram Stoker's Gothic vampire novel, *Dracula* (1897/1997).
17. Other recent Gothic tales using this trope include *The Somnambulist* (2007) by Jonathan Barnes.

Bibliography

Abel, Hirsch and Langland Abel, eds. *The Voyage In: Fictions of Female Development*. Hanover, NH: University Press of New England, 1983.

Adler, Dahlia, Ed. *His Hideous Heart*. New York: Flatiron, 2019.

Ahuja, Anjana. "'Frankenstein' still speaks to very modern fears." *Financial Times* January 15, 2018. n.p.

Baldick, Chris. "Introduction." *The Oxford Book of Gothic Tales*, edited by Chris Baldick, xi–xxiii, Oxford: Oxford University Press, 1992.

Barnes, Jonathan. *The Somnambulist*. London: Gollancz, 2007.

Botting, Fred and Catherine Spooner. "Introduction." *Monstrous Media/Spectral Subjects*, 1–11. Manchester: Manchester University Press, 2015.
Clemens, Kirsten. "Graphic Novels and the Girl Market." *CEA Critic*. 72, no. 3 (2010): 71–85.
Coats, Karen and Farran Norris Sands. "Growing up Frankenstein: Adaptations for Young Readers." In *The Cambridge Companion to Frankenstein*, edited by Andrew Smith, 241–56. Cambridge: Cambridge University Press, 2016.
Connors, Sean P. and Lissette Lopez Szwydky. "The Pre-Monstrous Mad Scientist and the Post-Nerd Smart Girl in Kenneth Oppel's *Frankenstein* Series." In *Young Adult Gothic Fiction: Monstrous Selves/Monstrous Others*, edited by Michelle J. Smith, Kristine Moruzi, 87–109. Montreal: McGill University Press, 2012.
de Bruin-Molé, Megen. "'Hail, Mary, the Mother of Science Fiction': Popular Fictionalisations of Mary Wollstonecraft Shelley in Film and Television, 1935–2018." *Science Fiction and Television* 11, no. 2 (2018): 233–55.
Dickinson. Tuning Fork Productions, Apple TV+. November 1, 2019–December 24, 2021.
Diedrich, Lisa. "Being-becoming-monster: Mirrors and Mirroring in Graphic *Frankenstein* Narratives." *Literature and Medicine* 36, no. 2 (Fall 2018): 388–411.
Emily. Embankments Films, Ingenious Media, Warner Bros. Pictures, September 9, 2022.
Friedman, Lester D. and Allison Kavey. *Monstrous Progeny*. New Brunswick: Rutgers, University Press, 2016.
Gaiman, Neil. "My Hero: Mary Shelley." *The Guardian*. October 18, 2014, n.p. https://www.theguardian.com/books/2014/oct/18/my-hero-mary-shelley-neil-gaiman.
Gelder, Ken. *Reading the Vampire*. London: Routledge, 2002.
Griffin, Bethany. *Masque of the Red Death*. New York: Greenwillow Books, 2012
Griffin, Bethany. *The Fall*. New York: Greenwillow Books, 2014.
Gustafson, Scott. *Eddie: The Lost Youth of Edgar Allan Poe*. New York: Simon and Schuster Books, 2011.
Hallett, Christine. "The Attempt to Understand Puerperal Fever in the Eighteenth and Early Nineteenth Centuries: The Influence of Inflammation Theory." *Medical History* 49 (2005): 1–28.
Hoeveler, Diane Long. *The Gothic Ideology: Religious Hysteria and Anti-Catholicism in British Popular Fiction, 1780–1880*. Cardiff: University of Wales Press, 2014.
James, Kathryn. *Death, Gender and Sexuality in Contemporary Adolescent Literature*. New York: Routledge, 2009.

Judge, Lita. *Mary's Monster: Love, Madness, and How Mary Shelley Created Frankenstein.* New York: Roaring Brook Press, 2018.
Kaplan, C. Victoriana: *Histories, Fictions, Criticism.* New York: Columbia, 2007.
Kohlke, Marie-Luise and Christian Gutleben. "The (Mis)Shapes of Neo-Victorian Gothic: Continuations, Adaptations, Transformations." In *The Neo-Victorian Gothic*, edited by Kohlke and Gutleben, 1–48. Amsterdam: Rodopi/Brill, 2012.
Kohlke, Marie-Luise. "Mining the Neo-Victorian Vein: Prospecting for Gold, Buried Treasure and Uncertain Metal." In *Neo-Victorian Literature and Culture: Immersions and Revisitations*, edited by Nadine Boehm-Schnitker and Susanne Gruss, 21–37. New York, Routledge, 2014.
Lee, Mackenzi. *This Monstrous Thing.* New York: Katherine Tegen Books, 2015.
Lewis, Matthew. *The Monk.* London: Oxford University Press, 1796.
Maier, Sarah E. "Portraits of the Girl-Child: Female *Bildungsroman* in Victorian Fiction." *Literature Compass* 4, no. 1 (2007): 317–35.
Maier, Sarah E. "Dark Descen(den)ts: Neo-Gothic Monstrosity and the Women of *Frankenstein*." In *Neo-Gothic Narratives: Illusory Illusions of the Past*, edited by Maier and Brenda Ayres, 23–40. London: Anthem, 2020.
Maier, Sarah E. and Brenda Ayres, eds. *Neo-Gothic Narratives: Illusory Illusions of the Past.* London: Anthem, 2020.
Mary Shelley. HanWay Films, BFI, Curzon Artificial Eye, September 9, 2017.
May, Antoinette. *The Determined Heart.* Seattle: Lake Union Publishing, 2015.
McCallum, Robyn. *Ideologies of Identity in Adolescent Fiction: The Dialogic Construction of Subjectivity.* New York: Routledge, 2012.
McInnes, Andrew. "Young Adult *Frankenstein*." In *Transmedia Creatures: Frankenstein's Afterlives*, edited by Francesca Saggini and Anna Enrichetta Soccio, 219–32. Lewisburg: Bucknell University Press, 2018.
Mitchell, Donna. "Of Monsters and Men: Absent Mothers and Unnatural Children in the Gothic 'Family Romance.'" Otherness: Essays and Studies. 4, no. 2 (2014): 105–29.
Murray, Christopher. "*Frankenstein* in Comics and Graphic Novels." In *The Cambridge Companion to Frankenstein*, edited by Andrew Smith, 219–240. Cambridge: Cambridge University Press, 2016.
Nosferatu. Prana Film, 1922.
Olson, Danel. "Introduction." In *21st Century Gothic*, edited by Danel Olson, xxi–xxxiii. Plymouth, UK: Scarecrow Press, 2011.
Oppel, Kenneth. *This Dark Endeavour.* Toronto: Harper Trophy Canada, 2012.
Oppel, Kenneth. *Such Wicked Intent.* Toronto: Harper Trophy Canada, 2013.
Priestley, Chris. *Mister Creecher.* London: Bloomsbury, 2011.
Pulliam, June. *Monstrous Bodies: Feminine Power in Young Adult Horror Fiction.* Jefferson: McFarland Press, 2014.

Radcliffe, Ann. *The Italian*. London: Oxford University Press, 1797/2017.
Ralston, Ramona, and Sid Sondergard. "Biodepictions of Mary Shelley: The Romantic Woman Artist as Mother of Monsters." In *Biofictions*, edited by Martin Middeke and Werner Huber, 201–13. New York: Camden House, 1999.
Sampson, Fiona. "Frankenstein at 200—Why Hasn't Mary Shelley Been Given the Respect She Deserves?" *The Guardian*. January 13, 2018: n.p. https://www.theguardian.com/books/2018/jan/13/frankenstein-at-200-why-hasnt-mary-shelley-been-given-the-respect-she-deserves-?CMP=Share_iOSApp_Other.
Sedgwick, Marcus. *The Monsters We Deserve*. Brookline: Zephyr Press, 2018.
Seymour, Miranda. *Mary Shelley*. London: John Murray, 2000.
Shelley, Mary. *Frankenstein. The Original 1818 Text*, 3rd ed., edited by D. L. MacDonald and Kathleen Scherf. Peterborough, ON: Broadview Press, 2013.
Skovron, Jon. *Man Made Boy*. New York: Penguin Juvenile, 2013.
Snodgrass, Mary Ellen. "Michel Faber, Feminism, and the Neo-Gothic Novel: *The Crimson Petal and The White*." In *21st Century Gothic*, edited by Daniel Olson, 111–23. Plymouth, UK: Scarecrow Press, 2011.
Spark, Muriel. *Mary Shelley*. London: Cardinal, 1987.
Spooner, Catherine. "'The Gothic is part of history, just as history is part of the Gothic': Gothicizing History and Historicizing the Gothic in Celia Rees' Young Adult Fiction." In *New Directions in Children's Gothic: Debatable Lands*, edited by Anna Jackson, 132–46. London: Routledge, 2017.
Stoker, Bram. *Dracula*. 1897. Ed. Glennis Byron. Peterborough: Broadview Press, 1997.
Szabo, Lucian-Vasile, and Marius-Mircea Crisan. "Technological Modifications of the Human Body in Neo-Gothic Literature: Prostheses, Hybridization and Cyborgization in Posthumanism." *Caietele Echinox Journal* 35 (2018): 147–58.
Thomas, Peyton. "Did the Mother of Young Adult Literature Identify as a Man?" *The New York Times*. December 24, 2022. https://www.nytimes.com/2022/12/24/opinion/did-the-mother-of-young-adult-literature-identify-as-a-man.html.
To Walk Invisible. BBC Cymru Wales, Lookout Point, The Open University, 2016.
Waxman, Barbara Frey. "Postexistentialism in the Neo-Gothic Mode: Anne Rice's *Interview with the Vampire*." *Mosaic* 25, no. 3 (Summer 1992): 79–97.
Weyn, Suzanne. *Dr. Frankenstein's Daughters*. New York: Scholastic, 2013.
White, Kirsten. *The Dark Descent of Elizabeth Frankenstein*. New York: Delacorte Press, 2015.
Whitlock, Gillian. "Autographics: The Seeing 'I' of the Comics." *MFS Modern Fiction Studies* 52, no. 4 (Winter 2006): 965–979.
Winters, Cat. *The Raven's Tale*. New York: Harry N. Abrams, 2019.

Wisker, Gina. "Gothic and Young Adult Literature: Werewolves, Vampires, Monsters, Rebellion, Broken Hearts and True Romance." In *The Edinburgh Companion to Gothic and the Arts*, edited by David Punter, 378–92. Edinburgh: Edinburgh University Press, 2019.

Wollstonecraft, Mary. *Vindication of the Rights of Woman*. 1792. London: Penguin, 2004.

CHAPTER 3

Mash(ed) Up: Maidens, Monsters, and Mad Scientists

Frankenstein is, perhaps, an unexpected companion text for this new century, a time of a new millennium, and the technologies that replicate exponentially as it moves forward. A blending of science and the arts, a kind of STEAM[1] production from 1818, Mary Shelley's novel empowered her—can she really have only been eighteen when she wrote it?—to inquire into the ethical questions of life, death, moral responsibility, and monstrosity posed by and to those who pursue scientific inquiry, to expose the hubris of a mad scientist, and to consider the ramifications of the creation of life in natural and unnatural forms.

Neo-Victorian fiction resonates with the "dense intertextuality" (Kohlke and Gutleben 2012, 3) that, as outlined earlier, also defines many neo-Gothic young adult narratives which rely upon long-nineteenth-century novels or others as their *Ur*-texts. Christine Wilkie-Stibbs delineates intertextuality as an embrace of discourses, where "in its uttered, illustrated, written, mimed or gestured manifestations … it includes images and moving images, the social and cultural context, subjectivities—which are the reading/seeing/speaking/writing/painting/thinking subjects" (2004, 179). In this case, the intertext is Mary Godwin Shelley's *Frankenstein*; it is, usually, identified as the first time an explicit attempt is made to create a fictional world that uses "known or imagined scientific principles, or to a projected advance in technology, or to a drastic change in the organization of society" (Abrams 1999, 279): a science fiction. In the realism of her particular world building, Mary Godwin Shelley astutely

© The Author(s), under exclusive license to Springer Nature
Switzerland AG 2024
S. E. Maier, *Neo-Victorian Young Adult Narratives*,
https://doi.org/10.1007/978-3-031-47295-4_3

maintains the standards of the early nineteenth century in her novel when only men participate in scientific endeavour while women do not. Several recent neo-Victorian young adult texts pose questions regarding the assumption of male dominion over science, women as objects of experimentation, and ethical concerns over transgressive scientific practices; indeed, narrators in those texts question whether the end justifies the means or, just because science can manipulate the natural world, should it. Megan Shepherd's trilogy—*The Madman's Daughter* (2013), *Her Dark Curiosity* (2014), and *A Cold Legacy* (2016)—and Theodora Goss' Extraordinary Adventures of the Athena Club—*The Strange Case of the Alchemist's Daughter* ([2017] 2018), *European Travel for the Monstrous Gentlewoman* ([2018] 2019), and *The Sinister Mystery of the Mesmerising Girl* ([2019] 2020)—contain the narratives of girl-children, adolescent girls, and young women who are the biological and/or literal product of their scientist fathers who have tread into the dark uses of such learning. It would be erroneous to think that young adult neo-Gothic narratives are akin to what Fred Botting refers to as "candygothic" which "no longer contain[s] the intensity of a desire for something that satisfyingly disturbs and defines social and moral boundaries" (2001, 134). These particular neo-Victorian works reconsider of science as the property of men—as those educated in and encouraged to investigate scientific questions—and to deliberate ethical questions—"Just because we can, should we?"—found in earlier literary texts and to suggest the potential occurrence of harm if they are left unaddressed.

Daughters as Legacies; or, the Sins of the Fathers

Megan Shepherd's The Madwoman Trilogy elucidates for the reader the ramifications of Victorian sciences if men, in their search for glory or power, forget questions of ethics and/or lose their altruistic positioning in relation to their experimentations. *The Island of Dr. Moreau* (1896), *The Strange Case of Dr. Jekyll and Mr. Hyde* (1886), and *Frankenstein* are explored in neo-Victorian narratives that consider the ramifications of perverting Charles Darwin's theories to cross ethical and moral boundaries. The neo-Victorian characters, the young men and women—the next generation(s)—who come in their wake, who weigh the moral implications of such achievements. The neo-Gothic narratives set in the neo-Victorian past enact their later generational characters as correctives to the sins of their fathers.

Juliet Moreau is the protagonist of all three novels; her story begins in *A Madman's Daughter* and revisits the traditional Gothic "intergenerational plot surrounding genealogy, inheritance, contested legacies, and family secrets" (Kohlke and Gutleben 2012, 10) found in historical Gothic books. Invoking *The Island of Dr. Moreau* as its central intertext, the title of the novel casts the female protagonist as dually marginalised—she is the girl-child of a madman.[2] Her father is Dr. Henri Moreau, the infamous scientist run out of England for his experimentation on live animals—vivisection—all of which he justifies as in the name of post-Darwinist evolutionary investigation.[3]

The compounding of Gothic representations of science's potential misuses and the neo-Gothic's perspective on its consequences is not surprising given both are "a genre and a mode emphatically concerned with otherness in its manifold shapes and monstrous misshapes" (Kohlke and Gutleben 2012, 4). Here, Shepherd begins a "feminist counternarrative[ ] of nineteenth-century science" (Heilmann 2014, 92); as Ann Heilmann suggests, neo-Victorian narratives with science-interested female protagonists act as an encouragement and a correction to the "rise of neo-essentialism in contemporary (popular) science discourse and the ongoing underrepresentation of women in the scientific world" (93).

The long nineteenth century, for example, was rocked to its core of faith by early scientific discoveries like the young but largely unacknowledged palaeontologist Mary Anning's ichthyosaur, plesiosaur, and pterosaur finds (1823) in Lyme Regis, Dorset and Darwin's assertions of evolutionary theory in *On the Origin of Species* (1859).[4] The film *Creation* (2009) poignantly creates a fictional moment where Darwin is confronted by Thomas Huxley's seeming delight that "You have killed God, sir. You have killed God" (14:10), a claim that leaves Darwin devastated, physically ill from his sense of responsibility. He recognises that society is bound together by faith. Potential developments in science were accompanied by suggestions of how or whether such a geological record could be paired up with the Biblical narrative, a challenge further confounded by clergymen who were also geologists—early palaeontologists—like Reverend William Buckland (later Dean of Westminster as well as President of the Geological Society in 1824) who searched for such a connection. The nineteenth-century establishment of the Geological Society of London (1807) and the Royal Geographic Society (1830, London UK) gatherings brought together learned men who were interested in the pursuit of scientific development and exploration. Women were, as modelled by the rest of patriarchal heteronormative society, excluded from the scientific societies based on the assumed inadequacy of their understanding and the inferiority of their intelligence. This assumption is a misogynist hypothesis given, to the contrary, women like Ada Lovelace, Marie Salomea Sklodowska-Curie, Marie Somerville, and others—Mary Anning included—were often autodidacts, or gifted students of math, physics, chemistry, physical sciences, astronomy, geology, or other disciplines who advanced science in a myriad of important ways which lead to binary systems for computer programming, radioactivity, and planetary and fossil discoveries, respectively.

The earlier parsing of the terms neo-Gothic and neo-Victorian allows for both terms to be applied to one text. Neo-Gothic and neo-Victorian narratives like Shepherd's are, fittingly, a hybrid between both genres and are able to bring the ideas of the monstrous to be considered in a self-aware critique to postulate the cost when science as the sole purview of men is challenged. Much of Shepherd's initial narrative is framed around Moreau's failure as a father and as an exiled scientist. Without the usual expectation afforded to young women of the upper class of patrilineal protection and status, Juliet is removed from the usual role of a daughter in society who moves from darling child to betrothed woman. Instead of participating in her first season at sixteen, she is on the street with no ability to fight against her circumstances other than to survive by becoming a maid. After her father is cast out of the scientific community—then from society—her mother dies when Juliet is just fourteen and "London society was not kind to the daughter of a madman. To the orphan of a madman, even less" (2013, 23). The elegant colleagues who had once treated her family with kindness were the "same men [who] were the first to brand him a monster" (23).

Cast aside by the scientific and social communities of her family by her father's disgrace, Juliet finds solidarity in female companions, a kind of girl squad who look out for each other. Although there may be an element of nostalgia to thinking of girlhood friendships, such "novels do not merely seek to revive the Victorian era or its literary modes; rather, they effect a transformation of it" (Hadley 2011, 181). Here, the people who surround Juliet are not all of her same age or class as would have likely been the case in a Victorian fiction. One person who continues to accept and love her is her friend, Lucy Radcliffe. When with her companion, Juliet admits, "I leaned in and pressed my cheek to hers. Her parents would be horrified to know she had snuck out to meet me. They had encouraged our friendship when Father was London's most famous surgeon but were quick to forbid her to see me after his banishment" (Shepherd 2013, 2). At another point, when afraid, Lucy "slid off her glove and found my hand in the dark" (14) to both give and receive comfort. No matter what her family or her social circle say about Juliet, or even despite how Juliet degrades herself, Lucy refuses to diminish her person or her intellectual capacity. The disgraced young woman wants to protect her friend, relieving her of their bond because, Juliet says, "I'm a *maid*"; Lucy bravely refuses the premise of the dismissal, reminding Juliet it is only a "temporary situation.... You come from money. From class" (7; emphasis in original).

Then, as now, young women are at risk when alone; assaulted at work by her boss, Dr. Hastings, Juliet strikes back to defend herself, maiming him in the process. In a reversal of logic, Juliet must flee the police. Hastings' injury casts Juliet as a criminal, while he is seemingly absolved of his predatory behaviour because of his position in society. With no father to protect her and with an old drawing by her father to lead her, Juliet eventually finds her family's childhood servant, Montgomery James, with his unusually large but gentle compatriot, Balthazar. Just before she meets him, she sees her reflection; she knows when she looks in the mirror that it shows her "face, wide-eyed and flushed.... like a madwoman" (28). This moment of self-recognition can break in two directions; first it could move Shepherd towards a story of madness inherited from one generation to the next—even Juliet admits, "Dead flesh and sharpened scalpels didn't bother me. I was my father's daughter, after all. My nightmares were made of darker things" (1). Madness, as a diagnosis, was used as a legitimate way to incarcerate women, so it would not be a stretch to do so with a daughter or an orphan, but Juliet's nightmares are not the product of an overactive imagination; they are memories from her childhood of her father's laboratory. Neo-Victorian texts often take to task this dismissal of troublesome women via the patriarchal medical establishment with narratives rewritten to historicise the move as intentional displacement of women's voices of protest.

The second possibility is to see how Juliet's reflectiveness—in the mirror and in her thoughts—is symptomatic not of madness but of her increasing confusion, disillusionment, and anger at her father's unrepentant behaviour which then drives the narrative impetus. The beginning of adolescence—remembering Juliet is just sixteen—coincides with the stage of development when young women might first "see the cultural framework, and girls' and women's subordinate place in it, for the first time" and this recognition might provoke "shock, sadness, anger, and a sense of betrayal" (Mikel Brown 1999, 16), all of which manifest in the trilogy's protagonist, particularly in relation to her father and his use of science.

Juliet uses reason to situate her unhealthy, disruptive relationship with Moreau. She soon realises that he is a failure as a father to her, as a father figure to Montgomery, and even as a god or supreme leader to the Beast People. The knowledge that her father deserted the family is compounded when she discovers "*Father was alive and had never tried to find me....* 'But I'm his daughter'" (Shepherd 2013, 41; emphasis in original) leads to her rejection of him with "He's no father!" (44). Symbolic of their detachment, Juliet comes to equate a science textbook—*Longman's Anatomical Reference*—with him.[5] It could be "The book of a scientist. A madman, too, perhaps" (99; emphasis in original). When Juliet meets him, there is no warm reception; rather, Moreau immediately labels her as if she is a specimen: "Juliet. Daughter" (106). He mocks her interests with "A girl interested in science? How *modern* of you. I suggest you find more appropriate interests" (156; emphasis in original) and pities her for being so smart.

The moment comes when Juliet is forced to confront her scientist father's increasingly erratic and bizarre behaviour on the island; she must decide if he is monstrous or misunderstood, "the madman or the misunderstood genius" (106), but she knows that she will be implicated as his daughter. Juliet rages, "I wanted my father's truth, not his science" (46). Moreau's truth is that Juliet was the first of his experiments. Born with a spinal defect, her mother begged Moreau to save her child; he operates, replacing her spine and some organs with those of a baby deer. Counter to the beast people's injections which keep them from rejecting their humanity or from devolving, Juliet must take them for her body to accept its animal nature. Moreau's death, in which Juliet plays a part, allows her an escape from the island and, she hopes, his legacy. Like any young woman, Juliet is confronted by her body and must come to terms with its physically changing and demanding nature.

One's relation to science is a defining feature of masculinity in the novel. Montgomery, once her family's servant, has been her father's *protégé*, and her friend, is now her confidant and protector. Juliet is both psychologically and sexually aware that he "wasn't a thin, silent boy any longer. In six years, he'd become a well-built young man with shoulders like a Clydesdale and hands that could swallow my own" with blonde, long hair (2013, 34). He could be perceived as either a man of society and means or, once on the ship, Juliet notices "He looked considerably less like a gentleman now. Sunburned shoulder. Salt ringing the hem of his trousers. Hair tangled and loose, and an edge in his handsome blue eyes. No wonder he bristled at the idea of staying in London—he was as wild as the caged animals" (2013, 65).

Invoking the duality of Stevenson's protagonist(s) for Edward as a point of neo-Victorian investigation of nineteenth-century standards of masculinity, the potential for complex personality is germane for Juliet. Early in the trilogy, her best friend Lucy tells her that young men will want to flirt with her, but in one of Juliet's few interactions with young men where she unselfconsciously demonstrates her intellect, one of those boys reminds her "Girls don't study science" because men "considered women naturally deficient" (Shepherd 2013, 10). Juliet immediately comprehends that "Lucy was wrong. He wouldn't want to marry me. I was cold, strange, and monstrous to those boys, just like my father. No one could love a monster" (21). To be able to separate her emotions from her intellect is, in the minds of such young men, equated with monstrosity, a kind of masculine mind in a feminine body. Edward Prince is first assumed to be a castaway, but is later revealed to be her father's crowning achievement. Juliet's fascination with him demonstrates that he meets the criteria of a Victorian gentleman; he "wore a fine suit … with a dark-gray vest that would have been at home in any London drawing room" (2013, 161) as a man with elegant manners and poetic diction. Moreau intends for Juliet to marry Edward, a plan disrupted by the regression and rise of the Beast People who assume control of the island, and Juliet's escape. In *Her Dark Curiosity*, Edward reappears in London, recreated as Mr. Henry Jakyll (Shepherd 2014, 69). Drawing on another recurrent interest in neo-Victorian fiction, mystery and crime, Shepherd reveals his alter ego to be the "Wolf of Whitechapel" (33), a man who kills in a manner reminiscent of both the historical figure "Jack the Ripper" and the literary intertextuality of Mr. Edward Hyde from Stevenson's *The Strange Case of Dr. Jekyll and Mr. Hyde*. He is, indeed, both Edwards—Prince and Monster. To the savvy young adult readership, he is also reminiscent of a third Edward, Edward Cullen, of the Twilight Saga who is, too, both gentleman and monstrous vampire.

Julian Wolfreys suggests that in the Gothic, "what returns is never simply a repetition … but is always an iterable supplement: repetition with a difference" (2002, 19). Edward has returned, taken up with Lucy, and appears as "gentleman type" (Shepherd 2013, 86) but increasingly, his behaviour demonstrates that he is "split into two selves that shared the same body: one a sharp-clawed monster, the other a tortured young man who wanted nothing more than to be free from his curse" (Shepherd 2014, 17) much like Stevenson's Dr. Jekyll, seeks to escape culturally assigned expectations. Like most educated Victorian gentlemen, Edward is comfortable with "Science, math, literature ... things easily learned from a book. He made a good show at social interaction, using lines and scenes from obscure plays" (94) but his identity is, like most young men, complex, awkward, and fragmented in its development between intellectual interests and physical desires. Edward shares Juliet's sexual desire; after they spend the night together, he wishes to find a minister to save her reputation, but when she disagrees, he expressly tells her that "What we did last night is only improper if you think it is" (147), casting aside Victorian social condemnation for love. Both Edward and Juliet are scientific products, transgressive to humanity and to social mores. He supports her decisions, a New Man to stand next to the New Woman into which she is developing as "no one's daughter. You can think for yourself, take care of yourself. You're Juliet, and that's enough" (149).

Victorian social Darwinists usurped and misused Darwin's theories of human groups and organisations for racist, imperial ends in order to assert dominance over colonial subjects, resources, and territory; in some cases, the aggressive forces believed that "indigenous populations unable to withstand the greater military and economic power of a colonising force must inevitably be pushed aside to make room for 'fitter' competitors" (Burdett 2014, n. p.). Arriving at the island, in her first encounters with the people who live there, Juliet notices their differences but does not yet know that they are the Beast People. It later becomes clear that these are the results and offspring of her father's arrogant colonial experiments to create a hybrid, or multiple, species involving both human and animal genetics, body parts, and instinctive temperaments, a state of liminality that is, from the perspective of the neo-Victorian project, "abjected, figured as precariously interstitial and hybrid, no longer definitely one thing or another" (Kohlke and Gutleben 23). As creator and coloniser, both Wells' and Shepherd's Moreau ignores critical questions of appropriate scientific method, as well as considered moral responsibility; further, he does not allow the subaltern subject to speak. According to Gayatri Chakravorty Spivak, "In post-colonial terms, everything that has limited or no access to the cultural imperialism is subaltern—a space of difference" (quoted in de Kock 1992, 45) like that populated by the Indigenous population of animals or othered animals who have been humanised. Montgomery, fully human, does not speak out against Moreau's inhumanity. Juliet and Edward, both animal enhanced, do give neo-Victorian voice to the subjected subaltern because the "oppositional and retributional stance can also be found in the postcolonial gothic where the other, the monster ... speaks out against her/his oppression and annihilation" (Kohlke and Gutleben 33). Here, the success of posthuman individuals is "not, or at least not primarily, ontological but essentially political, insisting on individual resurrections which always possess a collective or national dimension" (33) such as in reference to the undercurrent of writing back to the empire of the original text and pointed to, more overtly, in the twenty-first-century narrative.

Juliet "wondered what had made all the natives so disfigured. It was as though God had started here before he made man" (Shepherd 2013, 101), an implication that they might be "some collection of natives whom the theory of evolution—were Mr. Darwin to be believed—had skipped by" (118). They could also be delayed developmental examples or, alternately, degenerate humans, or "holdovers, evidence of Darwin's theories" (197). The othering of the Beast People reads as a lesson in post-colonial awareness; the young adult reader encounters how Indigenous populations were colonised due to their perceived inferiority and difference, a neo-Victorian intervention to remind the twenty-first-century reader of the arrogance of such assumptions. The inclusivity of the Beast People brings them together to mutiny against their creator and his disinterest in their intrinsic value.

Later in the trilogy, when she is cast as a murderer by the police, Juliet is subject to the same, dangerous racist science; a sketch artist represents her with a "jaw that was too wide, the brow too heavy, making me look like a degenerate" (Shepherd 2014, 73), a visual identification of the criminal man put forward by Cesare Lombroso in *L'Homme criminal* (1876) [*Criminal Man* 1911] where he suggested criminal types could be identified by phrenology (in Pick 1989, 112), a pseudoscience since discredited as racist.[6] Darwin wrote contrary to such assumptions in *The Descent of Man* ([1871] 2004); rather, he believed that while differences in facial and skeletal features could draw attention to the variability in aesthetic sensibilities between races: what was regarded as a marker of beauty in one race could be perceived as deformity by another (645–46), but it did not mean it was a sign of degeneracy. Such conjectures are clearly scientific racism and are pointed out to young adult readers; for example, Juliet's earlier assumptions are, again, proven wrong by the finesse and intelligence of Ajax the jaguar-man, now Jack Serra, a fortune teller who travels with the Romany, and Balthazar, their friend and protector because "His was not the face of a monster, as I'd first imagined, but it was disfigured nonetheless" (Shepherd 2013, 31). Disfigurement—or looking Otherwise—does not equate with degeneracy; rather, Moreau's appearance as a gentleman and a scholar hides his proclivities in plain sight.

Juliet is fully aware that danger is not determined by class or race. It lurks in every street where "men lurked.... The beasts that lurked here just had less fur and walked more upright" (Shepherd 2014, 5); degeneracy cannot be identified on sight but by behaviour. England is in danger from within not just the urban Gothic of the streets that provide "experiences of radical alienation, intense horror and sublime terror with potential threats lurking around every corner" a kind of "monstrous living entity" (Kohlke and Gutleben 26), but by its own aristocratic social leaders. The King's Club—two dozen men consisting of professors, upstanding scientists, a newspaper man, and an ambassador, as well as French, German, and other citizens who adhere to the motto *Ex scientia vera* (From Knowledge, Truth)—seek to weaponise Moreau's science and send it to France for a massive profit. Lucy, Edward, Juliet, and Montgomery challenge the King's Clubmen's plans a masquerade ball where they intend to trap Juliet.

The masked ball confirms the hypocrisy of society where a critical perspective of the young reader will see "one didn't have to be a creation to be a monster" (Shepherd 2013, 259) and raises the question of which appearance—authentic or socially presented personae—demonstrates the true character of an individual. Lucy and Juliet enter "arm in arm with a monster" behind their masks (Shepherd 2014, 174) but in the ballroom, all Juliet saw "were masks" including her own (176). Once there, Juliet sees a "beautiful masked girl [who] stared directly at me" until she starts because "it was a mirror, not a window. The girl was me.... Her mask—*my* mask—was split down the middle, white on one side, a deep red to match my dress on the other. That was how I felt—half a person" (177; emphasis in original). As an adolescent, Juliet is only half of what she will become, only half in society, and she believes only half Moreau's daughter. The other masks in the room hide the faces of the men of the King's Club, the puppet masters of patriarchal culture.

The trilogy's strength is in its consideration of scientific ethics in light of post-Darwinian scientific "progress" as usurped and distorted by the Gothic scientists, such malformative scientific experimentation is the central question of the third novel, *A Cold Legacy*. The ramifications of a legacy left by their fathers who seek power and profit are confronted by Juliet, Lucy—who is betrayed and ultimately killed by her father—and by Dr. Elizabeth von Stein. Elizabeth has her own monstrous family legacy, one kept secret by her family. She shares the secret with Juliet who is, then, her chosen heir. Descended from the family of a woman with whom Victor Frankenstein has a Scottish dalliance, it is the only existing lineage of his family. Mary Shelley's *Frankenstein* is the intertextual reference in *A Cold Legacy*, and the neo-Victorian narrative includes the questions that are not asked—but are suggested—in the *ur-text*. Both women, young Juliet and the older Elizabeth, act together to halt the conspiracy of their fathers who encourage Moreau's science in order to create an army of intelligent beasts, and profit from them with a sale to the French, a treasonous violation of Victoria's Empire and of the intense Francophobia of some people in the Empire.[7]

Elizabeth sends Juliet, Lucy, Balthazar, and Montgomery to safety in Scotland. Waiting there is a matriarchal community of women; the fugitives encounter only one elderly, possibly post-sexual man, Carlyle—a "gray-haired manservant with a thin face like a starved fox" (2015, 26)— who brings them into the home where they are evaluated for entrance by Valentina. She, too, is unusual in that she has "clover-honey skin" (24), "black hair and dark complexion, looked to be Romany" but is "dressed like a Puritan" including an "old-fashioned high collar around her neck" (25) and with hands that are a different skin tone than the rest of her. This house of women, where "*all* the servants were women, most of them barely more than children," is run by Mrs. McKenna, a woman with grey-shot red hair who wears "men's tweed trousers tucked into thick rubber boots" (32; emphasis in original) and whose "family has helped the von Steins with the management" (33) of the estate for generations. It quickly becomes apparent that conventional social standards set for women in non-rural society are questioned. At one point, Lucy is overwhelmed by the delicious food she is being offered, admitting her mother refuses to let her eat so much because "She says if I don't watch my figure, men won't give me a second look" to which Valentina responds "Girls weren't made to be trussed up like Christmas hens. A woman needs weight on her bones, especially in winter.… Any man who thinks otherwise would certainly not be welcome here" (57).

Young people, according to Gina Wisker, feel strongly the "underlying tensions between challenge and dis-ease, guidance and conformity" pulling them through a "sense of transition, of liminality, which can be expressed in ... boundary crossing" (Wisker 2019, 378). For Juliet, the significance of a place where women's voices are no longer sidelined but heard and encouraged, in a house that transgresses social conventions, is transformative in her yearning to become more confident and self-assured. Her admiration of Elizabeth, now her guardian and a woman of science, leads Juliet to ask a fundamental question for women that haunts much neo-Victorian fiction:

> I swallowed. "How do you do it?" I asked quietly. She cocked her head in question. I explained, "How do you ignore the voices in your head? The ones that won't let you just be happy. The ones that want more out of life. More like what men are free to do—study what they want, go where they want, *be* who they want." (2016, 77; emphasis in original)

For a young woman with a problematic past and an uncertain future, she seeks out wisdom from an earlier generation.

Shepherd's backstory for Valentina reminds the reader of how some young adults, particularly girls, will self-harm for relief when they are in emotional pain, a still too common occurrence, with one in four teenagers using it as a distressful method to deal with strong feelings (Baumgaertner 2018, n. p.). In one egregious example, Valentina is so desperate for a new life that when, at age fifteen and an orphan, she tells of how she heard of a "woman who lived as free as a man, and could perform miracles without witchcraft, and who would teach girls anything they wanted to know—but only girls with deformities. I knew that was the life I wanted. I did *whatever* I had to.... I cut off *my own hands* to gain admittance" (2015, 148; emphasis in original). The horror of her act points to the desperation endured by young orphan girls in Victorian society.

There is much about the house that is unconventional. Juliet learns the von Stein women have been the protector through six generations of Victor Frankenstein's Origin Journals (2015, 100) that delineate the process of reanimation. Elizabeth has used part of the process to heal those young women who arrive with injuries, but with humility and never to resurrect the dead. Like women of the past denigrated for their healing abilities, Valentina tells Juliet that "Elizabeth has a reputation for being able to cure ailments and illnesses, but only women are brave enough to come. The men think she's a witch" (2015, 86).[8] The women have created "strict rules for when the science may be used. A code. It's called the

Oath of Perpetual Anatomy. In one hundred eleven years we've never met the criteria" (101). Although her knowledge allows Elizabeth to heal the women and girls who come to her, is not a step to be used lightly.

Having proven her intellectual power, Juliet's self-determination is key to her *bildungsroman* as she sorts out her identity and chosen path. She is not her absent, abusive father's daughter but memories of him are bound to the monstrous. Nostalgia leads her to think of the past, but the remembrances are disturbing; at a carnival in Vauxhall Gardens when she is seven, her mother wants to see the "performing horses. Chinese jugglers. Ventriloquists" and Vivaldi, but her "Father scoffed. 'Vivaldi, that repetitive hack? I'm off to see the monstrosities, myself. The Dog-faced Boy. Hairy Mary'" (2015, 111). Other memories lead her to how her dog, Crusoe, went missing and she later hears his cries from her father's laboratory. Juliet turns to science for answers until she has "read enough research papers on genetics to know that a child naturally took on the properties of a parent" (2015, 64), a belief that deeply and negatively affects her self-perception. It is not until Montgomery tells her the truth, that she is not Moreau's biological child and counters with the fact that who her father was is irrelevant (307), that she frees herself from the burden and guilt of the ramifications of his mad science.

Relieved of her patriarchal family and its many faults, a period of doubt follows for Juliet as a young woman. Alison Waller, discussing adolescence for young women, remarks that "Adolescence is always 'other' to the more mature phase of adulthood, always perceived as liminal, in transition, and in constant growth towards the ultimate goal of maturity" (2011, 1); for Juliet, if she is not who she was told she is, then she must self-create to achieve agency. Juliet wonders, "I wasn't Henri Moreau's daughter. I wasn't a Moreau at all. And if I wasn't that, what was I?" (Shepherd 2014, 311). Her truth is now more fluid:

> "I'm not a Moreau," I said, testing out the words. "I'm a…Chastain, I suppose," I said, thinking of my mother's maiden name. "Or rather a James, since I married Montgomery."
> So many names, and none of them felt right.... "I was so certain I knew who I was and who I was supposed to be. I'm not certain of anything now." (314)

Balthazar, unexpectedly, provides the simple answer, giving her back her power of self-definition with, simply, "You're Juliet" (314).

Balthazar sees Juliet—as a self-defining individual—clearly; his affirmation leaves her emboldened with her own developing, strong sense of agency because, as she says, "I *wasn't* a madman's daughter. I wasn't a Moreau.... that very lack of identity left me stripped free of shackles. For the first time in my life, I could make my own decisions, unbound by the shadow of my father" (351; emphasis in original). Neither his science nor his DNA will be his legacy. Instead, Elizabeth sees Juliet has the heart of a scientist and that, despite Montgomery's warnings of "No more unnatural science. No more playing God, not even when there's a chance the ends could justify the means" (2016, 95), Juliet knows what is right. In retort, Juliet is adamant, "I've no desire to play God. The secrets I've sworn to keep have the power to save the world. There couldn't be any reason more noble" (2015, 106). Elizabeth encourages her to act for herself because "*Montgomery is a good man, but he'll never understand why women like us do what we must do.... If you want to know the real truth, I will teach you everything*" (2015, 106–7; emphasis in original). Elizabeth warns, "It's only a handful of scientists who are ever even faced with this decision. The smart ones turn back. Only the mad push forward" (2014, 419).

It is through her matrilineal teaching that Juliet comes to understand great learning and ability comes with responsibility. Elizabeth firmly reminds Juliet, "We don't do it to bring those we love back. There are rules, Juliet. A code.... When I'm certain your ethics are above reproach, then I'll let you be the one to pull the lever" (2016, 129). When faced with the choice, Juliet refuses to bring Lucy back to life, using her agency and knowledge to reset the ethical boundaries of science, and when Henley (a reanimated child) dies with Elizabeth in a fire that decimates the manor house, Juliet has a chance to save the Origin Journals but chooses to have the last remains of the dangerous science to turn to ash. Edward, too, decides to leave them to find Frankenstein's "monster"; Juliet reminds him "It wasn't a monster" and Edward takes comfort in the fact it occurs to him that "Frankenstein's creature and I, well, we could each use a companion" (385), to form a small family unit. Montgomery and Balthazar are Juliet's family of choice, and she leaves the estate in the hands of McKenna to continue the good work to educate young women left alone in the world. Both Victorian and neo-Victorian narratives come to a quiet end.

MALLEABLE MAIDENS

Another set of novels which grapple with scientific outcomes is Theodora Goss' trilogy, a complex neo-Victorian mash-up of the monstrous narratives of the long nineteenth century. The Gothic texts and characters of *Frankenstein*, "Rappaccini's Daughter" (1844) by Nathaniel Hawthorne, *Carmilla* (1872) by Sheridan Le Fanu, *The Strange Case of Dr. Jekyll and Mr. Hyde* by Robert Louis Stevenson, *The Island of Dr. Moreau* by H. G. Wells, and *Dracula* (1897) by Bram Stoker in addition to the characters of Mrs. Poole,[9] Irene Adler, Sherlock Holmes, and Dr. Watson come together for an investigative neo-Victorian purpose of another set of daughters.

In search of money to survive, one of the protagonists, Miss Mary Jekyll, has gone to Sherlock Holmes to help her find, she thinks, her father's murderous associate Mr. Hyde, so she might keep the household afloat with the reward money after her mad mother's death. Holmes takes the case, and as a result, Mary becomes serendipitously involved in his ongoing investigation into the death of five female unfortunates. These women are reminiscent of the victims of the killer known as "Jack the Ripper" who killed at least five women in the fall of 1888. Although each of these victims is missing various body parts from hands to head. Holmes and Watson are working with Inspector Lestrade to find the killer. Eventually, these murders are connected to Mary's case: the women are being reassembled to create a new bride for Adam, the still-existing Creature of Victor Frankenstein.

Goss' first novel, *The Strange Case of the Alchemist's Daughter*, begins the story of Mary's search for answers about her own father. Along the way, she discovers there are other "daughters" of the many immoral men who comprise *Le Société des Alchemistes*, an international organisation wherein the scientists have through scientific experimentation created or mutated their unknowing girl-children without their consents. In many of the twenty-first-century fictions, particularly those including Gothic elements, Catherine Spooner points out how the "freaks and geeks are no longer pushed to the edges of the narrative but become the protagonists" (2006, 103) which is certainly the case in Goss' novels wherein Justine Frankenstein, Mary Jekyll, Diana Hyde, Catherine Moreau, Beatrice Rappaccini, and Lucinda Van Helsing expose the monstrosity of the men who are their creators.

Ann Heilmann argues persuasively that in "revisionary accounts of nineteenth-century science … twenty-first-century women writers draw on the figure of the naturalist and explorer to raise feminist concerns about the gendered ethics of science, then and now" (2014, 108). In both Shepherd's and Goss' series, the novels maintain Mary Godwin Shelley's grounding idea, what Anne K. Mellor calls a contrast between "'good' science—the detailed and reverent description of the working of nature—to what she considered 'bad' science, the hubristic manipulation of the elemental forces of nature to serve man's private ends" (1987, 107).

Goss' narratives about scientific manipulation, like Shepherd's novels, are later regenerations or descendant of Victorian ur-text Gothics about mad men and their equally mad science, a thematic return that gives the new novels a sense of generational creation. This sense of historical inheritance is reiterated when, asked by Beatrice if she is Dr. Moreau's daughter, Catherine responds, "His daughter! I supposed you could call me that … I am, more accurately, one of his—creations" (2018, 187). The girls are fully aware of their unnatural attributes and are to various degrees ashamed, conflicted, or indifferent to their ancestry as well as their lived existence as monstrosities of science. "Here be monsters" reads the epigraph—or is it a dedication?—to the first novel; Mary instantly objects with "I don't think that's the right epigraph for the book" (2018, opening page). Sometimes to create alternative voices, nineteenth-century *fin-de-siècle* Gothic novels used a narrative technique that mimicked the "multi-vocal inter-textual forms which characterize *The Strange Case of Dr. Jekyll and Mr. Hyde*" (Smith 2017, 74). Expanding on this process, Goss' narrative structure exposes its postmodern metafictional position; self-aware as the constructor of a story, Catherine Moreau writes the life experiences of the young creatures who dialogically engage to interject questions, corrections, and denials based on their own recollections. It is, to some extent, a group narrative providing a multiplicity of reclaimed voices and perspectives.

The inquiry into monstrosity is at the core of the lengthy neo-Victorian narrative while postmodern praxis allows for the inner-textual questioning of the characters' creation, thematic elements, and narrative stylisation of a created neo-Victorian text. The story begins with Mary Jekyll staring at her mother's coffin with Mrs. Poole, the housekeeper, at her side; the omniscient narration is interrupted by text set apart and noted as Mary's voice.

MARY:	Is it really necessary to begin with the funeral? Can't you begin with something else? Anyway, I thought you were supposed to start in the middle of the action—*in medias res*....
	"Diana!" cried Mary.
MARY:	Not that *in medias res*! They won't understand the story I you start like that.
CATHERINE:	Then stop telling me how to write it. (Goss 2018, 3)

These first two intrusive interludes establish that the author of the girls' story is Catherine and that, throughout the novels, the other young women will question which narrative moments are included, offer commentary on politics and historical change, as well as provoke her to frustration. Catherine asserts that "all the best writers experiment with literary technique, like stream of consciousness" (2018, 243) reinforcing she is a young writer who also has her critics:

CATHERINE:	It's unbelievable, what authors have to put up with from their own characters. Remind me why I agreed to do this?
MARY:	Excuse me. We are not your characters, but fellow members of the Athena Club. And as to why you agreed ... we need money, remember? (2018, 88)

Indeed, the purpose of writing the novels is to make money because yet another sin of their fathers is to leave them all orphaned, destitute, and without a home.

Goss' novels consider how a young woman, in such circumstances and created as something other to society, will understand the concept of what is monstrous in relation to her own difference. These young women, like today's adolescents, are "Faced with the tensions and traumas of broken adult worlds" which leads them "instead learn to celebrate diversity, take on illegitimate power structures" (Wisker 2019, 381), ultimately seeing themselves as intelligent, self-defining, and agentic. Throughout the trilogy, the girls as well as Mrs. Poole, critique the narrative as written by Catherine, but each must write—take ownership—of her own story. Catherine fights off their protests because "this is what we agreed on. You would each write your individual stories" (Goss 2018, 94) but sees their self-creation as a way to find their voices through story and as a means by which to relinquish silence. To be monstrous is to negate their humanity; the term becomes, at first, a point of contention when Beatrice laments how she had once been loved, but "He [Giovanni] did not want to be a monster—that was the word he used.... That day, I realized what I was—a monster among men" (171). Mary interrupts the writing of the text with protests:

MARY: You're not a monster, Beatrice. I wish you would stop using that word.
JUSTINE: Why, if it's technically accurate. We are all monsters in our own way. Even you Mary. (171)

Their liminal existence as girl-adolescents between childhood and womanhood is complicated by their individualised monstrousness. Each of the young women, like any youth, has a moment of uncertainty. Mediated by the internal author, Catherine, Mary looks in the hall looking glass where she sees her pale face that makes her look like a corpse. Catherine, the author/narrator here admits,

> I have paused to show you Mary staring into the mirror because this is a story about monsters. All stories about monsters contain a scene in which the monster sees himself in a mirror. Remember Frankenstein's monster, startled by his reflection in a forest pool? That is when he realizes his monstrousness.
> MARY: I'm not a monster, and that book is a pack of lies. If Mrs. Shelley were here, I would slap her for all the trouble she caused. (4)

Mary Godwin Shelley's novel—her story—is the subtext. It is seen by the girls as responsible for detailing an ambitious scientist's journey to madness and for setting into motion the pre-history of the girls' own narratives; because she concealed information in her narrative, the girls recognise her as their kindred spirit and as an inaccurate historian of the past.

Mary Godwin Shelley is the foremother of these fictions and of these characters, the matriarchal lineage for the second generation's stories. She, too, had to bear the burden of her own father's betrayal. The Goss trilogy's lore explains how *Frankenstein* is not fiction; rather, it is a biography with a fictional ending because the young women discover that Adam, the Creature, did not die. He continues to live in search of a bride, Justine, and in his revenge desires to raise a powerful force of racially pure creatures who will dominate a new society. Catherine discloses that Shelley's *Frankenstein* is, in fact, an actual "biography" to which is added "a pack of lies" but she, as a young female author, is sympathetic because "We authors, have to stick together, even when one of us is long dead" (Goss 2017, 395). In one of many intertextual commentaries, Catherine points out that Shelley was only nineteen when she wrote "the *Biography*" (397; emphasis in original) and reminds her readers that Shelley was left motherless when early feminist Mary Wollstonecraft died in childbirth, and that she had a political rebel for a father, William Godwin. Shelley, too, is a product of her parents' radical thinking. Catherine reveals that Wollstonecraft was one of a few women of *Le Société des Alchimistes* alongside Godwin, Percy Shelley, Lord Byron, and Dr. John Polidori (396). For reasons unknown to the young women of the Athena Club, Mary Shelley was not a *Société* member.

As part of the complex narrative structure that evokes but does not copy Shelley's own novel's organisation, in an embedded narrative the young women—and, by extension, the readers—learn Polidori knew Ernest Frankenstein. Ernest Frankenstein told his story to the president of the *Société*, confirming that a female Creature was made, and that he advised his brother that "such an abomination should never have been allowed to walk the Earth. It is bad enough that my brother created Adam, but that he would create an Eve both stronger and more clever than man?" (397–98). Catherine wonders why Shelley lied and said Justine had never been created and posits "knowing of Justine, she did the best she could, for another woman. She erased her from the story" unlike Catherine who is trying to give "an accurate portrayal of a group of women trying to get along in the world as best they can, like women anywhere—even if they are monsters" (398–99) as she wonders what Shelley would think of her story. Justine, for one, considers Shelley as a kind of sister to herself and the others, a misfit young woman amongst men who have no understanding of her trials or tribulations.

One outcome of Shelley's *Frankenstein* biofiction—part fact, part fiction stitched together—is, according to Catherine, that Victor Frankenstein's success in creating his uber-progeny encourages the other male scientists to create offspring of their own, usurping both women's role and nature's process. They choose to pursue their scientific experimentation on their own girl-children once they are old enough to begin the process. Rappaccini confirms in a letter to Jekyll that Moreau was correct "to conjecture that the female brain would be more malleable and responsive to our experiments" (87) on transmutation.

The men feel righteous in their pursuit of transgressive scientific inquiry in their pursuit of progress, leading to their increased power, at a more rapid speed. Each scientist/doctor/man creates, in some form, a daughter. Moreau practises vivisection to recombine animals and humans (Catherine is his puma-woman); Rappaccini uses poisonous plants to create protective powers (causing Beatrice to breathe poison); Abraham Van Helsing seeks immortality (with Lucinda being, "against my will and sometimes without my knowledge, the subject of certain experiments" (393–94)) while Dr. Henry Jekyll had attempted to split man's nature (leaving his illegitimate daughter, Diana Hyde, as a consequence). These men, and the collective *Société*, seek to "direct evolution, to create the higher forms that man will become" (166) using their own theoretical, tested, and sophisticated methods to achieve their supposedly noble aims. Justine is the exception; created as Adam's companion, she is Frankenstein's daughter, but made out of protest.

Mary, a Victorian young woman with a modern perspective, wonders if any of their dangerous goals are possible, but acknowledges that this "was the nineteenth century, the age of science" even if the "ways of men are unaccountable" (2018, 83). The young women's insight is noted by Watson who admits—in a blending of the Victorian and the neo-Victorian moments—"There's nothing quite like the clear-sighted irony of a modern young lady to make one feel ridiculous" (31). For example, Van Helsing's desire for immortality becomes even more problematic and political when, in the third novel—*The Sinister Mystery of the Mesmerizing Girl*—Goss adds Professor Moriarty to the mix. Moriarty, too, seeks the powers granted by science and, in addition, he believes in the paranormal. Moriarty is described as "a nationalist and racial supremacist making money off people he regarded as vermin" (Goss 2020, 250), a social monster in any age if there is one. Mrs. Poole, with her experience, clearly sees each of the men as evil, "despite their fancy titles—doctors and professors! Evil is as evil does" (Goss 2019, 545).

European Travel for the Monstrous Gentlewoman moves away from the re/articulated narratives towards speculative fiction, but there is a moment where one woman, Ayesha,[10] is revealed to be the President of *Le Société des Alchimistes* and argues to continue the experiments giving Beatrice power on an oversight committee. Sandra Gilbert would see the significance of Ayesha's inclusion in this series about strong young women because, "Unlike the women earlier Victorian writers had idealised or excoriated, she was neither an angel nor a monster. Rather, She [Ayesha] was an odd but significant blend of the two types—an angelically chaste woman with monstrous powers, a monstrously passionate woman with angelic charms" (1994, 125). To that end, Ayesha refuses the demands of those around her: "I will not forbid experiments in biological transmutation—we cannot stop scientific progress, and the next century will see advances in the biological sciences that as yet we can barely conceive" telling Justine to read Frankenstein's papers because "Perhaps those will convince you how very special, how singular and extraordinary, you are" (Goss 2019, 671). The Athena Club representatives, Beatrice and Justine, remind her they are monsters, but that unlike her, they "did not choose. We were created without our knowledge and consent" (670). Their lives have been dictated by their lack of choice, a fact sure to raise the interest of young adult readers now hearing of gene splicing and cloning. Beatrice has unwittingly killed her lover with poison; Diana has been declared irredeemable at her convent school because of her lack of social graces and behavioural abruptness; Mary has been left destitute due to her father's insatiable spending on his secret science; Justine has lived alone for over one hundred years, without family, until she joined Catherine in the circus' freak show, and Lucinda has been robbed of her vitality through Van Helsing's blood experiments, all outcomes which have been beyond the young women's control. The young women, rather than becoming the damsels in distress of historical Gothic fiction, the young women assert their rights to individuality and agency.

The progressive ideas of the young women on rational dress, literary aestheticism, political suffrage, artistic movements, and isolation in marriage support the neo-aspects of these and are usually found in the voice of Beatrice, the most beautiful and forward-thinking of the young women who is, suitably, both a literal *femme fatale* and a New Woman for those persons who might potentially wish to harm her or her friends. Jeffrey Jerome Cohen has several captivating ideas in what he calls "Monster Theory," one of which is how "monsters ask us how we perceive the world, and how we have misrepresented what we have attempted to place. They ask us to re-evaluate our cultural assumptions about race, gender, sexuality, our perception of difference, our tolerance toward its expression. They ask us why we have created them" (2018, 54) and must be "examined within the intricate matrix of relations (social, cultural, and literary-historical) that generate them" (45). The concepts of fallenness, hypocrisy, and abuse are explored by Diana along with madness and women's traumatic suffering, just as the eighteenth- and nineteenth-century theories of Immanuel Kant, Georg Hegel, and other men are considered in the philosophical and generous thoughts of Justine which she brings to bear on the company's deliberations as they move forward.[11]

Enacting their progressive beliefs, they do, on occasion, The Athena Club members, on occasion, cross dress as boys or men to make their sleuthing easier or, in the case of Diana and Beatrice, for increased, personal comfort rather than the restrictiveness of conventional clothing. They are fully self-aware of their transgressive behaviour. In one exchange, Mary—like the Mrs. Grundy of Victorian values—reminds the girls of the need to be careful when out and about in society.

DIANA: I don't see the point of hats.
MARY: They're a social convention. One wears them because one is expected to, whether one needs them or not.
DIANA: How does that contradict what I just said?
JUSTINE: For once, I agree with Diana. I don't see the point of following social conventions. Why wear a hat unless it is cold outside? An umbrella keeps the rain off your head, a parasol keeps the sun out of your eyes. Why follow social conventions if they're silly?
CATHERINE: Because we're unusual enough without drawing additional attention to ourselves. (2018, 129)

They must remember they are experimental young women who, in some cases, bear the physical marks—including size, scars, bearing, and colouring—of the men's scientific work.

As monstrous young women, they must strategically hide in plain sight and Catherine is right to point out that performing femininity—or when necessary, masculinity—allows them to remain hidden to prying eyes. Irene Adler points out in one scenario, "'No one ever looks at a nun…. Especially not men. It's a very useful disguise, almost like being invisible'" (Goss 2019, 386), and Catherine notes how a habit "hides firearms and makes men uncomfortable. A perfect combination" (387). Justine crossdresses as a tall man, Justin Frank, if necessary; when returning to women's clothes, she laments that she can "no longer move freely and easily about in the world. She was aware of restrictions, limitations. Perhaps Beatrice was right, and our clothing did impact the way we thought and felt.... It was all rather confusing" (Goss 2020, 59) given a young woman may not be innately comfortable in women's clothing as society suggests.

The recognition of gender fluidity in Goss's novels reflects the twenty-first-century respect of LGBTQ+ young persons' clothing choices, gender presentations, sexual preferences, and pronoun uses. Arriving intertextually at the behest of Goss from *Carmilla* (1872), Sheridan LeFanu's Gothic novella, Carmilla is a powerful, female, lesbian vampire—sometimes known as Mircalla, Countess of Karnstein—who is involved with another woman named Laura. Young adult novels often "mediate history for young adult readers even as it challenges or problematizes conventional ways of knowing the past. ... they do so by using gothic metafictional techniques to draw attention to the process of writing and interpreting history, and gothic narrative motifs to restore a voice to those hitherto excluded from historical narrative" (Spooner 2017, 132), including strong lesbian characters. Even Mary realises, as "Carmilla strode into the room.... One really did need trousers to stride. There was no striding in layers of petticoats. Just for once Mary envied the striders" (Goss 2019, 475). Carmilla's stride—a term usually used for the authoritative walk of a male—signifies her social fearlessness, not just as a vampire but as a queer lesbian. Carmilla's human lover, Laura, is by her side just as her friend, Mina Murray, is comfortably in an illicit adulterous relationship with Count Dracula.

To be a strong young woman with character and agency, even as a neo-Victorian creation/daughter, is to be willing to stand righteously counter to culture and convention as demonstrated by Carmilla, and another mature, fulfilled woman, Irene Adler—Sherlock Holmes' "the woman" (Conan Doyle [1891] 2009, 161). The younger women learn from this couple that they must embrace their differences to mature successfully into individualised adulthood. Diana Wallace, in relation to the historical novel, considers how the Gothic "might provide a means for women writers to engage in political critique of the way they have been excluded" from official history; in response, young progressive women who are "Aware of their exclusion from traditional historical narratives, have used gothic historical fiction as a mode of historiography which can simultaneously reinsert them into history and symbolize their exclusion" (2013, 1). This action, then, "encourages a self-reflexive questioning of the individual's relationship to history and to collective identities" (Spooner 2017, 133). In the case of Goss' novels, "while the monstrous Other is represented as horrifying in the eyes of others," the character and/or reader might identify the possibility of resistance (Pulliam 2014, 16). For these daughters created by the hubris of scientific men, the revisioning of the supposedly monstrous is a transgressive act wherein recognition also comes with an understanding of one's difference from the socially constructed Other. In *The Strange Case of the Alchemist's Daughter*, this objective is overt.

If the "Subtext in both historical settings [Romantic and Victorian] tends to 'exceptionalise' Gothic heroines as they sometimes rebel against and transgress societal gender norms, while always returning in some shape or form to traditional forms of femininity and gendered identity, resulting in a recentring of the domestic sphere that remains possible (and even favourable) after transgressions of these boundaries" (Connors and Szwydky 2012, 91), then neo-Victorian narratives must respond to this submission or reversion. One of the main attractions for many readers of neo-Victorian and neo-Gothic literature, just like in young adult texts, might just be the space to "question established, flawed modes of behaviour in a flawed world, reconsider and repeat values and behaviours from historical times, and often then develop something new, diverse, hybrid, imagining forward" (Wisker 2019, 382). Shepherd's and Goss' texts contain exceptional young women who rebel, but counter to Connors and Szwydky's hypothesis, in these neo-Gothic narratives, the young women of the two fictional series do not regress to the domestic sphere but confront their origins to construct for themselves a future. In like fashion, young Victorian writers who pen alternate worlds must equally assert themselves as powerful and authoritative creators of their characters' lives in relation to society's expectations of young people.

Notes

1. "STEAM" is the anachronym for a kind of holistic learning where students should embrace Science, Technology, Engineering, Arts, and Mathematics; in a less holistic and humanities exclusive version, it is more often than not called "STEM" at the exclusion of the Arts (see Maier 2021).
2. This assertion may seem to be an overreach but a recent publication for adults, *The Daughter of Doctor Moreau* (2022), positions its protagonist—Carlota Moreau—much differently in that she grows up on an estate and is an adult when the reader encounters her.
3. In the original novel, H. G. Wells does not give Dr. Moreau a first name; however, in Shepherd's series, he is given a full name.

4. The full title is, more correctly, *On the Origin of Species by Means of Natural Selection, or the Preservation of Favoured Races in the Struggle for Life*.
5. It is likely that the book referred to is one known as *Gray's Anatomy* first published in London in 1858 by John W. Parker and Son but by 1863 and the third edition, the imprint is by Longman.
6. Ezechia Marco Lombroso—Cesare—was an Italian-born physician who expanded the study of phrenology and criminology using degeneration theory, psychiatry, and social Darwinism. His theory was that a person would be easy to identify as dangerous to society via physical deformities or congenital defects that would locate an individual as a criminal. Factually, these features and his photographic examples were often persons of Eastern European birth or Jews; the "evidence" of potential savagery was highly derogatory to persons of non-Western European and non-white birth.
7. Francophobia is expressed in novels of the period like Marie Corelli's *Wormwood* (1890); for an exploration of the topic, see Eugen Weber (1988) or Kirsten MacLeod (2000).
8. Another neo-Victorian narrative that confronts the alienation of the healing woman as a dangerous, malignant witch is the Cut-Wife in "The Nightcomers" episode of *Penny Dreadful* (Season Two, Episode Three) where she suffers from decades of persecution at the hands of the people who come to her for help when they are desperate.
9. Given the caretaking nature of Mrs. Poole, Goss might intend here a rehabilitative portrait or attempt to revision the madwoman's nurse in Charlotte Brontë's *Jane Eyre* (1847).
10. Ayesha is the powerful female figure who encounters the man of action, Allan Quartermain, in the Imperial Gothic novel *She: A History of Adventure* by H. Rider Haggard published in 1887, the first of a series.
11. Another neo-Gothic Victorian fiction for young adults, *The Dark Descent of Elizabeth Frankenstein* (2015) by Kiersten White, accentuates the philosophical and political progressive thinking of women so underdeveloped in Shelley's original novel (see Maier 2020).

Bibliography

Abrams, M. H. "Science Fiction." In *A Glossary of Literary Terms*, 7th ed., edited by Abrams, 278–79. Boston: Heinle and Heinle, 1999.
Baumgaertner, Emily. "How Many Teenage Girls Deliberately Harm Themselves? Nearly 1 in 4, Survey Finds." *The New York Times*. July 2, 2018: n. p. https://www.nytimes.com/2018/07/02/health/self-harm-teenagers-cdc.html
Botting, Fred. "Candygothic." In *The Gothic*, edited by Botting, 133–51. Cambridge: D. S. Brewer, 2001.

Brown, Lyn Mikel. *Raising Their Voices: The Politics of Girls' Anger*. Cambridge, MA: Harvard University Press, 1999.
Brontë, Charlotte. *Jane Eyre*. London: Smith, Elder, and Co., 1847.
Burdett, Carolyn. "Post Darwin: Social Darwinism, Degeneration, Eugenics." *British Library*. May 15, 2014. https://www.bl.uk/romantics-and-victorians/articles/post-darwin-social-darwinism-degeneration-eugenics
Cohen, Jeffrey Jerome. "Monster Culture (Seven Theses)." In *Classic Readings on Monster Theory*, edited by Asa Simon Mittman and Marcus Hensel, 43–54. York: Arc Humanities Press, 2018.
Conan Doyle, Sir Arthur. "A Scandal in Bohemia." 1891. In *The Penguin Complete Sherlock Holmes*. Foreword by Ruth Rendell, 161–75. New York: Penguin Books, 2009.
Connors, Sean P., and Lissette Lopez Szwydky. "The Pre-Monstrous Mad Scientist and the Post-Nerd Smart Girl in Kenneth Oppel's *Frankenstein* Series." In *Young Adult Gothic Fiction: Monstrous Selves/Monstrous Others*, edited by Michelle J. Smith, Kristine Moruzi, 87–109. Montreal: McGill University Press, 2012.
Corelli, Marie. *Wormwood: A Drama of Paris*. London: Richard Bentley and Son, 1890.
Creation. Ocean Pictures, HanWay Films, BBC Films, 2009.
Darwin, Charles. *On the Origin of Species by Means of Natural Selection, or the Preservation of Favoured Races in the Struggle for Life*. London: John Murray, 1859.
Darwin, Charles. *The Descent of Man*. 1871. London: Penguin, 2004.
de Kock, Leon. "Interview With Gayatri Chakravorty Spivak: New Nation Writers Conference in South Africa." *Ariel* 23, no. 3 (1992): 29–47.
Gilbert, Sandra M., and Susan Gubar. *No Man's Land: Sex Changes*. New Haven: Yale University Press, 1994.
Goss, Theodora. *The Strange Case of the Alchemist's Daughter*. 2017. New York: Gallery/Saga Press, 2018.
Goss, Theodora. *European Travel for the Monstrous Gentlewoman*. 2018. New York: Gallery/Saga Press, 2019.
Goss, Theodora. *The Sinister Mystery of the Mesmerizing Girl*. 2019. New York: Gallery/Saga Press, 2020.
Hadley, L. "Feminine Endings: Neo-Victorian Transformation of the Victorian." in Ed. B. Tredennick. *Victorian Transformations: Genre, Nationalism and Desire in Nineteenth-Century Literature*. New York: Routledge, 2011. 181–194.
Haggard, H. Rider. *She: A History of Adventure*. London: Longmans, Green, and Co., 1887.
Haggard, H. Rider. *Ayesha, The Return of She*. London: Ward Lock, 1905.
Hawthorne, Nathaniel. "Rappaccini's Daughter." *The United States Magazine and Democratic Review* 1844: 545–60.

Heilmann, Ann. "Reflecting on Darwin." In *Reflecting on Darwin*, edited by Eckart Voigts, Barbara Schaff and Monika Pietrzak-Franger, 91–111. London: Routledge, 2014.
Kohlke, Marie-Luise, and Christian Gutleben. "The (Mis)Shapes of Neo-Victorian Gothic: Continuations, Adaptations, Transformations." In *The Neo-Victorian Gothic*, edited by Kohlke and Gutleben, 1–48. Amsterdam: Rodopi/Brill, 2012.
Le Fanu, Sheridan. *Carmilla*. In *A Glass Darkly*. London: Richard Bentley & Son, 1872.
Lombroso, Cesare. *Criminal Man*. [*L'Homme criminel* (1876)]. London: G. P. Putnam's Sons, 1911.
MacLeod, Kirsten. "Marie Corelli and *Fin-de-Siècle* Francophobia: The Absinthe Trail of French Art." *English Literature in Transition, 1880–1920* 43, no. 1 (2000): 66–82.
Maier, Sarah E. "Dark Descen(den)ts: Neo-Gothic Monstrosity and the Women of *Frankenstein*." In *Neo-Gothic Narratives: Illusory Illusions of the Past*, edited by Maier and Brenda Ayres, 23–40. London: Anthem, 2020.
Maier, Sarah E. "STEAM(y) and Marvel(ous) Women: Agent Scully, Lisbeth Salander, Beth Harmon, and the Black Widow." In *Vindication of the Redhead*, edited by Maier and Brenda Ayres, 261–81. London: Palgrave Macmillan, 2021.
May, Antoinette. *The Determined Heart*. Seattle: Lake Union Publishing, 2015.
Pick, Daniel. *Faces of Degeneration*. Cambridge: Cambridge University Press, 1989.
Pulliam, June. *Monstrous Bodies: Feminine Power in Young Adult Horror Fiction*. Jefferson, NC: McFarland Press, 2014.
Shelley, Mary. *Frankenstein. The Original 1818 Text*, 3rd ed., edited by D. L. MacDonald and Kathleen Scherf. Peterborough, ON: Broadview Press, 2012.
Shepherd, Megan. *The Madman's Daughter*. New York: Balzer + Bray, 2013.
Shepherd, Megan. *Her Dark Curiosity*. New York: Balzer + Bray, 2014.
Shepherd, Megan. *A Cold Legacy*. New York: Balzer + Bray, 2016.
Smith, Andrew. "Reading the Gothic and Gothic Readers." In *Interventions: Rethinking the Nineteenth Century*, edited by Andrew Smith and Anna Barton, 72–88. Manchester: Manchester University Press, 2017.
Spooner, Catherine. "'The Gothic is part of history, just as history is part of the Gothic': Gothicizing History and Historicizing the Gothic in Celia Rees' Young Adult Fiction." In *New Directions in Children's Gothic: Debatable Lands*, edited by Anna Jackson, 132–46. London: Routledge, 2017.
Spooner, Catherine. *Contemporary Gothic*. London: Reaktion Books, 2006.
Stevenson, Robert Louis. *The Strange Case of Dr. Jekyll and Mr. Hyde*. London: Longmans, Green, and Co., 1886.
"The Nightcomers," *Penny Dreadful*. Desert Wolf Productions, Neal Street Productions, Showtime. Season two, episode three, 2015.
Wallace, Diana. *Female Gothic Histories: Gender, History, and the Gothic*. Cardiff: University of Wales Press, 2013.

Waller, Alison. *Constructing Adolescence in Fantastic Realism.* London: Routledge, 2011.
Weber, Eugen. *France, Fin de Siècle.* Cambridge: Harvard University Press, 1988.
Wells, H. G. *The Island of Dr. Moreau.* London: Heinemann, 1896.
Wilkie-Stibbs, Christine. "Intertextuality and the Child Reader." In *International Companion Encyclopedia of Children's Literature*, edited by Peter Hunt, 179–90. London: Routledge, 2004.
White, Kirsten. *The Dark Descent of Elizabeth Frankenstein.* New York: Delacorte Press, 2015.
Wisker, Gina. "Gothic and Young Adult Literature: Werewolves, Vampires, Monsters, Rebellion, Broken Hearts and True Romance." In *The Edinburgh Companion to Gothic and the Arts*, edited by David Punter, 378–92. Edinburgh: Edinburgh University Press, 2019.
Wolfreys, Julian. *Victorian Hauntings: Spectrality, Gothic, the Uncanny and Literature.* Basingstoke: Palgrave Macmillan, 2002.
Wollstonecraft, Mary. *A Vindication of the Rights of Woman.* London: J. Johnson, 1792.

CHAPTER 4

Illustrative Genii: The Brontës' Genius

The opening of the miniseries, *To Walk Invisible* (2016), written and directed by Sally Wainwright, is remarkable; the Brontë children come together in a large expansive room with a box. They hold the live miniature soldiers in hand with the fire of creativity hovering over their heads.

The grandeur of the room around them is a sign of just how vast their imaginations are. While the series is not created for a particular audience (rated PG) beyond Brontë fans, it would certainly appeal to young adult readers who are interested in how the Brontës desire to write began at such an early age. A consideration of neo-Victorian young adult narratives must include a consideration of texts by young writers for readers, and how those texts mobilise neo-Victorian patterns of revisioning both the young person and the texts they write. One important example of young writers—because of their excellence but also the ongoing interest in them—is the Brontë family. The recent Brontë bicentennials produced a great many narratives, biographies, biofictions, and graphic novels about the sibling authors, including an increase of work on their juvenilia. While Mary Godwin Shelley wrote as a teenager, the Brontës began even earlier, making them an important part of the connection between young authors and young readers; they were both at the same time. Like today's young people, the Brontës' childhood and teenage years included strong interests in literature, history, and politics helped to shape their intellectual development as adolescents. An author's juvenilia are the one chance the reader has to encounter an authentic young writer; in this instance, these

© The Author(s), under exclusive license to Springer Nature Switzerland AG 2024
S. E. Maier, *Neo-Victorian Young Adult Narratives*,
https://doi.org/10.1007/978-3-031-47295-4_4

juvenilia by the Brontë siblings explain their interest in a world beyond their own. Literature for young people is, most often, written by adults for them. In the twenty-first century, the interest in nineteenth-century authors and the use of their juvenilia in neo-Victorian young adult narratives, including the Brontës, creates an insightful juxtaposition of life and work, and a way in to how the space between their actual lives (in Howarth)[1] and their imaginative lives (in their juvenilia worlds of Glass Town, Angria, and Gondal) collapses. The Victorian authors and their neo-Victorian afterlives become intertwined in graphic novels and traditional narrative forms.

It may seem an odd combination—a Victorian family in a neo-Victorian graphic novel—but one of the "most significant transformations that took place in the realm of literature for children and young adults" during the rise of the Harry Potter series, paranormal romance, and dystopian young adult fiction as well as increase in filmic adaptations, was the "resurgence of comics geared toward a youth readership" (Tarbox and Abate 2017, 3), including increasingly complex graphic novels, manga, and anime.[2] Graphic works such as Glynnis Fawkes' *Charlotte Brontë Before Jane Eyre* (2019) and Isabel Greenberg's *Glass Town: The Imaginary World of the Brontës* (2020), and more traditional narratives in novel form, Lena Coakley's *Worlds of Ink and Shadow* (2016) and Catherynne M. Valente's *The Glass Town Game* (2017), show the intense interconnectedness between the siblings, their lives, and their works from a very early age. Biofictional graphic novels for adolescent readers engage with readers. Just as there are an increasing number of graphic novels which are autofiction, or the story of a person's life from their own perspective—like Art Speigelmann's *MAUS* (1980), Marjane Satrapi's *Perseopolis* (2000), or Alison Bechdel's *Fun Home* (2006)—there are also a number of powerful biofictions which also use the graphic format. Reading, and in this case seeing while reading, helps the reader possibly identify with the subject of the work because

> analogies, as well as incongruities, between the perception of reality and worlds of fiction play an important role in reception processes and reading experiences. Interviews, reading diaries, think-out-loud procedures, experiments, and observations have shown … that readers activate memories during reading, make comparisons with their own situations in the past or present, and recognize (or do not recognise) the world they live in. (Adringa 2004, 207)

Early readers might also be emerging creatives who seek confirmation of their abilities through the example of past others who were gifted and wrote their own juvenilia from a young age. By extension, there are "psychological processes during the exchange between the reader's world and the world evoked by a text or film" (Adringa 207) that may be assisted by the self-conscious interest of a neo-Victorian narrative about a nineteenth-century author.

Young Adults Writing

While juvenilia, as a genre, is defined loosely as "the literary or artistic works produced in the author's youth" (*OED*), scholar Christine Alexander rightly suggests the definition is necessarily fluid. "Juvenilia" per se "is not as stable as official dictionary definitions would suggest. As attitudes to childhood itself change, and as readers, students and editors discover the rich field of literary juvenilia, the negative connotations of the term begin to slip from the control of canonical writers of the past; but this is a slow process" (Alexander 2005, 70–2). Further, when the political or the social are "appropriated by the child-author [it] allows her to experience the adult world while at the same time challenging the ideologies it professes" that is, in many ways, "achieved partly through the protection that marginalization and difference allow" (162). For young adult readers, this project is often enticing; not only can the reader potentially understand the motivations of the Brontës as children growing into maturity, but also the connection and empathy any young writer might feel by creating other worlds and strong characters. Each bit of world building necessarily reflects on the world of the Victorian child author but acts as an impetus for the reader to reconsider their own world. Each character requires creativity and empathy, for the past society in which the character exists and for our neo-Victorian perspective of them in any rewriting of the narratives.

According to Charlotte, the initial impetus for the children's worlds arrived on June 5, 1826; after a trip away, their father brought a set of toy soldiers home to Branwell. Charlotte writes about their arrival in one of her first known writings from March 12, 1829, and famously, they each choose a soldier; telling their soldiers' stories would captivate their imaginations.[3] Their imaginations then spun fiction and non-fiction narratives, catalogues, speeches, poems, and fragments. By 1829, after the death of their sisters, the young authors were working in pairs—Charlotte with Branwell, and Emily with Anne—to create the powerful worlds of Glass

Town, Angria, and Gondal. Initially, the four small Brontës (ages ten, nine, eight, and seven respectively) become the omniscient and powerful Genii (Talli, Branni, Emmi, and Anni) of the West-African adventures.

Certainly, in each of these works, the young Brontës enter the world of their juvenilia, no longer aware of or caring about the boundaries between their imaginative lives and their lived existences. It is easy to see why the imaginary worlds of Glass Town and Gondal were comforting to the young Brontë children.[4] Too often, our present-day assumption is that childhood is and always has been an innocent, protected moment; for the Brontës, it was neither given the recurrence of illness and death just as it was for many young children in Victorian England. Marie-Luise Kohlke reminds us that "Biofictional subjects, thus partake of an uneasy liminal existence, an inter-subjective half-life between self and other, fact and fiction, embodiment and textualization" (2013, 5). Although it is clear that their father encouraged imaginative, robust, joyful play for the young family, it cannot be understated how the Brontës' world was full of trauma. Juliet McMaster argues the devastation of early loss would have been compounded by their need to write about their pain and, at the same time, being fully aware that, as children, they have, as yet, no voice (2005, 52). As siblings who approach adolescence, the sisters and brother continue to work in the worlds of their own creation; for Charlotte, the draw is even stronger. She keeps alive the characters of Glass Town until she begins to merge with them in her thoughts.

Picturing Charlotte

Fawkes' *Charlotte Brontë Before Jane Eyre* begins with a kind of prologue in which the post is delivered to Charlotte at Roe Head. A sister student assumes it is news from home or a letter from a sweetheart, but is rebuked harshly by Charlotte who denies it would be anything so petty. The rest of the day passes with her clear disgust at the pointless "talk and talk and talk" (2019, 2) around her. Once the students have all gone to bed, Charlotte reads a response to her poems, only to be reminded in increasingly dark panels that express her dismay that she "ought to be prepared for disappointment" (3). A full-page illustration follows the letter where only a candle burns in the darkness as, possibly, an expression of Charlotte's disappointment and depression. Ambiguous at best, one could argue that it represents the light that will not be extinguished in the young developing author. Post-title page, the images are blue and grey to demonstrate a flashback; it is now sixteen years earlier at the parsonage in 1821. The six siblings are busy, happy, interacting constantly under the watch of Maria, the eldest. They beg for her to read them "the part about the giant genie" (9) from *The Arabian Nights* as they debate the virtues of Napoleon Bonaparte and the Duke of Wellington, Arthur Wellesley. Their play is interrupted by the death of their mother who suffers to the end worrying about "my poor children!" (11).

These strong images begin the graphic novel, moving the narrative towards the young adult years of the children; school is attended, Maria and Elizabeth are lost in the deathly atmosphere of the school where the brutal teacher, Miss Andrews, abuses the girls with a switch in hand. When Maria's memorisation goes badly due to ill health, Miss Andrews demands her "Show me the back of your neck!" (Fawkes 15). The deaths of these two sisters pass and the remaining four children strike out into the moors, away from the parsonage and its graveyard. Charlotte's anger is palpable; she tells her siblings "When we are struck for no reason, we should strike back very hard! I'm sure we should! So hard as to teach the person who struck us never to do it again!" (19). These three panels have the children gathered around Charlotte as Branwell walks slightly ahead of the girls; it is to her that Emily asks, "Charlotte, are you the oldest now?" but only in a thought does the reader witness Charlotte's despairing answer at the responsibility now thrust upon her: "I'm only nine" (19). Her new status is a place she was not ever expecting to hold given she was a middle child of six.

The beginnings of the Brontë juvenilia begin a year later; a six-panel thread is given of the toy soldiers' arrival, as well as how they are chosen and named; the next pages are of "the Twelve Soldiers and the Four Genii," the initial story in the Glass Town saga. By the fifth and sixth panels, there is a blending of fact and fiction where Branwell and Charlotte appear as giant geni(uses) in the clouds, declaring themselves Genius Tallii and Branii Genius. Their young writer selves immediately have a conflict; Branii wishes to wreak havoc while Tallii intervenes on the characters' behalf. As creators, they are both cognisant that "We have the power of life and death over you mortals" (22). These scenes recall the real-life disagreements waged between the siblings over control of characters in Glass Town. Three years later, in 1829, Fawkes has the two eldest discuss the need to write down the many adventures of the Twelve Soldiers; metafiction inserts itself when Charlotte suggests the characters "themselves will be authors!" in the newly established *Branwell's Blackwood's Magazine* that will be character-sized, tiny so the soldiers might read it (23) but more importantly, so the adults in the house—their father and aunt—cannot.

Privacy and secrecy shield out judgement and dismissal feared by young people. For young adult readers who are creatives, the anxiety over intellectual ownership or the need to create can be overwhelming. The intensity of interaction is pictured as full of light and, as they walk the moors, the disparities between the siblings' interests begin to show. Emily and Anne—as Perry and Ross—begin to think of their own Lands in the juvenilia and how they would like them to be more grounded, without fancy palaces nor political intrigue "nor the decadent tyrants" (24). The illustration shows them literally drawing away from Branwell and Charlotte planning their own new adventures. Emily confronts Charlotte a year later, asking, "What do we know of palaces or the kind of people who live in them," and asks to write of "an isolated house" or the moors (25). Aunt Branwell often interrupts their "scribble scrabble" (24) but increasingly Charlotte becomes absorbed in her alternative world. Her eyes become darker as her thoughts are for Lord Charles but her reality involves being sent to school as the panels darken to match her mood. School responsibilities begin to usurp her time to write.

School is not described as an enjoyable place of learning; rather, it is titled "SCHOOLWORK" (31). Amongst the generically similar pupils, Charlotte is able to meet Ellen Nussey and Mary Taylor with whom she shares her thoughts. Sitting at night in a window box, reading in the dark, Charlotte is mocked for "Why would anyone want to read after a whole day of school?" (32). Mary understands there is an affinity between them such that Charlotte shares the facts about the tiny magazines. Mary believes the sibling writers should seek an audience because "All that writing and it never sees the light! It's like you're growing potatoes in the cellar!" (32). She transgressively tells stories to her fellow students in the dark, recalling the later Glass Town saga's heavy Gothic Romanticism as a woman walks on the castle wall on a stormy night—her story is so effective that sobs abound. Miss Wooler fines Charlotte for late talking but the girls want to know the ending to the story. The forbidden stories are, clearly, compelling which affirms her, and other adolescents', abilities to construct a narrative of interest, even at a young age.

At this point, the neo-Victorian graphic narrative establishes two points of focus: first, that the world of story into which the Brontës launch themselves is not constrained by their physical isolation; and second, Charlotte has begun to suffer under the weight of expectation and convention. The next section sees the end of school and the possibilities that await with Charlotte's declaration, "I want to have fun!" (36). She returns home to re-enter the mythic world where personalities and characters begin to blur. In a panel that shows the family at their most relaxed, they all lay about arguing how "Anne, you could be Marion … then Emily should be Zenobia" while Branwell wishes to be Rogue (38) as part of their routine. In a step towards pursuing a potential career, Branwell—as the male sibling—goes to London, the "City of Art & Culture!" where he declares, "I'm no more content with staying in this village than you sisters are content with being seamstresses" because "my inspiration carries me! My poetry rivals Byron's. My painting…" (40). Charlotte returns to teach at Roe Head and brings a resistant Emily with her. The attitudes of the girls are overheard in darkening drawings as Emily lays in the dark thinking of how "In dungeons dark I cannot sing … I'll never get used to it!" (42) accompanied by simple pencil lines which show her expression of sadness. She becomes more ill; in a panel that is reminiscent of a convict seeking light from a window high above her head (42), Emily hopes that "Gondal and Angria will still be there," although Charlotte is not certain if they will be, "Especially as we get older?" (42). Emily falls into dreamworlds of Gondal when the light fades knowing "And its joys fleet fast away" (43).

Victorian responsibility can be interrogated in the neo-Victorian revision of Charlotte as constrained by gender, and social obligation. She has slipped the bounds of ideal womanly kindliness and empathy. Increasingly Charlotte finds her time with her "dolt" students painful and questions if she is "to spend all the best part of my life in this wretched bondage, forcibly suppressing my rage" when "I felt as if I could have written gloriously. I longed to write. The spirit of all Verdopolis … came crowding into my mind" (45). A crucial panel appears; the fictional Marquis of Douro now exists alongside his author, asking, "Charlotte … Stay a moment…" (45). He then interrupts her days, coming in through her window, tempting her outside with "it's beautiful! Angria awaits!" (46) and crowding her thoughts while she tries to teach. Charlotte confesses in a letter to Ellen that "I keep trying to do right, repressing wrong thoughts—but still every instant I find myself going astray" (46). The contradiction between what life requires of her and where her dreams lie cause a crisis in identity and intention leading to "It does not matter where I am going … I am going and I know from whom I am going" (26). From Roe Head, Charlotte wrote to Ellen Nussey on May 10, 1836:

> Don't deceive yourself by imagining that I have a bit of real goodness about me. My Darling if I were like you I should have my face Zion-ward though prejudice and error might occasionally fling a mist over the glorious vision before me. for with all your single-hearted sincerity you have your faults. but I am <u>not like you</u>. If you knew my thoughts; the dreams that absorb me; and the fiery imagination that at times eats me up and makes me feel Society as it is, wretchedly insipid you would pity and I dare say despise me. … don't think me mad. (Brontë I:144)

This plea to her friend is an admission of despair that she does not fit in. Just newly twenty years old, Charlotte is a woman trapped by gender, class, and expectation, a scenario for which a modern young adult reader has been given the appropriate historical context and experiential distance to recognise as unfair.

The siblings must now decide, as all young adults must, on what will come next for each of their lives as well as for their characters. Seeking advice, this is the moment she writes to Southey; at the same time, Branwell writes to Wordsworth. Anne accompanies Charlotte back to Roe Head where she "endured teaching for another year" but after Anne becomes ill and returns home, Charlotte's "morbid nerves can know neither peace nor enjoyment" causing depression that lasts through "weeks of mental and bodily anguish" (Fawkes 51). The darkness of the panels begins to lighten up only once Charlotte returns to Haworth. Emily tries to teach but becomes physically homesick. In a move towards maturity of thought, and of leaving the juvenilia behind, Charlotte begins to think of a new story with "instead of a beautiful aristocratic heroine, I were to write of someone plain and sensible who will not be corrupted by society?" but her hero Arthur Wellesley, now styled the Duke of Zamorna, keeps reappearing in a kind of haunting to interfere with her work (53).

Charlotte and Emily go off to Brussels to learn French so they might open a school. While there, Charlotte encounters her real-life Monsieur Heger, who is drawn by Fawkes as tall, dark, and handsome. They are pictured by Fawkes working diligently; that said, Emily's strong will chafes under his direction, leading her to question "What is the good in imitating some other author's style—especially a sentimental one? We will lose all originality of thought and expression" (63). This panel shows the illuminated Emily, hair unfurling against the backdrop of a conformist classroom with rows of empty chairs lined up while Charlotte is desperate to please her Master falling into tears (Fawkes 64) when he critiques her writing. Emily objects. Her forceful, individualistic personality is developing in young womanhood and she thinks that rather than pleasing Heger, "It seems a far more profitable goal to please yourself" (66).

Much happens over the next year but during that return after the death of Aunt Branwell, Charlotte realises Emily and Anne have been continually writing; Charlotte breaks a house rule, goes into Emily's room and desk to read her poems. She runs to the moors and under a thunderous sky, Emily reacts to the invasion of her privacy; however, Charlotte counters with how the poems—paralleled with the background of the moors—"sent my spirits soaring" with their "peculiar music—wild, melancholy, and elevating" music (Fawkes 78–80). Their plan is created in secret in the contained dining room, the much-mythologised walking ground where their collection takes shape. They publish; they work towards their novels with focus and dedication; Branwell appears less and less in Fawkes' panels, an indication of how Branwell began his self-exclusion from the group. Although *The Professor* is rejected, *Jane Eyre* takes shape in a completely wordless panel (see Fig. 4.1) that is followed by the happy publication in 1847 of *Wuthering Heights* and *Agnes Grey* (see Fig. 4.2).

The end of adolescence for each of the young women comes with the fruition of their publishing efforts; the closing page is a full illustration of *Jane Eyre* hovering over a sketch of Haworth with a comment on its success. They are wedded to their pseudonyms—Ellis, Acton, and Currer Bell—and give birth to their novels.

Through Glass, Darkly

The graphic novel of story begins to tell the intricate, interwoven nature of the Brontës with each other and their creations; in Coakley's novel, *Worlds of Ink and Shadow*, the lines are not only intellectually but physically broken between the two worlds blur between authors and characters.

In an early piece of writing at the age of twelve, Charlotte explains her relation to her siblings and to the Glass Town world:

> It seemed as if I were a non-existent shadow—that I neither spoke, ate, imagined, or lived of myself, but I was the mere idea of some other creature's brain. The Glass Town seemed so likewise. My father … and everyone with whom I am acquainted, passed into a state of annihilation; but suddenly I thought again that I and my relatives did exist and yet, not us, but our minds, and our bodies without ourselves. … WE without US were

Fig. 4.1 Charlotte Brontë working on *Jane Eyre* in *Charlotte Brontë before Jane Eyre* (2019, 86). (Courtesy of Glynnis Fawkes)

shadows; also, but at the end of a long vista, as it were, appeared dimly and indistinctly, beings that really lived in a tangible shape, that were called by our names and were US from whom WE had been copied by something—I could not tell what. (Brontë in Alexander 1987–91, 257)

Coakley's narrative places the Brontës at the point where they began to break apart as writers and seek individual maturity. Branwell is on a male path to adulthood, and the girls find themselves imagining what freedom could be like. There is an abrupt beginning to this neo-Victorian novel that straightaway focuses on Charlotte's view of her own writing; she wants it to be transcendent and not like her brother's passionate scrawl. Charlotte sees his half full page and "she noticed with disgust" that he was

4 ILLUSTRATIVE GENII: THE BRONTËS' GENIUS   93

Fig. 4.2 Emily and Anne's celebration in *Jane Eyre* in *Charlotte Brontë before Jane Eyre* (2019, 87). (Courtesy of Glynnis Fawkes)

writing with his "left hand" which he only used when he wrote about "Rogue, his magnificently wicked villain" (Coakley 2016, 1–2). Branwell begins to see himself as an artist and an author and he attempts to annex the group study. Charlotte ascertains "that his mind was in that place where the real world falls away" with a "strange, ecstatic look" that she envies because she remembers she had "written like that once, for the sheer joy of being in invented lands, not caring whether the words were good. Whether they were *art*" (3; emphasis in original).

Now seventeen, Branwell finds his "words were still unspooling across the page" (4). Anne stares at the desk with a mix of "fascination and aversion on her face" and Emily admits the sight before them "was uncanny" because "Two papers sat on opposite sides of the desk writing themselves ... these words appeared in perfect silence" (7). The next chapter/scene opens in Verdopolis with Charlotte's eyes "shut, but she knew she was no longer at her desk; the little parsonage in Yorkshire was far away" (8). The reader is immediately uncertain about the veracity of the switch, whether Charlotte has figuratively—or literally—disappeared into Glass Town.

In the past, the four siblings had travelled into the invented worlds together of worlds inspired by their family reading, but they would sometimes open a "door of light ... one of them would make that mysterious hand gesture, and they would all go through" to the world which they were "enacting, not writing" (24). In that Glass Town world, Charlotte emerges out of the crimson curtain "where, for one horrible moment she was herself, a plain girl in a mouse-colored dress, too small, to ill-favored to belong anywhere in this world"; that said, she is powerful because when she begins to murmur under her breath "words appeared across Charlotte's story paper" (9). As young adult female author, Charlotte asserts control over her narrative, power she does not have access to at the Parsonage. The encounter Charlotte has here is with her two heroines: Mary Henrietta, the new bride of Zamorna, and Mina Laury, her maid. What becomes apparent is that Charlotte has changed genders in Glass Town because she is now a boy, is ten years old, and wears a blue velvet suit; she is, in this world, Charles Wellesley (9–11).

Unrestrained by gender as the younger brother of Lord Arthur Wellesley, Duke of Zamorna, both author and subject—Charlotte/Charles—command attention: "Stop! Charlotte said. The room fell silent. All were still" but she can move around the characters to adjust them, including her tall hero with a "high, noble forehead, loose curls, and arresting brown eyes. Even frozen" he was "so aloof, so arrogant, so aristocratic" with a "basilisk gaze" (13). Both references—to a plain young woman who foreshadows Jane and to the charismatic hero who bears striking resemblance to Edward Rochester—are neo-Victorian nods to Charlotte's future writing of *Jane Eyre*. Unlike in life, there is no fear in the character of a young boy-child "about being unladylike. After all, she wasn't a lady" (12) and with elder sisters here in Glass Town, she bears no responsibility. For the author, it is interesting that "*I made this ... All this is mine*" (Coakley 10; emphasis in original) but it gives her pause about the direction of her life. Perhaps she was "simply an eighteen-year-old girl from Haworth, England, a girl who was destined to be a governess someday soon ... *Perhaps I am only playing with the world's most exquisite set of dolls*" and "Perhaps it was time to put her dolls away" (15; emphasis in original).

Unlike an actual reading of the Victorian juvenilia, the neo-Victorian doubling of the character(s) problematise the idea of a prescribed role and allows for a reconsideration of a young girl/woman's restricted role in society that clearly favoured sons. The shifts between the narrator and her first-person perspective allow for entry of the twenty-first-century reader to be critical of such constraint that might be imposed on Charlotte's talent because of her gender and class.

Branwell, too, enters Glass Town but significantly he appears as Lord Thornton Witkin Sneaky, a "rich, young reprobate" (17). The young male author does not feel the need to change his appearance or gender while spending time with his character, Alexander Rogue. There is no need for Branwell to pretend or be concerned. Unlike Charlotte, Branwell "liked to let his plots go where they may" (19) even if his sister became fearful when "sometimes, in spite of her best efforts, her characters would drift away from the plot" (11) into areas of indiscretion. As a young man, Branwell's life could be successful and would unfold for him with even minimal effort; conversely, for Charlotte, Emily, and Anne, there are conventions of patriarchy that deny them inheritance from their father or financial independence and even more social mores that narrow their fields of potentialities as women.

BITS OF GLASS

Like any adolescent, the Brontës' writing as well as their character(s) must evolve as they move forward with ambition and creativity. Reading about the Victorian writers might help neo-Victorian readers with their own *Bildüngsroman* because developing young people often conceptualise their existence via "place, identity, and the body" as well as "barriers, boundaries, and binaries"; in addition, "issues of belonging, in and across space and place, are especially prevalent in literary representations of youth" (Hamilton-McKenna 2021, 308) or for youth. Learning about the world through stories is how children begin to understand their world. Here, in *The Glass Town Game*, the mythological tropes of the Brontës, as children who lived an isolated existence, are blended with the ideas of a fairy tale:

> Once, four children called Charlotte, Emily, Anne, and Branwell lived all together in a village called Haworth in the very farthest, steepest, highest, northernest bit of England. Their house stood snugly at the very farthest, steepest, highest bit of the village, just behind the church and the crowded graveyard, for their father was the parson. (Valente 2017, 3)

Each child is given a particular skill: Emily is an expert smuggler, Anne is a spy, Charlotte can lie to anyone and Branwell is a genius at badness, "both a vandal *and* a brawler" (6–7; emphasis in original). The subtlety of the gendered nature of these points is made manifest when Branwell knows "it was a boy's job to make things—furniture and machines and money and books and governments and art and such. It was a girl's job to sit still and let someone else make something out of *them*, and that was that" (8; emphasis in original) and he is not happy when the soldiers his father had chosen to "present to his only son" but his sisters, defying this bit of patriarchal preference, had "made a quick end to *that*" (9; emphasis in original) when they each claimed a favourite for themselves, an assertion they can make in the Glass Town world, but not in life. Their juvenilian or Glass Town world allows them a sense of agency they cannot access in the Haworth parsonage; hence, the girls' desire to frequent their imaginary world is understandable as a place of social mobility and self-actualisation even if, at times, in the guise of their characters.

Storytelling is cast as a playful activity even if Anne knows that you "had to mind your manners, she knew, when telling unreal stories about real people" (11). Writing stories has also become a kind of therapy for the children as they adopt the mantra "Buck up," "Be Brave," and keep "Busy hands" to make "bright hearts" (17) so they will not dwell upon "the Beastliest Day" (13)—the day they will be separated and sent to school. Their father is determined to educate their daughters but "would not dream of such a place for his only son" because Branwell "got all the good of the world as far as Emily could see it" (21). From the perspective of a modern reader looking back, Valente takes issue with the clear bias endured by the gifted sisters. At eleven, Branwell is "old enough to taste a little bit of manhood" that gives him "the responsibility, the authority, the *power*" with the duty "to care for soft, gentle girls and guide their soft, gentle minds. He would be their Lord, their general" (29; emphasis in original) when their father entrusts him with the money for a trip to Keighley. Emily's protests of this engendered power only to be reminded that "young ladies oughtn't to go about telling their fathers what to do, you know" (31) by her father. Branwell finds his sisters "bafflingly *female*. If only Charlotte had been born a boy, there would only be understanding between them" plus she could guide him into becoming a "different person, a better person, the perfect person" (35; emphasis in original).

The Brontës' imaginary worlds collide with their reality when they encounter a "man made entirely of books," the Magazine Man, came hurling towards them; Charlotte spots him and Anne wonders if anyone else sees him. When they ask from whence he came, the stationmaster bellows at them that "'Children ought to be seen and NOT HEARD, ORRIGHT?'" (42–3). The Magazine Man is "*magic*. It was all magic and they *knew* it was magic; they'd known it at once" (47; emphasis in original) and they told him "'You're made of *pages*, did you know?'" (48; emphasis in original). He retorts "'Well, *you're* made of *meat* … It's *disgusting*. I bet you've got … I bet you've got bones in there, And hair, too! Pah! How *grue*some!'" (48; emphasis in original). The character seeks to remind his creators of their difference; however, the rest of the narrative sees an intermixing of characters and creators.

This kind of conflation between the idealised fictional world and the real world is not unusual; further, it has led to literary scholars who are "examining how contemporary youth narratives not only blur but also transgress conventional spatial divisions" (Hamilton-McKenna 2021, 310). Certainly, as the older Brontë writings became more intense, the younger siblings were left behind and Anne finds it "remarkable … how one can become attached to fictional people" (Coakley 25). She views herself with "a tiny mathematician in her mind" who would "tell her unknowable things" about human nature like "*This person is lying. That person is afraid.* Today her little man told her that Emily was keeping secrets" (27; emphasis in original). Coakley significantly distinguishes the youngest girl-child, Anne, as the conscience and pragmatic sister of the group; Anne repeatedly sought employment to increase her self-sufficiency and the potential for independence even in difficult circumstances as well as being the most concerned with faith and consequences before God.

Like her siblings, Emily has her own sense of the otherworldy. In *Worlds of Ink and Shadow*, Emily is given a correspondence with the mystical, including the gytrash "ghost dog of the moors, who tore out the throats of unsuspecting travelers" which suits her vision of the impression of "unreality descending on the parsonage" that was "beginning to feel like a fairy tale" with "fairy hobs and ghost dogs" (29). Tabby makes clear that it is the "see-er who chooses the appearance, not the spirit" suggesting that fear creates form (31). The maturing Emily admits that she is drawn to darkness, drawn to Rogue and Zamorna but that "Rogue had done such cruel and terrible things. He was chaos. He was the black hound, tearing our throats on the moor. What sort of person could love that?" (33) she asks while the neo-Victorian narrative makes clear reference to her future character, Heathcliff, who is emblematic of her own creative spirit. Emily's writing is wilfully untethered to conventional expectations. When she eventually creates her own world of Gondal, breathing it into existence with a bargain made with "Old Tom," a place "like her own moor but wilder—more beautiful and horrible," full of "*Foxes and hawks. … Lightning and catastrophe*" (158; emphasis in original) where Rogue waits. Emily denies it has been made for him but rather for herself as she admits, "I'm really quite brilliant, aren't I?" (161). This recognition of her own genius comes at a price; when she returns to the Parsonage, she feels something has been "ripped away" and says "I felt something leaving me, draining away from me. I was so tired" and "I paid a price, but I don't know" other than it was very important; she asks Anne, "What if it was my soul?" (172–73).

Worlds Collide

The implication of Charlotte's need for control, Anne's careful watch on her sisters and Emily's fear is that each sister is on the cusp of womanhood, fully aware of what is expected of her but equally cognisant of their lack of desire to be conventional. Charlotte cannot raise their concerns with their father because even when he asks, she replies, "Nothing, Papa" (180), knowing that he cannot understand their plight.

This neo-Victorian narrative creates a metaphor in keeping with their juvenilia; if they keep returning to Glass Town and Gondal, "If we continue to pay the price for crossing over, we'll die young. It's as simple as that" (185) even though they are being called in spite of never saying they "would cross over forever. That wasn't the bargain" (184). The fluidity between childhood worlds and the road to maturity still exists; Mavis Reimer makes the case that in twenty-first-century texts for young people, "boundaries between the inside and the outside are porous and confused" (2013, 3). Caroline Hamilton-McKenna then extends that idea to argue that the "increasingly fluid conceptualization of space and place is evident in cultural analyses that bridge literary and real-world identities and communities" (2021, 310) to which one could add that stories encourage young people to move between real and literary worlds.

Young men, like Branwell, face their own challenges in the road to maturation. Charlotte explodes at Branwell's maudlin whining—"I cannot bear to hear you complain about your poor life. At least you'll be an artist. You'll be doing something fulfilling. If I had your advantages and expectations"—implying she would succeed with her ambitious work ethic (Coakley 185). Branwell strikes back, defensively, saying, "You are so lucky that no one will ever ask you to *be* anything" (185; emphasis in original). From a twenty-first-century perspective, the reader can see Branwell fights against Victorian expectations of traditional masculinity that include success as a son and future provider; nevertheless, he is still conceding his sister's perspective when he admits "I see that it is unfair that you will probably never be a painter or a writer or anything else you want to be because you are a woman" (186).

When the time for leaving behind childhood draws nearer, Emily's gytrash more regularly appears on the moors as a "black and threatening thing, howling up at them" as a "thing that shouldn't be real. It shouldn't be in their world" but she knew he would come (197). Charlotte believes *"there is something a little pagan about Emily"* (198; emphasis in original), but it takes a dark turn when Emily's world invades their own; Maria appears, grown into a woman" (202). At the same time, in her world, Emily confronts Rogue to tell him in spite of his growing power, that he is not alive, telling him "You're not alive. You are a story. We made you up" but Rogue pounded his chest with his fist with "'I *feel* alive. I don't *feel* like a story any more than you do!'" (257; emphasis in original).

Anne—often considered the least and the last—is the one to gain control over their submission to their creations. In her own bargain with Old Tom, Anne confirms she "did not wish to live longer than [her] sister Emily" and that he should "take as many days as lets me die within a year of her, and that if she ever crosses over again, he should add those days to my debt"; she tells them forcefully, "you *cannot* go, because every time you do, you will be bringing Emily and me closer and closer to our deaths" (311–12; emphasis in original). Anne refuses to allow her older siblings to risk their souls or their futures.

All four young Brontës continue to write; however, they no longer cross over. "Old Tom" has lost and Charlotte defies the character S'Death with her confident rage that "plain as I am, I will marry someone, and it will be for love. If I am to have a life of sorrows, I will not let them conquer me. I will be as brave as Emily, as honest as Anne, even as wicked as Branwell, if I must be, but I will be happy! Do you hear?" (335). The four siblings move forward, from young adulthood towards adulthood. The danger of remaining childlike risks their futures.

Revisioning Glass

The most recent narrative that conflates the young authors with their characters and settings is Greenberg's *Glass Town: The Imaginary World of the Brontës*, a graphic novel entirely cast in black, greys, browns, reds, and oranges, all reminiscent of earthy tones and heavily dependent on the colonial aspects of their writings which speak to the increased interest by current youth on issues of race and colonial reparations. The "Note to the Reader" offers an explanation that this book is historical fiction but only "some of the biographical details of the life of Charlotte Brontë and her siblings are accurate" and that, "especially in the Glass Town sections of the book," Greenberg has "embroidered, embellished, and indulged in a great deal of supposing" (2020, 2). Following this note, the *Dramatis Personae* are set forth and include both the Brontë family, family of choice, and the Glass Town characters. There is only a difference of place noted, either Haworth or Glass Town, but no indication of fictional or historical existence. This obfuscation between the real with the fictional is immediate. Charlotte, in 1849, is sitting on the moors sketched all in greys and black when she asks, "Is it you? After all this time?" as a tall, dark-haired gentleman approaches her, responding "I've always been here. … You just haven't wanted me" (Greenberg 8). After some thought, Charlotte shares with him that she is the only one left—her siblings are all dead. He reminds her that although Gondal is unreachable now, Glass Town remains if run-down from neglect. It is only well into the narrative that the gentleman is identified as Charles. A flashback begins to the "Weird Writings" of 1825–31 set in the usual desolate space of the graveyard-fronted and moor-backed Parsonage; the reader empathises with the four siblings who are leaving Elizabeth's funeral. The four remaining Brontë children vow to look out for each other. They retreat off to the moors to play and to walk which "left them raw and chafed but new" (24). A new day brings the toy soldiers; the panel has the newly opened chest of players within the circle of siblings and they consider if they are from "'Leeds, silly'" says Branwell "Or far-flung Africa" says Charlotte "Or another world" (37). Leeds slips into another world quickly as the children morph into the four great Genii on the next full page. Redressed as commanders, the siblings begin to interact with the main characters to build the Glass Town. The Genii write and write, papers crumpled and clear, destroyed, and rewritten, abound on a two-page spread while Zamorna and Quashia Quamina wait upon pedestals.

This neo-Victorian look at the Brontës is the only one to deal with the issues of colonialism and race that are a large part of their juvenile writings; awareness of race and the Othering of non-white, non-British subjects is, to a certain extent, part of their writings that is provocative for a modern, young adult reader and for their adult counterpart. From a young age, the Brontës' father encouraged them to engage with politics, parliamentary debates, and British concerns in contemporary periodicals as part of their reading; as a result, their juvenilia are full of references to political figures and current events compounded with their youthful—but not naïve or uneducated—opinions on these subjects. Rigorous family debates of issues found in *Blackwood's Edinburgh Magazine* or *Fraser's Magazine* find their way into the children's own developing prose on ideas of progress and history. Felipe Espinoza Garrido, Marlena Tronicke, and Julian Wacker, in their *Black Neo-Victoriana*, articulate the need for

> neo-Victorian fictions [to] understand the Victorian past as a rich archive for narratives to interrogate and destabilise rather than reproduce the racialised (and often gendered) biases that too often inform dominant understandings of "the Victorian". Black neo-Victoriana have the potentiality to critically intervene in the discourse of neo-Victorianism, which both in its cultural and academic manifestations has at times contributed to the imagination of a white Victorian Britain and a white global nineteenth century even when contesting it. (2022, 1)

Although this graphic novel is the creative recreation of white children's artistic understanding of a fictional African people, the African setting of the tales does demonstrate the young Brontës' "imagination of empire" providing "important early evidence of significance British Imperialism and racial conflict have" for the fledgling writers (Meyer 1991, 29); as such, the graphic novel points to the increased and necessary significance BIPOC issues—historical and neo-Victorian representations of them—hold for twenty-first-century young adult readers.

The story of Quashia is included in this graphic narrative under his own title banner to tell his story as the son of the King of the Ashantee people as one outside of the children's experience. Greenberg's explanatory commentary outlines how, when "the Duke of Wellington arrived with the Twelves, and the terrible Ashantee Wars began, they were driven from their homes. With the Duke at their head, the English troops ravaged and slaughtered and pillaged and enslaved" (58). Wellington finds Quashia, dressed in African attire, and declares, "I shall adopt you, little boy. And civilise you" into a "perfect little English boy you look. Almost, anyway" (26). Arthur, Wellington's son, even once Quashia has been redressed in European attire, denies the boy equal status due to class and race, even though they are both children. Arthur wonders if Quashia even speaks English before declaring, "I will never shake your hand, stranger" (26). Arthur's hatred grows, and he treats Quashia with "inexplicable cruelty"; he abuses the boy claiming "you are just an uncivilised Ashantee savage" but the African, now a young man, finally fights back with "My blood is nobler than yours will ever be. Yes, I will always be Ashantee. I am their king. And one day I will free my people. You will see" (61).

The savagery of Empire building is clear; neither the Brontës nor Valente's writings leave room for argument over their disgust with the colonising forces. In what surely must be one of the earliest depictions of a biracial relationship in juvenilia, Mary loves and wishes to marry Quashia, even though she is betrothed to Arthur. Here, in an elegant, simple frame, Quashia looks directly and defiantly out through the fourth wall at the reader, calling out passivity. The adopted son leaves Glass Town, declaring that "You will not see me again until I march into Glass Town at the head of a great army. And then we will drive the English from our land. I will free my people" (64). The Brontës and Greenberg have blended here to call out Empire.

The graphic narrative about the Brontës is, at one point, concerned with the period from 1831–35 that witnesses a break between the fantasy worlds and between the four Genii. Anne and Emily challenge their subordination to their older siblings which in turn leads to the creation of Gondal as Charlotte goes to Roe Head. There is a flash forward to the discussion taking place as the frame narrative where Charlotte confesses that, at school, "I made friends. ... I did well. I won prizes. I was normal" (Valente 76). Throwing themselves into writing is, for Charlotte, divided between the discussions with Charles about how the writings occurred, how decisions were made, and how some characters were of more importance to Charlotte (like Mary Percy) than others. Charles—ventriloquising twenty-first-century issues the young reader might have—takes Charlotte to task about "Beautiful, boring Mary. ... How you came up with a woman as pliable, as put-upon ... As two-dimensional as Mary ... I will never understand" (87). His disdain for her answer is clear when he waves about a white piece of paper with a flat drawing of Mary which he has taken from Charlotte's writing desk; the paper evokes an image of one-dimensionality, and of a white flag, the idea of Brontë's surrender to conventional constructions of young womanhood and a young woman's capitulation to patriarchal conformity. Mary Percy's painful story unfolds as both a testimony to her pain and as a warning. For a modern reader accessing the Brontëan character through the graphic novel, Mary is insipid in her submissiveness to Zamorna's abuse and is clearly used in her own father, Northangerland/Rogue's, schemes. Although Quashia returns to warn of her father's disloyalty, a chessboard in the background emphasises Mary's role as a pawn as well as how, extension, women were often used as objects of exchange in Victorian culture.

In direct contrast to this portrait of male need for power is the Lady Zenobia, a brilliant woman who speaks five languages including English, Angrian, Ashantee, Greek, and Enochian, "studied classics, and philosophy, economics and the science of modern warfare, needlepoint and archery and falconry and horsemanship" (100). Of African descent, Zenobia is fully attired as an Englishwoman and is the woman with whom Zamorna becomes obsessed even while betrothed to Mary Percy. Zenobia is wise; she sees Zamorna's duplicity and wishes Lady Mary luck because, she confides to the reader, "he's a snake. And he will eat that girl alive" (107). Charles sits with Charlotte listing off the dysfunctionality of how "Zenobia loves Zamorna. And Mary Percy loves Zamorna. And Quashia loves Mary Percy. And Zamorna loves Zenobia but is marrying Mary Percy" to make it clear the chess board—and Glass Town—is set for battle (108).

A very important moment in Charlotte's personal history is the focal point in a section entitled "Scribblemania" when she is at Roe Head. With the distance provided by a neo-Victorian narrative, the reader identifies that Charlotte Brontë (n.d.) is no longer just a scribbling sibling; rather, her reliance on the fictional world has moved to an uncontrollable slippage. In her journal on August 11, 1836, Charlotte recounts a frightening day.

> What I imagined grew morbidly vivid, ... All this day I have been in a dream, half miserable and half ecstatic: miserable because I could not follow it out

uninterruptedly; ecstatic because it shewed almost in the vivid light of reality the ongoings of the infernal world. ... Then came on me, rushing impetuously, all the mighty phantasm that we had conjured from nothing to a system strong as some religious creed. I felt as if I could have written gloriously—I longed to write. The spirit of all Verdopolis, of all the mountainous North, of all the woodland West, of all the river-watered East came crowding into my mind. If I had had time to indulge it, I felt that the vague sensations of that moment would have settled down into some narrative better at least than any thing I ever produced before. But just then a dolt came up with a lesson. I thought I should have vomited. (Roe Head Journal)

The twentieth- and twenty-first-century reader sees this feeling as mental illness caused by stress and anxiety, not uncommon in society. Goldberg's illustrations reflect the insecurity of Charlotte's reality as Charlotte articulates the feeling that the "world I inhabit ... this real world" has now "ceased to be as real to me as that other world" as she "catch[es] glimpses of Zamorna at the edge of my vision" (118) or "through the window" (120). The full-page spread conjoins the two worlds when the "Yorkshire hills fade away" into Glass Town and Zamorna appears as she ignores her students (122–23). In life, Charlotte returns to Haworth to re-establish her sense of normalcy.

Charles, again asking questions, pertinent to the reader of the neo-Victorian narrative who learns of the horrid portrait of a marriage; he wants to know why she mard Zenobia off to Rogue.

"It was a plot line that never made sense to me."
"I was jealous of her."
"Jealous ... of your own creation."
"Yes. You said it, Zamorna loved her, and I was jealous. So I punished her."
"Married her off to Northangerland. A drunkard."
"It's no wonder you turned down three marriage proposals."
...
"How could I marry a boring curate when I have known men like Zamorna, Rochester ... Heger." (132)

Two of the men are her own fictional creations, one is a married man who spurned her, and one—the curate—is real; that said, it is to Zamorna that her nightly dreams fly. Zamorna tells Charlotte, "I am you. And you are me" (147), a clear reference by Greenberg to another young Brontë author, Emily, whose character Cathy infamously and problematically claims, "I am Heathcliff" (Brontë, E. 1847; ch 9). A young adult reader, thinking about this narrative, would hopefully recognise the cost of such a loss of self, a hideous sacrifice for an undeserving person who threatens their personhood.

Charlotte's seduction by her characters has become perilous when she can no longer distinguish between the real and the fictional. She returns to writing about Glass Town to have Quashia and Mary Percy lay together awaiting a good end. Pulled back to reality by her companion teacher, Miss Wooler, Charlotte is shocked to see she has not noticed Anne's illness because, Charles warns, "things in Glass Town are spiralling out of … control. Get out Charlotte. You are in too deep. If you do not stop, Glass Town will consume you!" even though he knows he is "but a mere figment of [her] fine imagination" (Valente 182–83).

Charlotte escapes and nine years later, the sisters are all published authors. In one final neo-Victorian push into reality, Charles and Charlotte speak for the last time; she tells him of her losses and he tells her she must make a choice: return to Glass Town in her mind or move forward with her life. Charlotte returns one last time to see the degradation to which Glass Town has come without her guidance. With a burgeoning career, and after the death of her three sibling scribblers, Charlotte makes the decision to leave childhood behind for a future with her father's curate, Mr. Arthur Bell Nicholls,[5] who has proposed to her and for the sake of her writing. Before he takes his leave of his creator, Charles expresses his gratitude to her with "It has been a great honour … to be your creation" (211). The neo-Victorian young adult narrative makes clear these are, in life and fiction, metafictional conversations between Charlotte and Charles, but really between Charlotte and herself. Since childhood, her real-life siblings referred to her as Charles, and when she created her character from a soldier to enact her visions in the juvenilia, she chose to name him Charles Wellesley.

The recriminations throughout have been Charlotte's own awareness of the problematic moments in her own character(s) and her writing, just as they have been neo-Victorian explorations of the past to enlighten the modern reader about the complexity of the life of the Brontë children. One such Brontë life, that of Emily, is particularly well-situated to be the focus of neo-Victorian interventions to satisfy a young reader's curiosity.

Notes

1. The Brontës are a family of writers who lived at the Parsonage in Haworth during the children's young adulthood. Maria (née Branwell) and Patrick Brontë had six children—Maria (April 23, 1814–May 6, 1825), Elizabeth (February 8, 1815–June 15, 1825), Charlotte (April 21, 1816–March 31, 1855), Patrick Branwell (June 26, 1817–September 24, 1848), Emily Jane (July 30, 1818–December 19, 1848), and Anne (January 17, 1820–May 28, 1849)—of whom one four survived into adulthood.
2. One should also note the propensity of Victorians for illustrated books. See Catherine Golden's excellent work, *Serials to Graphic Novels: The Evolution of the Victorian Illustrated Book* (2017).
3. In Charlotte's letter it states: "Papa bought Branwell some soldiers from Leeds. When Papa came home it was night and we were in bed, so next morning Branwell came to our door with a box of soldiers. Emily and I jumped out of bed and I snatched up one and exclaimed, 'This is the Duke of Wellington! It shall be mine!' When I said this, Emily likewise took one and said it should be hers. When Anne came down she took one also. Mine was the prettiest of the whole and perfect in every part. Emily's was a grave-looking fellow. We called him 'Gravey'. Anne's was a queer little thing, very much like herself. He was called 'Waiting Boy'. Branwell chose 'Bonaparte'" (Brontë 1987, I:5).
4. For the purposes of this discussion, the reference will be to Glass Town, although there were several disagreements between Branwell and Charlotte over whether this was one word or two; most likely, it was more of an argument regarding who was in control.
5. Charlotte Brontë married Arthur Bell Nichols (January 6, 1819–December 2, 1906), her father's curate, June 19, 1854; she died nine months later from extreme morning sickness during her pregnancy. She was thirty-eight years old.

Bibliography

Adringa, Els. "The Interface between Fiction and Life: Patterns of Identification in Reading Autobiographies." *Poetics Today*. 25, no. 2 (2004): 205–40.

Alexander, Christine. ed. *An Edition of the Early Writings of Charlotte Brontë*. Oxford: Basil Blackwell, 1987–91.

Alexander, Christine. "Defining and Representing Literary Juvenilia." In *The Child Writer From Austen To Woolf*, edited by Christine Alexander and Juliet McMaster, 70–97. Cambridge: Cambridge University Press, 2005.

Brontë, Charlotte. *An Edition of the Early Writings of Charlotte Brontë Volume I 1826–1832*, edited by Christine Alexander. Oxford: Basil Blackwell, 1987.

Brontë, Charlotte. "Roe Head Journal: August 11, 1836." *bl.uk* https://www.bl.uk/collection-items/charlotte-brontes-journal, n.d.
Brontë, Emily. *Wuthering Heights*. London: Thomas Cautley Newby, 1847.
Coakley, Lena. *Worlds of Ink and Shadow*. Toronto: HarperCollins Publishers Ltd, 2016.
Fawkes, Glynnis. *Charlotte Brontë Before Jane Eyre*. New York: Disney Hyperion, 2019.
Garrido, Felipe Espinoza, Marlena Tronicke, and Julian Wacker. "Introduction: Blackness and Victorian Studies." In *Black Neo-Victoriana*, edited by Garrido, Tronicke, and Julian Wacker, 1–32. Amsterdam: Brill/Ropodi, 2022.
Golden, Catherine. *Serials to Graphic Novels: The Evolution of the Victorian Illustrated Book*. Gainesville: University Press of Florida, 2017.
Greenberg, Isabel. *Glass Town: The Imaginary World of the Brontës*. New York: Abrams Comicarts, 2020.
Hamilton-McKenna, Caroline. "'Beyond the Boundaries': Negotiations of Space, Place, Body and Subjectivity in YA Fiction." *Children's Literature in Education*. 52 (2021): 307–25.
Kohlke, Mel. "Neo-Victorian Biofiction and the Special/Spectral Case of Barbara Chase-Riboud's *Hottentot Venus*." *Australasian Journal of Victorian Studies*. 18 no. 3 (2013): 4–21.
McMaster, Juliet. "What Daisy Knew: The Epistemology of the Child Writer." In *The Child Writer from Austen to Woolf*, edited by Christine Alexander and Juliet McMaster, 51–69. Cambridge: Cambridge University Press, 2005.
Meyer, Susan. "Black Rage and White Women: Ideological Self-Formation in Charlotte Brontë's African Tales." *South Central Review*, 8, no. 4 (1991): 28–40.
Reimer, Mavis. "'No place like home': the facts and figures of homelessness in contemporary texts for young people." *Nordic Journal of ChildLit Aesthetics* 4 (2013): 1–10.
Tarbox, Gwen Athene, and Michelle Ann Abate. "The Varied Landscape of Contemporary Children's and YA Comics." In *Graphic Novels for Children and Young Adults*. Edited by Michelle Ann Bate and Gwen Athene Tarbox, 3–16. Jackson: University Press of Mississippi, 2017.
To Walk Invisible. BBC Cymru Wales, Lookout Point, The Open University. December 2016.
Valente, Catherynne M. *The Glass Town Game*. London: Margaret K. McElderry Books, 2017.

CHAPTER 5

The Odd(est) Brontë: Portrait(s) of Emily as a Young Author

Surprised by a room full of eager scholars and students ready to hear about biofiction, scholar Michael Lackey "started to realize, 'Oh my gosh, there's a hunger and an interest in this literary form'…. From that point forward, everything took off" (quoted in "Biofiction" 2020, n.p.). His own enthusiasm is relevant to the biofictions that have surfaced in young adult texts which take as their subjects Victorian authors; he says, "When I try to show them what a biographical fiction actually does, how the author actually changes facts, how the author is trying to give them not a biographical truth, but a higher truth about life—then they get really excited" (n.p.).

Novels, for any age of reader, written about real people in particular historical situations, combines biography and fiction—hence, biofiction. Author and scholar David Lodge claims that biofiction offers "interiority. If a novel is about a real person, it can use the clues that are available, the information that is available, to try and recreate what that person's consciousness was perceiving in any given situation" using the techniques of fiction (Lodge quoted in "Biofiction" 2020, n.p.). Of interest to young adult readers might be a person like Mary Godwin Shelley who was a teenaged mother and author whose *Frankenstein* (1818) contains the Creature that haunts the modern mind, or maybe the Brontës who were authors from childhood to adulthood and hid in their juvenilia's Glass Town when their lives became traumatic. Iconic fictional characters like Sir Arthur Conan Doyle's Sherlock Holmes are given full backstories, while Nancy Springer's next-generational character, Enola Holmes, is created to

© The Author(s), under exclusive license to Springer Nature Switzerland AG 2024
S. E. Maier, *Neo-Victorian Young Adult Narratives*, https://doi.org/10.1007/978-3-031-47295-4_5

demonstrate the ability of young people to solve difficult problems in hard circumstances.

A biofiction about a particular person allows for larger questions to be considered, in young adult as in adult texts. As a transitional phase in personal development, adolescent readers—particularly writerly creatives—can seek out stories of those authors who came before to watch their trajectories into adulthood. One such example is the rising interest in young adult portraits of the enigmatic Brontë siblings in works like Michaela MacColl's *Always Emily* (2014) and Jane Eagland's *The World Within: A Novel of Emily Brontë* (2015). Adolescent readers, like adults, are interested in who writers are as well as how and why they write; the same is true of the desire to know about real-life "characters" who enliven literary history and who invoke larger social issues through their own struggles.

More and more is being written about neo-Victorian fiction, but there is a parallel growing interest in writing and thinking about biofiction; recently, the two genres have increasingly come together in young adult fiction: as a blend of nonfiction—the facts of a person's life—and a fictional representation of the gaps between those facts. Such narratives are of great interest to some readers, both adult and adolescent. Ed Sullivan strongly argues that nonfiction, like memoirs, "is not just about information. The truth is that for many young adult readers nonfiction serves the same purposes as fiction does for other readers: it entertains, provides escape, sparks the imagination, and indulges curiosity. There's a lot more to a good nonfiction book than mere information" (2001, 44). In addition, in a report created for the National PTA in the United States, it outlines how reading "biographies help nurture children's empathy.... Honoring a real person's lived experience" can raise a young person's "awareness about races, cultures, religions or philosophies" (PTA 2021, 1). Another possibility is that learning about a particular persons' life acts as a catalyst for interest in a past moment in time or history, a way to re-enter or engage with history—and literary history—with a modern perspective central to the neo-Victorian project of self-conscious revisitation with an eye to inquiry.

A captivating image of a young woman who exists otherwise to society is one cast across the century in several biofiction: the idea of Emily Brontë—the odd one, wandering the moors, antisocial, bound to her home, a writer of tortured souls in the magnificent *Wuthering Heights* (1847) who dies far too young. The Brontës are one of the most written about and mythologised families of literature, but seemingly of particular interest lately in young adult narratives.[1] The fascination with the family has resulted in biographical myths, hagiographic portraits, and legendary status of the family members right from the time they were first published.[2]

Emily Brontë presents both a particular interest and an impossible task to a biographer; aside from three surviving letters, and fragments of diary notes written with her sister Anne on November 24, 1834, and June 26, 1837, as well as her birthday papers written on July 30, 1841, and July 30, 1845. This self-documentation, her poetry, and her novel are all the modern scholar has left from which to extrapolate a persona for an enigmatic young woman; it is a further expression of curiosity to sketch the earlier portrait of an adolescent girl's *künstlerroman*. Early biographer Charles Simpson recognises her compelling persona early on because readers "who have thought deeply about Emily Brontë may indulge in one speculation: what they would feel if they could for a moment see Emily in the flesh and compare her with the figure of their imaginations…. Seldom has a phantom so vast and so shadowy been raised above a personality so elusive" (1929, 1).

WHO ARE THEY … WHO AM I?

The enthusiasm of the authors who write neo-Victorian works matches the excitement of the reader, youthful or mature. Emma Donoghue, the author of several neo-Victorian fictions, when asked why she writes about historical persons makes several enlightening points; first, she admits "why I get so possessed by one particular dead nobody, I don't know. It's just like falling in love," but second, she elucidates:

> The reason I use a specific, real, named protagonist is because my original impulse was very much to represent the ones who'd been left out, like the nobodies, women, slaves, people in freak shows, servants, the ones who are not powerful. I felt an obligation if I was going to write about them at all, I wanted to give them their little moment in the sun. To name them, even if they were incredibly obscure figures. (Donoghue in Lackey 2018b, 81–2)

Donoghue freely admits that these intentions are shaped by the time and place of writing, as is what an author chooses to say about the person and how the author chooses to judge them, but the hope is to "make two periods resonate through this person. It's almost like the character I'm focusing on is a time traveler. There is a connection between the past and the present" but such fluidity does not create "a comforting or cozy genre. At its best … the biographical novel makes people uncomfortable" and asks important questions but relies on what she believes is an ethical commitment to people long dead (85–6). These questions are about time and place, age and gender, social conventions and confinement, family and orphanhood, childhood and maturity, uncomfortable but important questions that young readers will find relevant to their own lives.

Biofiction, at its most basic, is literature that takes as its protagonist an actual historical figure and does so to illuminate a particular perspective on a period in history. Michael Lackey puts it best: "Because authors of the genre name their protagonist after an actual historical figure, many readers wrongly assume that the work is either a form of history or biography…. But if readers understand that biofiction is fiction, and not biography or history, they will approach the text in a different way" where "the paper person and the real person" are not exactly one in the same (Lackey 2021, 1) but an illustration of plausibility for the life of the historical subject. Authors have "fictionalized both to give readers a way to think about and understand themselves and their world" (2), a way of historicising that matches the neo-Victorian desire Ann Heilmann and Mark Llewellyn see as to be "*more than* [a] historical fiction set in the nineteenth century" and necessarily "*self-consciously engaged with the act of (re)interpretation, (re) discovery and (re)vision concerning the Victorians*" (2010, 4; emphasis in original).

With those definitions comes a debate about the appropriation of the life of a real person for fictional ends. Biofiction "may lead authors to alter some biographical or historical facts, but this does not make the work 'untrue to history.' It just means that authors strategically package history in a particular way in order to maximize the effect on the reader" (Lackey 2018a, 6).[3] Biofiction enthusiasts embrace its possibilities when they find a gap in a person's biographical record that needs filling. Jane Yolen, too, sees such openings as places to tell a story but she reflects on a project much like neo-Victorian narratives with the claim that "many novelists are not just interested in a truth of one time. They are trying to get to a truth that can also apply to the other times and places" (quoted in Lackey 2018a, 16) via readers who are "curious, critical, and active readers of biography and history" (8). Indeed, "fictionalizing history and real people can pay great dividends" according to William Boyd; he continues, "Unlike the biographer or historian, the novelist is not constrained by documented facts or their frustrating absence, and is free to roam—always keeping authenticity and plausibility in mind—through character and motive, supposition and possibility" (2009, BR10).

What if, instead, biofiction is clearly "a more essentialized and embodied element of identity, a subject less than transcendent but more than merely discourse" (Kaplan 2007, 65), a kind of historical looking-glass that allows us to inform and investigate the past for young adult reader in a double move—or dialogue—between history and fiction, between person and character as well as the adult writing to and/or about the young adult of the nineteenth century and across to the twentieth and twenty-first centuries. Cora Kaplan, early on in neo-Victorian discussions, asserted in *Victoriana* that our—readers and scholars alike—obsession with creating new biographies of nineteenth-century authors might be due to "Biographilia ... our undiminished [twentieth-century] *fin-de-siècle* appetite for life histories" and for "biofictional treatments" as an "occasion for elegy in its capacity both to retrieve and to bury the past" (2007, 8). For an individual like Emily Brontë of whom there is a paucity of historical record, naysayers like Tom Winnifrith disagree, claiming that such biofictional rewritings cause a "fatal blurring of fiction and fact which has bedevilled Brontë studies" (1973, 1); at the same time, neo-Victorianist Mark Llewellyn sees the magnetic draw of authorial personalities and believes that if the author remembers that ethics are involved "in the decisions made about how the Victorians are represented in contemporary fiction" (2009, 30) they are important investigations of the past that can help us reconsider the present and the future, just as young people do to form their identities.

The Odd Brontë

The desire to speak for and about the Brontës in general, and Emily's personal development in specific, is her lack of knowability from historical documentation even if there are few basic facts. Emily Jane Brontë came into the world the fifth and penultimate child of Maria Branwell of Penzance, Cornwall (April 15, 1783–September 15, 1821) and the Reverend Patrick Brontë of County Down, Ireland (née Brunty, March 17, 1777). Baptised at the Old Bell Chapel by William Morgan on Thursday, August 20, 1818, Emily is the fourth daughter of the Brontës but when the family moves to Haworth Parsonage, the Brontë family structure drastically changes with the death of their mother from a painful battle with cancer.[4] The stories that surround the Brontës' childhood often forget that they were children, casting them as small adults full of gloom. Instead, the children had a routine of gathering in the morning for a family prayer then lessons before they burst out onto the moors for fresh air and exercise. Sarah Gars (?1806–99), one of the children's nursemaids, recounted that the Brontë's "afternoon walks, as they sallied forth, each neatly and comfortably clad, were a joy. Their fun knew no bounds. It never was expressed wildly.[5] Bright and often dry, but deep, it occasioned many a merry burst of laughter. They enjoyed a game of romps, and played with zest" (quoted in Barker 2012, 127). A significant part of Emily's day was spent with Tabby, the cook and housekeeper, in the kitchen, baking and hearing stories of the fairy folk and beasts of the moors.

In a progressive move, their father believed his daughters should have a solid education which he did not feel he could adequately provide so Patrick Brontë sends his first two daughters to the new Clergy Daughters' School at Cowan Bridge. Maria and Elizabeth attend the school. Charlotte and Emily join them with Emily described as "a darling child," a "little petted Em" who is "quite the pet nursling of the school"; the young one "Reads very prettily & Works a little" but "Knows nothing of Grammar, Geography or History and nothing of Accomplishments" (Barker, 155).[6] The two eldest sisters contracted tuberculosis and died within weeks of each other and their father brings the two younger girls home.

Content when she was at home, becoming homesick to the point of illness when she was made to leave, Emily spent her days working in the kitchen, baking, reading, and honing her writing as well as piano skills.[7] There is not much else known directly about her; unlike Charlotte who was an avid letter writer, there are few documents or factual accounts of Emily as she grows into a young woman of many talents, particularly as a writer. In a more specific definition of such neo-Victorian works, Marie-Louise Kohlke asserts that they are "the mainly literary, dramatic, or filmic reimaginings of the lives of actual individuals who lived during the long nineteenth century, in which said individuals provide the sole or joint major textual foci and narrated/narrating subjects, rather than serving as mere supporting characters or appearing only in brief vignettes to add period colour and interest" (2013, 4). These texts create a confluence of the past that is narrated and the present as written "while simultaneously testing the epistemological limits encountered in the (re-)construction of past lives and selves" (4). Emily, by her minimal—even spectral—presence in historical documentation invites the speculation of writerly reconstruction as well as the imagination of the young reader.

Emily is like one of "the oddballs, the marginalized people" whom Donoghue admits she can afford to make peculiar because, in some cases, "'they don't ever have to be purely representative of their type. They can afford to be odd individuals'" (quoted in Lackey 2018b, 87). Many critics and authors assume that "something must have *happened* to Emily to account for her creativity," but it may just be the case that the "real Emily remained reconstructable only by speculation" (Miller 2001, 225; emphasis in original) rather than in facts.[8] Mary F. Robinson, a very early biographer, even cast Emily as a possible mystic because hers was "an imagination of the finest and rarest touch, absolutely certain of tread on that path of a single hair which alone connects this world with the land of dreams" (1883, 4). The impulse to provide Emily with a story of her own has resulted in several biofictions and films—like the recent film *Emily* (2022)—that seek for Emily a man, a masculine presence to explain the obsessions and passions of her novel and the ensuing tragedies of its endings.[9]

Becoming Emily

Michaela MacColl's *Always Emily* is a young adult narrative of Emily's adolescent years; however, like most biographical or biofictional works on the Brontës, there is an intermingling of the close-knit siblings, particularly in their early formative years. Split into scribbling pairs as children, Charlotte with Branwell and Emily with Anne, the children writing and the children as their writing become confused, particularly with their juvenilia,[10] as modern writers attempt to elucidate the development of the isolated family of geniuses.

In MacColl's neo-Victorian narrative, Emily's early character—and Emily as a character—is in the transitional state of childhood to adolescence. Emily does not conform to social parameters. Emily is cast as an otherworldy child when at her sister's funeral, she seems to be a socially unorthodox girl of seven who sees an apparition of her sister; in addition, Emily asks the uncomfortable but honest question as to whether her sister's soul has been released after the remaining siblings open the coffin to peer in (MacColl 2014, 5). The connection between Emily and the world beyond, so often noted in neo-Victorian biofictions about her, is again raised later when Emily suddenly sits upright on the bed, and Charlotte notices as "Emily stared unseeingly toward the wide windows. 'Maria! Elizabeth! You've finally come!'" (33). The placement of religious questioning in the youthful words spoken by Emily places her belief system in contrast to both father's Protestant teachings and counter to cultural faith.

Emily's ongoing resistance to the gendered norms of the Victorian age is clearly presented as righteous questioning in MacColl's neo-Victorian text. When Emily is sent to Roe Head school, she openly flaunts the rules to push her own boundaries of development; she is unremorseful when caught climbing a tree; she has no interest in work as a governess or a teacher, nor does she have any interest in marriage, honestly asking, "What if I am not willing to surrender my dreams?" (11), a question silently shared by many young women. Emily is an artistically minded teenager who is aware that in adulthood, Victorian norms predestine the lack of agency of women in marriage and motherhood.

Self-contained, Emily is unwilling to share in the schoolgirl closeness encouraged by the teachers; even with her family, Emily is adamant that her writing is her own. Although Charlotte sees "Emily's defiant stance" (20), and knows "keeping Emily from speaking her mind was like asking the wind not to blow across Haworth Moor" (22). At the age of seventeen, Emily has the "courage of her convictions" and "so little concern for consequences" (25) that a modern reader can see how she contrasts strikingly with Charlotte who is cast as impatient, jealous, bitter and "absurdly righteous" (191). Both sisters, and the much younger Anne, are set apart from Branwell, a fledgling alcoholic who is unfocused, sexist, and "all promise and no accomplishments" (156) even though he is the favourite of his father. MacColl emphasises throughout the novel that, in spite of his patriarchally entitled male privilege, it is the adolescent girls who deserve encouragement and resources, not Branwell.

In 1833, Ellen Nussey—Charlotte's best friend—visited the Haworth Parsonage, and describes the real-life Emily. At fifteen, Emily was tall and had a

> lithesome graceful figure … hair which was naturally as beautiful as Charlotte's was in the same unbecoming tight curl and frizz, and there was the same want of complexion. She had very beautiful eyes, kindly, kindling, liquid eyes, sometimes they looked grey, sometimes dark blue but she did not often look at you, she was too reserved. She talked very little. (Smith 1995–2000, I: 598)

Unconcerned with fashion, or that her petticoats "lacking fullness, made her skirts cling to her legs, accentuating her height and thinness" refused to change her old-fashioned style of dress (Barker 462). Emily was not misanthropic but honest in that she had "no wish to please and no interest in doing so" but "She was quite capable of eloquence when the mood took her" (461) but was perfectly content at home as housekeeper and the silent simplicity of writing while fairly unconcerned with others. Biographer Juliet Barker posits how "it is curious that Emily should ever have gained the reputation for being the most sympathetic of the Brontës, particularly in her dealings with Branwell, as all the evidence points to the fact that she was so absorbed in herself and her literary creations that she had little time for the genuine suffering of her family. Her attitude at this time seems to have been brusque to the point of heartlessness" (537). Certainly, in portraits painted of her in young adult fiction, Emily is rough around the edges and introverted—not a typical heroine in a Victorian novel—and the neo-Victorian narratives approach her with fascination but with empathy for her artistic temperament and compassion for her oddities.

In *Always Emily*, "Lovely, reckless Emily" is defiant and strong willed (MacColl 26), perhaps a portrait in kind with the self-seeking reader of the neo-Victorian novel. As a pupil, Emily is so different, so unusual that when Miss Wooler asks Charlotte whether they can "rule out a malady of the mind?" (29), a recognition that Emily is contrary to Victorian expectations of young womanhood. In another scene, Emily has an "emaciated body" and has visions outside her window (33)—the description raises the modern concern with eating disorders in young women as well as Victorian constructions of non-conventional women as suffering from hysteria and/or madness,[11] all suppositions and creations of fiction. Katherine Frank, in her biography, *A Chainless Soul* (1990), does argue that Emily may have been anorexic because of "her refusal to eat and her extreme slenderness and preoccupation with food and cooking, but also her obsessive need for control, her retreat into an ongoing, interior fantasy world, and her social isolation" (3–4) made her slim, not the potential receptivity of a mystic; or, of course, Emily might have been naturally slender. Biofiction allows space for multiple considerations of possibilities, but at the very least, MacColl's neo-Victorian perspective allows the reader to both see the conventions in play but to empathise with—even celebrate—Emily's open resistance to classification or dismissal.

Appearance as an indicator of personality, then as now, is explored with Charlotte acting as aware of just how shocking Emily's indifference is to society. While Charlotte is appalled and constantly worried about the family's and each individual's appearance, Emily is not. She is unbothered by her own unpetticoated skirts and has "eyes [that] glittered with anticipation" when her father decides to teach her to shoot his pistol (MacColl 70). Emily unrelentingly walks the moors unaccompanied except by a huge mastiff, Keeper. Tabby's stories of a ghost dog, a *gytrash* who transfigures from man to beast (68),[12] excite Emily's expanding, highly unconventional imagination. Described as grounded and happy when at home in the Parsonage, she is self-assured that "her instincts were sound" (95) even if not in line with Victorian conventions. The neo-Victorian representation of the wild Brontë girl as confident and driven, not mad or mystical, is an evaluation of Emily's character in relation to Victorian standards of proper womanhood.[13]

Emily, in MacColl's text, is unrepentant in her self-definition as she matures, a lesson of growth to which Lackey's "higher truth" refers. Even Charlotte is aware that it is "Emily. Always Emily" (MacColl 25) who fascinates because she bucks against these gendered restraints. Emily is always ready to offer her opinions and has an astonishing intellect for creation. Charlotte, in contrast, is tiny and studious, ambitious for acceptance in society. Emily's character is, by nineteenth-century standards, too abrasive for an adolescent or mature woman, a kind of a virago. That said, by twenty-first-century standards, Emily is incredibly progressive in that she is aware she requires "space to think" (MacColl 22) and "physical exercise, not only for her body but also for her mind" (44). For example when Charlotte and Anne go to London to confront rumours of all three books having been written by one man, they assert themselves to George Smith as Currer and Acton Bell but, noticeably, Ellis/Emily is in no need of, nor does she desire, worldly confirmation of her abilities, even as a young woman. She prefers pseudonymity. Emily refuses to be outed and is only so after her death in the *Biographical Notice* (1851) that Charlotte reveals her sister to be Ellis Bell.

Capturing Difference?

Neo-Victorian biofictions, for the most part, seek to "recapture the past in ways that evoke its spirit and do honor to the dead and silenced" (Shiller 1997, 546), some of which can be found in one of the most interesting trends in neo-Victorian young adult narratives which are *kunstlerroman*, the stories of young writers or artists growing into their craft. Faced with the unknowability of someone like Emily, there is a degree of haunting in neo-Victorian narratives. *Always Emily* demonstrates Emily's liminal status as in, but not of, her time; as a young woman, she is variously considered eccentric, antisocial, misanthropic, or, most recently, a neuro-atypical young woman with Asperger's Syndrome, but what most scholars would call "exceptional" in every regard. Indeed, Claire Harman, Charlotte Brontë's most recent biographer, claims that Emily may have been autistic because, she says, "I think Charlotte and everybody was quite frightened of Emily, I think she was an Asperger's-ey person.… She was such a genius and had total imaginative freedom.… Containing Emily, protecting Emily, not being alarmed by Emily, was a big project for the whole household. She's an absolutely fascinating person—a very troubling presence, though" (qtd in Cain 2016, n.p.).

To a modern audience, the portrait of a potentially neuro-atypical person might raise interest in the neo-Victorian portrait of Emily although impossible to prove. To one Victorian historical person, Monsieur Heger of the Pensionnat Heger in Belgium, Emily's mind is troubling but whether it is because she is unusual in affect or just brilliant is unclear.[14] Elizabeth Gaskell recounts in her biography, *The Life of Charlotte Brontë* (1857), that Emily had formidable intellectual gifts; indeed, Heger admitted "Emily's genius as 'something even higher' than Charlotte's. She had … a head for logic, and a capability of argument, unusual in a man, and rare indeed in a woman" compiled with her "stubborn tenacity of will" (Gaskell, 205). He continued, "She should have been a man—a great navigator. Her powerful reason would have deduced new spheres of discovery from the knowledge of the old; and her strong imperious will would never have been daunted by opposition or difficulty; never have given way but with life" (Gaskell 205).

Impossible to prove with only anecdotes of Emily's non-normative behaviours, fiction allows for the author to fill in the elliptical moments relevant to the formidable nature of her intellectual genius who left behind a shocking novel seemingly far beyond her years and her realm of knowledge. In MacColl's neo-Victorian text, the thunderous passions of *Wuthering Heights* are key to her imaginative reconstruction of Emily's adolescence around it.

Rosario Arias and Patricia Pulham rightly argue that such a narrative "often represents a 'double' of the Victorian text mimicking its language, style and plot; it plays with the conscious repetition of tropes, characters, and historical events" while reanimating Victorian genres like the realist, sensation, or ghost story (2009, xv). MacColl does not endeavour to match the majesty of Emily Brontë's own novel, but she creatively considers the circumstances in which it was written.

In Victorian and neo-Victorian literature, attraction between individuals and the potential pairings of like-minded parties are often part of the plot. The expectation of a Victorian young woman is that any such feelings would be limited to and only admitted after marriage with the main influences on choice of husband would be an appropriate title, relevant class, and sterling reputation in a potential partner; however, in the neo-Victorian reconstruction of Emily's sense of self, the neo-Victorian perspective allows for personal exploration that might act as a mirror to the young adult reader's own uncertainties about gender roles and sexuality.

In MacColl's novel, Emily encounters Hareton Smith on the moors. He is the cast-out grandson of the recently diseased patriarch of Ponden Hall (a real-life location on the moors, but an imagined person). Emily is fascinated by him; he is around nineteen, dark-haired with cornflower blue eyes and "features roughened by wind and sun"; after investigating his deserted camp, she learns he reads Sir Walter Scott and George Gordon, Lord Byron; when he first sees Emily, Hareton is shocked into a youthful outburst, "'You're not a Gypsy…. You sound like a lady'" (MacColl 111). There is an assumption that there must have been some sort of heterosexual interaction in Emily's life in order for her to create such complex relationships in *Wuthering Heights*. MacColl posits their first interaction as a kind of intellectual kinship, with Hareton seeing Emily's passion for the moors on her face, telling her she is "luminous" (186); her reaction is not what is expected rather than simply fall to his Byronic charisma, "she mouthed the word, enjoying the way it pursed her lips" as she recognises that Hareton's appeal is in his choice of language, and that he smells of the "wood smoke and library dust" (186), two eccentric, traditionally masculine scents which she finds intoxicating.

Victorian conventionality descends immediately; Charlotte exclaims, "I arrived before you completely ruined your reputation" because "poor gentlewomen like us—with intelligence but no dowries—we cannot afford to tarnish our reputations" to which Emily fires back, with an empowered neo-Victorian voice, that she will not be one of the married women of Haworth who walk "hangdog at their husbands' heels, with bruised eyes and no freedom" (MacColl 188). The neo-Victorian critique of heteronormative marriage as a necessity for a young woman's future is clear: marriage does not equal happiness. Unlike the conventional marriage plot novel, the neo-Victorian biofiction does not contain a single representation of marriage that is not fraught with difficulty; in that regard, it is a parallel to Emily Brontë's own *Wuthering Heights*.

Emily's portrait—as a young author—makes clear that, like any other young adults, genius is still anchored in grit and determination. MacColl says in her Author's Note to the "Dear Reader"—breaking out the reader/author fourth wall in like fashion to Charlotte Brontë's "Reader, I married him" in *Jane Eyre* (1847, ch 38)—that "Every member of the family was a fascinating character" (266). MacColl even admits that as a writer, she believes "Emily was mesmerizing but also impossible to live with, while Charlotte tried so hard to be true to her artistic self while being the only practical person in a house full of brilliant lunatics" (266).[15]

MacColl's neo-Victorian narrative must find its way back to leave Emily as a loner, a nineteenth-century woman beyond her time, and an enigma to those who read *Wuthering Heights*. While the idea of romance might be tempting for the young adult reader, but if it is too far afield for the more knowing reader, MacColl leaves another clue to the possibility a young woman in the Victorian age might choose an asexual, artistic life over conventional endings. Playing Pirate King with Branwell in their youth, "Emily surprised Branwell by nimbly climbing down the tree to freedom" when he thought she was trapped; the narrator points out that "she had eluded captivity before; why not now?" (45). As "the parsonage walls had dissolved" around Emily, the moors offer her air that caresses her skin and a north wind that "felt like a familiar friend's embrace" (45) during the night; she is, explicitly, satisfied with her solitary life as her writing "poured from her fingers, filling page after page" (257). To be unpaired, alone with one's craft, is also a productive and valid choice for a young woman.

"If I Was a Man…"[16]

Another Emily Brontë biofiction teases the adolescent reader with the story of a character with whom they might empathise. The description on inner flyleaf of the Scholastic book cover for Jane Eagland's *The World Within: A Novel of Emily Brontë* (2015) promises "the story of a young writer struggling to find herself, and offers a window into the mind of the treasured by mysterious author of *Wuthering Heights*." This promise ignores Emily's Victorian context as well as erroneously assumes that her mind is transparent across the miles and decades but only needs to be elucidated by a modern teller of tales; the desired affinity is clear—a modern woman author explaining a young Victorian girl as author to young readers. Eagland has admitted she took liberties "to inform [the reader] about the inner world of that enigmatic person, Emily Brontë" and that she has not set out to "write an accurate history, but to explore my version, my vision" of Emily for which she apologises "to any reader who is disappointed because my Emily is not theirs" (2015, 330).

The concept that each reader might infer or construct an "Emily" is, as Lackey has pointed out, unethical in that this is a real, historical woman; in particular, it is hard for a young adult reader to have a sense of historical record without research—in other words, young people cannot know what they do not yet know. They might, rather, infer they are getting the whole story. Marie-Luise Kohlke and Christian Gutleben warn of the trap of moving too far away from the historical record because as readers and scholars, "we define the biofictional subject as a hybrid object of research, a field of investigation in which imagination must per force complement the lacunae of historical epistemology" (2020, 1). Eagland's admission of being inexact with the facts becomes more significant as a knowledgeable reader unpacking the novel sees it contains several points of ambiguity, particularly in the expectations placed on not only Emily but each of the Brontë children.

The World Within considers the early life of the remaining family members immediately after the death of their mother and sisters, a time referred to as "The Terrible Events," through to the first poem Emily writes as a youthful author. With clear references to both the many animals of the parsonage (multiple dogs, a falcon, two geese, and others) and to the opening of *Jane Eyre* finds Emily contemplating chaffinches, kestrels, and larks on the moors; the reader encounters Emily in her imaginary world of Gondal, created when she was a child, and demarcated in italics. Her Aunt Branwell demands her attention but in Emily's "imagination she [Emily] was her hero, Parry, the great explorer" who is disturbed at a critical moment in the journey in the wildness of the Arctic; Emily's reasoned, mental retort as given to us by the narrator who tells us that Parry is "unencumbered" by relatives and that "*He* never had to sew nightshirts, for sure" (Eagland 1; emphasis in original)—surely this voice is Emily's disgust. Her righteous indignation is not supported by society. Her Aunt Elizabeth Branwell, an unmarried woman from Penzance, is concerned about her poor and grubby sewing as well as how Emily has not brushed her hair. She is horrified by how Charlotte has become "dowly" after "an alarming experience—Aunt called it 'the start of womanhood'" (7)—and from "what [Emily's] seen her sister coping with, womanhood is a horrible, messy business. The very thought of it repels her" (66). Adolescence is recognisably difficult and unnerving in both Victorian and neo-Victorian worlds.

Questions of why Emily resisted conventional womanhood arise. If Victorian culture imprinted the idea that it is "natural for a girl to want to make the best of herself. It's…it's womanly" and, without missing a beat, Emily's intellectual retaliation tells her "women shouldn't adorn themselves with 'broided hair' but with good works" (Eagland 3), there is a strong break between assumptions of what is innately a young "woman" and a woman's actual character as she grows into maturity. Too wise to risk the argument, Emily realises that if "Aunt had any idea what went on in their minds, she'd be shocked. *An orderly mind.* How dull that would be" (4; emphasis in original). Emily's father knows her; he gifts her a wooden lion rather than a doll, and he does not mind that "she's a tomboy, outspoken at times and preferring to think things through for herself" even when climbing trees, fighting Branwell or challenging his own ideas (24). To gift a lion speaks of prowess, strength, and leadership, qualities usually associated with a boy-child. The Reverend Brontë's unexpectedly modern, progressive outlook—in Victorian reality and in Eagland's revisionary narrative—on his daughter's difference matches most young, modern readers' desire for assurance that their individuality will be supported.

The four sibling writers created their own worlds even while harsh and traumatic reality surrounds them. Reverend Brontë becomes ill; at that moment, Charlotte is the one to grasp the reality of their danger. If he dies, then they will unmoored, literally, in their eviction from the Parsonage. Charlotte, closer to responsible womanhood and the now-eldest child, tries to make Emily understand that she is not sure Aunt Branwell would "want us. Or could afford to keep us" (25). In fear, Emily retreats to the fantastic Glass Town narratives where it was "Safe? Was that it? Yes. As if between them all they spun a web, a safety net that held her, and for a while at least she could be part of those worlds, could escape from the desperate feelings that had engulfed her" (19) like a "box lid beginning to tremble as the monsters try to climb out" (25).[17]

Fraught with devastation, the memories of the Brontë children are problematised by the neo-Victorian perspective of the twenty-first novelist. The memories are not comfortable even if they have created their individualities. Any memory that "occasionally has recollections of a sensation—of being safe, of arms tight around" her is quickly darkened when "in this memory, there's no such comfort" because Emily feels memory "squeezing her heart" but "she makes herself remember. She's trembling, but she keeps hold of the feeling as long as she can, until she can't bear it a second longer" (Eagland 27). Adolescent fear of loss and change are poignant. For Emily to lose the memory would be to lose her mother, but to frame the time as nostalgia is challenged by her acknowledgement of the pain and sorrow of the time past;

> There is something she must do, something she must face, because if she doesn't, her fear will grow and grow and swallow her up.
> To give herself courage she thinks of the heroic Parry, bold, courageous, confronting the great unknown of the northern regions. Then in the darkness of the bedroom she says the word silently to herself, feeling the shape of it in her mouth.
> Death. (26)

Neo-Victorian narratives "display a metafictional and metahistorical concern with the process of narrating/re-imagining/re-visioning histories, and had to be self-conscious about its own position as literary … reconstruction" (Heilmann and Llewellyn 2013, 24); in Eagland's novel, the neo-Victorian depiction of the children's trauma as seminal in their development demonstrates their fear of illness was legitimate if only expressed in the fantasy world. When their Papa improves, Anne as the youngest rejoices, Charlotte "anxiously" follows him about the room with her eyes, but Emily feels "things aren't the same as they were before. Papa has changed" (31); she has changed. The potential death of the father, the patriarch, demonstrates just how vulnerable adolescents, particularly the young women, are in the mid-nineteenth century and parallels how twenty-first-century juvenile readers eventually come to learn of their own precarious position in society.

The challenge to Victorian culture that thought middle- and upper-class boys should be highly educated but girls only trained in accomplishments or pragmatic learning is one aread that often arises in neo-Victorian narratives for young people. Eagland points to how education was the one way the Brontë adolescent girls might secure their futures. Both their father and Aunt Branwell understand that an educational background will be necessary for Charlotte, Emily, and Anne; in reality and in fiction, until their brother secures his own future and is willing to support his sisters, or in the event he is not able to do so with his own earnings, they must be prepared to be teachers or governesses if not wives. Reverend Brontë acknowledges their debt to Aunt Branwell in Eagland's narrative, to which she replies, "Nonsense … I have little else to spend my money on. It would please me to assist in any scheme that might secure the girls' future" (33). Fiction engages fact here; their mother's unmarried sister did have a secure future and she played an active role in the education of all the Brontë children.

Much time, money, and effort are spent on the male heir, Branwell; as the boy of the siblings, he was in life encouraged to follow his talents such as when drafts a letter to the Royal Academy in London as a possible student. There is a debated story that he went in 1835 but intimidated by the world at large and his own ineptitude, he ends his time drinking away all his money before returning home with stories of a robber.[18] Eagland, with a modern eye on the past inequities of gender, uses this moment to show the inherent and ineffectual patriarchal bias towards the assumed abilities of a male heir often ventriloquised by Emily.

When Branwell goes through costly adolescent searches for his career including portrait painter, poet, and perhaps "a famous pianist," Emily sceptically replies, "I thought you were going to be a famous artist. Or a famous poet" (Eagland 59). As male heir, much stock is placed on his potentialities; in reality, he is a failure. Beyond this point in the Brontës' life narrative, Branwell began to drink and hold forth at the Black Bull on too many occasions; in addition, he becomes an opium addict. The combination of his addictions and his decrease in health that accompanies it leads, tragically, to his downfall, *delirium tremens*, tuberculosis, and death.

The World Within leans heavily on the stories of Charlotte and Emily and emphasises how Branwell's early arrogance leaves the girls' feelings ranging between jealousy, pity, and fear for his/their future. MacColl's novel imagines how frustrating it must have been; unable to voice her anger at her brother, a rage sublimated into the fantasy Glass Town. Charlotte creates a new character, Patrick Benjamin Wiggins. Sharing the first two initials with her brother, he is described as a "*low*, slightly built man…a bush of *carroty* hair" who as a "musician was greater than Bach, as a poet he surpassed Byron, as a painter, Claude Lorraine yielded to him," a bit of caricature that causes Anne to laugh out loud and Emily to smirk. The fictional Branwell claims "I'll achieve more than any of you silly girls" (Eagland 180; emphasis in original) but the real young man flails, gets involved with the Masons, demands publication by *Blackwell's Magazine*, and has a disastrous affair with his employer's wife, his life-path becomes a reactionary defiance of his father's temperance and against his sisters' obvious brilliance. Branwell exemplifies for the reader a young man, Victorian or otherwise, unable to find his own way under the ponderous weight of expectations placed upon him and due to his own inability to set to work. Eagland's Emily compares her brother with the Romantic poet, George Gordon, Lord Byron whose characters, like Manfred and Cain, are "dark defiant men with their inner loneliness and sorrow, [who] have committed dreadful deeds and feel no remorse" (118); sadly, her exemplars of Romantic genius and passionate masculinity are all doomed to destruction.

Emily's desire to have male freedom is equally a thought shared, perhaps, by the Victorian character and the modern reader who still combats gendered assumptions and tradition. Emily laments "if only she could be like them [men]… to do as you pleased and express your deepest feelings freely and fearlessly, and not have to be hemmed in by petty restrictions" (118). When Charlotte thinks of being an artist, Emily point-blank queries, "'Are there many women artists?' She means *any*" (125; emphasis in original). The sisters are fully aware of the sensitive issues surrounding gender and genius. Charlotte no longer pursued art, but she did reach out for poetic mentorship to the Poet Laureate, Robert Southey, in life; his return letter of March 12, 1837, Southey admits she does "evidently possess, & in no inconsiderable degree what Wordsworth calls 'the faculty of verse'" but he reprimands her ambition because "Literature cannot be the business of a woman's life, & it ought not to be" (Smith I: 166–7). Their father's belief and support of his girl children's education was, in life, unorthodox; refusing to limit their potential, the girls were allowed to read anything in his own library while encouraged to read the classics, Romantic poetry, political debates, newspapers, and novels.

In the neo-Victorian novel, Charlotte instead turns to her father who says, "writing wasn't a suitable profession for a woman and, even if I was determined to pursue that path" she would be "very unlikely to make any money" so she "shouldn't let it interfere with real life" (Eagland 271). It is, even from the most supportive parent, an unthinkable impossibility that a young woman could look to scribbling as a livelihood. The young women persevere, and they write at length and rewrite as a "new, engrossing interest" takes hold until the sisters "can't think about anything else" (284). In one instance, when a visitor comes to the door, Emily completely ignores mannerly protocol and is cold to him because she is so invested in a revision of her story; she must decide whether her character,

Augusta, will choose to reveal her illegitimate child or kill it and Emily was "struggling to convey the anguish of Augusta's inner conflict" (290). This creative thinking has no time for social niceties.

The neo-Victorian narrative suggests that subterfuge indulged in by the young women sisters become their acts of transgression so they might flourish in their future. Although Emily openly plays Beethoven masterfully, on three other occasions the sisters intentionally hide their abilities from Branwell and their father; they hide Charlotte's art, and then the publication of Charlotte, Anne and Emily's *Poems* (1846), and later, their first or only novels (1847). The neo-Victorian perspective on the limitations placed on talented adolescent and youthful women, or at least their perception that their possibilities would be curtailed, is expressed when focalised through Emily's fear of being at the centre of attention when "people who aren't family, expect you to behave in a certain way. If you don't, they give you that look—mostly disapproving, occasionally amused, but *always* judging you, criticizing you" (Eagland 142; emphasis in original), a fact that increases as young women come of age in Victorian society.

A Kindred Spirit

The Brontës did have friend, young women who in some ways act as precursors to possibilities, as a fast friend, or a kindred spirit. One young woman who was a friend to the Brontës was a sister student from Roe Head, Mary Taylor. Like Ellen Nussey, she visits Charlotte, but in *The World Within* significantly is portrayed as the kindred spirit of the young Emily. Mary's progressive ideas and disdain for convention make her discordant bluntness welcome by Emily at the Parsonage. Even her warning that "you must know that there's no guarantee that, by marrying, a woman will have a warm, close attachment" because convention dictates that "a wife would have to bend her will to that of her husband and subordinate her wishes to his" (Eagland 191) is not without merit for a modern reader having Victorian restrictions explained. Mary is clearly intended to voice the ideas of a young adult reader looking back to the past. Emily and Mary's conversations about inheritance revisit the limitations caused by a woman's financial insecurity as well as the complicity of many women's willingness to self-sacrifice their own potentialities to a patriarchal system. The literary world's complicity in young women's perceptions of life is exposed with recognition that "in books, it's all about love—But the books always end with the wedding and never go on to describe married life" (192–3). The never-married, folk-wise Tabby smiles about Mary's evaluation of convention because "The lass, she's a proper caution" (193), a foreshadowing about the real-life New Woman she was to become and, a reader notes, Tabby does not say Mary is wrong.[19] Emily and Mary bond over politics and self-made destinies rather than the trivialities encouraged as accomplishments by other women. Emily's connection to Mary is subtle but intense.

Like in *Always Emily*, there is a moment where Eagland wonders about Emily's liminal physical existence; so much of the mind, and of the body on the moors, but Emily's close connections beyond the family are a mystery to the scholar and storyteller alike. Before Mary leaves, Emily tells of her dark moods over the deaths of Maria and Elizabeth, after which they walk in comfortable silence. When they reach a brook, Emily "surprises herself by giving her companion a stiff bow, like a cavalier saluting his lady, and offers her hand"; Mary curtsies and Emily takes hold of Mary's hand as she jumps. They are only in contact for a second, but Emily experiences a "shock like a charge of electricity" after which she lies awake in bed thinking of Mary (202) astonished at herself for the first time in her life making a friend, or as suggested, seeing Mary as potentially attractive as a partner. The two young women become pen pals across continents, and Mary encourages Emily to "*Have courage, my dear, and don't let the tyranny of sewing, et cetera, prevent you from following your heart's desires*" (204; emphasis in original).

These are both neo-Victorian interventions created to demonstrate an expression of unconventional support and, perhaps, as yet unformed lesbian desire. There is no evidence in fact of such an emotional connection but provides another possible reason for Emily's lack of interest in any of the men who enter the parsonage. Emily then crafts a brave and passionate character, Augusta Geraldine Almeda, who will not "be beholden to any man, but strides about the world creating her own destiny" (Eagland 205),[20] a kind of future Emily or Mary making their own way. In this way, gender expectations are transgressed by Emily. She does not adhere to conventional gender norms, nor is she apologetic for her behaviour. Neo-Victorian fiction has the liberty to reconsider the constraint placed upon women, both literally and figuratively. Consistently throughout young adult narratives, finding one's sense of identity is crucial, no more so than in discussions of gender which is considered much more fluid now than in the past. The recognition that it is possible to "dispense with the priority of 'man' and 'woman' as abiding substances, then it is no longer possible to subordinate dissonant gendered features as so many secondary and accidental characteristics of a gender ontology" (Butler, 1990 24).

It is precisely this troubling of acceptable gender performance(s) limited to male/active or female/passive roles that Emily does in life and in several neo-Victorian representations. Emily—self-identifying as her male hero, uninterested in female attitudes of comportment, and highly invested in her own imaginative life—aspires to possess a creative, ambitious but private mind. MacColl describes Emily as increasingly emboldened by her growing self-knowledge, when

> alone in her bedroom, brushing her hair, she studies her face in the looking glass; wide-spaced blue-grey eyes, a long straight nose like Papa's, a determined set to her mouth. Does this amount to prettiness?
> As she gazes at herself, a realization strikes her like an electric shock.
> This is what she looks like.
> It's like meeting a stranger. For the very first time in her life, she's seeing *herself*. This is how other people see her—as a being, separate from all other beings on earth with her own unique recognizable identity.
> This is who she is.
> She nods to herself in the mirror: a greeting to the only Emily Jane Brontë in the world. (Eagland 112; emphasis in original)

For Emily, hers is a looking glass reflecting forward rather than a rear-view mirror (Joyce 2002, 3) just as when looking back at the impossible life of the young Emily, the reader's view is of a forward thinking young woman. Judith Butler is helpful here when she discusses gender as a performance usually produced along culturally established lines of coherence but asserts that these delineations are not definitive; rather,

> the exposure of this fictive production is conditioned by the regulated play of attributes that resist assimilation into the ready made framework of primary nouns and subordinate adjectives. It is of course always possible to argue that dissonant adjectives work retroactively to redefine the substantive identities they are said to modify and, hence, to expand the substantive categories of gender to include possibilities that they previously excluded. (24)

The postmodern nod is a critique of the limitations of seeing young women—Victorian or twenty-first century—as reflectors; rather, Emily sees herself—her self—in the mirror, standing in the steps of men looking at women. Emily casts aside convention when she moves beyond seeing herself objectified; the neo-Victorian move away from external construction leads to the foregrounding of subjectivity and self-awareness. Each young woman seeks to "go forward, secure in the knowledge that, as long as she has herself, she will survive" (Eagland 326). The sisters' investment in themselves, in their writings, in their own rights, plus the hard work they put into it is rewarded. Not unlike a usual didactic turn in a twenty-first-century young adult fiction, the neo-Victorian turn points to how under every circumstance that dictates the young women could not succeed they find, in spite of the odds, an infinite and stellar reputation.

The world(s) of the Brontës as children and young adults has them move easily in their minds between their lived life and their creative lives; they often see and consider themselves as characters like when the narrator tells us that although Hareton was kissing her hand like a "scene from one of her stories. Or, more likely, Charlotte's. But this heroine had more important things to do. She snatched back her hand" (MacColl 157) and then Charlotte faints into his arms, declaring "My Duke!" (160). Emily commits details of her life, particularly of the reclining Hareton reading Byron, for "a story someday" (173) because as she says to Tabby, "It isn't scribbling.... Writing is what makes life sweet to the tongue" (140).

The many neo-Victorian biofictions of Victorian young people and/as authors also spill over into the creation of fictional lives about Victorian characters; while characters are, by definition, fictional, there are parts of their lives—usually their youth—which are excluded from an adult text but are often explored in young adult narratives. These neo-Victorian biofictions of characters are, then, an extension of interest in significant individuals that allows young adult readers to explore a fascinating life.

Notes

1. Kohlke calls this celebrity biofiction which "infills" often "insufficiently documented lives" especially the "individual's pre-history (and sometimes post-history) to the events that brought her/him to public attention" to "provide a supplementary or compensatory effect, substituting fictional life for a lacunae in knowledge rather than reworking and adding a wealth of known detail" (2013, 8).
2. For a full discussion of these problematic constructions, see Maier (2016).
3. Michael Lackey raises the question of ethics with regard to biofiction for children and young adults since they are, as yet, possibly without the

knowledge to distinguish between historical fact and historical narrative (see 2018a).
4. During the illness, Maria's sister, Elizabeth Branwell (1776–1842), joins the family to care for her, then stays for the rest of her life to provide a stable, instructive female influence for the children, later to be joined in 1824 by Tabitha "Tabby" Aykroyd (?1771–January 6, 1859), the servant to whom the children often turn for comfort, rather than instruction.
5. Along with Sarah, her sister Nancy (1803–86) acted as nursemaid to the children.
6. The school was to be run by the well-known Reverend William Carus Wilson for students in need; they were placed under the tutelage of the headmistress, Miss Margaret Wooler (1792–1855) who became a lifelong friend of Charlotte, even giving her away at her wedding to her father's curate, Arthur Bell Nicholls (January 6, 1819–December 3, 1906), on June 29, 1854.
7. There are biographies aplenty of the individual Brontës and of their collective family from creating part of what has been called the Brontë industry. See Terry Eagleton ([1975] 2005).
8. This is not to say that important work has not been done on the known material lives of the Brontës; for further discussion, see Deborah Lutz's exceptional *The Brontë Cabinet* (2015) where she makes connections between physical artefacts in possession of and/or created by the siblings—such as Keeper's collar, or a painting of Nero by Emily—as a means to understand the family members in relation to their surroundings; in particular, these two objects demonstrate Emily's deep love of animals.
9. For a full discussion of the neo-Victorian adult narratives about Emily Brontë, see Maier (2018); for a discussion of Charlotte Brontë biofiction, see Maier (2016).
10. For a full discussion, see Chap. 3.
11. An earlier biographer, Robinson, warned her reader that "Emily's genius was set down as a lunatic's hobgoblin of nightmare potency" (MacColl 109).
12. A *gytrash* is defined as "An apparition, spectre, ghost, generally taking the form of an animal" (*OED*); further definition is found in this passage from Charlotte Brontë's *Jane Eyre*: "I remembered certain of Bessie's tales wherein figured a North-of-England spirit, called a 'Gytrash;' which, in the form of horse, mule, or large dog, haunted solitary ways, and sometimes came upon belated travellers" (1847, I xii).
13. John Ruskin tells us in his lecture "Of Queen's Gardens," in *Sesame and Lilies* (1865), that "man's power is active, progressive, defensive. He is eminently the doer, the creator, the discoverer, the defender. His intellect is for speculation and invention; his energy for adventure, for war" whereas "women's power is for rule, not for battle—and her intellect is not for

invention or creation, but for sweet ordering, arrangement, and decision" while "she is protected from all danger and temptation" (164–5). For a strong discussion of proper and "improper" womanhood, see Lyn Pykett (1992).

14. Charlotte and Emily go to Brussels in search of language skills to market for a potential school at the Parsonage since neither of them relishes becoming a governess.
15. Notably, there are two very recent adult books concerning the brother, *Branwell* ([2005] 2020) by Douglas Martin, and *Brontë's Mistress* (2020) by Finola Austin. The initially named *Taste of Sorrow* (2009) by Jude Morgan was changed to *Charlotte and Emily: A Novel of the Brontës* (2010), completely eliding Anne and Branwell from the titular discussion of sorrow and, by implication, the creative genius that arises from it; however, they are included in the novel itself. I have not yet found either an adult or young adult novel about Anne Brontë.
16. Refers to Taylor Swift's song, "If I was a man" (2019) that details the privileged position men enjoy in a patriarchal culture and the negativity placed on a woman who strives to succeed.
17. One such comparison of fear and emotional turmoil in a child or young adult facing the potential death of a parent is found in the Young Adult novel, *A Monster Calls* (2011) inspired by Siobhan Dowd and written by Patrick Ness.
18. In an excellent example of Brontë mythmaking, Juliet Barker argues that this story was instigated by Mrs. Ellis Chadwick but that this "supposedly disastrous trip to London" is unfounded (1036, footnotes 3 and 4). Chadwick's account is, at best, a series of assumptions: "Mrs. Gaskell had the impression that Branwell never visited London, and Ellen Nussey evidently had the same impression.... Branwell was the first member of the family to see the 'Great Babylon,' but it proved too much for him; he frequented the public-houses, amongst them the Castle Tavern in Holborn, then kept by Tom Spring, a well-known prize fighter. He was not twenty years of age, and before he really reached the City he had fallen a prey to 'sharpers,' and very soon the money which his father had so generously given him was either squandered or obtained from him by fraud" ([1914] 2011, 192).
19. Mary Taylor (February 26, 1817–March 1, 1893) was a remarkable woman and a lifelong friend of the Brontë sisters. Precocious from a young age, she left for New Zealand in 1845 where she became a businesswoman of note, a writer, a New Woman suffragette and, after she finally returned to Gomersal in 1859, she travelled and wrote about her travels as well as journalism on feminist issues of the day. Although radically different in

temperament, Charlotte and Taylor wrote regularly to each other even after Taylor emigrated.
20. For interest in a possible connection, that the Brontës lived within distance of Anne Lister and Shibden Hall, see Banerjee (n.d.).

BIBLIOGRAPHY

Arias, R. and Pulham, P. Eds. *Haunting and Spectrality in Neo-Victorian Fiction.* Basingstoke: Palgrave Macmillan, 2009.
Austin, Finola. *Brontë's Mistress.* New York: Atria Books, 2020.
Banerjee, Jacqueline. "Anne Lister ('Gentleman Jack') and the Brontës." *The Victorian Web.* n.d. https://victorianweb.org/authors/bronte/lister.html.
Barker, Juliet. *The Brontës: Wild Genius on the Moors.* London: Pegasus, 2012.
"Biofiction: Tweaking History to Reveal Greater Meaning." *University of Minnesota Research and Innovation Office* (2020): n.p. https://research.umn.edu/inquiry/post/biofiction-tweaking-history-reveal-greater-meaning
Boyd, William. "Saints and Savages." *The New York Times,* 24 June 2009: BR 10.
Brontë, Charlotte. *The Letters of Charlotte Brontë: With a Selection of Letters by Family and Friends,* edited by Margaret Smith. Oxford: Oxford University Press, 1995–2000.
Brontë, Charlotte. *Jane Eyre.* London: Smith, Elder, and Co., 1847.
Butler, Judith. *Gender Trouble: Feminism and the Subversion of Identity.* London: Routledge, 1990.
Cain, Sian. "Emily Brontë May Have Had Asperger Syndrome, says biographer." *The Guardian.* August 29, 2016. n.p. https://www.theguardian.com/books/2016/aug/29/emily-bronte-may-have-had-asperger-syndrome-says-biographer#:~:text=Emily%20Brontë%20may%20have%20had%20Asperger%20syndrome%2C%20according,the%20literary%20biographer%20Claire%20Harman.
Chadwick, Ellis H. *In the Footsteps of the Brontës.* 1914. Cambridge: Cambridge University Press, 2011.
Eagland, Joyce. *The World Within: A Novel of Emily Brontë.* New York: Scholastic, 2015.
Eagleton, Terry. *Myths of Power: A Marxist Study of the Brontës.* 1975. London: Palgrave, 2005.
Emily. Embankment Films, Ingenious Media, Tempo Productions, Arenamedia, 2022.
Frank, Katherine. *A Chainless Soul.* Boston: Houghton Mifflin, 1990.
Gaskell, Elizabeth. *The Life of Charlotte Brontë.* New York; Appleton and Company, 1857.
"Gytrash, n.". *OED* Online. Oxford University Press. https://www-oed-com.proxy.hil.unb.ca/view/Entry/82930?redirectedFrom=gytrash.

Heilmann, Ann and Mark Llewellyn. *Neo-Victorianism: The Victorians in the Twenty-First Century, 1999–2009*. London: Palgrave, 2010.
Heilmann, Ann and Mark Llewellyn. "Victorians Now: Global Reflections on Neo-Victorianism." *Critical Studies*. 55, no. 1 (2013): 24–42.
Joyce, Simon. "The Victorians in the Rearview Mirror." In *Functions of Victorian Culture at the Present Time*, edited by C. Kreuger, 3–17. Chicago: Ohio University Press, 2002.
Kaplan, C. *Victoriana: Histories, Fictions, Criticism*. New York: Columbia, 2007.
Kohlke, M. L. "Neo-Victorian Biofiction and the Special/Spectral Case of Barbara Chase Riboud's *Hottentot Venus*." *Australasian Journal of Victorian Studies*. 18, no. 3 (2013): 4–21.
Kohlke, Marie-Luise and Christian Gutleben. "Taking Biofictional Liberties: Tactical Games and Gambits with Nineteenth-Century Lives." In *Neo-Victorian Biofiction*, edited by Kohlke and Gutleben, 1–53. Amsterdam: Brill/Rodopi, 2020.
"Künstlerroman, n.". OED Online. Oxford University Press. https://www-oed-com.proxy.hil.unb.ca/view/Entry/104563?redirectedFrom=kunstlerroman (accessed July 26, 2020).
Lackey, Michael. "The Ethical Benefits and Challenges of Biofiction for Children." *a/b/: AUTO|BIOGRAPHY STUDIES*. 33, no.1 (2018a): 5–21.
Lackey, Michael, Ed. *Conversations with Biographical Novelists: Truthful Fictions across the Globe*. London: Bloomsbury Academic, 2018b.
Lackey, Michael. *Biofiction: An Introduction*. London: Routledge, 2021.
Layne, Bethany. "On the Limits of Biofiction: Behany Layne Talks to David Lodge." *LITHUB* (2018): n.p. https://lithub.com/on-the-limits-ofbiofiction-bethany-layne-talks-to-david-lodge/
Llewellyn, M. "Neo-Victorianism: On the Ethics and Aesthetics of Appropriation." *LIT: Literature Interpretation Theory*. 20, no. 1–2 (2009): 27–44.
Lutz, Deborah. *The Brontë Cabinet*. New York: W. W. Norton, 2015.
MacColl, Michaela. *Always Emily*. San Francisco: Chronicle Books, 2014.
Maier, Sarah E. "The Neo-Victorian Presence(s) of Emily Brontë." *Victorians: A Journal of Literature and Culture*. 134 (Winter 2018): 289–307.
Maier, Sarah E. "Biographical Myths and Legends of the Brontës." In *A Companion to the Brontës*, edited by Diane Hoeveler and Deborah Morse, 579–93. Chichester: Wiley Blackwell, 2016.
Martin, Douglas. *Branwell*. 2005. New York: Soft Skull Press, 2020.
Miller, Lucasta. *The Brontë Myth*. London: Jonathan Cape, 2001.
Morgan, Jude. *Charlotte and Emily: A Novel of the Brontës*. New York: St. Martin's Press, 2009.
Ness, Patrick and Siobhan Dowd. *A Monster Calls*. Somerville: Candlewick, 2011.
PTA. "Using Biographies to Grow Young Reader's Identities." *PTA Family Reading Experience*, 2021. https://www.pta.org/docs/default-source/files/

programs/pta-connected/2021/smart-talk/family-resources/activities/using-biographies-to-grow-young-readers-identities.pdf.
Pykett, Lyn. *The 'Improper' Feminine: The Women's Sensation Novel and the New Woman Writing*. Abingdon: Routledge, 1992.
Robinson, Mary F. *Emily Brontë*. Boston: Robertson Brothers, 1883.
Ruskin, John. *Sesame and Lilies*. London: Smith, Elder & Co., 1865.
Shiller, D. "The Redemptive Past in the Neo-Victorian Novel." *Studies in the Novel*. 29, no. 4 (1997): 538–60.
Simpson, Charles. *Emily Brontë*. London: Country Life Ltd., 1929.
Sullivan, Ed. "Some Teens Prefer the Real Thing: the Case for Young Adult Nonfiction." *The English Journal*. 90, no. 3 (2001): 43–7.
Swift, Taylor and Joel Little. "If I were a man." *Lover*. Republic, 2019.
Winnifrith, Tom. *The Brontës and Their Background: Romance and Reality*. London: Macmillan, 1973.

CHAPTER 6

Irregulars: Sherlockian Youth as Outsiders

The conflation of young men and crime during the Victorian age was ubiquitous from anonymous penny dreadfuls to Charles Dickens' novels, but there were also instances of boy detectives, so it is not surprising that the appearance and adaptation of the popular genres of sensation, and crime fiction in neo-Victorian literature and on screen is one of overwhelming prevalence.[1] Mystery is, perhaps, the most widely revisioned for a variety of audiences. It may be that the popularity of mystery novels for young readers are engaging because of "the genre's implicit command to readers to participate in the guessing game of detection" (Billman 1984, 30), but for adults, Louisa Hadley makes the case that in postmodern narratives, "the process of recovering the Victorian past [is] similar to that of a detective solving a case; 'clues' from the past need to be interpreted in order to make sense of what really happened" (2010, 59). In canonical detective narratives, there is a strong sense of conservatism because the intrusion of a perpetrator into the safety of the social context must be contained and explained. In order to reassert the status quo, a "conservative appeal to stabilising laws and rules" which constitute ideas of "unity and closure" (Priestman 1990, 21) that acts as a means of social integration (Mandel 1984, 47).

For both adults and younger readers, the appearance of Sherlock Holmes in neo-Victorian fiction was inevitable; the fifty-six stories and four novels written by Sir Arthur Conan Doyle between 1887 and 1917 have long filled the popular imagination with investigative puzzles, none more intriguing than to solve the enigma of the detective himself.

In particular, neo-Victorian young adult narratives have encouraged the immense interest in the teenage development of Holmes. Just as biofictions require an intent of fidelity—not always comprehensively—to an individual's known life facts, there are some cases of biofiction of a character that is intensely scrutinised to see if the older fiction matches up to the neo-Victorian biofiction. Several series now take as their point of departure the early life—or developing character(s)—of Sherlock Holmes: how did he become "the" detective? Andrew Lane's Young Sherlock series and Stephen Peacock's separate, but equally excellent, The Boy Sherlock series trace the developing and particularised nonconformist education of the young man in a manner that convincingly foreshadow the adult fictions of Sir Arthur Conan Doyle. In similar fashion, several series introduce young women detectives like Enola Holmes (*The Case of the Missing Marquess* in 2006 by Nancy Springer) and Charlotte Holmes (*A Study in Charlotte* in 2016 by Brittany Cavallaro), or characters like Abigail Rook (*Jackaby* in 2014 by William Ritter), Sally Lockhart (*Ruby in the Smoke* in 1985 by Philip Pullman), Mary Quinn (*Spy in the House* in 2010 by Y. S. Lee), or Evaline Stoker and Mina Holmes (*Clockwork Scarab* in 2013 by Colleen Gleason)[2] who are, literally and/or figuratively, intended to be the offspring of Sherlock Holmes. These neo-Victorian narratives explore how the experiences of nonconformist young adults of the nineteenth century, who are either immersed in or rejected by society, use their particular familial backgrounds, observational powers, and exceptional intelligence to take up the Sherlockian legacy.

The odds that a young adult audience having a specific and deep knowledge about the consulting detective is unlikely but the intrigue may be there to coax their interest; certainly, there are a plethora of Victorian-set mysteries in the Young Adult section of the bookstores just as there are in the adult sections. The question of why a neo-Victorian view of Sherlock Holmes is of interest to the current culture is striking. Holmes was introduced to the world in 1887 as a thirty-three-year-old confirmed bachelor, a mother descended from the French artist Vernet, and a previous life in the countryside with his family. For adults, the revisiting of Holmes in the neo-Victorian genre may have resulted in the release of popular renditions found in adaptations like Guy Ritchie's *Sherlock Holmes* (2009) and *Sherlock Holmes: A Game of Shadows* (2011) as portrayed by Robert Downey Jr, or the television shows *Sherlock* (BBC 2010–17), and even

Elementary (CBS 2012–19), but there are hundreds of Sherlockian texts, films, games, and other transmedia explorations.[3] For young adults, adaptations of *Enola Holmes* (2020) and *Enola Holmes 2* (2022) have appeared onscreen after the textual narratives, so the films may have sent young readers looking for more.

Hundreds of stories starring, explaining, exploiting, and even shipping Holmes exist; both corrective and complementary pastiches[4] abound. While "textual lineage—whether imagined or real—gives the text a special kind of credibility" (Nyqvist 2017, 2.8) it is clear that "the Sherlock Holmes pastiches are—despite their varying aims—fundamentally homages" (2.9). These neo-Victorian narratives are neither strictly corrective nor insipidly complementary; rather, these irregular homages seek to interject corrective possibilities into the canonical world while being complementary to it with the exploration of the youth of Sherlock Holmes or the possibility of his sister.

Holmes ... Sherlock Holmes

The Young Sherlock Holmes series is, as of now, the only Sir Arthur Conan Doyle Estate approved series, an enterprise initially intended to capitalise on the success of the Young James Bond books, by Charlie Higson and Stephen Cole published from 2005 to 2017.[5] The Estate has sanctioned various projects for young adults including the Young Sherlock series by Lane, and Ali Standish's forthcoming series, *The Improbable Tales of Baskerville Hall* (2023), will include Irene Eagle as the schoolmate of a young Arthur Conan Doyle and Jimmie Moriarty (2023, n.p.). According to the Estate, the forthcoming series "*Baskerville Hall* is a bold and thrilling reimagining of Arthur Conan Doyle's early life, filled with students and teachers who the world would later come to know so well, including Dr. Watson, James Moriarty and, of course, Sherlock Holmes" (n.p.). According to Lane, his literary agent Robert Kirby, who also represents the Conan Doyle Estate and approached them with the idea for a series because "the Young Adult market was desperate for well-written books with strong characters" (n.p.). Long interested in Conan Doyle's Holmes, he thought he "could make a strong argument that Holmes as an adult is mentally disturbed—suffering from obsessive compulsive disorder and certainly manic-depressive" so Lane saw the task was to try "to explain how a relatively normal boy becomes the dysfunctional adult" (n.p.). To critics of the idea, Lane has replied "I am trying desperately not to contradict anything that Conan Doyle did, and that I am attempting to explain how Sherlock Holmes came to develop all of those skills that Conan Doyle told us he had—the boxing, the fencing, the martial arts, the chemistry, the violin playing … he had to have a reason for learning them all" (n.p.).

In the neo-Victorian world created by Lane, Sherlock Holmes is a fourteen-year-old boarding student at Deepdene School. Expecting to return to his home for the summer, instead he is informed he will be going elsewhere. Holmes' father (Siger) has gone to India with his Regiment to "strengthen the existing military force" to fight "not the Indians" but "a mutiny" (Lane 2014, 9). With his mother unwell, his sister (Charlotte) too young, and his brother (Mycroft) too busy at the foreign office to act as guardian in London, Holmes is sent to live with his Aunt Anna and Uncle Sherrinford in the country. Once there, he meets and befriends his future sidekick Matty Arnatt, a young orphan boatman who prefers to be "out in the open" even at night (107) with his horse, Albert. To continue his education, Mycroft sends along Amyus Crowe, an American man from the "colonies"—a "big bloke" with an imposing stature, "funny voice and … white hair" (104)—who is employed to act as tutor for Sherlock. Crowe has a daughter, Virginia, who joins Holmes and Matty on their adventures. To be confused for a boy so she will have some mobility, Virginia uses disguise to her advantage when she "smoothed her hair up behind her head" and "slipped the cap on" with her "coat buttoned up" so she "might be mistaken for a boy" (242).[6]

A preliminary evaluation of Holmes' intelligence comes when Crowe challenges him to pick out which family painting is fake; the tutor wants to see if the young man can distinguish authenticity from artifice and to observe his level as well as range of knowledge. Sherlock stumbles, but Crowe uses it as a point of instruction:

> you can deduce all you like, but it's pointless without knowledge. Your mind is like a spinnin' wheel, rotatin' endlessly and pointlessly until threads are fed in, when it starts producin' yarn. Information is the foundation of all rational thought. Seek it out. Collect it assiduously. Stock the lumber room of your mind with as many facts as you can fit in there. Don't attempt to distinguish between important facts and trivial facts: they're all potentially important. (53)

The oddity of this explanation intended to foreshadow, the reader assumes, the "brain-attic" (2009 [1887], 21)[7] of the canonical Holmes, is exemplary of the tone of the series. Holmes is not necessarily uniquely gifted but has had an eccentric, American man educate him in skills of observation. Holmes also learns about China, bamboo, chemistry, tropical diseases, and bees from Professor Arthur Albery Winchcombe, Lecturer.

The nemesis conjured in the first of the series is Baron Maupertuis—a member of the Paradol Chamber—has bred a lethal genus of bee he intends for the destruction of the British Army. The bees will cause thousands of deaths and deal a "demoralizing blow directed at the heart of the British Empire" (Lane 2014, 256) because he feels the "boundaries of the British Empire have to be pushed back, if only so that other countries can get some breathing space, some room to live" (257) in a world that had "rolled over" (256) in the past. In the role of young detective, Holmes acts as a precursor to his canonical bee-keeping self, where he acts "as a figure who secures and stabilises the disparate spaces of home and empire" and is an "imaginative means of soothing late-Victorian anxieties about the permeable relationship between England and its colonies, however he may also be read as an unsettling presence, who makes visible the fragile distinctions between self and other" (Guest 2010, 73). In Lane's series, the concept of Empirical domination is taken to task by Maupertuis who, interestingly enough, escapes. Later it is revealed Crowe is an American spy of sorts; he was "retained by ... well, let's say the American government to make it easy, to seek out men who'd committed crimes" during the Civil War (Lane 2014, 222), one of whom is the Baron. The young Sherlock Holmes—much like James Bond—has assisted in an international case, an auspicious way to begin the series.

Sherlock Holmes, an Odd Boy

Shane Peacock's series was not initially conceived as a story of Sherlock Holmes; rather, it took shape as a specifically neo-Victorian story, he says, to

> deal with subjects I truly cared about—I wanted it set in the most intriguing place I know of (Victorian London); I wanted it to deal with racism and prejudice (mankind's greatest sins, in my mind), which meant discussing justice as well, I wanted there to be crows in it (brilliant, misunderstood birds who are themselves victims of a sort of prejudice); and I wanted the

novel to challenge my readers, to be a Young Adult novel that was essentially an adult novel with a kid as the hero. (Peacock quoted in Ue 2010, 34)

It was not until an early reader of the manuscript "asked if I thought I could make my boy hero Sherlock Holmes" to "increase its commercial potential" that Peacock pushed back, reluctant to "take someone else's character" and place him in his "gritty tale of racism and justice" (34). It was a "sexy suggestion" with "sensational" potential (Peacock 2008b, 18). He did not want to create a pastiche but "to seem very real, not a caricature of an old, famous character" (37). Peacock's observation, after rereading the Conan Doyle stories, was that Holmes "could not have been to the manor born, as many might suspect" because this "character was an urban sort, and messed up—cocaine addict, misogynist, manic depressive. What sort of childhood did he have?" (34–5). He realised Holmes "was a larger-than-life character like none other, filled with insecurities that must have had a fascinating genesis" (Peacock 2008b, 18). Peacock wanted to demonstrate that Holmes is flawed, which would appeal to a twenty-first-century audience and how he "grew and changed into the adult Holmes, and wasn't transported, fully formed, from one age to another" (35); the result is that the series is, in intent and purpose, the exposition of how the boy might have become the Master, demonstrating but not dumbing down the process of growing into adulthood for a young readership.

Beginning with *Eye of the Crow*, the series is haunted by the image and persona of the man the world understands to be Sherlock Holmes. John Watson tells us in *A Study in Scarlet* that "In height he was rather over six feet, and so excessively lean that he seemed to be considerably taller. His eyes were sharp and piercing, save during those intervals of torpor to which I have alluded; and his thin, hawk-like nose gave his whole expression an air of alertness and decision. His chin, too, had the prominence and squareness which mark the man of determination" (Conan Doyle 2009a [1887], 20). Further, he has several peculiarities that make him "a little queer in his ideas" (16) and is "a little too scientific for my tastes—it approaches to cold-bloodedness" but has a "spirit of inquiry" (17) according to Stamford, plays a Stradivarius violin, and seeks to use his talents for justice. Neo-Victorian Sherlockian narratives hope to explain the genesis of the irregular man.

The Boy Sherlock series begins in 1867 when Holmes is thirteen, and Peacock is clear that "The Sherlock Holmes series is a *bildüngsroman*, about a young man learning how to become an adult" (quoted in Ue 37).

The reader encounters "a tall, thin youth with skin the pallor of the pale margins" of newspapers, who "appears elegant in his black frock coat and necktie with waistcoat and polished boots. Up close, he looks frayed. He seems sad, but his gray eyes are alert" (2007, 1). Holmes is on the verge of his first case that changes both his life and his sense of self. From birth he has been "an observing machine" (2) who sizes up men from bearing to calluses, and women from bonnets to insteps, skipping school to read people and books, but more importantly, the police newspapers in Trafalgar Square as people walk by calling him "that dreadful boy" (2).

Holmes lives with his mother, Rose (née Sherrinford), and his father, Wilberforce who had anglicised his name for social acceptance when he arrived in England. Their home is above an old haberdasher shop in Southwark; their story is one of racism and hatred. Rose was an aspiring singer of the upper class and his father a scientific genius at University College London, who fell in love at the Opera. Their relationship "frightened his parents and infuriated hers" because "no Sherrinford could marry this Jew" so they eloped to Scotland (17) and returned to Rose being disowned by her family and Wilberforce without university opportunities. Rose teaches upper-class girls to sing while Wilber tutors in sciences, then chooses to become an ornithologist to work with the Doves of Peace at the Crystal Palace. Happy together, the couple have three children: Mycroft (born eight months after their wedding), Sherlock (born seven years later), and Violet who dies at age three. Holmes' family leads to his complex emotions where he "loves his mother and father, and despises the life they have given him" (18) full of abject poverty, racial injustice, and limited opportunities to rise above his station.

There is precedent for considering whether or not main characters in the canon of Sir Arthur Conan Doyle are Jewish, but the possibility is unlikely that his Holmes is a Jew. Liel Leibovitz has an interesting take on how, even though Conan Doyle made no reference to the consulting detective that identifies him as Jewish, and although Holmes—and, by extension, his author—has moments of anti-Semitism, there is one character who is often thought to be a Jew. Leibovitz discusses both issues:

> "The same afternoon," writes Conan Doyle in "A Study in Scarlet," brought "a grey-headed, seedy visitor, looking like a Jew pedlar." A notch above the author's Jewish peddlers are his Jewish money-lenders: "He is mad keen upon winning the Derby," Holmes informs Watson in "The Adventure of Shoscombe Old Place," speaking of a proper aristocrat. "He is in the hands

of the Jews, and may at any moment be sold up and his racing stables seized by his creditors." And while it is common to assume that Irene Adler—who in many recent adaptations, although not in Conan Doyle's original stories, is portrayed as Holmes' love interest—is Jewish, no specific mention of her faith is ever made. (2012, n.p.)

Noa Paz Wahrman agrees that the original books "are not kind to Jewish tradition, religion and culture. Although the books are not anti-Semitic, per se, Sir Arthur Conan Doyle indulged in mild anti-Semitism on occasion" (2013, n.p.). Leibovitz then puts forward that although Holmes is may not be Jewish, one "way would be to see him as, to borrow a phrase from Isaac Deutscher, a non-Jewish Jew" (2012, n.p.). Leibovitz takes this term from Isaac Deutscher to mean those who "don't announce their ethnic and religious identity; they simply embody it" and Lebovitz argues that the manner of Holmes thinking is Talmudic (n.p.). Melanie Pastor describes Holmes in *The Eye of the Crow* as a Jewish *siechel*; according to George E. Johnson, "*sekhel* in Modern/Israeli Hebrew and *syekhel* in Yiddish, it can mean intelligence, smarts, brains, reason, common sense, cleverness or even wisdom" and "*sechel*" is defined as "the spiritual ability to think, to weigh, the strength to judge and to come to a resolution" (2013, n.p.). Unclear as that characterisation may appear, it opens the possibility for considerations of, if only stereotypical, questions of racial discrimination as one of the defining reasons for the self-contained, emotionally removed Holmes, one explored by Peacock as a fundamental reason for Holmes' status as an outsider or as irregular to social norms.

This neo-Victorian strategy of making the young man Jewish seeks to explain, retroactively and contextually, why Holmes is alienated even by his peers and other young men with whom he comes into contact, and why he might feel Other in a Victorian society that was increasingly anti-Semitic towards the end of the century. His counterpart in the series is Malefactor, reminiscent of a young Moriarty, who runs the Trafalgar Square Irregulars; the boy is "dark-haired, tough-looking … dressed in a worn-out long black coat with tails" with "a dark stovepipe hat" and a "Crude walking stick" (Peacock 2012, 5). The two adolescents are

> skinny with large heads, though the leader has nearly an inch on the half-breed truant, his forehead bulges where Holmes' is flat, and his eyes are sunken while Sherlock's peer out. They both have a way of constantly looking about, suspiciously turning their heads—Malefactor the reptile, Sherlock

the hawk. Their hair, an identical coal-black, is combed as perfectly as they can manage. (40)

The Irregulars treat Homes with racist taunts of "'alf-breed Jew-boy!" and, in the later novels, others attack him with taunts like "Jew-boy will die. Hate Jews. Hate" (225). Rather than lower himself to respond to such epithets, it becomes clear that Holmes has an alternate focus; he "hates Malefactor; hates him with the deepest admiration" (Peacock 2007, 5) and the hateful respect is both mutual and discomfiting. There is no suggestion Malefactor is, too, Jewish, but it is known that he accepts Jewish boys into his followers. Although not the central focus here, Wiggins is the head boy of the Irregulars or "the Baker Street division of the detective police force" (2009a [1887], 42); they have been collectively recreated in several transmedia adaptations, not all of which are self-consciously neo-Victorian but which do revisit the concept of the young orphans who assist Holmes and Watson in their investigations.[8] There is, however, a vague similarity between the young men, Holmes and Malefactor, that "goes beyond their dark looks. It is in their way of expressing themselves and the careful manner they dress in their tattered cloths" but Malefactor refuses to grant him equality with, "You'll never be an Irregular. Not you, Sherlock Homes" to which Holmes replies, "And yet, I'm as irregular as I can be" (6).

In his home life, Wilber Holmes seeks to encourage his son with the example of Benjamin Disraeli and remind him that "Other Jews are getting places too" and so, too, might he; Holmes knows those who have success "have never lived in the slums of Southward or Whitechapel; their blood isn't mixed; their parents haven't suffered a great fall" (Peacock 2007, 28) but are middle-class converts who have been baptised in the Church of England. The toughs at school call him out as "Judas" or "Old Clothes" but Holmes early understands they "resent his many first-place finishes, his razor-sharp mind" (29) for which he suffers regular beatings. His father has taught him to "use his brain as his weapon in life" (37) but Holmes is ashamed when he does not fight back. Other boys hate him too, like Malefactor's minions who resent "the blue in his veins. They sense he isn't from the street, not truly. … He is neither with them nor against them" (38).

Thrown by interest into trying to solve the case involving Mohammad Adalji, a boy less than eighteen accused of the murder of an actress,

Holmes is then thought to be an accomplice—the thief who stole her purse. The two ostracised young men seem to understand each other:

> "…They want to think I acted alone. I am an Arab."
> "And I'm a Jew, a poor one."
> "A Jew?" There is hesitation in the accused man's voice.
> "Lower half Jewish, upper half English … respected part disowned."
> "That is not good."
> "Precisely." (60)

As his first case proceeds, it is a personal one wherein the reader encounters how and when Holmes builds his early skills. Malefactor's lectures on lock-picking (102) and disguise become part of his repertoire of skills. Encouraged by the elder boy, Holmes learns that "he must be whomever and whatever he needs to be" because, as Malefactor brags, "Disguise is an invaluable tool in the game of crime" and advises him "You must have some acting in your blood, Use it. Fit your movements, your whole person, to your costume" (106), a kind of whirlwind education on the use of the arts in detection. His father then teaches him to "listen to experts" and that while the ability to be keenly observant

> is not only the primary skill of the scientist, it is the elementary talent of life. Use your eyes at all times, my boy. They will not lie to you if you focus them fully. Use all your senses: hearing, smelling, tasting, and toughing. … Truly seeing things is a great power. It will give you strength even when fate seems to have made you weak. (71)

Since Peacock is building the circumstances of the young man who will become the man with his aloof presentation and his formidable intelligence, his father's encouragement to recourse to cold detachment is in keeping with his character.

His mother, Rose,[9] gives him a separate gift: music. They escape to listen through a grate at the theatre where they hear Opera and the violins that "tell us … of the tragedies of life" because "There are no instruments like them. Violins are sad; they are strong; they tell the truth. When they are slow, they make you cry. When they are fast, they press you forward, push you into the struggle of life" (45). When Rose is poisoned and dies, Holmes screams out in rage for vengeance; he is only restrained by "Something deep inside him, borne of the scientific wisdom of his decent father and the love of his beautiful mother, murmurs that this will *not* be justice. It will be murder. And he, Sherlock Holmes, will be as bad as the man he kills. His mother will have died in vain" (242).

This moment is the turning point alluded to in the Conan Doyle canon, where Holmes could have been a magnificent criminal had he so chosen. Dr. Watson writes in *The Sign of Four*, "So swift, silent and furtive were his movements like those of a trained bloodhound picking out a scent, that I could not but think what a terrible criminal he would have made had he turned his energy and sagacity against the law instead of exerting them in its defense" (2009b [1891], 112). Something in that moment of instant maturation changes in Sherlock Holmes. When next they meet, "Sherlock stares back at Malefactor. The criminal can see that there is no more fear in the half-breed boy's cloudy gray eyes. Something has changed. Forever" then "Malefactor nods at Homes, signals to his swarm, and melts into the crowd (Peacock 2007, 247) in recognition that their paths have just diverged, one to become the world's first consulting detective and the other to become a criminal mastermind known as Moriarty.

By the second book's beginning, six weeks after his mother's death, he has "grown much older"; Holmes has "little emotion on his face. His eyes are rarely cast down. He knows who he is and what he will be" (Peacock 2008a, 6). This neo-Victorian narrative over the series builds the future character of the consulting detective piece by piece in the attempt to fill in the massive gap of knowledge about a main character in the Victorian canon; it creates a biography for a fictional character or a fictional biofiction. While Conan Doyle's Sherlock Holmes comes to us fully realised, in Peacock's works the reader is able to fathom the possible circumstances that created him. By the time becomes an adult, he will have "rebuilt [himself] into a crime-solving machine. He would be a new sort of London detective" (7). In later narratives, Holmes gathers his signature abilities from various mentors including Sigerson Trismegistus Bell,[10] an apothecary who takes Holmes in as an apprentice and teaches him chemistry; as a sideline, Bell is interested in forensic investigation so enlightens Holmes to the developing sciences. As a means of self-protection, Bell has created a melding of "Eastern secrets of fighting, grappling, and striking … jujutsu and judo. … To these two Japanese arts I melded the Swiss craft of stick-fighting and England's own gentlemanly sport of pugilism to create the alloy I call Bellitsu!" (192–93) in which he instructs Holmes. Peacock shows how Holmes built his knowledge throughout his adolescence to become the detective of Sir Arthur Conan Doyle.

The Woman

Prequels, coquels, sequels, and descendent texts of Sherlock Holmes would, in some cases, have us believe that the man who disdained most women did, in fact, marry or seduce Irene Adler. In Conan Doyle's short story, "A Scandal in Bohemia," the reader learns that

> To Sherlock Holmes she is always *the* woman. I have seldom heard him mention her under any other name. In his eyes she eclipses and predominates the whole of her sex. It was not that he felt any emotion akin to love for Irene Adler. All emotions, and that one particularly, were abhorrent to his cold, precise but admirably balanced mind. … And yet there was but one woman to him, and that woman was the late Irene Adler, of dubious and questionable memory. (2009b [1891], 161)

In *Eye of the Crow*, Holmes encounters his own young woman, Miss Irene Doyle, when in jail. Unlike many references to women in Victorian texts where "References to girls are characteristically value-laden and stereotyped" (Dyhouse 2013, 116), the neo-Victorian Irene is anything but formulaic. She arrives with her Scottish father, Mr. Andrew C. Doyle, when they visit Adajli as members of The Society of Visiting Friends of London (Peacock 2007, 69). She is the antithesis of Irene Adler in appearance; she is "tall … She has long blonde hair … and dark brown eyes, darker than his own gray ones" (2007, 69). In most cases, "The Society of Friends" would refer to a local chapter of the "Religious Society of Friends" often referred to as "Quakers," a Protestant, Christian denomination founded in the seventeenth century by George Fox with a long-standing reputation as pacifists, abolitionists, and believers in spiritual equality. Irene appears; her "clothes are plain: a white blouse frilled a little near the neck where a red ribbon is tied, a beige woolen shawl, a dark cotton dress that hangs down almost to the top of her black boots, no crinoline" (2007, 69–70). Her clothes, from a neo-Victorian perspective, expose a "complicated cultural meaning of Victorian heroines dressed in Quakerish clothes. Contrary to the common understanding, Quakeresses in their distinctive clothing signified an instantly recognizable middle-class piety and demureness that was simultaneously coded as sexually attractive" (Keen 2002, 211) even if worn by a girl Irene's age.

In intention and intellect, the two Irenes challenge the two Sherlock Holmes. Here, Irene Doyle's father has taught her to be independent, live in a house that does things differently—no servants, no governess—than most families, and become "a strong, unique woman with a social conscience, and unusual, even unladylike ambition" (Peacock 2007, 74). Irene's ability to limn that "she shouldn't try to comprehend this remarkable boy, that that is the way to be his friend" and that "One understands him by not understanding, by trusting his mind" (128) is what makes them an unusual pair. In Conan Doyle's Irene Adler, the adventuress contralto who has sung at La Scala with a "soul of steel. She has the face of the most beautiful of women, and the mind of the most resolute of men" (2009b [1891], 166). The interested and knowing reader connects to the possible foreshadowing of who Irene Doyle might become. Like the original Irene Adler, Irene Doyle approaches "matters differently than [her] male counterparts because of a delineation of the sexes pervasive during the Victorian period" (Nolan 2020, 137) which was founded on the dichotomy of the active male and the passive female.[11] After her father's death, Irene Doyle is taken in by Jewish family and then given the name of which she is proud: Miss Irene Adler.

Another Woman? Enola Who?

Unlike the Young Sherlock Holmes series, the Enola Holmes films encountered a great deal of resistance; according to the Conan Doyle Estate, while "we welcome and support brilliant creative projects like Enola Holmes, mutual respect for copyrights is foundational to fostering creativity. Conan Doyle's ten copyrighted stories contain significant new artistic material about Sherlock Holmes, taking the character in a major new direction" (2020, n.p.). Their objection was to the portrayal of emotion in Holmes' character which does not occur until the end of the stories which are still under copyright. The odd point is that it was not the creation of an entirely new character—a sister!—to which they took exception.

As to why the recreation of the Holmes brothers, Sherlock and Mycroft, often includes the creation of a younger sister or a younger relation, is paralleled in adult fiction with the creation of a younger wife, a sister, or a woman who pretends to be the great detective.[12] One such engaging revision of the Sherlock Holmes has recently appeared in the Netflix film world so voraciously watched by Gen Z. *Enola Holmes* and *Enola Holmes 2* follow the desire of the young sister of the two elder Holmes to break out of the conventional life dictated for her by society and by brothers. Those two films are based on the ongoing neo-Victorian young adult series by Nancy Springer that spans from July 1888 to 1889 in London, "both splendid and gritty, heading toward an uncertain new century" (Solimini 2020, 41). Encouraged by an agent who wanted her "to do something that is set in darkest London at the end of the 19th century in the time of Jack the Ripper" (41), Springer began to think of what might have happened had Sherlock had a sister, reminiscent of the question first asked by Virginia Woolf of William Shakespeare's imagined sister in *A Room of One's Own* (1929).[13]

Springer emphasises the eclecticism of the family that produced Sherlock is now exposed to the reader in the raising of Enola. The series opens on Enola Holmes' fourteenth birthday; the narrative is a female *bildungsroman*, a first-person narrative of the difficulty of a girl-child growing up in the Holmes family; of course, the canonical Holmes stories contain no such sister.[14] The reader's initial encounter with Sherlock and Mycroft Holmes is at a train station, a transitional space, signifying the moment of change for their family. The men's material presentation makes clear their differences from their young sister. Usually Enola happily wears a "shirt and knickerbockers, comfortable clothing that had previously belonged" to the brothers and she constantly goes without a hat (8). Deborah Epstein Nord's insight, that this "kind of Gender disguise might provide an exhilarating sense of invisibility, interrupt the circuit of objectification, and deflect the attention habitually attracted by the lone female in a public place" (1995, 241), is—along with pure comfort—most likely why Enola dresses in this manner.

Even though Enola makes an effort to wear a dress—too long, too big—to meet her brothers, her attempt at socially acceptable behaviour is immediately crushed. They immediately comment on her lack of hat which leads to hair like "a jackdaw's nest" (Springer 2007, 33). In contrast, the brothers wore conventional gentlemen's attire of "dark tweed suits with braid edging, soft ties, bowler hats. And kid gloves. Only gentry wore gloves at the height of summer"; while Mycroft is "a bit stout, showing an expanse of silk waistcoat," Sherlock "stood straight as a rake and lean as a greyhound" (31). Enola reads the socially determined class superiority of their clothing and admits "I had no difficulty recognising two tall male Londoners who had to be my brothers" (31) even if she goes initially unrecognised by them. This moment exemplifies how, in Victorian literature, there is often a "lack of an obvious social space" for a young girl, which produces a "strain" or "complication" in that "a girl who has left the schoolroom lacks a clear location in her home or out of it" (Bilston

2004, 1–2). Here, the neo-Victorian girl has, apparently, not even been educated in social graces; appalled by her personal appearance and her appearance without a chaperone or brougham, they speak of her but not to her; Mycroft declares he has been paying for a seamstress and Holmes is appalled, noting, "You should have been in long skirts since you were twelve" (34), to both men a shocking breach of society protocols for a maturing young woman.

It is August of 1888; Enola's mother—their mother—has gone missing. Enola's *Bildüngsroman* is also the story of the struggle of her mother, Eudoria, who is a woman ahead of her time. Born when her mother was fifty, Enola believes she is her family's scandal, a burden, and a disgrace for having been "born indecently late" (10) to Eudoria. Born to "a gentleman Rationalist logician and his well-bred artistic wife," Enola intuits she keeps the "eyebrow-raisers" in society busy with their gossip (17). Raised by her mother—their mother—Enola feels "She does not belong here. The knowledge does not trouble her, for she has never belonged anywhere. And in a sense, she has always been alone" (3); indeed, her name reversed is "alone." Eudoria, fond of ciphers, constantly reminds her daughter, "You will do very well on your own, Enola" (5), and does not encourage Enola to have any connection with the brothers. Enola is encouraged to read books of logic, of political economy by Thomas Malthus, and evolutionary theory by Charles Darwin; she learns to ride a bicycle, and like her Mum, be "very much a free thinker, a woman of character, a proponent of female suffrage and dress reform" (21).

When Eudoria goes missing, Enola reaches out to Mycroft and Holmes, but their arrival brings consternation over questions of money and upbringing. Mycroft has sent money to his mother for staff and education that does not exist, suggesting Eudoria has used the money for other nefarious purposes. When her husband had died, a fight ensued over Eudoria's desire for independence, both financial and in the raising of Enola, resulting in the ten-year breach. When she disappears, Mycroft makes it horrifically clear that "legally [he] hold[s] complete charge over" both his own mother and his sister. He can "take whatever other measures are necessary in order to achieve" their compliance with convention because he "bear[s] a moral responsibility" for them (Springer 2007, 69). He is, in effect, his mother's keeper.

Enola's deductive skills are sharp and give her a sense of agency as a young woman on her own; rather than a Victorian waiting woman, Enola becomes a neo-Victorian woman of action. Using all of her senses and abilities, she attempts to track her mother to London beginning in her bedroom where Enola decodes ciphers left for her as presents. The use of encoding for messages and agony columns became a means of secrecy. According to Simon Singh, in the Victorian age as

> people became comfortable with encipherment, they began to express their cryptographic skills in a variety of ways. For example, young lovers in Victorian England were often forbidden from publicly expressing their affection, and could not even communicate by letter in case their parents intercepted and read the contents. This resulted in lovers sending encrypted messages to each other via the personal columns of newspapers. These "agony columns," as they became known, provoked the curiosity of cryptanalysts, who would scan the notes and try to decipher the titillating contents. (Singh 2000, 79–80)[15]

To have Eudoria create encrypted texts, with Enola capable of decyphering them, demonstrates significant intellectual ability, but also foregrounds the need for hiding women's abilities and concerns behind coded language.

Springer has declared, "Conan Doyle did me a tremendous favor by being a misogynist" because "Sherlock's weakness is that he doesn't pay attention to women whatsoever, so Enola can run circles around him simply by knowing all the feminine specialties and also how much one can stuff into a corset" (Springer quoted in Solimini 2020, 42). Springer's creation of a neo-Victorian sibling for the Holmes brothers allows the narrative to lean into femininity as a mode of performance that can be a form of subterfuge and transgression. To be "a woman—even now, but more so then—meant to stick on a whole bunch of stuff, simply add a great deal of surplusage" (Springer quoted in Solimini 42). Enola's need for pragmatic solutions leads her to adapt her mother's secret bustle and corset pouches for carrying valuables. Eudoria has left her home and her family with a purpose: to be free of constraint. Amy L. Montz writes that such "a fascination with the corset not for its erotic connotations ... but rather for what the contemporary audience believes that the corset represents to Victorian girls; propriety, constraint, and femininity" (2019, 89). Both Eudoria and Enola repurpose the corset to achieve their own ability to throw off social constraint, and in doing so, the "new ways of thinking about the corset become subversive, a reimagining of what it could represent beyond the confinement with which it is so often associated" (91).

It is Enola who decodes her mother's messages through flower meanings and ciphers. Eudoria had "felt trapped" and "had felt the injustice of her situation just as keenly. She had been forced to obey. ... She had wanted to rebel. ... In the end, she had managed it. Glorious rebellion" (72). To gain her independence, she had to leave, keeping in touch with Enola via encoded messages in the newspaper like

> Iris tipstails to Ivy
> ABOMNITEUNTNYHYATEUASRMLNRSML
> OIGNHSNOOLCRSNHMMLOABIGOE

If read in the manner of a meandering ivy, then it becomes
> BLOOMING IN THE SUN. NOT ONLY
> CHRYSANTHEMUM, ALSO
> RAMBLING ROSE. (212)

Through the mother and daughter's shared language of flowers and their intelligent encoding, Enola is comforted that her mother is now "a contented woman who is wandering, free, in a place where there are no hairpins, no corsets, no dress improvers: with the Gypsies on the moors" (212–13). The increasing maturity of Enola allows for a reinterpretation of her mother's actions as necessary, not negligent.

The continuing recurrence of the corset trope—as a physical marker of the constraint of women[16]—in neo-Victorian young adult literature is, in this series, not merely griped about by the protagonist, but female gadgetry and fakery is both exposed and used for pragmatic purposes by Enola. She later articulates what many Victorian women must have felt, that "To be a woman, all that was necessary was to put on false hair, various Patent Amplifiers, Enhancers, Improvers, and Regulators, and the necessary concealments: dress, hat, gloves" (195), conventional expectations of a well-raised woman that has, to the neo-Victorian mind, nothing to recommend it. At the very least, the contradictory impulses to both provoke the male gaze with enhancements of some attributes and then obscure others with coverings seemingly exemplify the confusion over a young woman's sexual nature, just as inadequately understood by men as is a woman's ability to think.

The Holmes brothers' acerbic comments on women represent their male, patriarchal sense of entitlement, and why Eudoria may have chosen to mislead the siblings in order to escape further control. For the Victorian Holmes, women "were admirable things for the observer—excellent for drawing the veil from men's motives and actions. But for the trained reasoner to admit such intrusions into his own delicate and finely adjusted temperament was to introduce a distracting factor which might throw a doubt upon all his mental results" (Conan Doyle 2009b [1891], 161). Springer is more direct in revealing the men's patronising, derogatory views of their own mother as an exemplar of her sex. Holmes thinks the mess of her room "could reflect the innate untidiness of a woman's mind" while Mycroft believes their mother has "progressed from oddness to senile dementia" (43). As the elder, indeed the patriarch of the Holmes clan, Mycroft feels responsible, and that the whole mess is his "fault. There's no trusting a woman; why make an exception for one's mother?" (46). Rather than empathising with Enola, and remembering her age, Holmes dismisses her intellect to Mycroft with "Pity the girl's cranial capacity" (49) on more than one occasion. Mrs. Lane, the housekeeper, overhears the boys she has known since they were children and sees their misogynistic opinions clearly. She speaks to the floor as she scrubs, aware of her role and of propriety, but she sniffs, "Small wonder they're bachelors. Must have everything their way. Think it's their right. Never could abide a strong-minded woman" (42).

Although Sherlock's burden of mind is exposed in retrospective moments where Enola admits, as a teenager, she "did not know then, had no way of knowing that Sherlock Holmes lived his life in a kind of chill shadow. He suffered from melancholia, the fits sometimes coming upon him so badly that for a week or more he would refuse to rise from his bed" (41). For Holmes to suffer from such culturally ascribed "feminine" weaknesses would be contrary to the robust masculinity espoused by Conan Doyle but, more directly, to the social expectations to which the Holmes' family must adhere as constituents of the Empirical Victorian family. Their entrenchment in society is exemplified by Sherlock as a consulting detective who provides the reassertion of cultural boundaries when he eliminates the deviant criminal from society, and by Mycroft, the shadow operator of various conservative and liberal governments who keeps scandal as well as danger at bay from Queen Victoria, her country, and her citizens.

Springer's neo-Victorian look at the Holmes canon is making a conscious intervention to provide female voices in a highly masculine, patriarchal, and Empirical Victorian story cycle. The Enola Holmes coquel series is a female *Bildüngsroman* in progress, insuring room for future progress in the following novels. Enola does not desire to be like her brothers;

rather, she asserts "*I* was a perditorian. Or I would be. ... The world first professional, logical, scientific perditorian. All in one gasping breath of inspiration, I knew this as surely as I knew my real name was Holmes. ... Let my brother be The World's Only Private Consulting Detective all he liked; I would be The World's Only Private Consulting Perditorian" (120–21; emphasis in original).

Enola's growing awareness of her difference leads to a refusal to limit herself by the comparison. Once in London, she revisits how six weeks previous, she had "made a mental list of [her] talents, comparing them unfavorably with his" (208). Now, Enola confidence brims over with "I found myself compiling in my mind a different list of my talents and abilities. I knew things Sherlock Holmes failed even to imagine" (208) including the significance of a bustle and a tall hat, ladies' underpinnings and adornments, disguise, encoded messages in flowers. Indeed, while Enola's brother "dismissed 'the fair sex' as irrational and insignificant" she asserts both emotional maturity and social awareness because, she says, "I knew of matters his 'logical' mind could never grasp. I knew an entire world of communications belonging to women, secret codes of hat brims and rebellion, handkerchiefs and subterfuge, feather fans and covert defiance" in a "cloak of ladylike conspiracy" (208–9) in which she could wrap herself in for a successful and politically aware life.[17]

To do so, Enola manipulates society. To be a good detective, Victorian or otherwise, one must have individual autonomy and be socially mobile but it involves the need for movement and re-presentation of one's self and the persona required. Like in Victorian fiction, the detective must "possess the ability to interact and move seamlessly among varying classes through atypical modes in order to collect evidence" (Nolan 136). Men can move in a sanctioned manner to do so, but in neo-Victorian detective fiction, women "freely interact with individuals of all social classes and take on roles outside their expected domestic duties ... despite the unlikeliness of such a favourability in the real world or even the literature" of the Victorian age (Nolan 136). Neo-Victorian young adult literature, however, is an early means to bring issues of social justice to a younger audience; it can provide a vehicle to consider the "thornier problems of the Victorian, modern, and postmodern eras, including gender roles and privileges, racial prejudice and the formation of racial consciousness, the significance and morality of wealth and capital, and the conflicting demands of privacy and social control" (Nickerson 1997, 744).

Turning to an alias, Enola Holmes becomes "Ivy Meschle," the ever prompt, modest, and capable secretary to "Dr. Leslie T. Ragostin," an unseen "Consulting Scientific Perditorian" in a "well-to-do neighbourhood" (Springer 2007, 211) of London. Enola knows that, for reputational authority and social credibility, a "scientist must of course be a man, and an important one, quite busy at the University or the British Museum" (211); consequently, Enola creates her alternate transgressive persona by the end of *The Missing Marquess* in order to pursue her chosen career.

Narratives of Sherlock Holmes as a non-normative, brilliant young person as well as his fictional and textual relation to the Conan Doylean intelligent and feisty offspring of Springer move the progression of postmodern considerations of Victorian expectations in an exciting direction, from rigid conservatism to an interesting place for the discussion of anti-Semitism, misogyny, and adolescence. From this point, other neo-Victorian young adult texts will be considered for how they provide a safe space for transgression in alternate readings of gender, as well as sexuality, for young women who are developing their own relationship to culture and society.

Notes

1. For a strong discussion of one such connection of interest here, see Lucy Andrew (2012).
2. Excluded from discussion here are Brittany Cavallaro's *A Study in Charlotte* and ensuing series which makes, perhaps, the most direct attempt to lure the twenty-first-century young adult audience by creating a neo-Victorian narrative that contains the duo of Charlotte Holmes and Jamie Watson, the great-great-great grandchildren of the Victorian sleuth and his friend, who attend a boarding school in Connecticut, a clear attempt to woo an American audience for the works. Another series beginning with *Lock & Mori* (2015) by Heather W. Petty have high-schoolers Sherlock Holmes and Miss James "Mori" Moriarty meet, fall in love, then become enemies. Neither author attempts a self-conscious neo-Victorian narrative even though they intentionally invoke Conan Doyle with the premise of their novels and the names of their characters.
3. Zelijka Flegar makes an interesting observation, that such films have "rendered famous literary protagonists as superheroes or, in the case of famous detectives, super-sleuths" (2022, n.p.).
4. Sann Nyqvist makes a useful distinction with corrective pastiches as those which "return to the world of the originals in order to account for the

inconsistencies and mistakes in the originals" (2017, 2.3) and complementary pastiches as those which "continue[ ] the original series in a straightforward manner" (2.4).
5. See Gardner (2020) or the complaint itself at https://www.documentcloud.org/documents/6956021-Sherlock.html. The Conan Doyle Estate and Netflix agreed to jointly dismiss the suit later in 2020.
6. Unlike in neo-Victorian fiction, Victorian female counterparts may use disguise but it is "a tactic reserved primarily for the lower-class women … as it would be frowned upon for a woman of the gentry to position herself as anything else" (Nolan 143) as a means of detection in the nineteenth-century fiction.
7. In *A Study in Scarlet*, Holmes remarks on his memory,

> I consider that a man's brain originally is like a little empty attic, and you have to stock it with such furniture as you choose. A fool takes in all the lumber of every sort that he comes across, so that the knowledge which might be useful to him gets crowded out, or at best is jumbled up with a lot of other things, so that he has a difficulty in laying his hands upon it. Now the skillful workman is very careful indeed as to what he takes into his brain-attic. He will have nothing but the tools which may help him in doing his work, but of these he has a large assortment, and all in the most perfect order. It is a mistake to think that that little room has elastic walls and can distend to any extent. Depend upon it there comes a time when for every addition of knowledge you forget something that you knew before. It is of the highest importance, therefore, not to have useless facts elbowing out the useful ones. (2009a [1887], 21)

8. Dominic Cheetham (2012) details the many versions, and for an interesting representation on screen, see the only season (eight episodes) of the Netflix creation, *The Irregulars* (2021).
9. In the Conan Doyle canon, Holmes' parents are without names.
10. The names of this character are significant; Jonathan Bell was the Scottish surgeon upon whom Sir Arthur Conan Doyle based the character of Sherlock Holmes. Several such connections via intertextual and metatextual elements are made in the series.
11. For an excellent discussion of how John Ruskin's theories on the sexes (1865) are interpolated in Victorian detective fiction, see Meghan P. Nolan (2020).
12. For novels, amongst others, see Mary Russell in the Russell and Holmes mysteries beginning with *The Beekeeper's Apprentice* (1994) by Laurie King, and Charlotte Holmes in the Lady Sherlock series beginning with *A Study in Scarlet Women* (2016) by Sherry Thomas; transmedia adaptations

include Eurus Holmes in *Sherlock*, and in *Elementary*, John Watson is now Joan Watson, and James Moriarty is now Holmes' past lover, Jamie Moriarty who has gone by the alias, Irene. The role of Irene Adler is vastly expanded in the films *Sherlock* and *Sherlock: Game of Shadows* where she is both past lover of Sherlock and unwilling cooperator of Moriarty, but the intent is neo-Victorian revision, not authenticity. In an interesting acknowledgement of the neo-Victorianism of her books, King has commented more directly, "Seventeen books later, I have learned a great deal about Russell, Holmes, and their world. I have learned even more about myself and my world, since a central *raison d'etre* of reading history, even fictional history, is that it is a mirror, reflecting unexpected sides of our times and ourselves" including "Politics, women's rights, religious expression, [and] governmental oppression" (n.p.).

13. Erin Temple also makes this point in her discussion of direct address and girl power in *Enola Holmes* (2021, 30).
14. The BBC *Sherlock* does include a mysterious sister, Eurus, who is one year younger than Sherlock, eight years younger than Mycroft, but who is—or is believed to be—locked away from the world due to psychosis and her psychopathic tendencies. The viewer is later shown that Eurus is a genius with an intellect agreed to be even higher functioning than her brothers.
15. As a point of note, Singh's bestseller was later adapted for a young adult audience (2000).
16. The corset is also adapted into a kind of weaponry or defence in texts not discussed here. For example, Enola finds the corset keeps her from harm, and see *The Girl in the Steel Corset* in The Steampunk Chronicles series (2011–14) by Kady Cross. For an excellent, extended discussion of the corset in such works, see Amy Montz (2019).
17. Just as Peacock has Holmes learn "Bellitsu," it would be thought provoking to see if Springer might have envisioned Enola learning "Suffrajitsu" from Eudoria, the Suffrage version of martial arts self-defence, had the story occurred in the 1910s (see Ruz and Parkinson 2015, n.p.).

Bibliography

Andrew, Lucy. "'Away with dark shadders!' Juvenile Detection Versus Juvenile Crime in *The Boy Detective; or, The Crimes of London. A Romance of Modern Times.*" *CLUES: A Journal of Detection*. 30, no. 1 (Spring 2012): 18–29.

Billman, Carol. "The Child Reader as Sleuth." *Children's Literature and Education*. 15, no. 1 (Spring 1984): 30–41.

Bilston, Sarah. *The Awkward Age in Women's Popular Fiction 1850–1900*. Oxford: Clarendon Press, 2004.

Cavallaro, Brittany. *A Study in Charlotte*. London: Katherine Tegen Books, 2016.

Cheetham, Dominic. "Middle-Class Victorian Street Arabs: Modern Re-creations of the Baker Street Irregulars." *International Research in Children's Literature*. 5, no. 1 (2012): 36–50.

Conan Doyle Estate. "Enola Holmes." June 26, 2020. https://conandoyleestate.com/news/enola-holmes

Conan Doyle Estate. "Cover Reveal! The Improbable Tales of Baskerville Hall." February 14, 2023: n.p. https://conandoyleestate.com/news/cover-reveal-the-improbable-tales-of-baskerville-hall

Conan Doyle, Sir Arthur. *A Study in Scarlet*. 1887. In *The Penguin Complete Sherlock Holmes*. Foreword by Ruth Rendell, 14–86. New York: Penguin Books, 2009a.

Conan Doyle, Sir Arthur. "A Scandal in Bohemia." 1891. In *The Penguin Complete Sherlock Holmes*. Foreword by Ruth Rendell, 161–75. New York: Penguin Books, 2009b.

Dyhouse, Carol. *Girls Growing Up in Late Victorian and Edwardian England*. London: Routledge, 2013.

Elementary. Hill of Beans Productions, Timberman-Beverly Productions, CBS Television Studios. 2012–19.

Enola Holmes. Legendary Pictures, PCMA Productions, 2020.

Enola Holmes 2. Legendary Pictures, PCMA Productions, 2022.

Flegar, Zeljka. "Mediating Girl Power: A Cognitive Approach to *Enola Holmes* on Page and Screen." *Children's Literature in Education*. (2022): n.p. https://link.springer.com/article/10.1007/s10583-022-09506-8

Gardner, Eriq. "Conan Doyle Estate Sues Netflix Over Coming Movie About Sherlock Holmes' Sister." *The Hollywood Reporter*. June 24, 2020. https://www.hollywoodreporter.com/business/business-news/conan-doyle-estate-sues-netflix-coming-movie-sherlock-holmes-sister-1300108/

Gleeson, Colleen. *Clockwork Scarab*. San Francisco: Chronicle Books, 2013.

Guest, Kristen. "Norbu's *The Mandala of Sherlock Holmes:* Neo-Victorian Occupations of the Past." 3, no. 2 (2010): 73–95.

Hadley, Louise. *Neo-Victorian Fiction and Historical Narrative*. London: Palgrave Macmillan, 2010.

Johnson, George. "Jewish Word/Sechel." *Moment*. Nov–Dec 2013: n.p. https://momentmag.com/jewish-word-sechel/

Keen, Suzanne. "Quaker Dress, Sexuality, and the Domestication of Reform in the Victorian Novel." *Victorian Literature and Culture*. 30, no. 1 (2002): 211–36.

King, Laurie. *The Beekeeper's Apprentice*. New York: St. Martin's Press, 1994.

Lane, Andrew. *Young Sherlock: Red Leech*. London: Macmillan, 2010a.

Lane, Andrew. *Young Sherlock: Death Cloud*. London: Macmillan, 2010b.

Lane, Andrew. *Young Sherlock: Fire Storm*. London: Macmillan, 2011a.

Lane, Andrew. *Young Sherlock: Black Ice*. London: Macmillan, 2011b.

Lane, Andrew. *Young Sherlock: Snake Bite*. London: Macmillan, 2012.

Lane, Andrew. *Young Sherlock: Knife Edge*. London: Macmillan, 2013.
Lane, Andrew. *Young Sherlock: Stone Cold*. London: Macmillan, 2014.
Lane, Andrew. *Young Sherlock: Night Break*. London: Macmillan, 2015.
Lane, Andrew. "Young Sherlock Faces His Deadliest Case Yet: Q & A with Andy" *Young Sherlock Holmes*. n.d. https://web.archive.org/web/20120322124624/http://www.youngsherlock.com/uncategorized/qa-with-andy/
Lee, Y. S. *Spy in the House*. Somerville: Candlewick, 2010.
Liebovitz, Liel. "The Jewish Sherlock Holmes." *Tablet*. September 27, 2012: n.p. https://www.tabletmag.com/sections/arts-letters/articles/the-jewish-sherlock-holmes
Mandel, Ernest. *Delightful Murder: A Social History of the Crime Story*. London: Pluto Press, 1984.
Montz, Amy. "Unbinding the Victorian Girl: Corsetry and Neo-Victorian Young Adult Literature." *Children's Literature Association Quarterly*, 44, no. 1 (Spring 2019): 88–101.
Nickerson, Catherine. "Murder as Social Criticism." *American Literary History*, 9, no. 4 (1997): 744–57.
Nolan, Meghan P. "The Socially Mobile Female in Victorian and Neo-Victorian Mysteries." In *Transnational Crime Fiction*, edited by M. Piipponen et al., 135–51. London: Palgrave Macmillan, 2020.
Nord, Deborah Epstein. *Walking the Victorian Streets: Women, Representation, and the City*. Ithaca: Cornell University Press, 1995.
Nyqvist, Sanna. "Authorship and Authenticity in Sherlock Holmes Pastiches." In *Sherlock Holmes Fandom, Sherlockiana, and the Great Game* edited by Betsy Rosenblatt and Roberta Pearson, special issue of *Transformative Works and Cultures*, no. 23 (2017): n.p. https://journal.transformativeworks.org/index.php/twc/article/view/834
Peacock, Shane. *Eye of the Crow*. New York: Tundra, 2007.
Peacock, Shane. *Death in the Air*. New York: Tundra, 2008a.
Peacock, Shane. "The Creation of The Boy Sherlock Holmes." *The Baker Street Journal*. 58, no. 4 (2008b): 17–21.
Peacock, Shane. *The Secret Fiend*. New York: Tundra, 2010a.
Peacock, Shane. *Vanishing Girl*. New York: Tundra, 2010b.
Peacock, Shane. *The Dragon Turn*. New York: Tundra, 2011.
Peacock, Shane. *Becoming Holmes*. New York: Tundra, 2012.
Petty, Heather W. *Lock & Mori*. New York: Simon and Schuster, 2015.
Priestman, Martin. *Detective Fiction and Literature: The Figure on the Carpet*. London: Macmillan, 1990.
Pullmann, Philip. *Ruby in the Smoke*. London: Oxford University Press, 1985.
Ritter, William. *Jackaby*. Markham: Thomas Allen & Son, 2014.
Ruskin, John. "Of Queen's Gardens." *Sesames and Lilies*. London: Smith, Elder, & Co., 1865.

Ruz, Camila and Justin Parkinson. "'Suffrajitsu': How the Suffragettes Fought Back Using Martial Arts." *BBC Magazine*. October 5, 2015: n.p. https://www.bbc.com/news/magazine-34425615
Sherlock. Hartswood Films, BBC Wales, WGBH. 2010–17.
Sherlock Holmes. Silver Pictures, Wilgram Productions, Village Roadshow Pictures, 2009.
Sherlock Holmes: Game of Shadows. Village Roadshow Pictures, Silver Pictures, Wigram Productions, 2011.
Singh, Simon. *The Code Book: The Science of Secrecy from Ancient Egypt to Quantum Cryptography*. New York: Anchor, 2000.
Solimini, Cheryl. "Sherlock Holmes' Smarter Sister." *Mystery Scene*. 116 (Fall 2020): 40–3.
Springer, Nancy. *The Case of the Missing Marquess: An Enola Holmes Mystery*. Toronto: Puffin, 2006.
Springer, Nancy. *The Case of the Left-Handed Lady*. Toronto: Puffin, 2007.
Springer, Nancy. *The Case of the Bizarre Bouquet*. Toronto: Puffin, 2008a.
Springer, Nancy. *The Case of the Peculiar Pink Fan*. Toronto: Puffin, 2008b.
Springer, Nancy. *The Case of the Cryptic Crinoline*. Toronto: Puffin, 2009.
Springer, Nancy. *The Case of the Gypsy Goodbye*. Toronto: Puffin, 2010.
Springer, Nancy. *Enola Holmes and the Black Barouche*. Toronto: Puffin, 2021a.
Springer, Nancy. *Enola Holmes and the Boy in Buttons*. Toronto: Puffin, 2021b.
Springer, Nancy. *Enola Holmes and the Elegant Escapade*. Toronto: Puffin, 2022.
Temple, Erin, "In Conversation with *Enola Holmes*: Neo-Victorian Girlhood, Adaptation, and Direct Address." *Victorians Institute Journal* 48 (2021): 24–42.
The Irregulars. Drama Republic, Netflix, 2021.
Thomas, Sherry. *A Study in Scarlet Women*. New York: Berkley Books, 2016.
Ue, Tom. "The Boy Wonder: Interview with Shane Peacock." *The Baker Street Journal: An Irregular Quarterly of Sherlockiana*. 60, no. 3 (2010): 33–40.
Wahrman, Noa Paz. "Becoming Holmes: The Boy Sherlock Holmes, His Final Case." *Jewish Book Council*. May 29, 2013. https://www.jewishbookcouncil.org/book/becoming-holmes-the-boy-sherlock-holmes-his-final-case
Woolf, Virginia. *A Room of One's Own*. London: Hogarth Press, 1929.

CHAPTER 7

The Mis(s) Education of Young Women

The genre of boarding-school books like Sarah Fielding's *The Governess; or the Little Female Academy* (1749), or the later Thomas Hughes' *Tom Brown's Schooldays* (1857), continues into the present day with private school paranormals, study abroad novels, haunted boarding school narratives, and others, a lineage that demonstrates an ongoing interest in both the development of education and the *Bildüngsroman* of young people in particular cultural moments. The move from child to tween to teenager and young adult might be what is now considered to be the normal progression of psychological and physical development for women, but any discussion of the same-age girl-child to young woman in the Victorian age must be contextualised differently. Carol Dyhouse traces the socialisation of British girls into the Victorian ideal of womanhood "Represented economic and intellectual dependence; its prescribed service and self-sacrifice as quintessential forms of 'womanly' behaviour" (2013, 2). From a young age, girls were "encouraged to suppress (or conceal) ambition, intellectual courage, or initiative—any desire for power or independence" which often produced "guilt and/or ambivalence which many strong intelligent women wrestled with in the attempt to reconcile their drives with what they had been taught to perceive as their 'feminine' social identity" (2).

The unconventional young women of neo-Victorian fiction embody uncomfortable social issues and/or political interests of unheard voices of the Victorian past, and Samantha J. Carroll argues that aside from being a way into the past of the Victorians, "neo-Victorian fiction's representation of the Victorian past is also the lens through which a variety of present concerns are examined" (2010, 180). Strategies of resistance—to social compliance when convention directly contrasts with personal fulfilment, personal safety when familial structures break down, and sexual preference when in contrast to heteronormative assumptions—that would have been silenced may, a century later, be explored. The neo-Victorian project takes as part of its mandate the "recovery of historically marginalized viewpoints" with an "ethical agenda of retrospective liberationist politics and witness-bearing to forms of historical oppression and un(der)acknowledged suffering" (Kohlke 2018a, 185).

In narratives like Libba Bray's *A Great and Terrible Beauty* (2003), *Rebel Angels* (2005), and *The Sweet, Far Thing* (2007), four girls of differing circumstances offer the reader an opportunity to rethink how "characters on the margins of a culture or society can offer positions from which to interrogate the social and cultural boundaries which limit subjectivity, and hence question dominant social and cultural paradigms of identity formation" (McCallum 1999, 118). In this case, there is an argument to be made for neo-Victorian narratives which foreground and grapple with various girl cultures[1] and girlhoods past and present, one of which is non-normative sexual interest. Sonya Sawyer Fritz makes an excellent case regarding the participation of Bray's Gemma Doyle trilogy and Nancy Springer's Enola Holmes series in "postmodern discourses on girlhood in order to address issues and develop themes that are pertinent to twenty-first-century girl readers" (2012, 39–40). Fritz argues the "construction of late-Victorian girlhood for its contemporary readers as, more than anything, a careful performance, a matter of maintaining a façade to hide one's true self from others" which creates "the trope of the Victorian girl's double-life" (39) central to the series. Such a reading is fruitful, but negates the ability of the character to become a coherent subject, instead relying on fragmentation and appropriate performance(s) to convince others of her persona rather than her authentic self. In the Bray series, the girls only become young women once they are aware of the conventions into which they have been educated but are willing to take risks to live authentic lives.

Abuse/MisEducation

While mindful that "tinges of twenty-first-century fantasies of defiance tend to invade" (Heath 2020, 83) in some neo-Victorian texts and with the modern desires of liberal readers, the characters in Bray's trilogy find that a young woman's ambiguous status—class, sexuality, intellect—invites a chance for subversion and agentic development.

From the early years the trajectories of Victorian girl children's lives were strongly prescribed. Girls were "taught that deference towards brothers was part of the natural order of things" and that they must "curb their spirits" because "natural exuberance" in a boy approaching puberty was "'hoydenish behaviour' in a girl" (Dyhouse 12). Society defined "maturity for men in terms of economic and occupational independence and actively discourages women from achieving economic independence *is* effectively condemning women to a permanently 'adolescent' state" (118; emphasis in original). Although boys and young men enjoyed some leeway to grow socially and intellectually into young men, girls, and young women "were much less likely than their brothers to have been allowed a period of legitimate freedom, however transitory, removed from adult surveillance and unencumbered by responsibility" (119).

Denied the path of young men to be fully educated and equal freedom to explore life, the expectation of a middle- to upper-class young woman was that she would strive to embody the idealised domestic feminine. Coventry Patmore's poem *The Angel in the House* (1854–62) outlines the virtues of his own wife; the "Angel" became emblematic of how a woman should fill her role in society as helpmate to her husband.[2] John Ruskin, in his volume, *Sesames and Lilies*, elucidates patriarchal culture's idealised aspirational characteristics for each sex.

> Now their separate characters are briefly these. The man's power is active, progressive, defensive. He is eminently the doer, the creator, the discoverer, the defender. His intellect is for speculation and invention; his energy for adventure, for war, and for conquest, ... woman's power is for rule, not for battle, and her intellect is not for invention or creation, but for sweet ordering, arrangement, and decision. She sees the qualities of things, their claims, and their places. Her great function is Praise: she enters into no contest, but infallibly adjudges the crown of contest. By her office, and place, she is protected from all danger and temptation. (1865, 146–7)

To assume these traits are innate is, from a twenty-first-century perspective, flawed, but such delineation of character traits and appropriate behaviour was a central convention of the production of embodied states of being within the heteronormative Victorian age. According to Lydia Vallone and Claudia Nelson, following these understandings for society "The Girl existed as raw potential, for she could embody either virtue (as wife/mother or spinster/sister) or a kind of depraved independence and sexual freedom (as 'fast girl' or 'New Woman')" (1994, 3). The expectation was that a girl would follow the first path, not the second; those girls who became women of the second order were thought to be unsexed viragos.[3] Girls might have been encouraged to have female friendships, but ideas of same-sex desire were not a part of that social progress.

The relevance to the past to the present, the relationship of the Victorian to the neo-Victorian, "can give us a clearer understanding of the origins of our present problems, showing how our tangles over education and class, gender and religion took root in the first place" (Birch 2008, 144) and how these considerations discussed in the neo-Victorian project might suggest ways to disentangle the past in order to improve the future. Presentism tugs the reader towards a feminist reading that would have left room for alternate representations of young women who may be trapped by situations beyond their control. Chandra Power defines presentism in two ways as it relates to historical fiction, particularly for young people; first, there is "writerly presentism, i.e., the imposition of a writer's modern values, beliefs, or awareness onto a past era" and second, there is "readerly presentism, i.e., the imposition of a reader's modern values, beliefs, or awarenesses onto a past era" (2003, 425). Neo-Victorian writing, which is both historical and is intended to be self-aware of such dynamics, must be particularly careful in locating and understanding where "projecting our ideas into the past" (Fisher 1970, 315) can be problematic even if tempting. Marie-Luise Kohlke such a desire is inevitable because "neo-Victorian works in particular are inherently presentist: they are grounded in the contemporary contexts of their production and recreate the past with historical hindsight that is part of the present's purview" (2018b, 389).

From early to mid-century, it would be unlikely that a girl-child, or a young woman, or even a grown woman, would completely reject "the understanding about femininity and the patterns of relationship between men and women learned in the family"; it would have been far more likely that women might be "consciously or unconsciously ambivalent" (Dyhouse 35) regarding society's expectations of women's passivity and/

or lack of imagination or ambition. Women who "stepped aside from convention and carved out careers for themselves outside the home—particularly those who became feminist—illustrate these conflicts in their attitudes and personalities, sometimes in an acute form" (35). In Bray's neo-Victorian young adult narratives, this potential ambivalence is pointed to and challenged by youthful protagonists Gemma Doyle, Felicity Worthington, Ann Bradshaw, and Pippa Cross who suffer from and see the dangers of patriarchal repression as well as of a male-only perspective on important issues like education, class, and abuse.

Schooling a Young Woman

Bray's trilogy of novels rests on the premise of the bildungsroman; however, unlike Victorian coming-of-age stories, these characters problematise the expected "becoming" of an individual if the outcome is predetermined by sex, age, and education. Eimear McBride's title, *A Girl is a Half-Formed Thing* (2013)—although neither neo-Victorian nor considered here—is a phrase that reflects the lot of many female individuals in Victorian fiction. Most novels of the long nineteenth century focused on male protagonists; the difficulty is that "Conventions dictate that a male *bildungsroman* is a conservative projection of the boy-child into male adulthood, following the necessary steps for education, growth and citizenry. For a girl-child to take that same path would, in fact, be extraordinarily progressive, and be an invitation to personal development beyond social accomplishments and wifehood, both of which—to some extent—framed the life of the real Victorian woman" (Maier 2007, 319). These neo-Victorian narratives consider what a young woman could achieve if fully formed, or at least given the option to pursue self-fulfilment. The difficulty is that "it becomes clear that female self-definition via a single identity is impossible when considered within the complex historical situation which, once experienced and witnessed by the female authors, then produces their complex heroines of fiction; woman's 'place' is, by definition, multiple—daughter, sister, teacher, lover, wife, surrogate mother figure—in both fact and fiction" (320). This idea of the female Victorian subject is then placed in the postmodern nexus of influences in twentieth- and twenty-first-century young adult fiction including a problematised socialising foundation of the narratives wherein "unconventional protagonists, subjectivity is perpetually fragmented and agentic development appears impossible" (Daley-Carey 2018, 468).

Gemma Doyle is a freckle-faced sixteen-year-old girl with an "unruly mane of red hair" (Bray 2003, 22) who begins the narrative in Bombay, India, where her father and mother are representatives of the Empire. Never having yet been in England, Gemma receives her grandmother's letters filled with gossip, scandal, and society; Gemma begs to go, using a proper education as the hook: "I am sixteen. *Sixteen*. An age at which most decent girls have been sent for schooling in London" (4; emphasis in original). Although her brother is at university, but her mother forewarns Gemma that educational expectations as well as social freedoms are not realistic for women because "It's different for men" (5). Sara Stickney Ellis, in her mid-Victorian text, *The Daughters of England, Their Position in Society, Character and Responsibilities*, advocates that "As women, then, the first thing of importance is to be content to be inferior to men—inferior in mental power, in the same proportion as you are inferior in bodily strength" (1843, 11–12).

The Report of the Schools' Inquiry Commission of 1867–68 noted, "Parents who have daughters will always look to their being provided for in marriage, will always believe that the gentler graces and winning qualities of character will be their best passports to marriage, and will always expect their husbands to take on themselves the intellectual toil and the active exertions needed for the support of the family" (quoted in Dyhouse 43). Certainly, the girls who attend the Spence Academy are of moneyed families—old and new—to be trained in subjects that will make them good wives. The purpose of such an institution was to equip young women with the "social gloss" (K. Hughes 2001, 18) that would allow them to both attract a husband and, later, manage his homelife and social requirements; to that end, the students had instruction in modern languages, music, dancing, and painting. To gain this requisite skill set, middle to upper-class daughters were sent to fashionable, expensive boarding schools—private establishments (Dyhouse 46)—with a select group of students in a sheltered environment with aims that were social and not academic. "Advice" manuals directed at girls were "emphatically explicit about one central feature" of the role of adult woman: they must accept limits and restraint and recognise male superiority (Gorham 2012, 101). They would then be educated into fiancées, wives, and mothers only to become "better companions for men" (Dyhouse 140) having been schooled in the characteristics of modesty, service, and selflessness (50).

Spence is "a very good school with a reputation for turning out charming young ladies" (Bray 2003, 21) with the "necessary skills to become

England's future wives and mothers, hostesses and bearers of the Empire's feminine traditions" with motto: grace, charm, and beauty (54). Felicity is angry with these expectations, even though the girls are so young: "They've planned our entire lives, from what we shall wear to whom we shall marry and where we shall live. It's one lump of sugar in your tea whether you like it or not and you'd best smile even if you're dying deep inside. We're like pretty horses, and just as on horses, they mean to put blinders on us so we can't look left or right but only straight ahead where they would lead" (Bray 2007, 601) whether or not the four friends wish to follow. In her own family, Gemma's brother, Tom, argues that "A man wants a woman who will make life easy for him" by being attractive, accomplished, and "above all" who "keeps his name above scandal and never call attention"; however, Gemma reminds him of a reality wherein "Mother was Father's equal.… He didn't expect her to walk behind him like some pining imbecile" (Bray 2003, 27). Gemma's response is an indication of the neo-Victorian at work in the novel; to speak up against patriarchal entitlement, embodied here by her brother, is a moment of resistance upon which a different future might be envisioned.

Becoming a (Marriageable) Woman

At the school, the four girls become friends. Outside of the family home, female friendships were considered important part of social development. Ann and Pippa attend the school alongside the much more outspoken Felicity and the inwardly confident Gemma; both Ann and Pippa have difficult personal circumstances which see them firmly under the control of their respective family. Whether "she chose to rebel against or to accede to the demands of her culture, a nineteenth-century girl could not but realize, withal her sex, that after childhood, gender (to paraphrase Freud) was inexorably destiny" (MacLeod 1994, 29). Ann is sent to Spence because her aunt and uncle wish for her to be educated in order to become governess to their children. Ann's family are not of the upper ten or even upper class, but part of the mercantile class, and they pay Ann's way to Spence on the understanding that she will come to them when summoned. With means but without social graces or rank, Ann knows her family will not rise to high society so she must be pragmatic. Bullied from her arrival, Spence's students evince intense condescension which was common in girls' schools where "Social snobbery … formed part of the 'hidden curriculum' of the school. There is no doubt that the girls were made fully aware both of their own privileged class position and also of the fact that their social status throughout life would depend on that of their fathers, brothers and future husbands" (Dyhouse 55). Felicity, the alpha girl—charismatic, rich, sensual—of the school, even admonishes Gemma for defending the new girl, reminding her that Ann's "life isn't going to be like ours. You think you're being so kind to her when you know very well that you can't be friends with her on the outside. It's much crueler to make her think otherwise, to lead her on" (Bray 2003, 69). Society dictates Ann's life will be different.

It is clear in most neo-Victorian fictions that, historically in the Victorian era, class predetermined path rather than individual determination. Regardless of Ann's rare vocal talent and desire to sing, she must go into service for her own family as a governess as repayment for her education. In that capacity, she must be "competent to instruct in a wide range of academic subjects, [while] her main task was to provide the round-the-clock moral and social supervision that her employer was unable to supply" (Hughes 21) due to social commitments increasingly assumed by the woman of the house. For any middle-class or newly moneyed family, a governess was an essential addition to the home, not just for the education of children; indeed, according to Kathryn Hughes, "one of the most important functions of the governess was to show off their own wealth and social prestige" (22).[4] When Ann dreams of a life as a popular actress, she is reminded that reputation is "all you have to recommend you as a governess" (Bray 2005, 45) and that the theatre is assumed to be full of morally corrupt individuals: theatre people. Felicity is the daughter of a socially ostracised woman; her mother, Lady Worthington, lives in Paris with a French artist, apart from her father and is the subject of much derisive society gossip. She is, perhaps more so than the other girls, fully aware of Ann's precarious social position with potentially "two-directional social mobility" wherein she might struggle up towards an advantageous marriage or drift down, losing status by being in, but not of, the family she will serve (Hughes 33) all dependent on keeping her reputation intact.

For the young women who necessarily required employment, or who had this role thrust upon them by family, the potential outcome was stressful. For some, "Becoming a governess was the only acceptable way of earning money open to the increasing number of middle-class women whose birth and education defined them as ladies, yet whose families were unable to support them" caused "emotional and social tension" the women were "obliged to negotiate" (Hughes xvi) while retaining their place. In addition, the nexus of social issues which "the governess seemed to embody—concerning social respectability, sexual morality and financial self-reliance—touched a raw nerve with a whole swathe of middle-class Britain" (xiii). Victorian fiction included portraits of governesses, with the two most known being Charlotte Brontë's Jane in *Jane Eyre* (1847) and William Makepeace Thackeray's Rebecca Sharp in *Vanity Fair* (1847). Unlike the romantic endings or outlandish manoeuvrings which provide Victorian closure in those novels, Bray's neo-Victorian narrative raises awareness—even in this limited depiction of Ann's impending service—of the significant and overwhelming pressure placed on a young woman without means to find security in the world, be it through marriage or employment.

Unable to speak up for herself on many occasions when she is demeaned by other Spence girls, Ann has internalised her passive position and their disdain. She wishes to be swept off her feet by a suitor because such a woman "who is considered the most fortunate in life has never been independent" but under the authority of her parents, then her husband (Tilt 1853, 15). Acutely aware that her education depends on financial assistance from and subservience to her Aunt and Uncle, Ann is reminded almost daily that she is not of the same class as the girls with whom she attends Spence. She refuses to fight back, and Gemma only fully realises Ann's pain when "A patch of wrist is exposed. I can see the red cross-hatching of welts there, fresh and angry. This is no accident. She's doing it to herself" (Bray 2003, 168). Searching for a way to help her friend through understanding, she asks Ann to explain why. Ann faintly replies, "I don't know. Sometimes, I feel nothing, and I'm so afraid. Afraid I'll stop feeling anything at all. I'll just slip away inside myself.... I just need to feel something" (177). Ann's self-wounding opens "a rhetorical space for the damaged body as a crucial juncture between notions of the public and the private" because Ann is, like other adolescent girls who self-harm, "inextricably connected to the sense of outsiderism and marginality experienced" (Gray 2017, 4) by other women forced into a life of conformity. Some women transformed "disappointment with women's social prospects into gestures of saintly martyrdom; and an idealization of self sacrifice" (Kucich 2002, 80) but Ann's gesture, in a neo-Victorian context read by twenty-first-century readers, can only be seen as despair with the sacrifice expected of her. Ann's fear in the nineteenth century—just like too many twenty-first-century young women—is that she is invisible, on the edge of madness or suicide, not fully aware of all the love and care which surrounds them. Her position is liminal; Ann exists between classes, places, ages, duty, and desire.

Pippa is equally bound to marry over her family's monetary concerns. Mr. Cross, her father, is an inveterate gambler, and his daughter's marriage has been arranged to an older man, Mr. Bumble, with the promise the lawyer will erase those debts. Pippa rightly feels she is a mere marker and a piece of collateral for homosocial exchange between men, a fact not uncommon in society marriages. Her sense of duty to her family is compounded by a devastating secret. The revelation of her physical illness, epilepsy, would make her a social pariah (Bray 2003, 188) and Pippa would remain a spinster with no long-term familial or financial security. Rather than being comforted with compassion and empathy, she is reminded that "she would be unmarriageable. It is considered a flaw in the blood, like madness. No man would want a woman with such an affliction" (190). While Ann has no prospects of marriage in spite of her romantic dreams, Pippa takes desperate measures choosing bodily death and a purgatorial existence in the Realms to avoid her arranged marriage to a wealthy lawyer, "the clumsy, charmless Mr. Bumble" (148).

Society's Masquerade

When Gemma returns home, there comes a point when she must go on social calls with her grandmother to establish her eventual place in society. Gemma articulates her opinion on the polite but unforgiving masquerade of society and her place in it; she acknowledges, "I'm under no illusions that this is simply tea; it is a market-place, and we girls are the wares" (Bray 2007, 49). The women of the upper class, like her grandmother, and their daughters, "work in concert to maintain the clear, pretty surface of this life, never daring to make a splash" (50). For example, on one visit, when asked about the notion of ladies learning Latin and Greek, Gemma measures her answer carefully because "It is not an innocent question. She is testing me" (Bray 2005, 217). The directness of the narrative allows for the neo-Victorian exposure of society as a "big lie. An illusion where everyone looks the other way and pretends that nothing unpleasant exists at all" (Bray 2003, 29). Behind these masks and behind the curtain are the reality of the season as "business" (182).

Gemma's feeling of alterity is enhanced when she is forced into settings with rote and expected interaction like social calls, or social events, adult events in which they must participate. Pamela Thurschwell calls this disruptive force of the adolescent's life as feeling "out of joint" in temporalities and locations (2010, 241). On one occasion, Gemma attends a demonstration of theosophy and spiritualism where she observes that the audience shows it's "breeding" (Bray 2003, 228) by wearing clothes and jewels that establish their position in the social hierarchy. In like manner, when in the audience at the Opera, Gemma identifies the hypocrisy of who and what is being watched—certainly not the stage. Rather, the "Opera glasses are used to spy covertly on lovers and friends, to see who is wearing what, who has arrived with whom. There is more potential scandal and drama in the audience than there could possibly onstage" (Bray 2005, 319).

Society is not without its secrets, nor is it necessarily a safe space for a young woman. At one gathering, the young man her brother wishes her to marry, Simon Middleton, has been charming and attentive until he dares the girls to join him in experimenting with Absinthe, a high-content alcoholic drink that was thought to have hallucinogenic properties.[5] Historical information is provided by Simon to assuage Gemma's confusion when he tells her it is the drink of "artists and madmen" and provides her with the tale of the green fairy who "spirits you away to her lair where all manner of strange and beautiful things can be seen" (Bray 2005, 409). He then asks, "Would you like to try living in two worlds at once?" after which she does not know "whether to laugh or cry" fully aware "I don't wish to try absinthe"; once under the influence, Gemma is unable to focus her thoughts because, in her head, a "lightness" makes it seem as if she is safe (409). The feeling makes Simon seem beguiling; he guides her as she stumbles to behind an ornate screen, knowing "I should be alarmed" as he presses against her and they go to the maid's room in the attic where he begins to seduce her even as she says she wants to "tell him to stop" but she can only mumble "I…I want to go back" (414). Gemma has clearly withdrawn consent; she dissociates while she feels she is falling into the Realms following three girls in white to The Temple while, in reality, she is screaming because he has his hand over her mouth to silence her; however, like many victims, Gemma turns inward to self-blame rather than anger, saying she "was foolish to have drunk the absinthe, to have gone with him alone" (416). Having Gemma's first-person narration delineate her thoughts during the assault, the neo-Victorian text outlines a possible encounter between two Victorian teenagers, or equally acts as a warning to modern adolescent readers to be mindful regarding potential trauma to their own bodies.

Girl Child(hood) Abused

Boarding schools and finishing schools were means through which to invigilate young women's transition from girl to woman through a conventional, controlled, and educated adolescence after which they would return to the safety of the family home. For girl children and teenagers, one of the implications of adherence to strict social codes and mores of class appropriate behaviour was to provide feelings of a secure, safe society of like-minded individuals and families wherein young women could maintain their innocence until such time as they entered the marriage market. According to Louisa Yates, "Families form the backbone of the neo-Victorian novel" that "present a complex array of kinship relations and marriages, but as a cultural practice and as a safe (or perilous) space for the child" (2011, 94). Neo-Victorian narratives, just like other current literature for adolescents,[6] frequently address taboo subjects, indeed increasingly so, in order to engage in discussions regarding the state(s) of girlhood, past and present. In both cases, narratives that present challenging social problems create a consistent adult anxiety, a "cultural impulse to sanitise or simplify literature within this genre" that "patronisingly assumes that developing readers are incapable of negotiating complex thematic concepts and textual forms" (Daley-Carey 2018, 469).

This belief is strongly challenged in the *A Great and Terrible Beauty* series. The darkest moment comes when Gemma reaches out to comfort a seemingly distressed Felicity. Moving from "silence to voice" Felicity "works through the traumatic incident" (Kokkola 2013, 176) in her past.[7] The always-in-control young woman begins to tell "A ghost story" (Bray 2003, 313), knowing that the autofiction she is going to tell belongs in the Gothic genre, long-filled with victimised women and predator men. Her tragedy—all the more so because it is true—begins, "Once upon a time there were four girls" who were "misled. Betrayed by their own stupid hopes. Things couldn't be different for them, because they weren't special after all. So life took them, led them, and they went along, you see? They faded before their own eyes, till they were nothing more than living ghosts, haunting each other which what could be. What can't be.... Isn't that the scariest story you've ever heard?" (314). There is no happy, fairy tale ending for this beautiful princess of society. Nowhere does the desire to recreate history loom larger than in relation to child sexual abuse; readers of such a neo-Victorian text are exposed to the social hypocrisy that perpetuated violence against children with its silence.

The concept of childhood sexual harm and abuse was still an emerging concept with the perpetrator painted in a Gothic manner as a monstrous stranger rather than a family member or known individual. Ailise Bulfin reminds us that "emerging scientific definitions of abusers could not be fully articulated without recourse to atavistic conceptions of monstrosity, producing a category of experience which, due to its moral nature, resisted medicalisation" (2021, 228). This pervasive denial, a refusal of the reality that children were and are abused in their own homes, was and is a horrific psychological betrayal and physical trauma. Dismissed as a problem only of the impoverished, overcrowded lower classes, such classist distancing allowed child sexual trauma to be marginalised; in addition, it allowed for incest and intra-family abuse within middle- and upper-class families to be denied. Discourses of sexology and criminology, sensational journalism, and popular fiction (223) fed the conventional conception that "the sex abuser was commonly evaluated as 'deviant' in relation to notions of 'respectable' masculinity in the Victorian and Edwardian judicial systems. The 'normal' father and breadwinner who protected and provided for his family remained beyond reproach" (Jackson 2000, 81) even if he was not.

Victorian fiction contained scenarios of child abuse via poverty, neglect, mistreatment, and exploitation but without much direct discussion of child sexual abuse or its perpetrators. Kohlke counsels the scholar to be aware that looking back in this way at difficult subjects because, if not done critically, might be "linked to more questionable nostalgic and prurient impulses" because although there is a prominent focus in neo-Victorian fiction on sexuality, particularly non-normative forms such as prostitution, homosexuality, and paedophilia that might lead to "vicarious consumption of sexual trauma" in a kind of "perverse nostalgia" (2018a, 184). In other work, Kohlke has additionally warned about "*reading for defilement*" (2008, 55; emphasis in original) where the "trauma of child sex abuse becomes both crucial facilitator and targeted goal of literary consumption, with the neo-Victorian novel providing a prurient peephole onto the past's transgressions" (2018a, 188). In Bray's novels, child abuse is handled in a manner in keeping with the neo-Victorian project whereby the narratives' silenced voices of past and potentially future abuse victims are portrayed and heard with empathy as well as compassion, not with voyeurism or salacious representation.

Felicity has a complex relationship with her father, the much-admired naval hero Admiral Worthington. It is not until the second volume, *Rebel Angels*, that she obliquely tells Gemma of the sexual abuse she has suffered. Felicity's trauma is introduced when her father takes in a young girl, Polly, who is to live with the Admiral and her mother. When she hears the news, Gemma noted Polly "looks a good deal like Felicity" (2005, 273), the possibility the Admiral is bringing home his illegitimate child. Beyond the point of adultery, which seems to pass by Gemma, the fact that "Felicity has gone pale" but "Her mother pretends she hasn't noticed" (167). The phrasing is provocative; it is not that her mother has not noticed, it is that she chooses to look away from what she knows to be true just as she has done in the past when she ignored Felicity's divulgence of the truth. The reader is encouraged to dismiss Felicity's mother as an accomplice rather than as a protector.

Felicity increasingly fears that the cycle will repeat itself when, at a gathering, the six-year-old Polly is encouraged to climb into the Admiral's lap. The Admiral, whom Polly calls Uncle, asks her for a "true and proper kiss"; Polly's response is telling—"the child squirms a bit, her eyes darting from person to person. Each one gives her the same eager expression: *Go on, then. Give him a kiss*.... Murmurs of approval and affection float about the room"—and Felicity intervenes (Bray 2005, 418; emphasis in original). Rather than see this scene as innocent, here society can be seen making an "effort to flatten the narrative of the child into a story of innocence" which "has some very queer effects. Childhood itself is afforded a modicum of queerness when the people worry more about how the child turns out than about how the child exists as a child" (Bruhm and Hurley 2004, xiv). Only another child, now a "knowing"[8] child, can interrupt this placation of social deviance.

Linking the Victorian depiction of perpetrators with folkloric evil, using the same language adopted by Victorian medical men, Felicity warns Polly to lock her door at night in order "To keep out monsters ... you must keep Uncle out" (Bray 2005, 418). Polly's story matches Felicity's own horrific childhood; Polly has been told her doll tells lies about her Uncle, just as Felicity says "they said she [her doll] was wicked, too. But she wasn't. She was a good and true doll" (Bray 2007, 251) in a world of lies and liars. An instant, "full horrible understanding" overwhelms Gemma like a dark shadow; she listens when Felicity defiantly tells her, "It's not his fault. The blame is my own, I bring it out in him. He said so.... He didn't mean it. He loves me. He said so.... That's something, isn't it" as she cries (Bray 2005, 419). Victorian subjects may not have been able to articulate their childhood trauma, but in her neo-Victorian narratives, Bray is mindful to be clear that Felicity's self-blame and shame is misplaced. Gemma is adamant: "Fathers should protect their children" (419).

Gemma reflects on that statement and knows that her own father has let her down. An opium addict who has lost himself in grief for her mother, he has entrusted his parental responsibility for Gemma to others in the family. Without his support, she becomes vulnerable to her brother's jealousy and failures. Felicity, too, knows Gemma's emotions regarding her father are fragile; when shame overtakes Felicity, she lashes out at Gemma, asking "how does your father protect you in his laudanum stupor?" (419). She is, of course, right. Gemma's father exists in an opium-laden state, plagued by nightmares, and surrounded by only a hazy understanding of their day-to-day life. The neo-Victorian position—in both the retrospection of time and in relation to the age of the protagonists—is framed by Gemma who admits, "Fathers can wilfully hurt their children. They can be addicts too weak to give up their vices, no matter the pain it causes. Mothers can turn you invisible with neglect. They can erase you with a denial, a refusal to see" (512). Between girlhood and womanhood, Gemma and Felicity have been given burdens that should never have been theirs to bear.

These scenes make clear what Christian Gutleben calls the "recriminative purpose" (2001, 169) of neo-Victorian narratives because the assault of Gemma, her father's drug use, and particularly the parallel discussions of Felicity's past—and Polly's potential—trauma avoid titillation while they instigate witness-bearing as well as provide an educational purpose for the adolescent, and any other, readers. Such fictional moments "can both reflect its own cultural moment as well as the cultural moment of the Victorians it represents" (Wilson 2012, 120) while the denial in the Victorian past is juxtaposed with the hoped-for vigilance of the present day.

Girls Existing Other-Wise

Gemma acknowledges that, for men—family members or otherwise—that they are "all looking glasses, we girls, existing only to reflect their images back to them as they'd like to be seen. Hollow vessels of girls to be rinsed of our own ambitions, wants, and opinions, just waiting to be filled with the cool, tepid water of gracious compliance" (2003, 305). This idea parallels Virginia Woolf's *A Room of One's Own*:

Women have served all these centuries as looking-glasses possessing the magic and delicious power of reflecting the figure of man at twice its natural size.... Whatever may be their use in civilised societies, mirrors are essential.... That serves to explain in part the necessity that women so often are to men.... How is he to go on giving judgement, civilising natives, making laws, writing books, dressing up and speechifying at banquets, unless he can see himself at breakfast and at dinner at least twice the size he really is? (1929, 53)

Gemma sees herself as a "*girl in the mirror*" (Bray 2005, 397; emphasis in original), only a reflection of whom she might become for someone else; by contrast, the matriarchal realms offer wish-fulfilment, where she can "Imagine a world ... where women rule, where *a girl* could have whatever *she* wished" (158; emphasis added).[9]

In the parallel world of the Realms, women—Gemma, her friends, her mother, and others—are powerful. A neo-Victorian boarding house narrative juxtaposed with a fantasy storyline allows for a space in which the adolescent girls can explore their desires in what Marla Harris refers to as an "alternative community" where young adults, Bray's four girls and others before them, can "join together to form a community that explores alternative versions of home and family" (2002, 64). Librarians have noted how young adult readers embrace fiction that is a mash-up "fusing elements of fantasy, science fiction, or other genres with historical fiction" (Rabey 2010, 38) as a means of escaping their everyday lives. Melissa Rabey makes an interesting point, that mash-ups are often dismissed as a "low-brow pop culture fascination" and young adult literature has been disdained in the same way, maybe "its authors are more willing to try a disdained format like the mash-up ... fully exploring what this technique can achieve" while making it a "respectable" genre (40). It is significant that many neo-Victorian narratives embrace the mash-up of genres including melding the Victorian with fantasy, Gothic, detective, and steampunk.

Bray's trilogy is such an example wherein the daughters of society breach into a magical realm full of freedom and power, the kind they do not have in their own day-to-day existence. The Realm world suggests multiple possibilities of life paths where the young women feel empowered. The girls' forays into the Realm world provide perspective on the primary world, and perhaps the reason young women must be restrained; Gemma guesses, "Why our parents and teachers and suitors want us to behave properly and predictably. It's not that they want to protect us; it's that they fear us" (Bray 2003, 207). The Realms, although not discussed at length here, give a matriarchal space where they "realize their desires" but they "still must confront the realities of life in Victorian England" where they must learn to "balance conformity and rebellion" (Wilson 2012, 128).

The one progressive teacher at Spence, Miss Moore (who is a member of the Order in the Realms), has encouraged the girls to embrace the role of New Woman. She believes that young women should demand the life they want, happily declaring, "Oh, my, I see I've started a little fire" (Bray 2003, 130) akin to the more vocal suffragettes whom the girls see in the street but each in her own way. Ann admires and hopes to join the company of Lily Trimble (née Lilith Trotsky), a Jewish actress who even had to take on a new identity that is "more suitable name for the stage—and for the well-bred patrons who come to see famous actresses" (Bray 2007, 199). For her part, Felicity declares "how liberating it is to be without layers of skirts and petticoats…. When I am free of these shackles and living in Paris on my inheritance, I shall never wear a dress again" (109) because "That is freedom" (Bray 2007, 813). She admits, "I wish to live for myself. I should never want to be trapped" (187) like she was in the past, and Felicity plans to take Polly with her (251). Gemma lays out her own plan; she wants to be an educated, independent woman. She is relieved when, finally, "Father has spoken to Grandmama about my decision. She is scandalized…. I shall go to university" but since "[I] truly desire independence, I shall need to work. It is unheard of. A black mark" (801), but one she is happy to wear.

Miss Moore warns the girls that "Women who have power are always feared" (Bray 2003, 126). They discuss the condemnation of Eve and her desire for knowledge (267), plus the sculptural friezes of strong women in the Realms that show

> women of all sorts. Some are as young as we are; others are as old as the earth itself. Some are clearly warriors, with swords held aloft to the rays of the sun. One sits surrounded by children and fawns, her hair flowing in loose waves to the ground. Another, dressed in chain mail, wrestles a dragon. Priestesses. Queens. Mothers. Healers. It is as if the whole of womanhood is represented here. (Bray 2007, 81)

It is an unusually proud material construction intended to preserve a lineage of matriarchal power where "Goddesses have been carved into the rock. They stand, possibly fifty feet tall … naked and quite sensual, hips cocked at an angle, an arm placed behind the head just so, lips curved into a smile. Decency tells me I should look away, but I find I keep stealing glances" near the Caves of Sighs (Bray 2005, 180–81). Entranced by the women's defiant stance, one not lauded in Victorian culture, Gemma appreciates their beauty and strength, as well as the empowered celebration of the various women's bodies and accomplishments. A modern reader is invited to understand how these young women, constrained and without choices, yearn to live other-wise. The actions of these young women question "entrenched power dynamics, and thereby challenges normative assumptions about adolescence, thus tends to provoke opposition and controversy" (Daley-Carey, 470), all with the desire to be celebrated for their authentic selves.

Notes

1. The use of the plural for girl cultures and girlhoods is intentional; Lynne Vallone and Claudia Nelson are correct in that "Girls' culture was not monolithic but multivocal" (1994, 2). Although this chapter focuses on one trilogy to make specific comments on the culture of the finishing school, but not on all the diversity of girls or schools.
2. The "Angel in the House" has become a kind of shorthand for these characteristics as aspired to in life but also described in fiction, particularly as opposed to the other end of the dichotomy, the "Whore." For a full consideration of the polarization of women as binary oppositions of character, see Nina Auerbach (1982).
3. There are many excellent discussions of the New Woman, including the following seminal texts: Gail Cunningham's *The New Woman and the Victorian Novel* (1978), Linda Dowling's "The Decadent and the New Woman" (1979), Lyn Pykett's *The Improper Feminine* (2003), Ann Heilmann's and Margaret Beetham's *New Woman Hybridities* (2004) and others.
4. The profession of governess was an important one, particularly for young women with education but without means; according to the 1861 census, there were 24,770 governesses in England and Wales (Hughes 22).
5. Absinthe, a high alcohol anise flavoured spirit made from wormwood is sometimes referred to as *la fée verte* and is most often associated with the *belle monde* of the *fin de siècle* in Paris or of Bohemian life. It was particularly used and/or described by artists and authors like Charles Baudelaire, Edgar Degas, Édouard Manet, and Henri de Toulouse-Lautrec. A scathing indictment of the drink was written by Marie Corelli in *Wormwood: A*

Drama of Paris (1890). Usually depicted as a drink among degenerates during the late Victorian age, in Bray's novel it is easily acquired by a young man and distributed to his friends with its use mirroring that of a date-rape drug. For a full discussion, see Doris Lanier (2004).
6. Difficult subjects have increasingly appeared in young adult fiction with novels that address BIPOC issues including race, LGBTQ+ gender and sexuality conversations, teen suicide, self-harm, abuse, sexual assault, and others.
7. Following Christine Wilkie-Stibbs observation that loss of language makes victims into non-subjects, in her chapter on "Queer Carnalities" Kokkola reverses the direction of language loss to consider the move from silence to voice "the dominant trope of trauma literature" (176).
8. On the "knowing" child, Kokkola laments that the "abused child is not a blank slate" (203) as envisioned by the Romantics. Rosemarie Bodenheimer writes about how a Dickensian childhood is defined by its abnormality; rather than protected, it is inadequately taken care of and suffers physical and psychological abuse or exploitation, leaving the child feeling alienated (see 2015).
9. Danielle Russell discusses the powerful figure of the witch in relation to the expectations of family in Bray's trilogy (see 2016).

Bibliography

Auerbach, Nina. *Woman and the Demon*. Cambridge: Harvard University Press, 1982.
Birch, Dinah. *Our Victorian Education*. Oxford: Blackwell, 2008.
Bodenheimer, Rosemarie. "Dickens and the Knowing Child." In *Dickens and the Imagined Child*, edited by Peter Merchant and Catherine Waters, 13–27. London: Routledge, 2015.
Bray, Libba. *A Great and Terrible Beauty*. New York: Random House, 2003.
Bray, Libba. *Rebel Angels*. New York: Random House, 2005.
Bray, Libba. *The Sweet Far Thing*. New York: Random House, 2007.
Brontë, Charlotte. *Jane Eyre*. London: Smith, Elder, and Co., 1847.
Bruhm, Steven & Hurley, Natasha. Eds. *Curiouser: On the Queerness of Children*. Minneapolis: Minnesota University Press, 2004.
Bulfin, Ailise. "'Monster, give me my child': How the Myth of the Paedophile as a Monstrous Stranger Took Shape in Emerging Discourses on Child Sexual Abuse in Late Nineteenth-Century Britain." *Nineteenth-Century Contexts*. 43 no. 2 (2021): 221–45.
Carroll, Samantha J. "Putting the 'Neo' Back into Neo-Victorian: The Neo-Victorian Novel as Postmodern Revisionist Fiction." *Neo-Victorian Studies*. 3 no. 2 (2010): 172–205.

Corelli, Marie. *Wormwood: A Drama of Paris*. London: Richard Bentley and Son, 1890.

Cunningham, Gail. *The New Woman and the Victorian Novel*. New York: 1978.

Daley-Carey, Ebony. "Testing the Limits: Postmodern Adolescent Identities in Contemporary Coming-of-Age Stories." *Children's Literature in Education*. 49 (2018): 467–84.

Dowling, Linda. "The Decadent and the New Woman." *Nineteenth-Century Fiction*. 33 no. 4 (1979): 434–53.

Dyhouse, Carol. *Girls Growing Up in Late Victorian and Edwardian England*. London: Routledge, 2013.

Ellis, Sarah Stickney. *The Daughters of England, Their Position in Society, Character and Responsibilities*. London: Fisher, Son, and Co., 1843.

Fielding, Sarah. *The Governess*. London: The Author, 1749.

Fisher, D. H. *Historians' Fallacies: Toward a Logic of Historical Thought*. New York: Harper and Row, 1970.

Flegel, Monica. *Conceptualizing Cruelty to Children in Nineteenth-Century England*. Farnham: Ashgate, 2009.

Fritz, Sonya Sawyer. "Double Lives: Neo-Victorian Girlhood in the Fiction of Libba Bray and Nancy Springer." *Neo-Victorian Studies*. 5, no. 1 (2012): 38–59.

Gorham, Deborah *The Victorian Girl and the Feminine Ideal*. London: Routledge, 2012.

Gray, Alexandra. *Self-Harm in New Woman Writing*. Edinburgh: Edinburgh University Press, 2017.

Gutleben, Christian. *Nostalgic Postmodernism: The Victorian Tradition and the Contemporary British Novel*. Amsterdam: Rodopi, 2001.

Harris, Marla. "Bleak Houses and Secret Cities: Alternative Communities in Young Adult Fiction." *Children's Literature in Education*. 33, no. 1 (2002): 63–76.

Heath, Michelle Beisel. "Reveling in Restraint: Limiting the Neo-Victorian Girl." *Children's Literature*. 48 (2020): 80–104.

Heilmann, Ann and Margaret Beetham, Eds. *New Woman Hybridities*. London: Routledge, 2004.

Jackson, Louise. *Child Sexual Abuse in Victorian England*. London: Routledge, 2000.

Hughes, Thomas. *Tom Brown's School Days*. London: Macmillan, 1857.

Hughes, Kathryn. *The Victorian Governess*. London: Hambledon and London, 2001.

Kohlke, Marie-Luise. "The Lures of Neo-Victorianism Presentism." *Literature Compass*. 15, no. 7 (2018a): n.p.

Kohlke, Marie-Luise. 2018b. "Perverse Nostalgia." In *Reinventing Childhood Nostalgia* edited by Elisabeth Wesseling, 184–201. New York: Routledge, 2018.

Kohlke, Marie-Luise. "Sexsation and the Neo-Victorian Novel: Orientalising the Nineteenth Century in Contemporary Fiction." In *Negotiating Sexual Idioms*, edited by Marie-Luise Kohlke and Luisa Orza, 53–77. Amsterdam: Brill, 2008.

Kokkola, Lydia. *Fictions of Adolescent Carnality*. Amsterdam: John Benjamins Publishing Company, 2013.

Kucich, John. "Olive Schreiner, Masochism and Omnipotence: Strategies of Pre-Oedipal Politics." *Novel: A Forum on Fiction*. 36 no. 1 (2002): 79–109.

Lanier, Doris. *Absinthe*. Jefferson: McFarland and Co., 2004.

MacLeod, Anne Scott. *American Childhood*. Athens: University of Georgia Press, 1994.

Maier, Sarah E. "Portraits of a Victorian Girl-Child: Female *Bildungsroman* in Victorian Fiction." *Literature Compass*. 4 no. 1 (2007): 317–35.

McCallum, Robyn. *Ideologies of Identity in Adolescent Fiction*. New York: Garland Publishing, 1999.

Patmore, Coventry. *The Angel in the House*. London: John W. Parker and Son, 1858.

Power, Chandra L. "Challenging the Pluralism of Our Past: Presentism and the Selective Tradition in Historical Fiction Written for Young People." *Research in the Teaching of English*. 37, no. 4 (May 2003): 425–66.

Pykett, Lyn. *The "Improper" Feminine: The Women's Sensation Novel and the New Woman Writing*. London: Routledge, 1992.

Rabey, Melissa. "Historical Fiction Mash-Ups: Broadening Appeal by Mixing Genres." *YALS*. (2010): 38–41.

Ruskin, John. *Sesames and Lilies*. London: Smith, Elder, and Co., 1865.

Russell, Danielle. "Liberating The Inner Goddess: The Witch Reconsidered in Libba Bray's Neo-Victorian Gemma Doyle Trilogy." *Gender and Fantasy*. no. 57 (2016): 48–63.

Thackeray, William Makepeace. *Vanity Fair*. 1847. London: Bradbury & Evans, 1848.

Thurschwell, Pamela. "The Ghost Worlds of Modern Adolescence." In *Popular Ghosts and the Haunted Spaces of Everyday Culture*, edited by Esther Peeren and Maria del Pilar Blanco, 239–51. London: Bloomsbury, 2010.

Tilt, Edward John. *Elements of Health, and Principles of Female Hygiene*. London: Bohn, 1853.

Vallone, Lynn and Claudia Nelson. "Introduction." In *The Girl's Own: Cultural Histories of the Anglo-American Girl, 1830–1915*, edited by Claudia Nelson and Lynn Vallone, 1–10. Athens: University of Georgia Press, 1994.

Wilson, Cheryl A. "Third-Wave Feminists in Corsets: Libba Bray's Gemma Doyle Trilogy." In *Inhabited by Stories: Critical Essays on Tales Retold*, edited by Nancy A. Marta-Smith and Danette DiMarco, 119–36. Newcastle-upon-Tyne: Cambridge Scholars Press, 2012.
Woolf, Virginia. *A Room of One's Own*. London: Hogarth Press, 1929.
Yates, Louisa. "The Figure of the Child in Neo-Victorian Queer Families." In *Neo-Victorian Families: Gender, Sexual and Cultural Politics*, edited by Marie-Luise Kohlke and Christian Gutleben, 93–117. Amsterdam: Brill, 2011.

CHAPTER 8

~~Deviant~~ Young Womanhood: Liminal Queerness, Mad Femininity, and Spectral Subjectivity

In the *Medical Review* of August 27, 1892, a devastating juxtaposition was made: "We cannot avoid believing that … if she had been taken in hand early by those in authority … she would not have become a Lesbian lover or a murderess" ("lesbian" *OED*). The false equivalence of these two ways of being sets both terms, lesbianism and murder, as criminal activities. This Victorian definition lays blame on the woman's upbringing—most likely by women—which, they presume, caused such deviant behaviours. "If only she had been raised right" invokes "then she would be straight and well-behaved" or "then she would be attracted like she is supposed to be to men" and "then she would be an angel in the house." None of these assumptions are accurate, and the linking of queerness and criminal behaviour is still, sadly, believed by some people. These positions do, however, point to how the nineteenth century conceptualised heterosexuality as normal and ostracised queerness. Any woman whose sexual preferences or social behaviour deviated from this prescribed pattern would be viewed with suspicion, even if a young adolescent woman.

Libba Bray's Gemma Doyle Trilogy (2003, 2005, 2007), Jane Eagland's *Wildthorn* (2009), Cat Winters' *The Cure for Dreaming* (2014), and Mindy McGuiness' *A Madness So Discreet* (2014) exemplify the struggles of young adult females who know they are outside the norm, especially in sexuality or politics. Neo-Victorian fictions, as in these novels, "take a revisionist approach to the past, borrowing from postmodern historiography to explore how present circumstances shape historical narrative"

© The Author(s), under exclusive license to Springer Nature Switzerland AG 2024
S. E. Maier, *Neo-Victorian Young Adult Narratives*,
https://doi.org/10.1007/978-3-031-47295-4_8

(Shiller 1997, 539). In such a revisionist and redemptive past, it is then possible "to recapture the past in ways that evoke its spirit and do honor to the dead and silenced" (546). Young adult neo-Victorian narratives often seek to be inclusive of LGBTQ+ characters who revision the possibilities of queer individuals under Victorian circumstances; such a move makes modern readers aware of the many difficulties faced by queer youth of the past. These neo-Victorian narratives investigate the burden of expectations and negotiate the liminal space of adolescence often "marked by ongoing uncertainty, marginalisation, trauma, and crisis" (470) without simple solutions. Since to be liminal is "characterized by being on a boundary or threshold, esp. by being transitional or intermediate between two states, situations, etc. ... characterized by liminality" ("liminal" *OED*), the female protagonists of these novels are liminal in both being between places and spaces, but also between rules and rebellion as adolescents on the verge of becoming.

One of the defining features of the passage from girl-child to adult woman includes the transitional phase of adolescence where the individual is betwixt and between in both mind and body. Adolescence is, indeed, "Marked not only by an anticipatory relation to the future and a haunted relationship to the past, but also by something even less assimilable to teleological notions of time and progress" where sometimes, "Ghosts resemble adolescents in that they are defined by their liminality, caught between timeframes" (Thurschwell 2010, 240) that "partakes of both backward-looking haunting and forward-looking desire" (239). No longer a child but not yet an adult the transformation of the individual is further complicated by the limitations placed on sexual curiosity and on political expression. For those adolescents who transgress society's heterosexual norms or conservative ideologies, this development is fraught with difficulty. Ebony Daley-Carey sees any "Understandings of subjectivity as fluid, fragmentary, and constantly evolving are central to the development of young adult fictions that validate disruptive and transgressive ways of being" (2018, 468). This concept is particularly *apropos* when a Victorian character in a neo-Victorian narrative works within the normalised conventions of contextual society but finds they cannot adhere to those norms. In other words, it is the transgression of the neo-Victorian character which allows for a reconsideration of the Victorian prescriptive conventions so central to a young woman's life.

Spectral Subjects

Julian Wolfreys, in *Victorian Hauntings*, outlines how spectral traces of the past, and the trope of haunting, are "transgenerational" because "There can be no narrative ... which is not always already disturbed and yet made possible from within its form or structure by a ghostly movement" (2002, 3). This movement, a kind of Gothic influence, "manifests itself as both a subversive force and a spectral mechanism through which social and political critique may become available and articulable, as we come to apprehend material realities, political discourses and epistemological frameworks from other invisible places" (11). In a neo-Victorian narrative, then, the movement is twofold; first, it provides acknowledgement of a fluidity that is not usually found in Victorian novels and therefore should be considered for what it attempts to accomplish and second, the sense of ghostliness and spectrality, while not necessarily manifested in actual form does parallel the liminal existence of female adolescent characters. Like ghosts, adolescents "uncomfortably unsettle" society and space, "dismantling the difference between public and private space" (Thurschwell, 240). The female protagonists of these young adult novels create a lack of comfort for other characters and the potential disruption of traditional society through their queerness.

In young adult fiction, the evocation of historical atmosphere provides the opportunity to contextualise the Victorian characters who may then be seen as enacting, imagining, and interpreting similar situations perhaps familiar to modern adolescents. Rosario Arias and Patricia Pulham theorise that "the Victorian age is spectralised and appears as a ghostly apparition in contemporary literature; in returning as a revenant, it opens up multiple possibilities for re-enactment, reimagining, and reinterpretation" (2010, xix). This ghostliness of the Victorian in neo-Victorian fiction combines with how, in any historical moment, adolescents are in a state of flux, childhood being left behind but not yet situated as social participants, sexualised beings, or political actors.

What is at stake in this reading back into history and forward to today is "the way in which the past and the contemporary age establish a dialogue, a two-way process, a dual relationship by means of which the Victorians come to life in neo-Victorianism, and contemporary revisions of the Victorian past offer productive and nuanced ways of unlocking occluded secrets, silences and mysteries which return and reappear in a series of spectral/textual traces" (xx). Here, the traces include queer sexuality and progressive politics, and how those significant factors in a young adult woman's life can lead to extreme ostracism to the point where alienation makes some characters feel they exist in a liminal space, even separated from themselves. The resolution of this liminality is in and of itself a neo-Victorian act since the Victorian age encouraged silence. The ghost—or the liminal young woman existing between social acceptance and authentic selfhood—"functions as a powerful metaphor for the dynamic relationship maintained between Victorianism and neo-Victorianism" (xxv).

Gemma, Felicity, Pippa, and Ann all live in home and educational environments which limit their authentic self-development. Aside from anxiety and lack of esteem that cause the girls to feel out of step with society, they each have moments where they see themselves as non-existent or, if present, as the unseen ones in scenarios which will decide their lives. For example, when forced into obligations of duty, she feels herself separated from the acts she must perform to secure her future; instead of experiencing happiness or pride in her social graces, Gemma feels she has become "a ghost of a girl who'll nod and smile and take her tea but who isn't really here" (Bray 2003, 30). At another society event, dressed up for the opera, Gemma even wonders if she has become spectral because a man "stares, boldly, as if I am an apparition" (Bray 2005, 313) rather than because she is a striking red-headed young woman. The highly talented Ann sings beautifully but when she sings for a room full of society matrons, she is acutely aware "It's as if she doesn't exist for them. She's no more than a ghost" (40) appearing in front of them, with her lack of class position or family money causing her to be equated with nothingness. Felicity is unseen by her mother who ignores the sexual abuse she endures at the hands of her perpetrator Admiral father, and Pippa's physical illness, epilepsy, erases the possibility of marrying for love in favour of quickly for money and security.

When the four friends become aware that, in a previous generation, young women have disappeared or died at Spence, their upper-class finishing school, it piques their interest to discover more about them. With the discovery of pictures, they see the uncanny similarity between those girls and themselves, all "grim-faced ghosts in white dresses" (Bray 2003, 72) and "half-erased women" (327). Another young woman who has been negated is Eleanor "Nell" Hawkins, a previous student and attempted sacrifice, of Miss Moore's who, because of her truthful but disruptive ideas, is sent to Bedlam (Bray 2005, 238). Nell is one of the many women

8 ~~DEVIANT~~ YOUNG WOMANHOOD: LIMINAL QUEERNESS, MAD… 189

who are made to perform their illness for society at the yearly mad women's ball (346) where society comes to "peek behind the curtain at despair, horror, and hopelessness" with its "taint" far from their own lives (356). To look at the women who have lost their way through mental illness or have been sent away by their families for nonconformist behaviour is reassuring to society; it also keeps the Realms hidden by casting Nell as a hysteric.

Liminal Lesbians

Gemma becomes increasingly aware of Felicity's sense of her own sexuality. Not only does she catch her friend in a stolen moment alone with a young man from a group of Travellers that has sometimes lived on the Spence grounds for decades, but Felicity is unapologetic about the encounter or being caught. Felicity enjoys the physical contact with him and, on several other occasions, demonstrates she understands the rituals of flirtation and appropriately adjusts her female performance to suit the situation be it at school, in a social club, or when she is presented to the Queen at Court. Gemma's assumption is that Felicity is purposely acting recklessly with the boy outside of school rules and boundaries of class. Neo-Victorian texts, whether adult or young adult, often extend their narratives into "liberating explorations of what is typically repressed, oppressed, dark, and/or hidden in nineteenth-century texts—such as explicit sexuality and deviations from heteronormative expectations" (Heath 2020, 80). This lack of nineteenth-century restraint on the new generation of young women—as embodied by the four friends at a crucial moment of their transformation from girl to woman—can be and is used to "explore the contemporary cultural moment" (Rodgers 2016, 220) as much as it cross-examines the past.

During the adolescent development of a young woman in the Victorian age, the nurturing of female friendships was a crucial aspect of social becoming and networking; indeed, "the first serious female friendship in a girl's life was seen as a significant turning point" because they could encourage "empathy and expressiveness, and should develop the capacity for sustained intimacy" (Gorham 2012, 113). This encouragement of female friendship came with a warning that a young woman should not "take a sudden and violent liking" (113) to another girl.

Even now, adolescents whose "desires fall within the range of 'queer' (a political term which covers more than same-sex desire) are doubly marginalised in the sense that they must overcome prejudices against both their age and their orientation" (Fuoss 1994, 154). Eve Kosofsky Sedgwick reminds us that the "shift in European thought from viewing same-sex sexuality as a matter of prohibited and isolated genital acts ... to viewing it as a function of stable definitions of identity" (1990, 82–3) was crucial to a change in conception of lesbianism. Reclaiming nineteenth-century love between women is part of an ongoing project of recovering queer history; debates continue regarding what, exactly, constitutes romantic friendships or lesbian love and whether or not sex must be involved. Terry Castle's "apparitional lesbian" accounts for the liminal position of women as present but not always seen:

> When it comes to lesbians ... many people have trouble seeing what's in front of them. The lesbian remains a kind of ghost effect ... elusive, vaporous, difficult to spot—even when she is there in plain view, mortal and magnificent, at the center of the screen. Some may even deny she exists at all.—Why is it so difficult to see the lesbian—even when she is there, quite plainly, in front of us? In part because she has been "ghosted"—or made to seem invisible—by culture itself. (1993, 2–4)

Same-sex desire in adolescents, particularly young women, challenges a kind of patriarchal protocol (3) on two fronts; first, they disrupt the heteronormative binary around which culture is organised, and second, they exist in a realm of negated adolescent sexuality unless it is in the service of social organisation. Cheryl A. Wilson identifies one feminist issue in Bray's neo-Victorian novels as the expression of sexuality, and discusses Gemma's relationship with a Rakshana young man, Kartik, as outside the usual boundaries—literally in a different realm—away from Victorian sexual context (2012, 129–32). Outside of her experience in the realms, Gemma knows women are to control their sexuality so it may be bartered in the marriage marketplace by her family rather than personally explored unless it is kept quiet and subversive.

Queer desire is subversive to both patriarchal binaries and adult assumptions about young adult sexuality but it is not unheard of at Bray's school. The previous generations of women, including Gemma's own mother, have had very close bonds both at the school and in the Realms. The subject of Sapphism arises in a discussion when Pippa directly asks Ms. Moore, the school's progressive teacher—and later antagonist in the Realms—what, exactly, a Sapphist is. Felicity scoffs at her lack of knowledge but explains that the word itself is derived "From the Greek Sappho, a lady poet who enjoyed the love of other women" and "prefer the love of women to men" (Bray 2003, 167). It seems two past Spence girls who also had the power to enter the Realms, Mary and Sarah (201), might have had such a relationship which creates an ongoing queer history at the school that has been suppressed; in the present, Gemma admits she is surprised with her own reaction when Felicity "kisses me full on the lips. I have to put my hand to them to stop the tingling, and a blush has flooded my entire body" (143). This moment gives Gemma thoughtful pause but leads to another discovery.[1]

The queerness of two of the main characters, Felicity and Pippa, or the surprise—but not shock—of Gemma at witnessing their authentic feelings for each other, as well as her own queer—and pleasant—encounter with Felicity. Gemma has long realised—with a degree of jealousy—that for Felicity and Pippa, when they are together, "it is as if the rest of us do not exist. Their friendship is exclusive. I am envious of their closeness" (Bray 2007, 355). That said, it is not until Gemma finally sees them in a private moment that she fully grasps the extent of their attraction to each other. Gemma describes how Pippa "pulls Felicity to her. Something I cannot name passes between them, and then Pip's lips are on Fee's in a deep kiss, as if they feed on one another, their fingers entwined in each other's hair. And suddenly, I understand what I must have always known about them—the private talks, the close embraces, the tenderness of their friendship…. How could I not have seen it before?" (664).

Gemma has seen the depth of emotion between them but her education as a young woman has never included the possibility of lesbian love. When Felicity defensively attacks Gemma—with "Why did you come…. Did you come to see the degenerate? … Go on—say it. I'm a degenerate then. My affections are unnatural" (667)—she sparks questions, not revulsion. Gemma admits, "What I feel is confused. I have questions I do not yet know how to ask: Has she always been this way? Does she feel this same affection for me? I have undressed before her. She has seen me. And I have seen her, have noted her beauty. Do I harbor these secret feelings for Felicity? Am I just as she is? How would I know if I were?" (668).

In what is potentially a move towards a wider inclusiveness in Bray's novels, the Realm folk include a multi-spirit person. In a revelation of difference, Gemma is awed when "Before us is the most magnificent creature I have ever seen. I do not know whether it is a man or a woman, for it could be both. It is slight, with skin and hair the dusty color of a lilac bloom and a long, trailing cape made of acorns, thorns, and thistle. Its eyes are vivid green and turned up at the corners like a cat's" with paw and talon, but speaks in "a voice that is like three-part harmony, the tones distinct but inseparable at the same time" (Bray 2005, 187). The blending of genders, attributes, and expressions come together in a being who embodies liminality.

~~Mad~~ Angry Young Women

Spectral spaces, places not seen or spoken of in society, are sometimes occupied by those women who are maltreated in the name of a "cure" for seeing a future life that leads them to be designated as abnormal, hysterical, and/or ill by society. Elaine Showalter, in *The Female Malady*, made the case for how "As women sought opportunities for self-development outside of marriage, medicine and science warned that such ambitions would lead to sickness, freakishness, sterility, and racial degeneration" (1991, 39). Many neo-Victorian novels for adults have addressed questions of how madness, insanity, criminal insanity, hysterics, and other mental health issues were handled—and the gross malpractice towards and ill-treatment of women that occurred in the name of medicine—during the Victorian age. Sarah Waters' *Fingersmith* (2002), Victoria Mas' *The Mad Women's Ball* (2021), Wendy Wallace's *The Painted Bridge* (2012) and other neo-Victorian novels of "madness" contain similar material for an adult reader but their categorisation rests on the age of their adult-age protagonist; however, this critical response to the invalidating of women, and young women, as "mad" when inconvenient, progressive, or outspoken is also thematically present in young adult literature.

McGuiness, in *A Madness so Discreet*, begins her narrative with the immediacy of trauma; in the Wayburne Lunatic Asylum of Boston,[2] a new woman's screams fill the ward where "They all had their terrors" (2015, 1). Grace Mae, the protagonist, has learned "the efficacy of silence, the art of invisibility. Grace had given up speech long ago. Once the words *no* and *stop* had done nothing, the others refused to come out"; instead, though her imagination vividly remembered the past, "the acuity of her memory was a dark artist at work in her mind, painting pictures without her permission" (2; emphasis in original). The images are neither joyful nor nostalgic but of "her father's face twisted into a paroxysm no daughter should ever witness" (3) which results in both her pregnancy and incarceration by him, United States Senator Nathaniel Mae. Grace tells her mother, a woman with "lips permanently stained with wine" (3), but she—like Felicity's mother in Bray's trilogy—is in denial; with "words tasting like the vomit" of morning sickness, she confronts her mother: "I told you and told you and YOU WILL NOT LISTEN" (125). From that point on, Grace chooses silence because "no words were big enough to encompass her past" (125).

Unable and unwilling to speak of the sexual abuse she endured, the attendant physician, Dr. Heedson claims she is "an aristocrat of loose morals" (21); ironically, the doctor must be reminded by another patient, Mrs. Clay, to keep his hands off Grace. Like with her father, Grace sensed the "smell of him [Heedson], the maleness surrounding her, the wine-soaked words in her ear" (24) that fill her with anger and dread; she stabs his hand with a fork after which she was wrapped in steamed-hot sheets and miscarried her child. For punishment Grace has been sent to a dark, damp, rain-filled basement. Once there, she hears Dr. Falsteed, another patient kept in solitary confinement and who remains in the dark. He evaluates, then immediately understands, Grace: "Dear child, do you even know all the rage that is inside you?" (41). Able to read her silence and her post-partum body, he confidently diagnoses her quiet demeanour is a result of "the wrongness of all that's been done to you by hands familiar and those of strangers. You chose to stop acknowledging a world that has treated you foully. What's saner than that?" (47).

Dr. Thornhollow has been asked to the asylum; his profession is surgery, specifically neuropsychological surgery: the lobotomy.[3] Asked to perform the operation on those patients who are unruly to calm their actions and distress, he has studied extensively in both pseudosciences (like phrenology), sciences (including brain studies), and forensic science (such as crime scene investigation). Falsteed, having agreed to help Grace escape from the asylum with Thornhollow. Heedson's fear of Mae's reaction to the error will force him to declare her dead. Falsteed and Thornhollow agree that she must enact the symptoms of a post-lobotomy patient which include lethargy and a lack of emotional affect. Grace had already learned to dissociate from her surroundings, particularly when she would hear familiar footsteps in the hall and a hand on her bedroom doorknob. To dissociate, in psychological terms, causes a "disconnection and lack of continuity between thoughts, memories, surroundings, actions and identity" which, when extreme, can fall into the category of Depersonalization-derealization disorder that involves a "sense of detachment or being outside yourself" ("Dissociative" Mayo Clinic). The "click" Grace heard in her mind lets "her emotions leave her in a rush, all cares exiting with her exhalation, not to return until she allowed them" as her "eyes glazed over, her muscles became torpid" (82) and she slouched into a kind of lifelessness, a liminal purgatory of endurance and survival.

This neo-Victorian novel throws into question the contextually biased nature of ideas of abuse and madness as well as indicts a lack of punishment for predators or justice for their victims. Dr. Thornhollow tries to explain how there are "discreet types of madness" used by some on others that include "power and pain" (48) and how, for society, "using the words *sane* and *insane* is a way ... to draw a safe line through humanity" (135; emphasis in original). Dr. Thornhollow tells Grace that some people are labelled insane because they are "simply people who have chosen not to participate in the world in the same manner as the majority" (136) but are not necessarily mentally ill. For example, the medical man tells Grace that another girl, Nell, has been admitted to the asylum because she is a young woman who enjoys the company, perhaps sexual encounters, of men and "feels no shame in it. The world can't understand this behavior; therefore the girl must be insane" (137).

In contrast, the abuse Grace has suffered at the hands of the predatory Mae is not questioned; he is powerful, charismatic, and dangerous. The reality of Grace's trauma—along with the physical repercussions of incestuous pregnancy—has been denied by her mother who has come to see her own daughters as "competitors for his [her husband's] attention" (287). The reader later learns that there have been many other women whom Mae has raped and abused, but it his next potential victim that is appalling to Grace. In the wording of letters Grace receives from her little sister, Alice, Grace identifies clues that he is now following the same pattern of enticements he had followed with herself; he tries to "comfort" Alice (170) and promises to keep bringing her a present, but this time Alice will "have to do him a special favor to get it" (283). Grace recognises the process of predatory grooming which she suffered through and is fully aware that her little sister "lives in a more refined pit, but a viper's nest nonetheless" (177). Thornhollow, unsure, asks if Grace realises the danger her sister is in, and Grace responds with both guilt and shame. She confesses, "I had thought that when the temptation was removed he would no longer" act in such a manner but he tells her directly and without equivocation, "The fault does not lie with you. It never did. You are not a temptation but simply a target for another's black sin" (192).

For Grace, society—as the replication of her own mother's denial—will not punish Mae for his incestuous sexual abuse of his own daughter or for his sexual assaults on other women. Not willing to wait for court justice, Nell, infected with syphilis by a young man, takes her own vengeance by sleeping with every man in his family to pass along the curse of illness, ugliness, insanity, and ultimately a justified death. Unlike Nell, Thornhollow notes of Grace, "Your brain is your strength, your quickness of wit the one thing that will deliver you" (73); the result is that Grace, Thornhollow, Nell, and Lizzie hatch a plan to frame Mae for murder and, during the trial, his victims testify about their own experiences of his violent actions, and with his own daughter dealing the final evidence of a port wine birthmark by his genitals which is verified by the court, further proof that Grace has always told the truth. The narrator's tone certainly suggests a certain amount of admiration for Nell's determined and poetic vengeance, but intense, profound sadness at her suicide by drowning. Predators must be punished, and a re-visioning of Victorian justice in MacGuiness' novel allows readers to feel satisfaction at the appropriate punishment being determined by the victims.

The Glow of Suffrage

Winter's *The Cure for Dreaming* opens with raven-haired Olivia Mead on her seventeenth birthday headed to a hypnotism demonstration by Henri Reverie and his sister, fifteen-year-old Genevieve, in Oregon 1900. Earlier in the day, she admits to watching a suffrage rally where "rotten eggs [had] smacked my arms and chest" while "Fierce-eyed men ... barked at us to go back to our homes where we belonged, and I ran off to scrub away the filth and my guilt" (2014, 13). Her father, "Mad Mead" the dentist, has found out about her "chanting *with* the women" and has declared, "My hope for you since the day your mother left was that you would grow up to be a rational, respectable, dignified young woman who understands her place in the world" (37; emphasis in original) not that she would ever "humiliate yourself by standing in that crowd of hysterical women" (36). In spite of his anger, Olivia goes to the birthday show with her friends and is called as a volunteer where she is hypnotised, lies stiff and flat as a board.

The young man whom her father wishes her to marry, Percy Acklen, said during the show she seemed "as lovely as Sleeping Beauty"; his father, too, agreed, "Now that's womanhood perfected, Percy my boy. That's the type of girl you want. Silent. Alluring. Submissive" (26). Percy infantilises Olivia just as he ridicules his ex-girlfriend, Nanette, because her parent's believed in free love and a utopian society, and their unorthodoxy leads Percy to question if her father is her father (121). The irony is that Olivia sees "The only other evidence of mischief on my body, the only sign my seventeenth birthday wasn't quite as proper as it should have been, was a dusty pair of footprints on my dress, right above my stomach and thighs" (39). On her birthday, she has been figuratively, and literally, stepped on by men: Reverie, egg throwers, Percy, his father, and her own father. Olivia's unspoken anger continues to build.

The "cure" Mead wishes to find for her with the help of Reverie is, he believes, available by making her an empty vessel to be filled with patriarchal wisdom; he asks Reverie to "help her" with her "rebelliousness" to ensure she will not become her mother, and to free Olivia of "unladylike dreams" for her own good (46). Reverie agrees to raise money for his sister's breast cancer operation and after his hypnosis session with Olivia, when she is about to speak her anger, she can only say "All is well" no matter the circumstances or whether she is in physical or sexual danger. Mead desire Reverie to "Teach her to accept the world the way it truly is.... Make her clearly understand the roles of men and women.... Her rebelliousness has got to be removed if she's going to survive" (63).

Olivia is exemplary of the New Girl, a "modern girl, who, like the New Woman, may or may not have existed in reality; in narratives, the image provided symbolic potential and imaginative power" (Rodgers 2016, 220) to readers who are formulating their own futures. The slippery nature of the term "girl" is as difficult as the late-nineteenth-century term "adolescence." Such an adolescent girl might be, "depending not only upon her age but also upon her class, educational attainments, and marital or biological status," a "home daughter" who might be in her early twenties, "a wife and mother aged seventeen, or a self-supporting member of the workforce at twelve" or a student, a nurse, a prostitute, or a factory hand (Nelson and Vallone, 3). Viewed differently according to social class, a chaste young lady was assumed to be of the moneyed classes while girls of the working classes were "thought to be sexual beings at puberty" (3).

Suffragettes—particularly the New Girl and her potential to be a suffragist—created a great deal of anxiety in the periodical press at the time; not seen as a young woman of advanced mind, instead she was cast by some writers as a disruptive influence. The periodical press in England was full of arguments for both sides of the New Woman debate, and there was a great deal of anxiety over the place of the New Girl's interest in suffrage. Eliza Lynn Linton in "The Girl of the Period" (1868), Sarah Grand's "The Modern Girl" (1894), and others worried about what would become of womankind if young women were allowed to be educated and independent.

Understandably, Olivia's repressed resentment causes her to lash out with a comment seemingly intended to emasculate her father's claim to wisdom with "You're angry because you couldn't keep my mother inside this home" (Winter 45). Although he sent her, as a young woman, to a school that was both integrated and coeducational, "a progressive school," she admits she is confused and angry that "my lunatic father was still considering hiring a stranger to obliterate my thoughts" (47). Olivia confronts his inconsistency with "You actually hired this person … to extract my thoughts in your operatory, as if my brain were a decayed thing, like Mr. Dibbs's disgusting bicuspid? Do you know how cruel and horrifying this is?" (60).

Although Reverie reluctantly places Olivia under hypnosis, his agreement with her father is to show her the world as it is. Immediately after the session, Olivia awakens into a liminal world where she sees spectral images; her father is a brute fiend with red eyes, canine teeth "as sharp as the fangs of a wolf" with jutting facial bones (66), much like a vampire. She flees and is horrified by an establishment that is caging up women in a gilded cage. The women, rather than fight back, passively read pamphlets without regard for "the freak-show absurdity of their situation" accentuated by a female carnival barker pointing out to passers-by that containment was "the only proper place for women and girls" (68). Olivia watches women with blood on their necks walk down the street, followed by a businessman reminiscent of a vampire. Reverie has contained her ability to retort. When she tries to express her feelings, she is only able to say "All is well." While her verbal response is limited, she retains her own opinion, silently—and sarcastically—articulating "*My life is so much better now that I hallucinate and can no longer articulate my anger*" (84; emphasis in original).

The argument for women's emancipation in this neo-Victorian novel is not anti-male; it does, however, cause the adolescent reader to challenge discourses that single out feminine complicity over masculine responsibility. Like Bray's trilogy, written at moment of backlash and confusion in young women of the early twenty-first century, Winters' narrative uses "intertextuality and historical double vision to offer adolescent female readers a way to connect with a feminism they both resist and need"

(Wilson 2012, 123). In no way does such a reading, or resistance, or need, exclude potential male readers; Reverie, in fact, is in sympathy with the social status of women and with Olivia's desire to lay claim to her own life. Rather than hypnotise her into submission as her father desires, Reverie implants the suggestion to Olivia's mind that "*You will see the world the way it truly is. The roles of men and women will be clearer than they have ever been before. You will know whom to avoid*" (Winters 71; emphasis in original). His desire is that she has protection from those people like her father or Percy or others who would harm her or take away her imagination. Although when Olivia refuses Percy, his friend John accuses her of being "a lesbian" and says, "I'll thrust the masculinity straight out of you myself. I'll break you like the wild filly you are" (183), Winters balances the view of gendered interaction. Not all men are considered a threat; Henri is subversively supportive, and Frannie's bookish father, appears in Olivia's truthful vision as "regular" (72) with his shop and home full of books with air "rich with the perfumes of paper and ink" (74) because he is a learned man who is fully supportive of his own daughter.

Olivia is a strong, critical reader of several kinds of texts. Like many neo-Victorian novels, *A Cure for Dreaming* is transmedial and intertextual. Several Victorian photographs are included as are cartoons, drawings, and posters, perhaps to enhance the reading experience providing context and texture. Intertextually, Olivia has read *Dracula* (1897) and *Trilby* (1894), and the novel includes quotations from Susan B. Anthony, Elihu Root, Mark Twain, Kate Chopin, and others. She has also read nonfiction, including Nellie Bly's *Ten Days in a Mad-House* (1887), an investigative report on the Women's Lunatic Asylum on Blackwell Island, and is an avid reader of periodicals.[4] The clear respect Olivia holds for the work Bly has done leads Olivia to be a careful reader of texts; as a result, she remains interested in the arguments in the press regarding the Woman Question—the "problem" of woman demanding political suffrage, social freedom, and sexual choice in a rapidly changing era. Olivia's support of women's suffrage is a clear point of contention with her father and his friends One piece against a woman's right to vote finally caused her rage to spill over. Written by the crusading anti-suffrage Judge Percival Acklen, the piece declares there is a "*staggering wealth of scientific research that proves women were created for domestic duties alone, not higher thinking. A body built for childbearing and mothering is clearly a body meant to stay in the home*" rather than "*muddle their minds*" which would "*trigger the downfall of … society*" (85; emphasis in original). Olivia's response is both carefully considered and well-reasoned; as "*A Responsible Woman*" (87–89; emphasis in original), her argument is that if men would only understand all the skills women use to run a household, men would necessarily see the "reason" of Woman; certainly, the many women who write letters to the paper in response to her column.

Once Reverie's "cure" allows Olivia into the spectral world, she begins to see "Certain women" disappearing. One woman's dinner companion had "said something to her that made her blur and fade into fog and shadow" (145), while her neighbour, Mrs. Stanton, becomes "a ghost … translucent … a cobweb woman. Barely there. Almost gone. A nothing person" (96). In contrast, the Mead family maid refuses to stand by and watch Olivia's torment and abuse at the hands of her own father: Gerda quits. Reverie's sister has breast cancer which causes Olivia to see her light dimming; courageously, rather than allow men to refuse her treatment because she cannot afford it, Genevieve self-advocates and performs with her brother to raise money to preserve her life. Last, when walking by the crowd of women gathered to rally for their right to vote, Olivia sees "Lanterns switched on inside all the women's bodies. Their hair glistened with breathtaking luminescence—a light that reflected off the surrounding wood. Their skin flushed with a brilliance that rivaled our candle's flame. I sucked in my breath and watched in awe as they glowed—literally *glowed*—before my eyes" (146–47). These women, unlike the frightening Gothic images Olivia sees from those who might cause her harm, shine from their inner worth and strong commitment to their righteous cause.

Olivia decides to leave home to strike out on her own. Her connection to her mother is only remembered through her father's bitterness—"Father's favorite saying about my mother's strawberry curls: *Red hair is a symptom of dangerous, fiery passions*" (2; emphasis in original)—and a yearly birthday letter with money. Aside from the oft-used pejorative towards red-haired women,[5] Olivia's mother is a Shakespearean actor who now lives near Barnard College. When she writes, she says she thinks of Olivia every time she sees "*those smart young women walking around with books*" and asks, "*Does your father allow you to be bright? Or does he still insist young ladies out to be silent idiots?*" (109; emphasis in original). With her letters, this stereotyped ginger with passions that may just be a desire to have a life full of meaning sends her daughter money which, now accumulated, provides the means for Olivia's escape from her father's dominion and to advocate for change.

Wildthorn foregrounds its interest in Victorian issues, particularly women's issues, on its cover. Like with Bray's *A Great and Terrible Beauty*, the first encounter a reader has with the book is to see the cinched, distorted waist of a tight-laced corset, with no head and no body, emblematic of how a young woman—or any woman—is constricted in breath, movement, and freedom. Eagland's novel centres on the strong-willed and inquisitive Louisa Cosgrove who has been sent away from her family; she believes she is going to be a companion. Two issues are of concern to Louisa: will she have time to continue her studies, and whether her cousin, Grace, has kept their secret (2010, 4–5). The narrative quickly turns and at the last moment, Grace has realised "Something is wrong" (6) and that she is to be locked away in an asylum, Wildthorn Hall, without her consent. Interviewed by Mr. Sneed, he refers to her as "Miss Childs" but when she corrects him—"That *isn't* my name. I am Louisa Cosgrove" (9; emphasis in original)—he replies as if to a confused child, "You only think you are Louisa Cosgrove.... You are Lucy Childs" (10). He assures her that "we are used to dealing with unusualness of all kinds" (10).

Louisa is, perhaps, unusual, but the inference throughout the novel is that she is representative of other girls who aspire to a life other than one of passive acquiescence to patriarchal influences. A flashback to the age of six has her receiving a fancy doll from her Aunt Phyllis (Grace's mother) named Evelina, but Louisa wishes that, like her brother, she had received a "folding penknife with blades, a corkscrew, and a pair of scissors. Compared to that, what use was a doll? Not for the first time, I wished I was a boy" because he was allowed to climb and fish and swim (13).

This early paradigm of gendered gift-giving and expectations leads to Louisa's biggest transgression; she wants to be a physician. After accidentally melting her new doll, she decides to conduct a kind of autopsy, confirming her actions as acceptable when she remembers, "Papa said scientists have to be bold sometimes" (17). Her mother confronts her in embarrassment mixed with horror, but her father stifled a laugh and defends Louisa's activity as the productive outcome of "natural curiosity ... not naughtiness" (20). Her father, understanding Louisa has a precocious mind, asks his wife, "Why should she be thwarted?" (44) since she is "keen to learn" (57). Having an understanding father was Louisa's means of support to a different life, but he dies, and with him goes her champion. Her "tomboy" (58) behaviour is met with a physical caning by her mother (37) and, seven months later when her father dies of typhoid, being sent away. Tom steps into power as the patriarch of the family; he believes he has the right to declare, "I won't let my sister embark on an improper course that will bring shame on her and all the family" (124) even though it is his own failure at medical school and his addiction to opium that is, in fact, the family disgrace.

A twenty-first-century reader of a neo-Victorian text will, hopefully, make the connection between the material culture's representation of a woman via her clothes and her persona. Immediately upon entry into the asylum, she is stripped of her identity along with her clothes, just as the corset which defines the book on its cover also defines the constriction of Louisa's rights. Several scholars discuss the function of the corset in neo-Victorian fiction; Cheryl A. Wilson sees the corset as a way to offer "readers historical context about Victorian clothing, and highlights body image issues as central to feminism" (2012, 126), while Amy Montz argues that corsets for a contemporary audience represent Victorian expectations of "propriety, constraint, and femininity" (2019, 89). In addition, steampunk and speculative fiction offers images of "the need for the corset as armor, to protect the bodies of the wearers from external, not internal threats" (90) as protection from, not restriction by, society. Louisa admits that ever since childhood, she had "eyed the corset with suspicion … It's like a suit of armour" in which "my rib cage [was] imprisoned" (74). Conversely, at the asylum, she admits "I've always hated its whalebone ribs but now I don't want to lose its protection. When the last hook is released, I hold the corset to me for a moment before dropping it on the bench" (23) because "Bit by bit, I am losing more of myself. Soon I won't exist" (24). Her adolescence is losing its anticipatory relation to the future but is in a haunted relationship to the past where her understanding of family and of protections was clear; now, in the asylum, her existence lacks in teleological notions of time, progress, space, and desire.

The severe abuses of women in Victorian asylums have been well documented,[6] and neo-Victorian fiction is steadfast in its judgement of the maltreatment and convenient incarceration of those young women and others. Eagland's narrative is scathing in its stark realism, a strong example of the neo-Victorian impulse to speak for silenced victims. Dropped in a bath while restrained by straps and unable to move, the first-person perspective tells the reader how "Water fills my mouth and nose. I can't breathe" in the hot steam (108), but she is suspended by her head in a canvas cover until she hallucinates from the cold. Willing herself to stay awake, Louisa focuses on medical procedures and instruments—like tourniquets, forceps, or cutting through soft tissue—to keep her from unconsciousness. When it does not work, she dreams of being seduced by Grace and being "utterly happy"; her dreamworld turns into a nightmare when she believes a "voice hisses in my ear, 'You're a bad girl, a very, very bad girl, and you must be punished'" (110). Louisa's same-sex desire both saves her and, in her subconscious mind, condemns her to live in a kind of purgatory until escape is possible.

Pamela Thurschwell builds the case for the popular representations of twenty-first-century adolescents "who similarly occupy haunted spaces and unsettling temporalities" where "adolescence is marked not only by an anticipatory relation to the future and a haunted relationship to the past, but also by something even less assimilable to teleological notions of time and progress" and the "fear or desire that those (past and future) times will never come, or have never been?" (240). To preserve a semblance of herself, she "tried to control it by concentrating on something clear and calm. I recall mathematical formulae, I recite the symptoms of diseases and medical procedures, the discipline of it helping me to keep hold of a sense of myself. I am still me. I am Louisa Cosgrove" (Eagland 221).

Louisa's first-person narration and flashback sequences while in the asylum confirm that the secret she has held with Grace involves her confused feelings and fumbling action. She sees Grace's beauty, a lovely young woman who "gave me a strange, fizzing sensation" which "wasn't unpleasant, but at the same time I felt unaccountably frightened" (96). Later, declaring she does not want to be married, Louisa's self-questioning leads to "Whatever was the matter with me?" (97). Such specific phrasing underlines the strength of social construction of correct femininity and how it acts upon an adolescent without the parameters for understanding the fluidity of sexuality; to ask what is the matter is to assume something is wrong or unexplained—i.e., she may not be heteronormative—with her sexual awakening. Sharing a bed as they had in the past, Louisa is now "painfully aware of her body lying next to mine. If I moved a fraction of an inch, we would be touching. *Touching*" (100; emphasis in original). She wonders if "*I felt about her in the way that she felt about Charles! ... It can't be true, it can't*. But even as I was denying it, I knew I was deceiving myself" (102; emphasis in original); consequently, Louisa's denial is of her own queer identity.

Two other young women are in the asylum with stories of significance for Louisa and act as examples of the Victorian plights of victims that can be viewed effectively in the rear-view mirror[7] of neo-Victorianism.

Triggered by the arrival of a photographer who has come to document the inmates,[8] Louisa learns the story of Beatrice, a girl who had been pregnant. Beatrice, too, has been sent away to hide what others call her shame. Louisa learns that from the age of eleven, Beatrice had been photographed by her stepfather for other paedophiles. He, too, groomed her with the bribery of "a pretty glass paperweight and said *Don't Tell Mama*" (183; emphasis in original). Beatrice's mother was complicit in her daughter's abuse because "he said if I didn't Mamma would send me away like the others" (184), the implication being that there had been other girls, siblings or otherwise, who had also been victimised. The stepfather, too, in another act of power, had renamed his victim from Beatrice to Bella, ignoring and erasing her identity to assuage his own deviant proclivities. Beatrice has been sent away because she couldn't stop crying, but "they say it's all in my mind, my imagination" (191). Although the reader had been unsure of the extent of her delusions, when she refers to a doll named Rosalie over whom she obsessively worries, the inference becomes that, in fact, Rosalie may have been her baby who now is "lying at the bottom of the river" (191).

The second young woman of significance is an assistant at the hospital, Eliza. She has watched Louisa suffer, and it becomes clear that Eliza cares for Louisa. At one point they slide into awkward silence; Eliza moves to leave but Louisa reasons it is because "She's embarrassed now and probably thinks she's offended me. But I'm not offended at all. I feel as if I'm floating, light and free" (241). Eliza loves her, a fact Louisa reads in her tone "that makes me look at her hard, and she's looking at me and in that moment something happens.... As if it was the most natural thing in the world. As if it was *all right*" (241–42; emphasis in original). Eliza has assured her that she has done nothing wrong by kissing Grace, adamant that "no it weren't. You were just showing your feelings. That's not a crime" and Louisa realises Eliza "*understands*" (289; emphasis in original) her queer desire. The two young women are the novel's love story; Louisa is now able to integrate her entire personality, pursue life as a physician, and love a woman.

The newly self-empowered Louisa's confidence leads to her confrontation with her family over her confinement in the asylum. The documentation of her committal to the institution records a litany of one family member's observations—and signature—of "Facts indicating insanity observed":

> *An interest in medical matters inappropriate for one of her age and sex.*
> *A neglect of appearance and personal toilet, and wearing unsuitable clothing for a young lady of her status.*
> 2. Other factors indicating insanity communicated to me by others:
> *Excessive book-reading and study leading to a weakening of the mind.*
> *Desiring to ape men by nursing an ambition to be a doctor.*
> *Self-assertiveness in the face of male authority.*
> *Obstinacy and displays of temper.*
> *Going about unchaperoned....* (238; emphasis in original)

To use these criteria as the basis for a diagnosis of insanity and committal reflects the social climate of the mid-to-late nineteenth century. Women and those others who believed in and advocated for a wider understanding of women's roles in society should be enriched and expanded were often cast as abnormal or neurotic. Charles, Grace's fiancé, had been open about his thoughts on women, proudly declaring that he was "with Maudsley.... You know what he says—a girl who is educated beyond what is necessary for her role as wife and mother cannot possibly reach the perfect ideal of womanhood" (277). Uncle Bertram agreed with Charles, "These women—they hardly deserve the name! They're a disgrace to their sex! Aping men!" (278).

Women's complicity—here exemplified by the actions of Grace as well as Louisa's mother, aunt, and cousin—is clear; in fact, Louisa is shocked to find she has been committed by a woman—Aunt Phyllis—who signed the papers with the intense urging of Charles and Bertram. Having been told by Grace of her interaction with Louisa, her Aunt Phyllis commits the latter young woman to maintain her own daughter's reputation within the patriarchal fold and to maintain the security of her upcoming, advantageous marriage. Charles successfully convinced both her aunt and Grace that Louisa suffered from "moral insanity" (302) while Bertram rejects Grace on the basis of her unfeminine behaviours. Louisa makes clear the unacceptability of such judgement on her as a person and confronts her aunt: "Let me get this clear. Because I refuse to conform to the role expected of me, because I long to lead an independent life and be of service to others ... that makes me mad?" (304).

Louisa's mother is confused; long confined to her gender role as wife and mother, the yearning of her daughter for education, and to be a doctor, is beyond the scope of her own upbringing. As a member of an earlier generation, she tries to understand and attempts to right a wrong by admitting to Louisa that the inheritance was consciously divided equally in three by her father; he had made certain to provide for his wife and his daughter who would, strictly speaking, be under the monetary control of Tom. Last, Louisa tells her mother the truth of who she is. Although the money is in trust until she is twenty-one, together the women decide Louisa should go to medical school.

The two young women, Louisa and Eliza move together to London; fully aware of the potential for society's condemnation of their relationship, Eliza agrees to come to the boarding house as her "true companion" (342) but is concerned about "other folk—what will they think?" (342). Those afraid of the "lesbian menace" would find their union frightening because it presents a kind of "threat of another kind, a threat that 'mistresses and maids' might indeed challenge the social and domestic order by claiming to be 'woman and woman only'" (2008, 109) They manipulate society's assumptions and live together in their own ruse for protection. Eliza shares the house, seemingly as Louisa's maid, because Eliza—more mindful than Louisa—that, at their particular historical moment, it "is the way things are, the way they have to be" but Louisa looks forward and is "determined that one day we'll live together openly, as equals, in a home of our own" (349). The successful, healthy couple in these novels is comprised of two women, one upper class and one lower class, educated and world-wise, who create a life of love and happiness. Forward-thinking and determined, Eliza and Louisa give neo-Victorian readers a glimpse into how such women might have lived in Victorian companionship.

Notes

1. Cheryl A. Wilson identifies one feminist issue Bray's neo-Victorian novels as the expression of sexuality, and discusses Gemma's relationship with a Rokshana young man, Kartik, as outside the usual boundaries—literally in a different realm—away from Victorian sexual context (2012, 129–32).
2. McGinnis refers here to the historical Athens Lunatic Asylum in southeast Ohio, known as The Ridges (373).
3. The lobotomy was an intrusive, controversial neurosurgical procedure that severed most of the prefrontal cortex from the rest of the brain to cut off communication between these areas to alleviate mental distress. It was used on patients who had been deemed, by the doctors, to be violent or morally

insane. It would make patients passive and confused as well as emotionally limited.
4. "Nellie Bly," née Elizabeth Jane Cochrane, was an investigative journalist for the *Pittsburgh Dispatch* where she wrote on issues like women's right to work, to not marry, and to divorce and ongoing problems like the lives of female factory workers for poor wages. After leaving the paper, she went to the *New York World*; once there, she went undercover at the Women's Lunatic Asylum (Blackwell's Island) to expose the cruel mistreatment of women in asylums.
5. See Brenda Ayres and Sarah E. Maier (2021) for a lengthy discussion of the stereotypes of redheads and the disruption of the same tropes in literature and film, including neo-Victorian narratives.
6. For example, see Cara Dobbing and Alannah Tomkins (2020).
7. Simon Joyce uses this idea of twenty-first-century society looking into the rear-view mirror of history to see what it reflects about us (2007).
8. This trope of a photographer visiting a mental hospital is based in history and has precursors in adult neo-Victorian fiction. In the nineteenth century, Jean Paul Charcot famously had photographs taken of his hysterics at the Sâlpetrière Hospital in Paris to record hysterical movements (see Georges Didi-Huberman 2003); in addition, the hospital held the mad women's ball to raise funds for the hospital and to give the inhabitants of the asylum a reminder of being in society. One British photographer, Hugh Diamond, used the newly invented technology of the camera to be objective and accurate regarding the visual indicators of mental illness; it was "based on the idea that one's face reveals one's mental state—with the goal of identifying visual signs of mental illness" (Wetzler 2021, n.p.).

Bibliography

Arias, Rosario and Patricia Pulham. Eds. *Haunting and Spectrality in Neo-Victorian Fiction: Possessing the Past*. Basingstoke: Palgrave, 2010.

Ayres, Brenda and Sarah E. Maier. *A Vindication of the Redhead: The Typology of Red Hair in the Literary and Visual Arts*. Basingstoke: Palgrave, 2021.

Bly, Nellie. *Ten Days in a Madhouse*. New York: Ian L. Munro, 1877. https://digital.library.upenn.edu/women/bly/madhouse/madhouse.html.

Bray, Libba. *A Great and Terrible Beauty*. New York: Random House, 2003.

Bray, Libba. *Rebel Angels*. New York: Random House, 2005.

Bray, Libba. *The Sweet Far Thing*. New York: Random House, 2007.

Castle, Terry. *The Apparitional Lesbian: Female Homosexuality and Modern Culture*. New York: Columbia University Press, 1993.

Daley-Carey, Ebony. "Testing the Limits: Postmodern Adolescent Identities in Contemporary Coming-of-Age Stories." *Children's Literature in Education*. 49 (2018): 467–84.

Didi-Huberman, Georges. *Invention of Hysteria: Charcot and the Photographic Iconography of the Salpêtrière*. Cambridge: MIT Press, 2003.

"Dissociative Disorders." *Mayo Clinic*. https://www.mayoclinic.org/diseases-conditions/dissociative-disorders/symptoms-causes/syc-20355215.

Dobbing, Cara and Alannah Tomkins. "Sexual Abuse By Superintending Staff in the Nineteenth-Century Lunatic Asylum." *History of Psychiatry*. 32, no. 1 (2020): 69–84.

Eagland, Jane. *Wildthorn*. Boston: HMH Books, 2010.

Fuoss, Kirk. "A Portrait of the Adolescent as a Young Gay: The Politics of Male Homosexuality in Young Adult Fiction." In *Queer Words, Queer Images: Communication and Construction of Homosexuality*, edited by Jeffrey R. Ringer, 159–74. New York: New York University Press, 1994.

Gorham, Deborah, *The Victorian Girl and the Feminine Ideal*. 1982. London: Routledge, 2012.

Grand, Sarah. "The Modern Girl." *The North American Review*. 158, 451 (June 1894): 706–14.

Heath, Michelle Beissel. "Reveling in Restraint: Limiting the Neo-Victorian Girl." *Children's Literature*. 48 (2020): 80–104.

Joyce, Simon. Victorians in the Rear-View Mirror. Athens: Ohio University Press, 2007.

"liminal, adj.". *OED Online*. June 2022. Oxford University Press. https://www-oed-com.proxy.hil.unb.ca/view/Entry/108471?redirectedFrom=liminal (accessed June 12, 2022).

Mas, Victoria. *The Mad Women's Ball*. New York: Harry N. Abrams, 2021.

McGuiness, Mindy. *A Madness So Discreet*. New York: Katherine Tegen Books, 2015.

Montz, Amy. "Unbinding the Victorian Girl: Corsetry and Neo-Victorian Young Adult Literature." *Children's Literature Association Quarterly*. 44 no. 1 (Spring 2019): 88–101.

Rodgers, Beth. *Adolescent Girlhood and Literary Culture at the Fin de Siècle: Daughters of Today*. London: Palgrave, 2016.

Shiller, Dana. "The Redemptive Past in the Neo-Victorian Novel." *Studies in the Novel*. 29 no. 4 (1997): 538–60

Sedgwick, Eve Kosofsky. *The Epistemology of the Closet*. Berkeley: University of California Press, 1990.

Showalter, Elaine. *Sexual Anarchy: Gender and Culture at the Fin de Siècle*. London: Penguin, 1991.

Thurschwell, Pamela. "The Ghost Worlds of Modern Adolescence." In *Popular Ghosts and the Haunted Spaces of Everyday Culture,* edited by Esther Peeren and Maria del Pilar Blanco, 239–51. London: Bloomsbury, 2010.

Vallone, Lydia and Claudia Nelson. "Introduction." In *The Girl's Own: Cultural Histories of the Anglo-American Girl, 1830–1915,* edited by Claudia Nelson and Lydia Vallone, 1–10. Athens: University of Georgia Press, 1994.

Wallace, Wendy. *The Painted Bridge.* New York: Scribner, 2012.

Waters, Sarah. *Fingersmith.* London: Virago, 2002.

Wetzler, Sara. "Hugh Diamond, the Father of Psychiatric Photography—Psychiatry in Pictures." *The British Journal of Psychiatry.* 219, no. 2 (August 2021): 460–61.

Wilson, Cheryl A. "Third-Wave Feminists in Corsets: Libba Bray's Gemma Doyle Trilogy." In *Inhabited by Stories: Critical Essays on Tales Retold,* edited by Nancy A. Marta-Smith and Danette DiMarco, 119–36. Newcastle-upon-Tyne: Cambridge Scholars Press, 2012.

Winters, Cat. *The Cure for Dreaming.* New York: Amulet Books, 2014.

Wolfreys, Julian. *Victorian Hauntings: Spectrality, Gothic, the Uncanny and Literature.* Basingstoke: Palgrave, 2002.

CHAPTER 9

Things as Yet Undone: Encountering the Past Through the Present

For anyone who has loved *Jane Eyre* and then gone on to read *Wide Sargasso Sea*, the fascination of moving from a canonical Victorian novel to an enlightening reconsideration is likely intriguing. The questions lingering in the back of scholars' minds are manifested in the new work, a nuanced change that opens new possibilities through alternate perspectives, allows a reader to consider past and ongoing issues of concern at a careful remove, and encourages a rigorous return to the original texts with self-conscious intent to be mindful of nuanced readings of those texts.

Neo-Victorian Young Adult Narratives seeks to enter this conversation via an enquiry into the growing curiosity in the neo-Gothic and neo-Victorian found in the narratives for adolescent readers who are interested in the literary and historical past while artfully and awkwardly negotiating their present's confusing intersection of discourses and expectations. Texts, both fictional and graphic, that explore the life of Mary Godwin Shelley foster ties to a young woman who wishes to live differently but pays an enormous, devastating social and personal price to do so encourage twenty-first-century young women to evaluate comparatively their own lives' challenges. Aspiring young writers can think about their own relationship with characters like themselves in some way. These narratives may introduce them to the young Brontës and how, as the family members increase their creativity, each scribbling sibling manages expectations differently. The modern reader may encounter in-depth biofictions about individual lives giving greater access to the factors supporting or

© The Author(s), under exclusive license to Springer Nature Switzerland AG 2024
S. E. Maier, *Neo-Victorian Young Adult Narratives*,
https://doi.org/10.1007/978-3-031-47295-4_9

detracting from the creative impulse of an author like Emily Brontë. This conversation between centuries expands to fictional characters like Sherlock Holmes or the girl-children of the nineteenth-century mad scientists who are, in and of themselves, awkwardly growing into adulthood while consulting issues of parentage, lineage, legacy, and resentment in portraits of abused children, marginalised young women, predatory (young and older) men, as well as non-normative lives and sexualities. Discussions of women's desire for suffrage, the misogyny of hysteria or mad diagnoses, the patriarchal biases of society, the anti-Semitism of the past and present, the lack of individual agency, and other questions of the past illuminate young people's desire for independence, mental illness, societal racism, LGBTQ+ sexual identities, and others in the present day.

While this project engages with neo-Victorian young adult fiction, graphic novels, biofictions, and other narratives, it has only managed to barely touch on the multiple areas of interest—so many questions remain. To see how young adult fiction embodies steampunk, or how neo-Victorian paranormal worldbuilding works—indeed, how young adult literature continues to connect with neo-Victorianism in a contscientious irreverent manner—leaves so much more to read and see. Ideas begun here will naturally lead off to cinematic adaptations—what about the Netflix Enola Holmes? Surely she is even more feisty than the textual one and how does it affect the viewer to see Helena Bonham Carter embody Eudoria? Does the TV show or other novel revisitations of Holmes' Irregulars remain faithful to the stories very limited exploration of their characters?

Two interesting neo-Victorian young detectives evoke the spirit and intent of Holmes. Veronica "Sally" Lockhart is, like Enola Holmes, an intervention into the Victorian past. Philip Pullman's Sally Lockhart mysteries, beginning with *The Ruby in the Smoke* (1985), are set in the Victorian age and they with common issues of neo-Victorian interest like the colonial thievery of gems, the opium trade, the treatment of children, the temperance movement, and the status of a young woman without a father, while William Ritter's series, starting with *Jackaby* (2014) set in 1892 New England involves the investigator, R. F. Jackaby, a haunting Jenny Kavanagh—the spectral woman he loves—as well as a young, intrepid woman named Abigail Rook who would rather be a palaeontologist, and another parallel world thrown into epic battle. What about novels that address young adult characters involved in criminal investigation— think Kerri Maniscalo's *Stalking Jack the Ripper* (2016)—or that revisit

Dracula, or other mythologies in a way reminiscent of a neo-Victorian Buffy the Vampire Slayer?

Is *Dickinson* (Apple TV) a good representation of the young, possibly lesbian, poet—historically and literarily important, likely encountered by young adult viewers, should we present her life in a comedy? There are books like Michaela MacColl's *The Revelation of Louisa May* (2015) a biofiction wherein Louisa May Alcott becomes a character, while in another narrative, one of Jo's sisters, Amy March, becomes the focus in Elise Hooper's *The Other Alcott* (2017); there is even a novel giving voice to the concerns of a mother in *Marmee* (2022) by Sarah Miller. For those unhappy with the ending of the fictional *Little Women* (1868), there is the sequel *Jo & Laurie* (2020) by Margaret Stohl and Melissa de la Cruz that begins in 1869.

The early ideals of masculinity and queerness combine in pre-neo-Victorian novels, like *The Gentleman's Guide to Vice and Virtue* (2017) by Mackenzi Lee, where young men are much more fluid in their identifications than developing Victorian ideas of robust Christian masculinity suggest. Other biofiction narratives have been written for characters; in *The Fall* (2014), Bethany Griffin make a new storyline for Madeline Usher while the protagonist in *The Raven's Tale* (2019) by Cat Winters combines author and character when readers meets a seventeen-year-old Edgar as he encounters his Lenore, and short story writers have recently reworked his tales in *His Hideous Heart* (2019). For more paranormal texts, there are the massive Victorian-sized tomes of Cassandra Clare's Clockwork series where the Downworld is full of vampires, warlocks, magic, and supernatural conflict—does this step outside the purview of neo-Victorianism?

There is so much more to do in the discussion of neo-Victorian young adult narratives than what has been managed here and I look forward to carrying on! Certainly, my work here in *Neo-Victorian Young Adult Narratives* hopes to encourage an expansion of the rigorous readings and theorisation into the neo-Gothic and neo-Victorian into the realm of children's as well as young adult texts. These important life stages as investigated in young people's narratives evoke different ideas, considerations, concerns, and responses that deserve equal attention to their adult counterparts.

Bibliography

Adler, Dahlia. Ed. *His Hideous Heart*. New York: Flatiron Books, 2019.
Griffin, Bethany. *The Fall*. New York: Greenwillow Books, 2014.
Hooper, Elise. *The Other Alcott*. New York: William Morrow, 2017.
Lee, Mackenzi. *The Gentleman's Guide to Vice and Virtue*. New York: Katherine Tegen Books, 2017.
MacColl, Michaela. *The Revelation of Louisa May*. San Francisco: Chronicle Books, 2015.
Maniscolo, Kerri. *Stalking Jack the Ripper*. New York: Jimmi Patterson Publishing, 2016.
Miller, Sarah. *Marmee*. New York: William Morrow, 2022.
Pullman, Philip. *Ruby in the Smoke*. Oxford: Oxford University Press, 1985.
Ritter, William. *Jackaby*. New York: Workman Publishing, 2014.
Stohl, Margaret and Melissa de la Cruz. *Jo & Laurie*. New York: G. P. Putnam's Sons, 2020.
Winters, Cat. *The Raven's Tale*. New York: Harry N. Abrams, 2019.

Index[1]

A
Absinthe, 173, 180n5
Abuse, 36, 76, 87, 102, 103, 165–167, 174, 175, 181n6, 181n8, 188, 193–195, 199, 201, 203
Adolescence, 4, 7, 12, 13, 17, 26, 59, 67, 86, 91, 115, 119, 123, 147, 156, 174, 180, 186, 196, 201, 202
Adolescent, 7, 10–12, 15, 22, 26, 41, 48, 56, 64, 71, 83, 84, 88, 95, 110, 111, 115, 116, 118, 121, 124, 125, 127, 144, 165, 171, 173, 174, 177, 178, 185–187, 189, 190, 196, 197, 202, 209
Agency, 10, 12, 16, 26, 27, 67, 68, 75, 77, 96, 116, 151, 210
Alcott, Louisa May, 27, 49n8, 211
Angel, 75, 165, 185
Anti-Semitic, 144
Anti-Semitism, 143, 144, 210

Assault, 173, 177, 181n6, 195
Asylum, 193, 194, 200–203, 206n4, 206n8
Authentic, 16, 64, 83, 164, 180, 188, 191
Authenticity, 113, 140, 158n12

B
Beast People, 60–63
Bildüngsroman, 11, 17n5, 27, 67, 95, 142, 150, 151, 154, 163, 167
Biofiction(s), 12–15, 29, 30, 32, 49n8, 73, 83, 84, 109, 110, 112, 113, 115, 117, 118, 121, 130, 130n1, 130n3, 138, 147, 209–211
BIPOC, 3, 101, 181n6
Blume, Judy, 1
Boarding house, 178, 205
Boarding school, 16, 23, 156n2, 163, 168, 174

---

[1] Note: Page numbers followed by 'n' refer to notes.

INDEX

Bray, Libba, 16, 164, 165, 167–176, 178–180, 181n5, 181n9, 185, 188, 190–193, 197, 200, 205n1
  A Great and Terrible Beauty, 16, 164, 174, 200
  Rebel Angels, 16, 164, 175
  The Sweet, Far Thing, 16, 164
Brontë, 7, 14, 15, 33, 49n8, 83–105, 106n1, 109–130, 131n7, 131n8, 132n18, 132n19, 133n20
Brontë, Anne, 27, 33, 49n8, 85, 88–91, 93, 95–100, 102, 105, 106n1, 106n3, 111, 115, 116, 118, 124, 125, 127, 132n15
Brontë, Branwell, 33, 49n8, 85, 87–93, 95–97, 99, 100, 106n1, 106n3, 106n4, 115–117, 121, 123, 125–127, 132n15, 132n18
Brontë, Charlotte, 27, 33, 49n8, 79n9, 85–100, 102–105, 106n1, 106n3, 106n4, 106n5, 114–127, 130, 131n6, 131n9, 131n12, 132n14, 133n19, 140, 171
  Jane Eyre, 79n9, 91, 94, 121, 122, 131n12, 171, 209
Brontë, Emily, 15, 27, 85, 87–91, 93, 95–100, 102, 105, 106n3, 109–130, 210
  Wuthering Heights, 91, 110, 119–121

C

Class, 11, 13, 58, 59, 64, 90, 95, 102, 120, 124, 143, 150, 155, 165–167, 169–172, 174, 175, 188, 189, 196, 205
Clothing, 46, 76, 77, 148, 150, 201, 204
Coakley, Lena, 14, 84, 91–94, 97, 99
  Worlds of Ink and Shadow, 14, 84, 91, 97
Code(s), 13, 66, 68, 155, 174

Colonial, 62, 100, 210
Colonialism, 7, 12, 101
Companion, 55, 58, 68, 74, 105, 128, 168, 199, 200, 205
Companionship, 205
Complicity, 127, 197, 204
Conan Doyle, Sir Arthur, 15, 77, 109, 137–140, 142–144, 147–149, 152, 154, 156n2, 157n9, 157n10
  "A Scandal in Bohemia," 148
  The Sign of Four, 147
  Study in Scarlet, 142, 143, 157n7
Corset, 152, 153, 158n16, 200, 201
Creature, 7, 13, 14, 21–49, 68, 70, 72, 73, 91, 109, 191
Crime, 12, 16, 61, 137, 141, 146, 193, 203
Criminal, 59, 63, 79n6, 147, 154, 185, 192, 210

D

Darwin, Charles, 56, 57, 62, 63, 151
  evolution, 63
  The Origin of Species, 57, 79n4
Degeneration, 79n6, 192
Detection, 137, 146, 157n6
Detective, 15, 16, 137, 138, 141, 143, 145, 147, 149, 154, 155, 156n3, 157n11, 178, 210
Deviance, 176
Doppelgänger, 22, 25, 27, 43
Dream, 29, 34, 37, 39, 43, 45, 47, 89, 90, 96, 103, 104, 115, 116, 170, 172, 196, 202

E

Eagland, Jane, 15, 16, 110, 121–130, 185, 200–202
  Wildthorn, 16, 185, 200
  The World Within, 122, 125, 127

Education, 15, 17n5, 23, 27, 42, 114, 124–126, 138, 140, 146, 151, 163–180, 191, 204
Ellis, Sara Stickney, 168
The Daughters of England, 168
Empire, 63, 65, 102, 141, 168, 169
Encoding, 152, 153
Enola Holmes, 139, 149
Epilepsy, 172, 188

F

Fantasy, 2, 21, 25, 102, 117, 124, 125, 165, 178
Father, 14, 23, 24, 31, 33, 35, 37–39, 42, 44, 46, 48, 50n14, 56–69, 71–73, 75, 85, 86, 88, 91, 95–98, 101, 103, 105, 106n5, 114, 116, 118, 123, 124, 126, 127, 131n6, 132n18, 140, 143, 145–149, 168–170, 172, 175–177, 179, 188, 192, 193, 195–200, 205, 210
Fawkes, Glynnis, 14, 84, 86, 87, 90, 91
Charlotte Brontë Before Jane Eyre, 14, 84, 86
Femininity, 16, 29, 76, 78, 152, 166, 185–205
Feminism, 23, 197, 201
Fuseli, Henry, 30

G

Gaiman, Neil, 21
Gender, 7, 9–13, 16, 27, 45, 75, 77, 78, 89, 90, 94, 95, 112, 120, 125, 126, 128, 129, 150, 155, 156, 166, 169, 181n6, 192, 204
Genii, 14, 83–105
Ghost, 7, 8, 21, 25, 38, 39, 49n6, 97, 118, 120, 131n12, 174, 186–188, 190, 199

Girlhood, 14–16, 23, 58, 164, 174, 177, 180n1
Glass Town, 85–88, 91, 94–96, 98, 100–105, 106n4, 109, 123, 125
Godwin, William, 23, 33, 49n1, 73
Political Justice, 29, 30
Gondal, 84, 86, 89, 98, 100, 102, 122
Goss, Theodora, 14, 56, 69–78, 79n9
European Travel for the Monstrous Gentlewoman, 14, 56, 74
The Sinister Mystery of the Mesmerising Girl, 14, 56
The Strange Case of the Alchemist's Daughter, 14, 56, 69, 78
Gothic, 8, 9, 12, 14, 21, 22, 24–28, 30, 33, 35, 42, 44, 45, 49, 50n15, 50n16, 50n17, 57, 61, 63, 64, 69, 70, 75, 77, 78, 79n10, 88, 174, 175, 178, 187, 199
Governess, 23, 94, 116, 125, 132n14, 149, 169–171, 180n4
Graphic novel, 12–14, 26, 32, 33, 38, 50n10, 83, 84, 87, 91, 100, 101, 103, 210
Greenberg, Isabel, 14, 84, 100, 102, 105
Glass Town, 14, 84, 100

H

Haunting, 25, 35, 38, 90, 119, 174, 186, 187, 210
Hawthorne, Nathaniel, 69
"Rappaccini's Daughter," 69
Heteronormative, 58, 120, 164, 166, 189, 190, 202
Historical novel, 77
Historiographic metafiction, 4
Homosocial, 172
Hypnotism, 195
Hysteric, 29, 189, 192, 206n8

I

Ideal of womanhood, 163, 204
Identity, 9, 10, 12, 22, 25, 26, 28, 33, 38, 42, 62, 67, 68, 77, 78, 89, 95, 98, 113, 128, 129, 144, 163, 164, 167, 179, 190, 193, 201–203, 210
Incest, 175
Insanity, 192, 195, 203, 204
Irregular/irregulars, 15, 137–156, 210

J

Jew, 79n6, 143–145
Jewish, 143–145, 149, 179
Judge, Lita, 13, 22, 32, 33, 35, 37–41, 46
  Mary's Monster, 13, 22, 32, 33
Juvenilia, 14, 33, 83–88, 90, 95, 98, 101, 102, 105, 109, 115

K

Künstlerroman, 11, 17n5, 111, 118

L

Lane, Andrew, 15, 138–141, 154
  Young Sherlock Holmes, 15, 139, 141
LeFanu, Sheridan, 77
  Carmilla, 77
Lesbian, 77, 128, 185, 189–192, 198, 205, 211
LGBTQ+, 3, 77, 181n6, 186, 210
Liminal, 9, 17, 67, 72, 86, 119, 128, 172, 185–205
Liminality, 14, 17, 22, 26, 33, 62, 66, 186, 188, 192

M

MacColl, Michaela, 15, 110, 115–121, 125, 129, 130, 131n11, 211
  Always Emily, 15, 110, 115, 117–119, 128
Mad, 14, 43, 48, 55–78, 90, 118, 143, 185–205, 210
Madness, 7, 8, 12, 38, 43, 44, 59, 72, 76, 117, 171, 172, 192, 194
Marriage, 23, 42, 75, 104, 116, 120, 121, 168, 170–172, 174, 190, 192, 204
Masculinity, 60, 61, 76, 99, 126, 154, 175, 198, 211
Mash-up, 69, 178
Mask, 64, 172
Masquerade, 64, 172–173
May, Antoinette, 13, 22, 29–32, 46
  The Determined Heart, 13, 22, 29, 31, 32
McGuiness, Mindy, 16, 185, 192
  A Madness so Discreet, 16, 185, 192
Metafiction, 4, 87
Mirror, 8, 37, 59, 64, 72, 120, 129, 158n12, 178, 202, 206n7
Monster, 9, 21, 22, 28, 30–32, 34, 41, 42, 55–78, 123, 176
Monstrosity, 13, 14, 21–49, 55, 61, 67, 69, 70, 175
Mother, 23, 24, 28–31, 33–39, 42, 46, 58, 60, 65, 67, 69, 70, 87, 109, 113, 122, 124, 125, 138, 140, 143, 146, 147, 151–154, 166–170, 176–178, 188, 190, 192–197, 199, 200, 203–205, 211

N

Neo-Gothic, 7–9, 13, 14, 25–29, 33, 37–39, 42, 44, 49n7, 55–58, 78, 209, 211

Neo-Gothic Victorian, 21, 22, 24–27, 33, 79n11
Neo-Victorian, 1–17, 25–28, 49, 55–59, 61–63, 65, 68–70, 74, 77, 78, 79n8, 83–85, 88, 89, 92, 94, 95, 98, 101, 104, 105, 110–121, 123, 124, 126–130, 131n9, 137–142, 144, 145, 147–149, 151–156, 156n2, 157n6, 158n12, 163–167, 169–178, 185–190, 192, 194, 197, 198, 201, 205, 205n1, 206n5, 206n8, 209–211
New Woman, 62, 75, 128, 132n19, 166, 179, 180n3, 192, 196
Non-heteronormative, 3, 9, 27
Nostalgia, 58, 67, 124, 175

O
Oppel, Kenneth, 41–48
  Such Wicked Intent, 41, 48
  This Dark Endeavour, 41, 47, 48

P
Paedophile, 203
Paranormal, 74, 84, 163, 210, 211
Patmore, Coventry, 165
Patriarchal, 28, 31, 35, 45, 58, 59, 64, 67, 96, 103, 125, 127, 132n16, 153, 154, 165, 167, 169, 190, 196, 200, 204, 210
Patriarchy, 95
Peacock, Shane, 141, 142, 144–147, 149, 158n17
  The Boy Sherlock Holmes, 15
  Eye of the Crow, 142, 144, 148
Performance, 129, 152, 164, 189
Performativity, 41
Predator, 174, 194, 195
Predatory, 45, 59, 194, 210

Presentism, 5, 166
Presentist, 166
Pseudoscience, 63, 193

Q
Quaker, 148
Queer, 16, 77, 106n3, 142, 176, 186, 187, 189–191, 202, 203

R
Rational dress, 46, 75
Rider Haggard, H., 79n10
  She, 79n10
Ruskin, John, 131n13, 157n11, 165

S
Salinger, J. D., 3
  The Catcher in the Rye, 3
Sapphism, 190
Sapphist, 190
Sappho, 191
Science, 7, 14, 21, 31, 37, 39, 42–44, 48, 55–58, 60–68, 70, 74, 75, 103, 143, 147, 178, 192, 193
Shame, 177, 194, 201, 203
Shelley, Mary Godwin, 7, 13–15, 21–24, 26–35, 37–39, 41–47, 49n4, 49n5, 49n6, 50n14, 55, 65, 70, 72, 73, 79n11, 83, 109, 209
  Frankenstein, 13, 21–26, 28, 31–33, 38, 41–49, 50n10, 55, 56, 65, 69, 72, 73, 109
Shepherd, Megan, 14, 56–64, 66, 67, 70, 78, 78n3
  A Cold Legacy, 14, 56, 65
  Her Dark Curiosity, 14, 56, 61
  The Madman's Daughter, 14, 56

Sherlock Holmes, 15, 16, 69, 77, 109, 137–149, 154–156, 156n2, 157n10, 210
Society, 7, 9, 10, 24, 29, 35, 39, 45, 48, 55, 57–60, 64–66, 71, 73, 76–78, 79n6, 85, 90, 95, 104, 110, 118, 122, 124, 127, 138, 144, 149, 151, 154–156, 164–166, 168–170, 172–174, 176, 178, 186–189, 192, 194–196, 198, 201, 204, 205, 206n7, 206n8, 210
Somnambulist, 46, 47
Spectral, 8, 9, 30, 37, 38, 46, 114, 185–205, 210
Springer, Nancy, 109, 138, 150–152, 154, 156, 158n17, 164
  Enola Holmes, 109, 138, 156, 164
  The Missing Marquess, 156
Stevenson, Robert Louis, 61, 62, 69
  The Strange Case of Dr. Jekyll and Mr. Hyde, 61
Stoker, Bram, 50n16, 69
  Dracula, 50n16, 69
Subaltern, 62, 63
Suffrage, 75, 151, 158n17, 195–205, 210
Suffragette/suffragettes, 132n19, 179, 196

T

Trauma, 8, 10, 25, 27, 71, 86, 124, 173, 175–177, 181n7, 186, 192, 194
Traumatic, 9, 33, 76, 109, 123, 174

V

Valente, Catherynne M., 14, 84, 96, 102, 105
  The Glass Town Game, 14, 84, 95
Ventriloquising, 102
Ventriloquist, 67
Victorian, 4, 6–8, 10, 12–17, 21, 24–28, 43, 56, 58, 61, 62, 66, 68, 70, 74–76, 78, 84, 85, 89, 95, 99, 101, 103, 109, 112, 113, 116–124, 126, 127, 129, 130, 137, 138, 144, 147–153, 155, 156, 156n2, 157n6, 157n11, 163–167, 170, 171, 173, 175–178, 180, 181n5, 185–190, 192, 195, 200–202, 205, 205n1, 209–211

W

Wells, H. G., 62, 69, 78n3
  The Island of Dr. Moreau, 56, 57, 69
Winters, Cat, 16, 185, 195, 197, 198, 211
  The Cure for Dreaming, 16, 185, 195
Wollstonecraft, Mary, 23, 29, 30, 33, 35, 37, 46, 49n2, 73
  A Vindication of the Rights of Woman, 30, 35
Woolf, Virginia, 150, 177
  A Room of One's Own, 150, 177

Printed in the United States
by Baker & Taylor Publisher Services